# LUCK

## OF THE

# DEVIL

# Other Books By Denise Grover Swank

***Harper Adams Mystery***
Probable Cause (short story)
Little Girl Vanished
Long Gone
Luck of the Devil
Lost in the Dark
(Coming Winter 2026)

***Maddie Baker Mystery***
Series complete

***Magnolia Steele Mystery***
Series complete

***Carly Moore Mystery***
Series complete

***Rose Gardner Mystery***
Series complete

***Darling Investigations***
Series complete

**Rose Gardner Investigations and Neely Kate Mystery**

# LUCK OF THE DEVIL

## Harper Adams
### Mystery #3

DENISE
GROVER SWANK

*To my mother, our relationship was complicated, but I'm so grateful to have spent so much of your last month and a half with you. I hope I gave you comfort and peace.*

*Carolyn Sue Grover*
*February 28, 1942 - March 25, 2024*

Chapter 1

They said my mother's funeral was one of the largest in Jackson Creek's since my murdered sister's twenty years prior.

My mother would have been bursting at the seams with pride, while saying in her smug tone, "Well, of course it was."

The thing was, there were few *true* mourners in attendance. Most people were there because it seemed the right thing to do given her social status. The fact that it was the perfect place for people to gossip about her death was pure bonus.

"*I* heard," a woman said in a not-so-hushed tone to several of her friends, "she *purposely* drove off that bridge. That her *daughter's* scandal pushed her into it."

I was lurking around the corner, on my way back from the restroom after making sure the bruises from my own car accident, days before, were still covered with makeup. I'd also snuck a sip of vodka from the flask tucked in my purse. If Harper from last fall—the me prior to my *scandalous* incident —could see me now…

But I'd only had one drink that morning and my hands had begun to shake as sweat pooled at the nape of my neck. I couldn't look like the wreck I was, so I'd taken a healthy sip, despite the fact I'd sworn to give it up.

My mother would have said it was rude to plaster my back to the hallway wall, eavesdropping, but my mother was no longer here to police my behavior like the manners sergeant she'd always been. She would have loved to know her influence had lived on, not that I was moving from my position.

"So, you think she actually, *you know*," a woman who sounded like she had a stuffy nose said. Had she been crying? For such a large attendance, there had been very few tears. "You think she actually…" Her voice trailed off, then she whispered, "*killed* herself?"

"That's what I heard," another woman said in a snooty tone. "That she drove right off that bridge." I could only imagine her adding a hand motion to dramatize her statement.

"I heard it was her husband that pushed her over the edge," a fourth woman said.

"He pushed her car off the bridge?" the woman with the stuffy nose asked in horror.

"No, don't be ridiculous," the snooty woman said. "I heard he left her and was filing for *divorce*."

I stepped around the corner and they all froze, their eyes widening in silent horror. Whether it was because I'd caught them maligning my mother or because I was the infamous Harper Adams, I couldn't be sure. Maybe both.

"If she killed herself," I said in a reasonable tone, "then why were there skid marks on the road?" I lifted my brow.

None of them answered, still frozen in shock.

"And if she planned to kill herself," I said, taking a step toward them as my voice took on a slight edge, "then why did she have a suitcase packed with a week's worth of clothes? Do you think my mother was *stupid enough to think she had to pack for the afterlife?*"

"Harper," my friend Louise said as she walked up from

behind, wrapping an arm around my shoulders. "Why don't we go take a rest in the family room?"

The women took that as their cue to bolt, scattering into the crowd like cockroaches caught in the light. I would have found it hilarious under any other circumstances.

I could practically hear my mother saying, "Harper, really. Must you be so uncouth?"

*Yes, Mother. Why is this a surprise?*

"I know this is hard," Louise said, tears swimming in her eyes. "People are so mean."

"I didn't want a funeral," I said. "Not like this. Not with the sharks circling. I wanted something private."

"I know," she said, squeezing my shoulder before dropping her arm. "But your father did."

We'd had a fight about it. I said I couldn't deal with the backstabbers who would show up with their fake niceties. I guess I'd gotten the niceties part wrong.

Dad had insisted this was what my mother would have wanted. To let the town pay tribute to her. The joke was on my parents. To our faces, we heard what a great woman she was, but in the corners, they were dragging out every misdeed she'd ever done, from how she'd cheated Betty Jean Hendrix out of the presidency of the garden club to how she'd dominated the church auxiliary to the way she'd spread rumors about a woman—her name long forgotten—and run her out of town.

And those were only a few stories I'd heard whispered. Still, a few people had shown up and offered me true condolences.

Louise, of course, who had been by my side for the past several days when her schedule as a deputy sheriff allowed. And my friend Nate Davis, the owner of Morty's Bookstore, although I'd only seen him at the funeral. Betty, who owned Betty's Diner, walked up after the service. Although I'd only known her a week, she gave me a warm hug and told me to come by for pie anytime I liked. Vanessa Peterman, who'd been my sister's best friend when she'd died, came and hugged me, telling me how sorry she was and how grateful she was to me for helping get her daughter back a little over a month ago, a kidnapping very few people knew about.

The employees and partners from Dad's law firm had come of course, mostly for my father, but I'd worked there for nearly a month, so many knew me and offered me sincere condolences as well, even though they likely knew what a nightmare my mother had been to live with. Several of the paralegals had been there since before my sister's kidnapping and murder twenty years before and knew me from when I was a little girl, visiting my father's office with Andi.

Misti, the bartender at Scooter's Tavern, and a few other employees had come. None had approached me, but they'd given me solemn nods from the back of the church. Their boss, James Malcolm, was noticeably absent, not that I was surprised. I hadn't expected him to show up. Hell, I hadn't expected his employees to show up. James Malcolm attending would *not* have been a good thing. In fact, it would have been very, very bad.

James Malcolm was a known former crime boss who had done several months in a federal prison before he was released. He'd gone on to open up a tavern here in Lone County. While the Lone County Sheriff's Department and the Jackson Creek Police Department couldn't find any current dirt on him—and Lord knows they'd tried—I knew he was far from innocent.

He'd committed four murders in the last month alone, and I'd been privy to all of them.

Very few people knew I had any association with James Malcolm, and I preferred to keep it that way.

To say I'd been peopled out was an understatement. Most of the town believed I'd murdered a fourteen-year-old boy five months ago while I was on duty as a Little Rock police detective. I'd lost my job and my reputation, along with my house, which I'd sold to help pay my legal bills. Other than my father and my friend Louise, a Little Rock patrol officer who'd moved to Lone County shortly before I'd moved back myself, no one wanted me here.

My mother certainly hadn't been happy to have me back.

Louise was still watching me with concern, so I wrapped my arms over my chest and said, "I just need to make it through the graveside service, then I'm going home. I'm not going to the luncheon."

Louise offered me a look of understanding and gave a nod. "I'm sure your father will understand."

I wasn't so sure of that, but he wouldn't guilt me into going like my mother would have. Then again, maybe it would be easier for him if I wasn't there. He was currently the center of attention in front of my mother's casket, getting sympathy from multiple middle-aged women. He did look handsome in his black suit, crisp white shirt, and black tie. Sure, he had some gray at his temples, but my father was a good-looking man, an attorney, and newly single. I suspected he wouldn't have to worry about meals for months. The local women would take turns bringing him casseroles in the hopes of becoming the next Mrs. Paul Adams.

The thought of my father with another woman made me want to reach for my flask and drink enough alcohol to forget.

I'd picked a hell of a time to try and stop drinking.

The funeral director walked up to my father and whispered in his ear. My father nodded, then lifted his head, scanning the room, and I took that as my cue.

"Looks like you need to go," Louise said. She'd make detective in no time with her observation skills. She gave me a hug, holding me close for several seconds. I wasn't a hugger, so I was stiff, but then my body relaxed and I hugged her back, grateful to have her as a friend.

"I won't be able to go to the graveside service," she said

apologetically. "I only got the morning off, but I'll drop by the house to check on you later tonight."

"Thanks."

Then I headed toward my father, ready to bury my mother. If only I could bury my guilt with her.

## Chapter 2

My father was understanding when I told him I was skipping the luncheon, and I was pretty sure I saw a flicker of relief in his eyes. Having me here in town was fairly new and likely stressful. Hell, he'd left my mother over it. Besides, he was tired and worn out from the grief and funeral preparations. He didn't need to be worrying about me.

I drove back to my mother's house, parked in her driveway, then headed for the apartment over the detached garage at the back of the property. I'd moved into the studio apartment upon my return. It had been my mother's stipulation to my homecoming, not that I'd complained. I'd wanted my space.

Her house was sitting empty now, but I'd only slept in there one night since I'd been back, and that was only because the door to my apartment had been destroyed by gunfire.

Why was my door shot up? Long story ... but I was back in my apartment two nights later, and I'd been here since, quite literally. I had barely left other than to go to the funeral home with my father—and then to my mother's bedroom to pick out a dress for her to wear in her casket.

I trod up the wooden steps, casting a glance at my mother's back door. In the summer, my mother had flower beds surrounding the house that burst with color, and a few bulbs were shooting green stalks into the cool March air. They'd bloom soon, revealing whether they'd be tulips or daffodils, and my mother would have cut them and put them in a vase on the marble top table in her living room.

This year they'd die and decay. Just like her.

*Lord, I'm morbid.*

I unlocked my front door and headed toward my espresso machine, pressing the button to turn it on. My fingers were itching to open the cabinet door under my sink to grab a bottle of alcohol, but I steeled my back. I could make it through a fucking day without alcohol. Or at least *the rest* of a day.

Sure, I hadn't gone a day without a drink for four months, but lots of people had a drink a day—a beer to unwind after work. A glass of wine at dinner. A cocktail with friends.

The way I'd been drinking lately, though… It was like there was a prize at the bottom of the whiskey or vodka bottle. I'd known it was getting out of control, but I'd told myself that I would stop soon. That I had it under control. I'd been fooling myself, of course, and the last week had proven it.

Maybe if my mind hadn't been so muddled with alcohol, I would have realized sooner that my mother was missing. Maybe her body wouldn't have been at the bottom of the Red River for three days.

I swore I'd never take a drink again, because if I hadn't been drunk the past month, I might have been able to stop my mother from running off. And if she hadn't run off, then she'd still be alive.

Wanting to remain sober and actually doing it were two very different things. But my mother had always said I had a strong will. It was time to prove her right.

Fighting the urge for a drink, I gripped my fist so tightly I felt a sharp pain. I glanced down and found red half-moons with beads of blood on my right palm.

No one had said this would be easy.

I rinsed my hands off in the sink, then grabbed a paper towel and held it with my fist while I started to make a latte. A few minutes later, I carried my steaming mug with slightly shaky hands to my small round table. I'd just taken a seat when I heard a knock at the door.

My brow lifted in surprise. Everyone in town was at the funeral luncheon. Who could be at my door? I knew Louise was worried about me, so maybe she'd taken the rest of the afternoon off to sit on my futon and watch romcoms like we'd done the last two nights.

I got up and opened the door, surprised when I saw James Malcolm standing on my front porch. He was wearing a pair of faded Levis that hung low on his hips with a black t-shirt.

I stared at him in surprise while he studied me with his usual detached stare.

"What are you doing here?" I blurted out.

"The same could be said for you," he said. "I suspect half of Lone County is at your mother's funeral lunch."

I suspected he was right. "How did you know I was here?"

He gave me a look that screamed, *please…* Over the last month, I'd worked with him on two cases and learned he knew plenty of things about this town *and* its people. It wouldn't be a stretch for him to know my whereabouts—or at least for him to know where I wasn't.

"Okay," I conceded. "*Why* are you here?"

His gaze dipped to my right shoulder, then back up to my face. "Your stitches need to come out."

I'd gotten injured when two men had broken into my mother's house last Thursday. They'd proceeded to ransack my apartment. I'd been hiding in my mother's house, but I'd followed them out here and tried to lock them into my apartment by tying the door handle to the porch railing. When they'd realized they were stuck, one of them had shot at the doorknob to get free. I'd still been on the porch and a four-inch piece of metal had lodged itself under my collar bone. Malcolm had shown up a few minutes later and taken me to a twenty-something woman in the woods who'd called him Skeeter, a nickname tied to his hometown. She'd had honest-to-God suture kits, and enough medical knowledge to stitch me up.

Which, of course, had raised a ton of questions, only a few of which had been answered, and poorly at that.

That was the thing about James Malcolm. He wasn't fast and loose with information. Then again, when you used to be the crime boss over a whole county, even a small one like Fenton County, Arkansas, I supposed you had to be.

I released a dry chuckle. "Are you here to drive me to your friend in the woods? I thought she said she was done doing you favors."

The corner of his lift lip hitched slightly. "I planned to do it myself."

My brow shot up. I wasn't surprised he knew how to remove stitches. I was sure a big, tough guy like him had acquired more than his fair share of them, and he didn't strike me as the kind of man who'd condescend to visit a doctor unless he was bleeding to death. So, it stood to reason he knew how to remove sutures. The real question was why he was here wanting to remove *mine*.

"Are you gonna let me in?" he asked dryly. "Or do you want me to do it out here?" He nodded to my shoulder. "Seems like you're gonna have to take that off for me to get to them."

My black dress was short sleeved with a rounded neck. It came to an inch or so above my knees and had a zipper down the back.

I considered telling him I could remove them on my own, but I'd have to do it with my left hand, and I wasn't particularly ambidextrous. Add in my sporadically shaky hands and the task seemed impossible—and painful.

I took a step back to let him in, glancing at the back of the house to see if my mother was watching a man walk into my apartment, which was strictly against her rules. Then I remembered I could do whatever the hell I wanted. She wouldn't ever spy on me again.

I expected a wave of grief to hit me, but all I felt was numb.

He brushed past me, and I shut the door, turning to face him. "I'll need to change."

He gave a sharp nod, and I walked over to the dresser and pulled out a tank top and a pair of yoga pants, then headed to my small bathroom. Only as I was about to shut the door, I realized I couldn't reach the zipper. Louise has helped me zip up before the funeral.

Great.

I turned around and gave him a sardonic look. "I need help with my zipper."

I expected him to throw out a barb about not being interested in undressing me, but he simply motioned for me to turn around as he took a couple of steps toward me.

I stepped out of the bathroom and turned around, raising my left hand to move my hair out the way. It had grown longer since I'd moved to Jackson Creek, but it was only an inch or two past my shoulders. Long enough to get in the way.

I still expected him to say something, but he didn't. The only sound was the zip of the metal. When he reached the small of my back, his knuckle brushed my skin, sending a shiver up my spine.

My breath caught in my throat, but I regained my senses and hurried into the bathroom and shut the door.

Sure, I'd noticed James Malcolm was a good-looking man, and sure, I'd also noticed he was in amazing shape for a man in his early forties. And, okay, *parts* of me had noticed those things as well and responded to them, but those previous instances were nothing compared to what I was feeling at the moment, and I wasn't sure what to do with that.

I let my dress drop to the floor, then sat on the toilet to put on my yoga pants as my mind reeled.

I could *not* sleep with James Malcolm. Talk about bad decisions. But it was a moot point since he'd made it crystal clear he wasn't interested in me that way.

After taking several deep breaths, I tugged the spaghetti-strap shirt over the strapless bra I'd been wearing since I'd gotten the stitches, then got to my feet.

I hesitated as I reached for the doorknob. Had Malcolm noticed my reaction? If he had, would he believe it if I said I was ticklish?

My emotions were raw, and as much as I hated to admit it, I was probably suffering from alcohol withdrawal. That had to be what this was about.

The back of my neck was sweaty again, and I briefly considered putting my hair up, but I didn't want Malcolm to think he made me nervous. I opened the door and stood in the opening, giving myself a moment to gauge his reaction. Malcolm was standing next to the table, and he'd set a blue cloth out on the table with a couple of stainless-steel tools on top of it.

"You brought your own tweezers and scissors?" I asked as I moved closer and took inventory.

"You think I'm gonna use the tweezers you use to pluck your eyebrows?" he scoffed.

I couldn't suppress the smile spreading across my face. The forceps he'd brought looked medical grade and nothing like the pair I'd picked up at the drugstore. "I suppose that wouldn't be very hygienic. Where do you want me?"

He turned to look at me. "You can sit at the table." He took in my bare shoulders and upper chest, but didn't say anything as I walked over to the table. He'd turned the chairs so they were facing each other, one in front of my coffee mug and the other next to his medical kit. I sat in front of my latte and took a sip. It was still warm, but more importantly, I was hoping the caffeine would help take my edge off. Not likely, since caffeine typically had the opposite effect.

Malcolm watched me, still standing.

"Would you like me to make you something?" I asked.

"You can when I'm done," he said.

"I don't have any to-go cups."

"Won't be needin' one," he said, taking a seat in the chair opposite me. Then he started to pull on what looked like a pair of nitrile gloves.

So, he planned to stay after he was done. Why? We weren't friends, something he'd insisted both times we'd worked together, but there was no denying he'd saved my life last week when Skip Martin had kidnapped me to find out what I knew about the finances of Hugo Burton, the man he'd murdered five years before. Skip had also made it clear he intended to kill me and leave my body somewhere so Malcolm would be accused of my murder. That's why it could be argued that Malcolm had only burst into the cellar to save his own hide by saving me.

But we both knew better.

He'd eliminated the threat to my life when he'd killed Skip and his underling, Pinky. I wasn't in any danger other than the mild concussion I'd suffered after Pinky had run my car off the road and I'd crashed into a tree. But he'd taken me to his office at his tavern and woke me up every few hours to assess my status.

Those were the actions of a friend.

His bartender Misti and his attorney Carter Hale had told me that Malcolm took care of his own, meaning his employees, and that I had come into the fold. I wasn't sure what that meant exactly since he hadn't hired me. We'd only worked together to fulfill our mutual *business* needs, and I'd been too numb over the past five days to give it much thought.

But now, as Malcolm picked up a pair of fine-tip scissors, my mind fully went there.

What did his presence here mean?

He must have seen the cogs in my head grinding, because he said gruffly, "Don't read too much into me being here. We have things to discuss, and I knew you wouldn't be bothered with removing the sutures, so, two birds with one stone."

"Yeah," I said, as I slipped the strap of my gray camisole down over my shoulder. "Makes sense." But I wasn't sure what we had to discuss. We'd solved the case of who killed Hugo Burton, so I didn't think he was here for that.

He studied my healed wound, then lightly probed around it with both hands. "It looks like it healed okay. No sign of infection."

I didn't see any reason to say anything since he wasn't asking a single question. The *true* wonder was that I hadn't pulled out any stitches during my car accident and kidnapping. Or that, other than Malcolm and the nurse in the woods, no one else knew I had them.

He lightly rested a hand on my shoulder as his scissors slipped under the first suture and snipped. He reached for the forceps and grabbed the knotted end, then gave a tug.

I drew in a breath as a pain shot through my shoulder blade.

"Sorry," he murmured, dropping the suture onto the blue cloth. "Only eight more to go."

"Okay," I said. "No big deal."

He started to work on the second suture, then caught me by surprise when he said, "I was sorry to hear about your mother."

"Yeah," I said, surprised when it came out sounding choked. I hadn't shed a tear since hearing the news, but his offer of sympathy seemed to have ripped a tear through the thorny thicket encircling my heart.

"From what little you said, you seemed to have a complicated relationship."

"That's an understatement," I grunted, wishing I had a drink.

"You got someone to talk to?"

I jerked my gaze up to him in shock, only to gasp again as he pulled out the other stitch. When I recovered, I narrowed my eyes. "You don't seem like the kind of guy who likes to hear women unburden their souls."

The left corner of his mouth ticked up. "I've had my ear bent a time or two."

That shouldn't have been surprising. Malcolm was forty-four. One would hope he'd had at least one significant relationship, and to my surprise, I hoped he'd been a considerate partner—the kind of man who'd listen. I nearly laughed. What had prompted *that* thought? Not that I had a great frame of reference. I was thirty-six years old and had never had a relationship rich enough to share deep feelings. The closest I'd come to it was my relationship with Keith, my Little Rock police detective partner, and the last thing he'd been interested in were my deep feelings. Still, I was struggling to make the empathetic Malcolm and the emotionally detached Malcolm fit together. Or why he seemed to be making the offer to *me*.

He snorted. "The look on your face suggests you find that hard to believe."

"Maybe it's because I've never been good at listening to men unburden their souls."

He chuckled. "That doesn't surprise me."

"You think I'm incapable of having a relationship?"

"Oh, you're capable," he said. "You just have too much to hide to be in a committed one."

"Now you're a relationship expert?" I asked in a snotty tone.

He chose that moment to pull out the third stitch, which seemed to hurt a bit more than the other two.

"Besides," I added. "Pot meet kettle."

"We aren't talkin' about me. We're talkin' about you," he said, dropping the suture onto his cloth. This one seemed to have more crusty skin around it, so maybe he hadn't purposely hurt me.

"How convenient for you," I said, still pissed, especially since my forehead seemed to be sweating now and I had to grip my hands in my lap to keep them from shaking.

He moved to the next suture and was quiet for several seconds before he asked in a hushed tone, "How long has it been since your last drink?"

I jerked my gaze up again and found myself staring into his softened deep brown eyes. "What?"

"How long?"

I considered telling him it was none of his business, but he was the only one who had noticed my drinking had grown out of control. Why lie? "I had a sip from my flask before the graveside service."

"And before that?"

"A shot in my coffee before the funeral." Before Louise had shown up to check on me.

"Nothin' else?" I felt a tug and realized he'd just taken out the fourth suture.

"No."

He was silent again as he dropped the stitch onto the cloth, then moved to the next one. "Why stop now?" he finally asked.

"I have my reasons," I said in a huff. I wasn't about to confess my guilt over missing the signs that my mother had been missing. Sure, I'd caught on, but not until the day before they'd found her. I should have noticed the signs the first day. Then again, I *had* noticed. I'd just blown them off.

He gave a slight nod before he pulled out the next suture. As he got to work on another, he nonchalantly said, "What would you say if I told you that I'm not so sure your mother's accident was an accident?"

Anger burned in my chest, and I gritted my teeth as I looked up at him. "So you're like all those other idiots in town and think she killed herself?"

He stared back, his face blank, as he said, "No. I think she was murdered."

# Chapter 3

"What?" I blurted out. I supposed I now knew why he'd planned to stay, but his statement didn't make any sense.

I shook my head. "First of all, why would you think that? And second, *why the fuck would you care?*" My voice rose, practically shouting at him as I finished the sentence.

He turned back to his task. "To answer your second question," he said calmly, "I have my reasons, but as far as the first, I looked at the evidence."

"What are you talking about? It was an accident."

"Let me finish with this, then you can make me that coffee and we'll talk."

I nearly pressed him to talk now, but I suspected my brain was still too dazed to listen to anything he presented as evidence.

Who would want to murder my mother? Okay, dumb question, I suspected most of the town hated her, but I also doubted most of them had the stomach to actually kill someone, even her. Besides, she had run off the road. There were skid marks on the bridge. There was water in her lungs. She'd drowned. Sure, the official autopsy report wasn't out, but no one in the Lone County Sheriff's Department was suspicious that she'd run into foul play. The idea had never even come up.

But the skid marks could have also meant someone had run her off.

I was still lost in my stupor while he finished removing the last stitch, and mercifully, he hadn't said anything else about his suspicions. By the time I got up and started my espresso machine on autopilot, I'd already come to my own conclusion.

"I'm sure you think you're helping, and I actually appreciate it more than you know," I said in a slow, even tone. "It's not uncommon for families to search for reasons for their loved one's death. They think something sinister happened because they can't accept that someone they love *just died*, through no fault of their own. There *has* to be some external force that caused their death, because they can't accept that it was random. That someone could be here one moment, then gone the next." I looked him dead in the eye. "But I'm not like those people. I've seen the randomness of death. I've accepted my mother's death for what it was: an accident. She was a terrible driver, and she ran off the road. I don't need you to try to make this more palatable for me. I've accepted it just fine." That wasn't the complete truth, but believing it was murder wouldn't make me feel less guilty that she'd been in the river two days longer than she'd needed to be.

"That's not what I'm doin', Harper," he said softly, still sitting in his chair, his legs spread apart in a relaxed posture. "Finish makin' the coffee, and I'll explain my reasoning. "

I lifted the heel of my hand to my forehead. I could at least hear him out. "What do you want? Same as last time?"

"Sure."

I went through the motions of making him a vanilla latte, then set it in front of him then returned to my chair. "What is your reasoning?"

He picked up his mug and took a sip. Something like appreciation filled his eyes, but he didn't comment as he set it back down on the table. Was he buying himself some time before responding, or was I imagining it?

"What have you heard from the autopsy report?" he finally asked.

"That she had some bruising and water in her lungs."

"What specifically do you know about the bruising?"

I shook my head. "I didn't ask, and they didn't say. Detective Monahan said it was consistent with the car accident. Her car dropped from a thirty-foot bridge into a twelve-foot-deep river. Bruising was to be expected."

"What about the toxicology report?" he asked.

"It hasn't come back yet."

"There's a preliminary one."

"And it didn't show anything," I said, my head beginning to throb.

"Harper, she had Sertraline in her system." His brow lifted. "Did she take Sertraline?"

A strange numbness crept over me, like my brain refused to process what he'd just said. Sertraline was the pharmaceutical name for Zoloft. "No way. Absolutely not. She would have considered it a sign of weakness."

But had I missed something? My mother had always been so controlled—rigid, even. Could she have been self-medicating?

A flicker of a memory surfaced—her fingers shaking slightly when she set down her wine glass last week, but I'd brushed it off.

I considered asking him how he knew all of this, but figured now wasn't the time. It was no surprise he had access to information even I wasn't privy to. At the moment, I didn't see how it mattered who'd fed it to him.

"Would your father know?"

"Uh…" My head was spinning. I asked myself, again, where she'd been going. She'd had that suitcase with her…

"Maybe," I said, distracted. "Maybe not. I take it they weren't very close."

"You take it? You don't know?"

"My mother pretty much kicked me out of the house the day I left for college. I wasn't home much, so no, I don't know. I came back for the summer after my freshman year, and got the message loud and clear that she didn't want me around. So, I only came back for holidays after that, and over the past decade, I didn't even do that much. All I know is that he left her a month ago."

"Did she have a medicine cabinet?"

"No. She kept some medication in a kitchen cabinet, but only Tylenol, antibiotic ointment, and things like that. Besides, she had a suitcase with her, like she was going out of town. She would have taken any prescription medication with her."

"Did they return her belongings to you?" he asked.

"Yeah." I was trying to wrap my head around the possibility that she'd been murdered . "It was all wet and soggy. I didn't go through it."

"Where is it now?"

"In a plastic bag in the garage. My dad didn't want it and it didn't seem right to just throw it away, even though everything had to be completely ruined." I narrowed my eyes. "Surely you're not basing your theory on the fact she had a Zoloft in her bloodstream."

"Remember the bruising? She had a contusion on the back of her head."

"Maybe she hit it on the head rest," I countered. "Or maybe she turned her head when the car was falling and hit it on the window."

"The indentation in her skull fits blunt force trauma better than it does cracking her head on a window or head rest."

I gave him a hard stare. "Where's the report with this information? It seems unlikely that the sheriff's department would overlook blunt force trauma. Everyone knows they're leaps and bounds better than the Jackson Creek police."

"The preliminary report doesn't state she had blunt force trauma. I had my own expert talk to the pathologist."

My blood iced in my veins. "Why?"

He reached over and picked up the mug. "Why what?" He took a sip, as though we were discussing the weather and not my mother's potential murder.

"Why would you have someone look at the report?" A new thought hit me. "I'm not paying you for that, and I sure don't owe you a favor."

He took another sip and shook his head. Tsking, he said, "So cynical."

I snorted. "Coming from you, that's laughable."

He lowered the cup but held onto it. "The timing of her death seemed suspicious."

"Because I was looking into Hugo Burton's murder? The last time I talked to her was around noon last Tuesday when I was on my way out to meet with Hugo's widow. I didn't see her lights on in the house when I headed out to Scooters around seven that night, and they were still off when I came back well after ten. I suspect she left that afternoon. The timing makes it unlikely her accident had anything to do with my investigation into Hugo."

He shook his head. "I'm not necessarily talkin' about Hugo. I'm talking about you bein' back in town, diggin' shit up. Your father was involved with J.R. Simmons, who had some very mean and deadly people in his back pocket. Your parents were in the process of going through a divorce. What if she dug something up and it made someone nervous?"

I shook my head. "Sure, she dug up dirt on people, but they were rumors, whispered into the right ears. Nothing serious enough to get her killed."

He cocked an eyebrow. "It wouldn't be the first time someone was murdered for destroying someone's reputation.

Had your mother been nervous lately? Acting out of character?"

I didn't have to consider it to reluctantly admit, "She seemed super needy. She wanted me around all the time in the evening. I ate dinner with her most nights, and she wanted me to stay late. I figured she was just lonely after my dad left."

"I thought your parents weren't close," he said. "So why would she be lonely?"

"I suspected she was probably doing it to manipulate me."

"How so?"

I pushed out a sigh of frustration. "She liked to control people, and *I* was usually uncontrollable." I ran my hand over my head. "Look, I don't want to get into the details of my family trauma, but suffice it to say, my mother and I didn't get along before my sister's kidnapping, and after, well, she blamed me, and she made no secret that she hated me."

I took a breath, then reached for my cup with shaky hands.

Malcolm's gaze, of course, followed my movement. "You're in withdrawal."

"Bullshit. I'm not an alcoholic."

"You're shaking. You're sweating. You're anxious. You have a headache."

"I have a headache because I had to suffer fools at my mother's funeral, and I'm anxious because you're at my kitchen table, accusing me of suffering DTs."

But I could see that he might be right, and it scared the hell out of me.

He lifted his shoulder in a half shrug. "I call it as I see it."

I hated his smug sneer. "You don't know everything, James Malcolm."

"Never claimed to, but I've seen a few drunks detox in my time, so I recognize the signs."

"Fuck you."

He just continued to smirk at me.

"I can't do this right now," I said, my voice breaking. It was all too much. Him in my personal space… His insinuations that my mother might have been murdered because of me… Him claiming I was suffering from alcohol withdrawal…

My breaths were coming in short bursts, and I felt like my chest was going to explode.

He got to his feet in one fluid motion. "Come on."

I glared up at him. "What? Where do you think we're going?"

"Somewhere you can breathe."

# Chapter 4

I stood on the wooden porch, watching as Malcolm descended the steps, my stomach twisting. I hadn't decided whether I wanted to follow him.

Stubbornly, I refused to believe my mother had been murdered, but my stomach still lurched. I told myself I didn't trust him, and yet I did.

What if he was right?

There was no way he was, of course, so wouldn't it be great to prove him wrong?

There was no doubt he wanted answers, and now I did too. Sighing, I gave into the inevitable. I followed him to his car and got in on the passenger side, then fastened my seat belt. I started shivering from the chill, and I realized I'd just walked out in fifty-degree weather wearing a spaghetti strap top.

What an idiot.

But I was too proud to say I needed a jacket. "Are you taking me out to the country to kill me and bury my body?"

He let out a derisive snort. "Do you take me to be that stupid? My car was likely captured by a half dozen video doorbells. If I was going to kill you and go to the trouble of hiding your body, I would have been a helluva lot more discreet."

"Wow. That makes me feel a whole lot better."

"Good," he said in that irritating smug tone as he backed his car into the street before starting down the road, away from downtown.

"Where are we going, Malcolm?"

"Guess you'll see when we get there."

I sank back into the plush leather seat and closed my eyes. If I was on my way to my murder, at least I was going out in style. Not that I really thought he was dangerous to me. We'd reached a kind of truce, and even before then, I'd felt safe enough with him. Sure, I'd seen him murder two men in cold blood, but I didn't fear for my own life. He'd done it out of his own form of justice. I wasn't a threat to Malcolm. Especially not in this state.

My hands had begun shaking so hard I shoved them under my legs to keep them still, and the sweat on my neck and back was making me stick to the seat.

Malcolm shot a glance at me, then held out his silver flask.

"I'm not drinking that," I said, turning to look out the window.

Sighing, he pulled it back, unscrewed the cap, then took a small sip. "It's not poisoned. See?"

"I never thought it was poisoned. I just don't want a drink."

It was a bald-faced lie. I was dying for a drink, and sitting on my hands was doing double duty—not just controlling the shaking but preventing them from snatching the flask out of his grip. I was stronger than my need for a drink, and I wasn't giving in.

"You can't just quit cold turkey," he said in a softer tone. "You need to taper off."

"I didn't know you had an M.D. after your name."

"It doesn't take eight-plus years of school to know that quitting abruptly like that is hazardous to your health."

My stomach cramped. He wasn't wrong, but admitting he was right would be admitting I'd fallen down the slope further than I'd realized, and I wasn't ready to face that yet. Not out loud.

"Give it a rest, Malcolm," I snapped. "I'm not an alcoholic."

"So why are your hands shaking?"

Goddamn him. "Because I'm cold!"

He didn't respond, which only pissed me off more.

I glanced out the window and saw we were headed toward Wolford, the town north of us. "Are you planning to dump me at a treatment center?"

"And who the hell would pay for that?" he mocked. "You're flat-ass broke, and I'm not sure your daddy's in much better shape."

Between my job at the law office and the money Vanessa Peterman had given me for finding her daughter, I wasn't flat-out broke, still I doubted I had enough to pay for rehab. But it was the latter statement that caught my attention. I jerked my head to face him, instantly regretting the sudden movement. "What's that supposed to mean?"

"Maybe your father isn't as well off financially as he'd like people to believe."

"What?" I shook my head. I almost asked him how he knew, but at this point I believed he knew just about everything that went on in this town. The real question was whether he was bluffing about my father's finances. Then again, Malcolm didn't bluff, at least not with me.

How financially bad off was my father? I felt sick thinking about the implications. Suddenly, this all felt like too much.

"Never mind," I said, grabbing the arm of the door and looking out the back window. "I want out of this stupid field trip. Take me home."

"Too late for that, Detective."

"The hell it is. If you don't take me home right now, I'll press charges for kidnapping."

He let out a genuine laugh that caught me by surprise and somehow loosened the cord of dread squeezing my heart.

"You don't think I'd do it?" I demanded hotly.

"I think you'd rather kick my ass yourself," he said with a grin. "You wouldn't get the same satisfaction if you handed me off to the sheriff's department."

I had to admit he had a point. In a little over a month of working with him, my moral compass had shifted. The satisfaction from vigilante justice was hard to deny.

He cast a glance at me, his smile fading. "I have a job for you to do."

"Oh," I said, understanding finally sinking in. "This doesn't have anything to do with me or my near panic attack. This has to do with what I can *do* for you."

"Of course," he said with a snide grin.

I wanted to slap it off his face, only he'd likely laugh at me and tell me violence was another symptom of detoxing.

Smug bastard.

"What do you expect me to help you with and why were you so willing to let the issue of my mother's potential murder drop so fast?"

"There's nothing potential about it," he said, keeping his gaze on the road. "There's no doubt she was murdered, and whoever did it is very good at covering their tracks, which makes me think it's related to your father and his own illegal connections."

Which meant—if she was murdered—that it might not have been because of me. "My father didn't know who J.R. Simmons was when he started doing business with him and he regretted it."

"Not enough to *stop* doing business with him."

"He stopped when Simmons was killed."

"He only stopped *because* the man was dead." He shot me a glance. "And don't you try to deny his involvement or the fact he knew he was dealing with a dangerous man. Simmons told him to let one of his stooges into Hugo Burton's office the day after his disappearance, and he did it. He let the guy clean it out."

"One could argue that my father was only cooperative because he knew he *was* dangerous," I snapped.

"Exactly."

I nearly countered that his statement didn't make sense, but everything in my head was so muddled, I couldn't be sure if it did or not. "What do you want my help with? Don't tell me you want to help me solve my mother's supposed murder, because I don't know what it could possibly have to do with *you.*"

Only I did. He didn't trust my father, and he'd already said he thought her possible murder was linked to him. But that still didn't make sense. Why would he give a rat's ass about my father other than his link to Malcolm's deceased boss?

"All in good time," he said good-naturedly.

"Your interest in her death has something to do with Simmons."

"Nice to see your brain is still workin'." He shot me a look, his brow lifted.

I ignored his insinuated *despite the fact you're in withdrawal.* "I'm not helping you with your vendetta against a dead man, Malcolm."

"I didn't ask you to."

"Then what am I doing in a car with you?"

"Getting some air."

"More like getting hot air," I muttered under my breath, then my blood ran cold as I realized the bridge over Red River was looming in front of us.

While I knew this was where they'd found her body, I hadn't been here yet. I hadn't been prepared to face it.

"What are we doing here?" There was no way he didn't hear the panic in my voice.

"Getting some air," he repeated, but with more kindness than I was used to from him. He pulled over on the side of the bridge and turned on his hazard lights, then opened the door and got out.

I watched him through the windshield, my stomach twisting in knots. Was he playing some kind of game with me, suggesting my mother had been murdered? To what purpose?

But my stomach sunk as the truth hit me that whether she'd been truly murdered or not, I owed it to her to look at any evidence Malcolm had uncovered. And if there was something to it, then I owed it to her to find the truth and bring the perpetrators to justice.

I got out and instantly regretted not grabbing a jacket. The overcast sky kept the air chilly and there was a slight northern wind.

Malcolm was on the shoulder in front of the car, surveying the road, or more accurately, the black skid marks that still marred the concrete.

"It looks to me that she hit the brakes right here." He pointed to the road in front of us. "And then the marks get darker as they get to the side of the bridge." He pointed to the end of the bridge, where the bridge met the road on the other side.

Something in my brain shifted, and Detective Adams took over, shoving Grieving Harper out of the way.

I frowned. "That doesn't make sense."

I scanned the skid marks again, then the landscape or the riverbank on the northern side. My heart began to hammer in my chest.

*There's no way her car went into the river from that side.*

Shoving my rising panic down, I walked the length of the bridge, studying the trajectory of the markings. The angle was wrong. Everything about it felt wrong. I knew it in my gut, and

I felt my instincts take over. I trusted them far more than my grief.

"These skid marks aren't hers." I said out loud, letting it sink in.

Malcolm didn't react, just stood there for a moment as though he'd been waiting for me to get on the same page.

"Her car would have run off into the trees on the other side, not the water."

"Could it have hit the river bank, then rolled in?"

I studied the bank. "Do you happen to have any photos or diagrams of how her car landed in the water?"

He slipped his phone out of his front jeans pocket and swiped the screen a few times, then handed it to me.

Of course he had photos of the crime scene. The first photo showed a huge wrecker with an extendable crane was parked on the bank, the arm hanging over the murky water. A thick cable was attached to the bumper of my mother's Lexus, the front end of the vehicle still submerged in the water. The next photo showed the car being pulled toward the river bank, the water inside the interior barely visible through her tinted windows. I looked up at him. "How did you get these?"

"I have my sources."

"Like, seriously, Malcolm. This is a huge breach."

He gave me a sardonic look, then said, "Does that mean you don't want to look at the evidence?"

"I never said that. I just asked how you got them and you refused to answer." My head was pounding, and I decided it wasn't my problem that the sheriff's department had a breech. Especially if it worked to my advantage. I studied the images again, then compared them to the river, the northern river bank, and the direction my mother's car had supposedly traveled.

I was even more convinced.

"This doesn't line up," I said. "The car was more in the middle of the river, not close to the bank. And for argument's sake, let's say it hit the bank, then rolled into the river, it would have gone in back end first." I studied the photos, then moved onto a drawing of the car in the river. "I think it went in from the other side."

"Which doesn't line up with the skid marks at all."

"Exactly. Because they didn't come from my mother's car." I took out my phone and checked for traffic before walking out into the road and taking multiple photos. "Happen to have a tape measurer?" I asked.

He didn't respond; instead, he walked to the driver's door and leaned over.

Shivering, I turned back to the road and studied the marks. I'd guess them to be a few weeks old, maybe a month. How had the sheriff's department gotten them wrong?

I felt something slip onto my shoulders and felt the warm weight of Malcolm's leather jacket settle over me. I stared up at him in surprise, unsure what to say, but he held out a metal tape measure. "This work?"

So, we were pretending he hadn't just done something nice? I was good with that.

"Perfect. Can you extend it and hold it up to the skid marks there?" I pointed to a mark in the road.

A car was approaching from the Jackson Creek side, so we both moved to the shoulder. I ignored the curious stare of the man driving past, trying to ignore the smell of Malcolm's jacket, a mixture of leather and cedar.

Malcolm moved back onto the road and held the extended measuring tape over the first skid mark while I took a photo.

"You gonna compare the width to the tires on your mother's car?" he asked, glancing up at me while he squatted next to the markings.

I had to stop thinking about what he'd just done, and I *definitely* had to stop thinking about how much the jacket smelled like him. "Yep. I need to prove her tires didn't make these marks." I walked down the road and motioned for him to follow so I could take more measurements. "They're not fresh."

"The preliminary report says they faded due to weather."

I shook my head. We'd had snow, rain, ice, and cold weather over the past week, but it wouldn't account for this amount of fading. "They should still look fresher than this. Nevertheless, the skid marks insinuate a car could have gone off the road here. I need to look up recent accident reports."

"I'll get Carter on it." He reached for his phone, which I was still holding, and used voice command to call Carter Hale.

I slipped my left hand into an armhole of the jacket, then the other, hoping Malcolm wouldn't read anything into it. I needed to use my phone, and the jacket might fall if I didn't wear it. Once it was on, I opened my phone and looked up my mother's Lexus model and year so I could look up the tire width.

"I need you to do some diggin'," Malcolm said when Carter presumably answered. He paused for a second, then said, "Pull any auto accidents that occurred on the bridge over the Red River over the last…" He gave me a questioning look, his gaze dropping for a slight second to my leather-clad arms, then back up to my face. "How long?"

"Make it six months." That seemed too long, but it couldn't hurt to check. Plus, this wasn't a heavily traveled road. I suspected there wouldn't be that many.

My search results popped up, showing me her tires were between 215 to 235 millimeters wide. Then I pulled up a chart to convert the inches on Malcolm's tape measure to millimeters. My mother's tires would have been nine and a quarter inches or less, but these marks were nearly ten and a quarter inches wide.

"Send them to my email when they're available." Malcolm said, then hung up.

"Would it hurt you to say 'please'?" I asked sarcastically,

inexplicitly feeling the need to be difficult. Was it because him giving me his jacket threw me off guard?

"In theory, no, but it's his job to do what I ask, which makes the please unnecessary."

"Still…"

His brow lifted with its trademark asshole look. "Did you typically say please and thank you to all your buddies on the Little Rock police force before they threw you out on your ass?"

I gritted my teeth. "Fine. Be shitty to your employees. What do I care?"

"I pay him well, so I wouldn't call that treating him shitty."

"Money isn't everything, Malcolm."

"But it's a whole helluva lot."

"Besides," I said, still feeling salty, "they didn't throw me out. I quit."

"*Right.*"

I shot him a half-hearted sneer that he ignored.

"We were right about the marks," I said grudgingly, then told him the results of my search.

He nodded grimly but didn't respond.

I moved to the side of the bridge, staring down into the water. We'd had a lot of rain the week before, and I knew the water had been higher and rougher when they'd pulled her car out. Now it was deceptively calm, as though satisfied from purging its latest victim.

I was still struggling to believe someone had murdered my mother, let alone dumped her car into the river. "There are a lot easier ways to get away with murdering someone," I said, thinking out loud, as I hugged my chest. A sudden wind gust hit hard, and I tugged the edges of the jacket closer—trying desperately to ignore the fact the jacket smelled so much like him it was like he was wrapped around me.

I nearly ripped it off and threw it on the ground from the thought pissing me off.

I was not going to fall for James Malcolm. I wasn't that much of an idiot.

"Maybe, maybe not," he countered, moving next to me.

Thank God, he seemed oblivious to my inner torment. I needed to get control before I made an even bigger ass of myself than I already had.

He continued, "Maybe the sheriff's department found the skid marks and presumed they were hers, which sent them looking in the water. It stands to reason whoever did it pushed her car into the water from the south side. I suspect they hoped she wouldn't be found for a long, long time. We got a lot of rain last week, but usually the water level doesn't change that much, and they don't dredge this river much either. It stands to reason they might not have expected her to be found for years. Or ever."

"So, why *did* they find her?" I asked. It was crazy that they'd thought to look at all. No one had reported her missing and skid marks on the road wouldn't necessarily motivate them to check the river. "I was in too much shock to ask."

"I don't know," he admitted. "It wasn't in the report." He turned to face me. "I can try to find out."

"No," I said, turning around with my back to the water. "I'll ask Louise."

"Are you gonna tell her you suspect your mother was murdered?"

"No." I drew in a breath. "I'm still struggling to believe someone killed her."

"Why?"

I turned to face him. My cold detective facade slipped, allowing my grief to rush in, coming out in the form of anger. "Because, if I accept that she was killed, I have to wonder if she was murdered because of *me*!" I shouted. "What if I turned up something in Hugo Burton's case that made people worried enough to try and stop me?"

"You thinkin' they murdered your mother to interfere with your investigation?" he asked in disbelief.

"It wouldn't be the first time something like this has happened," I insisted.

Sympathy filled his eyes as he shook his head. "Harper, we already determined it didn't have anything to do with Burton. You hadn't even started investigatin'."

*Right.* I closed my eyes for a moment, trying to get my shit together.

His reaction only made me even angrier, or at least that was what I told myself. Because what else could I be pissed about? "She seemed anxious when I talked to her last Tuesday afternoon." I ran my hand through my hair, trying to remember how the conversation had gone down. "She was upset that I wasn't taking her to her historical society luncheon." I shook my head. "Dammit, why can't I remember what she said? Why did I just blow her off?"

He studied me for a moment. "Take a moment, and let's—"

"Fuck you, Malcolm!" I shouted, then pointed my finger at him. "Don't you fucking try to placate me!"

"Placate you?" he scoffed. "You're hysterical, and I'm trying to get you to calm down and think rationally."

"Hysterical?" I screamed, realizing that I *was* hysterical, but I was also past the point of caring.

He took a step back and gave me a patronizing look.

"Fuck you!"

"You already said that."

"Arg!" I shouted into the air.

"There you go again, losing control. I thought you were some kind of hot-shot detective," he sneered. "When you were in Little Rock and things didn't go your way on an investigation, did you just shout at your partner and throw fits?"

"It's my fucking mother, Malcolm!" I shouted. "My mother was *murdered*!" I said, choking on the word, and then the anger was replaced with an overwhelming grief that stole my breath and made me dizzy.

I stared up at him, whispering, "Someone murdered my mother."

"I know," he said, lowering his voice as his face softened.

I'd spent the past five days trying to accept that she was gone. That it was over.

But it wasn't over. It had only just begun.

I took a deep breath, subduing my grief, and shoving it back into the box where it belonged. Grief had no place in an investigation. I needed to be cold and calculated, and the truth was, I was very good at both.

"I'm going to find out who did this," I said, my voice as hard as steel.

Malcolm's eyes darkened. "Then let's get started."

## Chapter 5

I shot him a dark glare. "You plan to work this case with me?"

Disgust flashed across his face. "I thought that much was obvious by now."

"Why?" I demanded. "Why are you so interested in this?"

He propped his hands on his hips and turned to look out at the water, the wind blowing pieces of his dark brown hair. "Because despite your narcissistic tendencies, I highly doubt her death had anything to do with you. I'd bet money it's tied to your father, and he's likely the tip of the iceberg. Your mother just got caught in the fallout."

Was he right? Malcolm wasn't the sort to offer consoling lies. He believed in facing the cold, hard truth, just like he'd made me do on this bridge. If he'd thought it had something to do with me, he would have told me so. I had to believe he was right, which also meant he was likely correct about my father.

As much as I hated to admit it.

"Do you think my father's next?"

He turned to face me, watching me for several seconds. "I don't know."

"I have to warn him." I lifted my chin, prepared to fight him on this.

"You don't think he's already on alert?" he asked dryly.

"Why would he be?"

"You said your mother never went out of town or on vacation, yet she'd packed a bag and was on her way out when she was killed. Your father knew that was unusual. Right? You called him the day we found Hugo after you noticed her suitcase was missing."

"Yeah."

"He knows, Harper. Has he been acting more paranoid lately?"

He'd been paranoid the day I'd cornered him at his law office and demanded answers about his connection to J.R. Simmons. Had he been acting paranoid since her death? I'd been too self-absorbed to notice. I'd learned about her death a full day after my father, so I had no idea what his reaction had been. Had he been shocked or looked guilty? "I'm not sure. I was kind of too busy drowning in my own misery to notice his."

I expected some smart-ass answer, but he simply nodded. "He's a big boy, and he's taking care of himself. Has he tried to take care of *you*?"

"I can take care of myself too."

"But at least *he* knows he's in danger. Has he warned *you*?" He held up a hand to stave off my imminent protest. "We both know the answer is no."

I'd never felt more lost and alone. Everything Malcolm had said was true. My father had grown more reserved since her accident. More guarded. I'd thought he was simply upset about her death, especially since they weren't on good terms, but what if it was because he suspected she'd run into foul play? Why hadn't he warned me? Did he think I'd call him crazy and declare it impossible, just like I had when Malcolm presented his case? Or more likely, he'd hoped to hide his possible tie to her death. He'd tried to downplay his connection to J.R. Simmons when I'd quizzed him about it last week. But there was no denying Simmons had been dead for four years. And dead men weren't threats.

But their successors could be.

Wasn't that Malcolm's true motivation? To find Simmons's successor? He'd pretty much admitted it while we were digging up Hugo Burton's body.

Malcolm had hinted that Simmons's successor might be worse than the original. I knew Simmons had ordered Malcolm to murder a child who could testify against Simmons. Malcolm had refused, so Simmons had done it himself. How much worse could the new man be?

"I don't think you should stay at your house," Malcolm said, catching me off guard. "Not until this is said and done."

I narrowed my eyes. "Why?"

"I know you're a little slow at the moment, given the fact you're grieving *and* in detox, but if the person who killed your mother did this because they were afraid of what she might know, then it stands to reason they might think you have the information too and want to eliminate *you*."

I hadn't connected all the dots to get to that conclusion yet. I told myself he'd had multiple hours, possibly days to reason it out. I refused to believe my brain was sluggish because of withdrawal.

Still, I hated to admit he might be right. About any of it. "You think I should stay in my mother's house?"

He grunted. "I don't think you should be anywhere near that property."

I heaved out a sigh. "While there's a possibility I'll inherit *something* from my mother's estate, my parents weren't divorced, which means everything will go to my father. I have some money, but I'm trying to save it, so I don't want to stay at a motel, and I don't feel comfortable asking Louise if I can stay with her." Especially if I really was going to investigate my mother's possible murder. If the Lone County Sheriff's Department had covered it up, I could be putting my friend in danger.

"You're gonna stay with me."

I blinked. For a second, I thought I'd misheard him. I'd expected him to suggest a cheap motel off the highway or guilt-trip me into calling Louise. But instead, he was offering to put me up—like it was nothing. Like it was the obvious choice.

I finally got my wits about me and said, "No offense, but I'm too damn old to be sleeping on the sofa in your office. No matter how comfortable it is."

"You'll be comin' to my house."

I stared at him in shock, then quickly recovered. "I'm not staying with you!"

"Why the hell not?"

I started to say because I didn't trust him, but that wasn't true. I wouldn't be here on a bridge with him if I didn't. He'd proven multiple times that I could, but the idea of staying at his house still felt weird. Wrong.

Or maybe too right.

"Okay, then," he said with a small grin of triumph when I didn't present a reason. "That's settled." He glanced down at his phone. "I've got to be getting to the tavern to work the evening shift."

"Great. You can just drop me off at my apartment."

He snorted. "What part of you not staying at your place do you not understand?" When I started to protest, he said, "I know your laptop was stolen, and I doubt you already bought a new one. You can work on my laptop in the tavern office while I'm workin'."

When I didn't respond, he gave a satisfied nod. "Good, it's settled."

"Fine," I said in disgust, trying not to look too agreeable, otherwise he might get suspicious, but deep down, I was grateful to not have to stay at my place. Besides, if I stayed with him, I could watch him like a hawk to make sure he wasn't keeping things from me. "But I need to get some things from my apartment."

He started walking toward his car. "Once we get there, you have ten minutes to get some shit together."

"Generous," I muttered sarcastically as I followed him.

"More than you know."

<hr>

He actually gave me nine minutes because he counted the time it took me to climb up the stairs and unlock the door. Not that it mattered. I didn't have much to pack other than some toiletries, a few days' worth of clothes, and my phone charger.

I was dying for a drink, and it felt like Keebler Elves were building an industrial-sized cookie factory in my head, but I resisted the pull to my kitchen sink cabinet and instead grabbed a bottle of water from the fridge with shaky hands along with a couple of aspirin. Malcolm noticed, because he seemed to notice everything, but he wisely kept his mouth shut. After I packed my bag, I slipped off Malcolm's jacket. Even though I threw on a pullover sweater, I was already feeling partially naked without the jacket. I told myself it was because it had warmed to my body temperature, not because of who it belonged to.

I gave Malcolm a smug look and held out the jacket. "Six minutes."

He took it and studied me for a moment before pivoting and heading wordlessly to the door.

We drove to the tavern in silence while I stared out the window, going over the last month with my mother. She'd started acting strangely after my dad moved out.

And then there was my father. He'd claimed he'd moved

out because of how my mother was treating me. But what if there was some other reason?

I sat up and turned to Malcolm. "I need to speak to my dad."

"We already decided he was safe. We don't want to tip him off that you think she might have been murdered."

"I don't want to warn him," I said in frustration. "I want to ask him more details about why he left her. I think she got scared after he moved out. What if she discovered something dangerous about my father and *that's* why he moved out?"

He frowned. "You think she found out he was working for Simmons?"

"Maybe, I don't know. But I *do* know my father's desk in the home office is completely empty, so he took everything with him when he left." I shrugged. "What if she found something before he cleaned it out?" A slimy feeling coated my skin. "This feels wrong. Sure, my father had a business dealing with Simmons, but that doesn't mean he's crooked."

He was my dad. The man who'd made pancakes every Saturday morning before Andi died. The man who'd taught me how to play basketball in the driveway and how to build a campfire. *That* man wouldn't have murdered anyone. But what if I didn't really know him at all?

The look Malcolm shot me suggested he thought my father was very crooked. "Frankly, I'm happy you're lookin' at all the options. I expected you to need more of a push."

I could understand why he'd thought so, but at the moment, my father was the most obvious place to start.

"If I were with the LRPD, I wouldn't interview him first. I'd probably start with searching her suitcase and house."

He cocked a brow. "Well, you're not with the Little Rock PD, are you? Good thing too since your mother died in Lone County."

It took a couple of seconds to realize what he was insinuating—that the LRPD was out of Lone County's jurisdiction. "Wow," I said dryly. "That was sort of a joke."

He gave me a wry grin. "I'm just sayin', you're not bound to any rules about how you go about this. If you want to start with your father, then go ahead, but take everything he says with a grain of salt. You can't trust him to be truthful, but hear what he has to say and we can sort it out later."

"Yeah." I rubbed my temple, trying to ease the pain in my head.

"Ask him to meet you at the tavern."

"So you can eavesdrop?" I asked sarcastically.

He snorted. "No, so I can make sure you don't get murdered."

"Gee, thanks," I said, wondering why I was being snotty when he was obviously trying to help me.

But he took it in stride, twisting his hand on the steering wheel. "Don't go gettin' the wrong idea. This is purely for business reasons. I need you to dig up shit for my own investigation."

"Of course." But I couldn't keep a tiny grin from lifting the corners of my mouth. I knew he didn't want me dead—and also that it was for more than business reasons. I had no delusions that the man was interested in me sexually—he'd made it pretty clear he wasn't—but I considered him a friend. You couldn't go through the crap we'd gone through together unless there was a tiny smidgeon of friendship there.

When we got to the tavern, we walked through the back door and headed straight to his office. I was now familiar with the dark wood paneling, the mahogany desk, and the comfy leather sofa. Maybe too familiar given our respective backgrounds, but there was no putting this partnership back in the proverbial bottle.

Malcolm got me set up on his laptop, because we both knew I wouldn't be snooping through any secret files. The week before, he'd told me there wasn't anything incriminating on there.

He studied me for a moment. "If you get hungry, come out front and Misti'll feed you. Better yet, ask your dad to meet you for dinner so you can get food *and* answers."

"Yeah," I said, sinking into the leather sofa. "I'll call him in a minute."

He nodded, then stood in the doorway for several seconds. "For what it's worth, I truly am sorry about your mother, but we're gonna make it right."

I watched him turn around and disappear around the corner, wondering how you made someone's murder right. Sure, we could find who had done this to her, but it wouldn't make it right. It wouldn't bring her back. She'd still be dead, lying in the Jackson Creek cemetery.

And yeah, I'd been through this with my sister. Andi had been kidnapped and murdered, which had been its own special hell, but they'd found her killer within days. There had been a trial, and we knew we'd saved the lives of her murderer's other potential victims.

But this felt different. Messier. I wasn't sure it would give me closure, not if she'd been killed because of my father's secrets. And what if it turned out that he'd been directly responsible for her death? What would I do then?

But I was jumping ahead before I had enough facts. Or really any evidence. I didn't know that my father was involved, directly or indirectly, so there was no use letting my mind go there. Not yet. I needed to be objective and stick to the facts.

I had a new sympathy for families of murdered loved ones. Somehow, they always seemed to find a way to blame themselves, even if they went through convoluted hoops to get there. Of course, they wanted justice, but that wasn't the only thing they usually wanted. Many seemed desperate for information, any information at all, about their loved one's final moments. Even if the details were excruciatingly painful.

I was experiencing all of those things right now. Feeling guilt at the thought that I might be in some way responsible. Wanting the person who hurt my mother to face justice. But right now my thoughts were filled with what her last moments must have been like. Had she panicked when she'd realized her car was going into the river? Had she tried to get out? The detective who'd investigated the crash had told me she was still wearing her seatbelt. Had that been true? And if she was wearing it, had she tried to unbuckle it? Had she been too confused or her adrenaline so high that she couldn't? Or, if she really had blunt force trauma to the back of her head as Malcolm suggested, had she been unconscious or too disoriented to save herself?

Had she been filled with terror as she drew that first breath of water into her lungs?

Had she thought of me?

What a stupid thought. My mother wouldn't have spent her last moments thinking of me. She never would have spent her last moments thinking about the daughter she *wished* had been kidnapped and murdered instead of the other.

I drew in a deep breath and stood, shaking out my hands. My skin felt like it had a million bugs crawling over it, but I ignored the little voice in the back of my head that said my symptoms were about to get a lot worse. That I'd been drinking more than I realized.

That I truly was a drunk.

At least my mother wasn't alive to find out her daughter had one more fault to add to her lengthy list. I could only imagine her horror if people found out I was an alcoholic.

I shook myself out of my reverie. This was getting me nowhere. It was time to start getting answers.

It was time to call my father.

## Chapter 6

I grabbed my phone and texted him.

> Sorry I just took off this afternoon. I couldn't deal with all those people

To my surprise, he answered within seconds.

> I understand, Harper. I'm sorry you had to go through that.

Since I knew he was by his phone, I called him, deciding this was better than communicating through text.

"Hey," he said when he answered. "I was hoping you'd want to talk."

"Yeah," I said, a lump filling my throat. "I figured it would be better this way."

"How are you doin', kiddo?" he asked in a gentle tone.

Tears swam in my eyes. A new nickname. He'd been trying them out over the last month, saying he wanted to get closer. Surprisingly, this one didn't grate against my nerves like the others had.

"Um…" I looked up and blinked. I needed to keep it together. "I'm hanging in there. How about you? I'm sure this couldn't have been easy given how you'd moved out last month."

"No matter what happened between us, I never would have wanted this for your mother," he said emphatically.

Was he talking about not wanting her dead, or was he suggesting he had something to do with it? "I know. I never thought otherwise."

"Good." He was silent for a moment. "I'm sure you're dealing with a whole host of feelings right now."

"Yeah." I cleared my throat, then took a breath. While I'd planned to ask him to meet me for dinner, I doubted he'd want to come here, and I wasn't so sure I wanted to look him in the eye when I asked him some hard questions. A number one rule in interrogating a suspect was to do it in person. Body language often said more than their actual words, but then again, he wasn't a suspect, and this wasn't an interrogation. It was a daughter asking her father questions. There was also the thought that if he did have something to do with it, I wasn't sure I could face him.

"I keep going over the last month," I said, struggling to find the words that would get him talking without making him suspicious. I couldn't tip him off. If he was innocent, I didn't want to destroy our fragile truce. But if he did know something, I couldn't give him a reason to hide it better. "She just seemed so off."

"Well," he said, gruffly. "Keep in mind I moved out and asked for a divorce. As far as she was concerned, I also stole her identity, which was being the wife of a prominent attorney. She thought she was nothing as a divorced woman."

"That's ridiculous," I muttered, not that I didn't believe him. I wasn't surprised by her antiquated view.

"*You* and *I* and everyone else knows that, but she put her entire being into being a wife and mother. Not to mention, she was raised to believe divorce was wrong, and her parents have been married for decades."

"But she hadn't been in contact with her mother in years."

"Maybe," he said carefully. "Maybe not."

"Wait," I said, sitting up straighter. "She *was* in contact with her?"

"After Andi…" His voice broke and he took a moment before he continued. "Your mother had a falling out with her parents and they went no contact. I can't be sure, but I think she still talked to her parents from time to time."

"And she kept it a secret from you? Why?"

"Part of the reason they stopped talking was because her mother blamed me for Andi's death."

"*What?*"

"And to my surprise—your mother, who was looking for scapegoats wherever she could find them—actually stood up for me and cut contact."

That was because *I* had been her scapegoat. Maybe she couldn't handle adding my father to the list and alienating everyone around her. "That's crazy. Why would it be *your* fault?"

"Why did your mother blame *you?*" he asked softly. "Sometimes there's no rational reason."

He was right, of course, but her reaction had still shredded what was left of my heart. Still, I couldn't make sense of why my grandparents would turn on him. They'd seemed to love him before Andi's murder. I'd never been my mother's favorite so it was easier to understand why she'd blamed me.

Had my father done something to rouse their suspicion? It had happened years before his involvement with J.R. Simmons, not that Simmons had anything to do with John Michael Stevens. But what if Simmons wasn't the first criminal my father had struck a deal with?

"Mom's parents liked you. Why did they blame you?"

"I really can't get into it tonight, Harper," he said,

sounding exhausted. "We can talk about it some other time, okay? We buried your mother six hours ago."

I nodded, even though he couldn't see me, because my throat was clogged with emotion. "Yeah," I finally choked out.

"I was going to broach this with you later," he said slowly. "But since we're sort of on the topic, I thought I'd bring it up."

Was he going to make a confession? It seemed highly unlikely given he'd proven his cowardice just last week, refusing to own up to his involvement with Simmons until he was cornered. But I was still curious to hear what he had to say. "I'm listening."

"As you know, your mother was quite depressed." He paused and cleared his throat.

"Actually, that's what *I* wanted to talk about," I said. "She seemed anxious and worried. Like a boogeyman was out to get her. Or maybe both of us. At the time, I blew it off as manipulative behavior. I figured she was lonely without you, so she decided I was suddenly an acceptable alternative. She wanted me with her almost every night, and she'd asked me to go to two historical society luncheons with her. She seemed off."

"It was all due to her depression," he said. "And I'm sure you're right that there was a manipulative component."

"How do you know she had depression?"

"Well, it stands to reason that she was depressed," he said defensively. "As far as she was concerned, I blew up her life."

"But it seems weird that she'd want to be with me, when I was the cause of you blowing up her life."

He remained silent.

"I know you said you left because of how she was treating me, and it means more than you could possibly know that you said that, but I can't help wondering if something else was going on with her."

"Why would you think that?"

I didn't want to come out and insinuate she'd been murdered, so I pushed the conversation in a different direction. "When do you think she started talking to her parents again?"

"I don't know."

"If she was talking to them again, then why weren't they at the funeral?"

He paused. "Because I didn't invite them."

I gasped. "Why not?"

"Because of how they treated me," he said defensively. "And of course, how they treated her. She needed them after Andi died and they made her choose—me or them."

Did my mother regret choosing him? Look where they'd ended up. Then again, she could have had me in her life—I would have done anything to have her interest and love—and she'd tossed me aside like garbage. Worse than garbage. Like I was evil.

"Do they even know she's dead?" I asked.

"I don't know."

"You don't intend to tell them?"

"No," he said, his voice cold as ice. "I'll never speak to those people again."

"They need to know, Dad."

"Then *you* can tell them."

"Fine. Do you at least have a number for them?"

"You're a hot shot detective," he said in a hard tone. "Use your skills to find them."

The words landed like a punch, sharp and unexpected. For a second, I was ten years old again, sitting in my room with my arm around Andi, listening to him yell at Mom about something I didn't understand—his voice cold and clipped, just like this. I'd spent years forgetting this side of him. Pretending he was only the man who used to bring Andi and me to his office and spoil us rotten.

"So, this is how you really feel about me?" I asked, my

heart breaking. "Has all this *I want to be closer to you and I'm sorry for everything I've done* act been bullshit?"

He released a long groan. "No, Harper. I didn't mean it like that, I swear," he pleaded. "I'm so sorry. I'm just on edge, and you're dragging up all of these feelings about your grandparents. They should have been here for the funeral, but their choices kept them away." He paused, then his voice broke as he added, "It's just been a horrible, horrible day."

"Those words didn't come out of thin air," I said, tears burning my eyes. "You must have actually thought them at some point. Is this because I pressed you about your involvement with Hugo Burton and J.R. Simmons?"

"I can't do this right now, Harper."

"Yeah, you mentioned that," I said, my bitterness slipping through.

"Harper, I'm sorry," he said, sounding panicked. "I swear I didn't mean anything by it. I was just frustrated. But before you go, I *do* need to share a concern I have."

I froze. Had he found out about my drinking? Or that I'd spent the afternoon with Malcolm? I steeled my back. "Go on…"

"As we both noticed, your mother was depressed and several of her friends say she wasn't acting like herself."

"You mean scared?"

"She wasn't scared," he scoffed. "They think her depression had an anxiety component." He drew an audible breath. "In any case, we have reason to believe that perhaps she did this herself."

My heart skipped a beat. "You mean she might have driven off that bridge on purpose?"

"We have no proof…" He hesitated. "But that's our concern."

"When you say *our,* who exactly are you talking about?"

"Me and Detective Monahan. He knows the status your mother held in town and given my career and your recent troubles, he agreed to keep things quiet. She didn't have a life insurance policy, so it's not like we're defrauding anyone. This protects us."

"Why are you telling me this now?" I asked. "Why not tell me when you found out?"

"I was trying to spare you. I didn't want you to blame yourself."

I blinked. "Why would I blame myself?"

"Because I was the one who insisted you come home, and we both know she wasn't happy about the whispers and the gossip about you."

My chest tightened. "Wait, let me get this straight. You're saying that my return was so distressing she couldn't live with it anymore and drove her car off a bridge?"

"That's not the *only* reason, Harper," he said sympathetically. "In her eyes, my leaving was much worse. She said I abandoned her." He paused. "I considered not telling you, but I also know you're curious by nature and you might start asking questions. I wanted you to hear it from me instead of someone in the sheriff's department."

"I see."

He hesitated. "Maybe I shouldn't have told you."

"No," I said in a tight voice. "I would rather live with the heartbreaking truth than a cold lie. Especially since I heard several women gossiping about it after the service today."

"Oh," he gasped. "I'm so sorry you had to hear that."

Where had the rumor come from? Had *he* spread it? Would he tell me if he had? "Like I said, I'd rather have the truth."

"I knew you'd see it that way." He sounded relieved.

He'd be less relieved if he knew what I really meant. I wanted the actual truth, not his bullshit story.

"I just wish she'd tried to get help," I said, trying to bait him. "If only she'd gotten some medication, maybe it wouldn't have come to this."

"She was on Zoloft," he said. "But obviously it wasn't enough."

According to Malcolm, there'd been Zoloft in her bloodstream. Did she have a prescription or had my father known she was drugged?

"So that's how you knew she was depressed?"

"Yes, she told me she'd started taking it a couple of weeks ago."

"So, you knew she was depressed because she was taking Zoloft," I said, trying to make my voice sound neutral. "Why didn't you tell me sooner?"

"She didn't want people to know. You know how she was. She never wanted to admit weakness."

Which wasn't entirely true. She picked and chose which weaknesses she would cop to. But I suspected taking an anti-depressant would be on her secret list.

"Did she get it from Dr. Albright?" My mother had been going to our family practice doctor forever, and I couldn't imagine her willingly going to a psychiatrist.

"Of course," he said. "He always took good care of her."

Would Dr. Albright tell me if he'd prescribed it? "They returned her suitcase," I said. "Do you know if her prescription bottle was in there?"

"It's not," he said. "Detective Monahan took it." After a moment, he asked, "Why?"

"I didn't want the pills sitting around in your garage," I fibbed. "If the wrong people found out they were in there, they might break in and steal them."

"Good point," he said, sounding relieved. "But no one else knew she was taking the pills, so I think we're safe."

"I'm surprised she told you," I said. "It must have really gotten under her skin to take them."

"She was hesitant about filling the prescription," he admitted. "And I think she told me as a way to try to get me to move back. More manipulation."

His words sat heavily on my heart. While everything he'd said was plausible, I wasn't sure I believed him. I wanted to be able to trust him, but I couldn't.

"Thanks for telling me all of this," I said, trying to sound grateful. "It means more than you know."

"Of course, kiddo," he said, sounding more light-hearted. "I'm just sorry you're going through this. I love you."

I closed my eyes, my heart quietly shattering. He sounded like the dad I used to know before Andi's death. Warm. Protective. But that man had lied to me before. How many times would I let myself fall for that voice before I learned better?

"I love you too." Because I did love him. He was my dad, imperfect as he was. Would I still love him if he'd had something to do with my mother's death? Did you just stop loving your parent? Or was it easier when they weren't the parent you'd needed? My heart was so tightly locked that even I didn't know.

I hung up and leaned forward, feeling like I was going to be sick.

I wasn't buying the suicide story, even if I'd seen plenty of evidence that my mother's death had been no simple accident. If there was one thing I knew about Sarah Jane Adams, it was that she was a fighter. She'd proven that with Andi. She *never* would have just given up. She would have fought.

I knew without a shadow of a doubt that she'd been murdered. Now I needed to find out who'd killed her.

Chapter 7

Once I collected myself, I headed out to the dining area and sat at the bar in front of Malcolm.

He gave me his attention while he filled a glass with draft beer. "You look like you just talked to a ghost."

"I talked to my father."

"Ah… I take it you didn't like what he had to say."

I leaned closer and lowered my voice. "He claims she committed suicide."

His brow shot up.

"He said he and Detective Monahan agreed to keep it quiet. She didn't have a life insurance policy, so they figured they weren't defrauding anyone."

"That's bullshit. They would have been defrauding *you*," he said gruffly. "You would have had a right to know."

I was surprised by the outrage in his voice. "You're not buying that she committed suicide, are you? I mean, the evidence you dug up could partially corroborate it."

"Fuck no, I don't buy it," he growled. "How did the subject of suicide come up?"

"I told him she was acting weird after he left."

"So he blamed it on depression and claimed she killed herself because of it."

"Pretty much. Yeah." No need to tell him my father had partially blamed it on me.

"What about the suitcase? Why would she have bothered packing a bag if she'd planned to drive off a bridge?"

I shook my head. "I didn't ask. I didn't want him to realize we were suspicious."

"Good call." He set the mug he'd been filling on the counter and gave me a cursory glance. "How're you doin' after talking to him?"

I released a bitter laugh. "Not good."

He started to reach for a shot glass, then hesitated. "You want a drink?"

"More than I want oxygen, but no." I'd stopped shaking for the moment, so maybe the worst was over.

He leaned closer and lowered his voice. "While I applaud your decision to give up drinking, you can't just quit. Your body is addicted to it. You need to taper off, or you're gonna deal with some nasty side effects." When I started to protest, he said, "All I'm sayin' is, if you want to keep your wits about you, you might need one at some point."

Shame filled me. "How pathetic is that?"

He shook his head, his jaw tightening. "You're not gonna start feelin' sorry for yourself now, are you?" But his words didn't carry their usual bite. "Are you a whiner or a fighter, Detective?"

"All I know at the moment is that I'm gonna find out what happened to my mother."

A glint filled his eyes. "See? You're a fighter."

Was I? I felt like I'd rolled over and played dead after the Little Rock Police Department had thrown me under the bus. I knew the kid I'd shot had pointed a gun at me, but sometime between the shooting and the investigation, the gun had disappeared. Someone had obviously set me up, but I hadn't seriously considered it might be the department before Malcolm had made me question the possibility. Being a part of that department had meant everything to me, and losing my job and reputation had taken away my purpose. The only thing that had numbed the pain was alcohol. Which is how I'd gone from sipping a few glasses of whiskey at night to pouring it into my coffee first thing in the morning.

Part of me was terrified of who I was going to be once the detox ran its course. Maybe I *wasn't* a fighter. Maybe I never had been. But I wanted to be one.

"You're sure your father doesn't suspect you think she was murdered?"

I shook my head. "I was careful. The topic of her taking antidepressants came up, but he was the one who mentioned it, not me."

Surprise filled his eyes. "To cover the Zoloft in her bloodstream?"

"Maybe?" I raked my top teeth over my bottom lip. "I think…" I had to be Detective Adams, not my father's daughter, even if it meant facing some hard truths.

I started again. "If my father had something to do with her death, I'm not sure she was collateral damage." I held his gaze. "The way he suggested it was suicide and then played up her depression … it makes me think he had something to do with it."

"And if he did?" Malcolm asked. "What will you do about it then?"

"I don't know. But I'm not letting him get away with it."

He gave a curt nod. "Carter called a short bit ago about reports of accidents on the bridge." He took a beat. "There hasn't been an accident out there in over two years."

"But the skid marks."

His mouth tipped into the hint of a grin. "Teens like to go out there and race. Carter says they are likely from that."

"But the skid marks *do* go toward the embankment."

"Yep, and Carter called around and got Roy from RM Towing to admit he pulled a kid's car off the hill and didn't report it to the cops. That was last fall."

That helped back up our theory, but it also sobered me. My mother was *murdered*. But it reminded me of the other piece of information I needed to tell him.

"I have to drive to Jonesboro tomorrow."

"What's in Jonesboro?"

"My grandparents. My mother had been estranged from them since my sister's death, but my dad said that he thought she'd been in contact with them in recent years."

"Why were they estranged?"

"Honestly? At the time, my mother and I weren't talking, so she never told me why they were no longer part of our lives, and I was buried too deep in my own guilt and depression to really notice. I thought it was strange we weren't seeing them around the holidays, but when they didn't come to my high school graduation, I finally asked why. My dad wouldn't talk about it, and my mother said they wrote us off years ago. But on the phone call with my dad, he said they'd stopped talking to us because they needed someone to blame for Andi's murder."

Malcolm's eyes narrowed. "Why blame him?"

"I asked," I said. "At least my mother's reasons for blaming me for what happened had some merit."

"Bull-fucking-shit," he grunted, "You were *not* to blame, and any real mother would have *comforted* her daughter instead of blaming her."

His outrage on my behalf caught me off guard. He'd known about my mother's reaction to Andi's murder since our first case together, but while he'd insisted it wasn't my fault before, he'd never sounded this pissed about it.

"Well, maybe so," I admitted, "but there's no changing what's done. All I'm saying is that she had some basis for her resentment. I was with my sister when she was kidnapped, and I let her be taken."

"You were a child."

"I could have tried to stop him. If we'd both fought him, if we'd—"

He leaned closer, his face inches from mine. "Stop."

Surprisingly, I did, my breath coming in rapid pants.

"Goin' down that path won't change what happened," he said with surprising gentleness. "You're only beatin' yourself by doin' it."

He had a point, but maybe that was exactly why I kept at it. I sucked in a slow breath before saying, "My father had absolutely nothing to do with my sister's death."

His brow cocked. "You sure about that?"

I eyed the half-full bottles lining the back wall, my palms itchy with the need to hold a glass of whiskey. A cold sweat broke out on the back of my neck and my stomach churned. But I forced myself to focus on his question.

"Sure that my father had nothing to do with her death? I don't see how he could have been involved. My sister was randomly targeted. It had nothing to do with him."

"And nothing to do with you," he asserted.

*But I let him take her.*

He shook his head as though reading my mind but remained silent.

"In any case," I said, with more force than necessary. "My father didn't tell my grandparents about my mother's death, and I think I should inform them in person. It's the least I can do, and maybe I can find out why they stopped talking to her." Then I added, "And if my mother was in contact with them again."

He leaned back, resting the palm of his hand on the edge of the bar. "I'll take the day off. We'll go together."

My lips parted in shock. I knew he'd planned on helping

me investigate, but I hadn't expected him to take this road trip with me.

"I'm not going to hide anything from you," I said, meaning it. "I'm not trying to protect my father, if that's what you're afraid of. I'll tell you everything they say. I'll even record the conversation if you like."

He studied me so closely, I was sure he could see the blackness swirling in my soul. He didn't flinch. Maybe he saw something familiar. "So you say, but I'm goin' anyway."

"Why?"

He started to say something, then stopped, a hard look filling his eyes. "Because while you claim you intend to keep me in the loop, past experience proves otherwise. Besides, your car's in the shop and you're too poor to rent one. I'm goin'. End of discussion." Then he carried the beer to the other end of the bar and placed it in front of a patron.

This nicer version of Malcolm had me on edge. Sure, he'd practically called me a liar, but in the past, he would have told me to fuck off. What was with this softer version? Was he playing me? No, not playing me. But he clearly thought my mother's death played into his grand scheme somehow. Maybe I should be warier, but as far as I was concerned, as long as he helped me, then I could help him. It had worked for us before. I really did intend to tell him anything I learned from them. Sure, he hadn't reciprocated, but that didn't matter. My best chance of finding the person or persons behind my mother's murder was by teaming up with Malcolm. He could do whatever he wanted with the information we dug up.

I'd come a long way since last February. When my investigation to find Ava Peterman, Vanessa's eight-year-old daughter, kept crossing paths with the notorious James Malcolm, I'd expected he'd shoot me for crossing him. I sure hadn't expected him to suggest we pool resources.

That had been the drunk, sloppy version of me. What

would Detective Harper Adams, the strict, by-the-book detective I'd been before last October think of what I was doing now? She would have bitterly denied that she could become someone who let a man get away with literal murder.

More than once.

I'd witnessed Malcolm kill Ava Peterman's kidnapper. And I knew without a shadow of a doubt that he'd also killed Ava's kidnapper's brother, who'd watched while my own sister was tortured years before and kept quiet about it, but I hadn't turned Malcolm in for either crime. Even after he'd staged their deaths to make it look like Ava's kidnapper had committed a murder suicide.

Justice had been served, right?

Maybe the Harper before last October hadn't been the real me. Maybe I didn't know myself at all.

Then there was Skip Martin. I could have turned Malcolm in for killing him, and insisted, quite rightly, that he'd done it to save me. But I hadn't. And when he'd carried me out of that cellar, then turned his gun on Skip's crony, Pinky, I'd told him to pull the trigger.

And I hadn't had an ounce of remorse. Not even a minuscule amount of guilt.

Both men had gotten exactly what they deserved.

I stared at Malcolm at the end of the bar. I was more like him than I cared to admit.

So, what did that make me?

But now was not the time to have an identity crisis. I needed to put all my effort into getting justice for my mother, even as a voice in the back of my head shouted that justice might be a lot different from what I'd believed it to be six months ago.

I'd deal with that later too.

I still had work to do before tomorrow, so I pushed away from the counter and headed down the length of the bar toward the door leading to the back office.

Misti called my name as I passed by, so I stopped and moved closer to the bar.

"Sorry to hear about your mom," she said with a sad smile. "I know we don't know each other very well, but if there's anything I can do, let me know, okay?"

A lump filled my throat, and I forced out, "Thanks."

She leaned her forearm on the countertop. "Petey made his world-famous chicken parmesan tonight. How about I make you a plate?"

"You don't need to do that. I'm not very hungry."

She cocked her head. "When was the last time you ate?"

"Um…" I'd heated up that muffin after the funeral, but I was pretty sure I'd only had a few bites.

"That says it all," she announced in a smug tone. "You're gettin' some food."

I smiled. "Okay. Note to self: Don't cross Misti."

A smile spread across her face. "Best advice I've heard all week. I'll go grab your plate. Wait right here."

I stood at the counter, staring at the bottles of top-shelf booze on the wall, my mouth watering at the thought of taking a sip of whiskey. My fingers tightened into a fist.

I did *not* need a drink. I'd be damned if I caved. I could do this, despite what James Malcolm thought.

A few seconds later, Misti came out with a plate heaped with enough food to feed two large men.

I released a short laugh. "I can't eat all that, Misti."

"Maybe not, but you're gonna give it a try. There's always plenty of work to do after someone dies, and you need your strength."

She was right, but not in the way she thought. "Sounds like you know from personal experience," I said softly.

She gave a quick nod. "My daddy. I had to clean out his place and handle closin' all his accounts." She drew a breath, tears filling her eyes. "It's not for the faint of heart."

"I'm sorry you had to go through that," I said. "I hope you had someone to help."

"Not really, but that's okay." A sad smile on her face. "I'm glad you have James."

My eyes flew wide. "It's not like that with us."

Her smile brightened. "He's helpin' you, ain't he?"

"Well, yeah, but not how you think." Not that I was about to tell her what he was doing.

"Help is help, right? And James Malcolm is one of the most loyal people I know. Once he's your friend, the man has your back."

I was struck speechless, unsure how to respond.

"In any case," Misti said, seemingly unaware of my inner turmoil, "try to eat as much as you can, okay?"

I took the plate and offered her a tight smile. "Thank you."

She pointed a finger at me as I walked toward the back. "I'll be back to check on you later. No runnin' off without tellin' anyone like last time!"

A mere five days ago, I'd been working in Malcolm's office when I'd gotten a text from Detective Matt Jones from the sheriff's department, asking me to meet him somewhere for an important discussion. I'd thought it was related to my investigation into Hugo Burton's disappearance. But if Pinky hadn't run me off the road and kidnapped me before I made it to the meeting, Detective Jones would have told me that he'd pulled my mother's body out of the river late Friday afternoon instead of Saturday.

"He drove me here, so I won't be going anywhere."

"Good."

I meant it too. I was sticking to Malcolm like white on rice. He might be using me, but as long as I got my answers, I didn't care how they were acquired.

Further proof that I was no longer Detective Harper Adams, if I'd ever been her at all.

## Chapter 8

I sat at Malcolm's desk to eat. Just thinking about how much I wanted a drink made sweat break out on the back of my neck. I needed to keep busy and stop thinking about it.

I knew I had to eat, but based on the way my stomach was churning, there was no way I could eat even a fourth of what Petey had made for me. I cut off a piece of the chicken and took a bite, groaning with satisfaction.

There was no doubt Petey's culinary talents were wasted as a short-order cook in Malcolm's kitchen. Scooter's Tavern didn't have much of a menu, which meant Petey made most of his good stuff for staff dinners. It didn't seem like Malcolm to squander talent, which made me wonder if he had some master plan in the works. Was he planning to open an upscale restaurant under a dummy LLC? I wouldn't be surprised.

But I'd spent entirely too much time thinking about James Malcolm. I needed to get to work.

I pushed the plate aside and moved the laptop in front of me, then opened the lid and entered the simple password to wake it up.

Maybe I should find a notebook to keep track of my notes —especially since I wasn't in top shape. I could have opened a word document on the laptop, but something about hand-writing my notes had always helped sink them deeper into my head when I was working cases before. And considering the fact that my back was damp with sweat, and the ringing in my ears was back, I needed all the help I could get.

Earlier, I'd wanted to blame my shaky hands on low blood sugar, but it was time to be honest with myself.

Malcolm was right—I had a drinking problem, and there was a very strong likelihood I was suffering symptoms of withdrawal. A person couldn't drink as much as I had the last few months then abruptly stop with no consequences.

I opened a search tab and looked up alcohol withdrawal and squirmed when I saw symptoms I'd definitely experienced over the last day or two.

Sweats, tremors, anxiety, irritability, and loss of appetite—although the last three could be attributed to grieving, I had to admit everything fit.

Great.

This meant Malcolm was probably right about something else—I couldn't go cold turkey if wanted to spend the next few days investigating my mother's death. I was going to have to taper off. The problem was I didn't trust myself to take one drink and stop. I needed someone to help monitor me.

I could only imagine what Malcolm would say when he realized I needed a babysitter.

I shook my head, ignoring the fresh wave of pain that slammed into my temples. I was supposed to be finding a notebook. I'd gotten off track.

I opened a few of the desk drawers and found a clean legal pad with white paper in the middle drawer on the right side. Despite the fact I was starting to feel feverish, I pushed on and grabbed a pen with the Scooter's Tavern logo on the side and started a list of what I needed to do.

*Confirm my mother had been prescribed Zoloft*
*Find my grandparents' contact information*

*Dig into my father's financial information*
*Dig into my father's other possible business dealings*

I considered contacting Detective Monahan about my mother's supposed prescription, but if the deputy told my father that I'd asked, he might get suspicious. Besides, I couldn't trust that the detective would tell me the truth.

I could wait until tomorrow to call Dr. Albright's office, but it might not be necessary. My mother had used a chain drugstore for her prescriptions for years, one where you could sign up for an online account and refill your medications. If I could figure out her login information, then I could see if she'd filled the Zoloft there.

Her username was easy—her email address—but it was the password that threw me. She'd given me her password for her online banking a few weeks ago, when she'd had trouble signing into her account. Since my father had handled all the bills, it was an entirely new process for her. He'd opened an account of his own and left the old one for her, but she'd become responsible for her own bills. I'd been buzzing pretty hard that night, though, and now I was struggling to remember the password.

One more example of how I'd let drinking screw with my life.

Of course, there was a good chance I wouldn't have remembered even if I'd been ten days sober, but being drunk hadn't helped.

I'd blamed stress, blamed grief … hell, I'd blamed *every-thing* to excuse my drinking and justified it by claiming it was equivalent to taking medication. But there was no more denying the dirty truth: my body was screaming for what I'd denied it.

It would have to keep right on screaming. I was a strong woman, and I could push through this, and then I'd never, ever take a drink again.

I needed to focus on breaking into my mother's pharmacy account.

I tried the first idea that came to mind, and the screen popped up with an "Invalid Password" message.

Some websites gave you a limited number of attempts before locking you out, so I needed to be careful with my next guesses.

I closed my eyes and willed the memory to surface. It hadn't been any of our names, which had surprised me. I'd expected her to use a combination involving Andi's name, but it had been a plant and numbers instead of a random set of letters and characters.

After a few minutes, I was feeling worse and considered lying down for a bit, but I had work to do, and I wasn't going to let my problem interfere with my investigation. I just needed to focus and figure out this password situation. I made a few more attempts, getting all of them wrong.

The solution was to go to her house and open her laptop. I'd taught her how to save her logins and passwords onto her browser, so I could instantly gain access—but I was impatient. There was no way Malcolm would let me go to my mother's house on my own, so I'd have to wait for the end of his shift. And if I were honest, at the moment, the thought of going to my mother's house and trying to sort through her laptop sounded like climbing up a hill with ten cinder blocks strapped to my back.

My phone vibrated on the desk, and I realized I hadn't checked it since I'd called my dad. Louise had tried to call me three times while I'd been up front, and she'd just sent a text.

*Harper, I'm really worried about you. You're not home and you're not answering your phone. Where are you?*

I called her immediately. "I should have let you know I wasn't going to be home," I said as soon as she answered. "I'm so sorry."

"You've got a lot on your mind," she said. "I was just worried about you. Where'd you go?"

"I'm with my dad." The lie fell out before I could think twice, not that I could tell her I was sitting in James Malcolm's office at the tavern. "I guess I lost track of time. I should have been more considerate."

"No, don't worry about it," she said reassuringly. "I'm just glad you're not alone. Maybe we can get together tomorrow."

I pressed the heel of my hand to my forehead as a wave of pain hit and a shiver ran through my body. I was sure I was running a low-grade fever. "Actually, I'm going to be gone for a few days."

"Oh? Where're you going?"

I understood her surprise. She knew I didn't have anyone else other than her and my father. Kara, my roommate in Little Rock, had stopped talking to me after she'd moved out. "I need to go see my grandparents in Jonesboro. After Andi died, my mother and my grandparents had some kind of falling out, and they weren't in contact. I just found out my father never notified them about her death. They have no idea."

She gasped. "Oh, my God. That's horrible."

"I know, which is why I think I need to go and tell them in person."

"Yeah," she said, sounding distracted. "Of course. I didn't realize you had grandparents." Then she hastily added, "I mean, of course, everyone has grandparents. I just didn't realize they were still alive. While I can understand your dad not getting along with them—mother-in-law horror stories are a dime a dozen—I still can't believe he didn't tell them."

"I know. I haven't seen them since Andi's funeral, so I could call or have law enforcement in Jonesboro contact them, but that just seems wrong. Besides"—my voice broke—"I feel like I need to see them."

"Of course! It's a way for you to feel a connection to your mom."

Not exactly, but I wasn't going to confess that I also wanted to ask questions about my dad. If I told her I suspected my mother had been murdered, I'd have to explain where I'd gotten the idea. And there was no way I could confess that.

Which gave me pause. If you felt the need to hide something, it meant you were either ashamed or knew you were in the wrong.

Was either acceptable?

"I think it's a good idea," Louise said. "But you shouldn't go alone. I can try to get off work and go with you."

Would I have wanted her to go under different circumstances? It wasn't like it was a girls' trip. But it was a moot point.

"I think I need to do this alone," I said. "Plus, I'm not sure how long I'll be there. The law firm told me and Dad to take off as much time as we need."

"You aren't working on any cases?"

"PI cases?" I'd only gotten my PI license a couple of weeks prior, and I hadn't told many people other than Louise, one of the law firm partners, and Malcolm. In fact, just last week, I'd considered opening my own office instead of working for my father's law firm.

That seemed like years ago.

She released a soft laugh. "Of course. What else?"

I tried to laugh too. "Sorry. My brain's moving a little slow right now. No, I don't have any cases, but then again, I haven't really hung out my PI shingle yet. I found out about my mother's accident practically moments after I wrapped up the Hugo Burton case."

"That makes sense," she said. "But I'm not sure sitting around dwelling on what happened is good for you." She took a beat. "In fact, when you're ready to work again, maybe you should ask the law partners if they have any investigative work you could do. Something simple, like an adultery case or something."

"Good idea," I said. "I'll ask them."

"Good," she said decisively. "Keep me updated on how long you're gonna be at your grandparents. We'll do something when you get back."

"I'll let you know," I said. "You're the best, Louise. Thank you for being there for me."

"Of course. That's what friends are for." I thought she was going to hang up, but then she said, "Before you go…" She drew out the words, like she was weighing what she was about to say. "Have you talked to Nate? I saw him at the funeral, but I was surprised he didn't come say something to you."

*I* wasn't surprised. Disappointed, but not surprised. "Maybe he had to get back to the bookshop."

"Yeah, maybe," she said. "I'm struggling to understand it. You two are friends."

"Yeah…"

She heard the hesitation in my voice. "Did you guys have a fight?"

"No, but I had a couple of weird run-ins with him last week."

"Neither of you have mentioned that," she said. "What happened? Did you finally tell him you aren't interested in dating him?"

"I never said I wasn't."

She sighed. "Well, it's obvious you're not. And not telling him is only going to hurt him."

I picked up the fork next to my plate and twirled it between my fingers. "You know I've told him that I'm not ready and he should date other people."

"Not being ready and not being interested are two very different things," she said bluntly, "and you and I both know you're *not* interested. If you want to keep his friendship, then you need to tell him before it gets too awkward when you do."

She was right. While I really liked the idea of having someone like Nate as a significant other, the fact was, he was too normal for me—no matter how much I *wished* I could be happy with normal. It stung that Malcolm had been the one to point it out last week—bonus points to him that he was right.

"It doesn't help that I showed up in his bookstore kind of a mess twice last week."

"What?" she asked in surprise. "What happened?"

"I stopped by his shop after getting some bad news." I released a bitter laugh. "I don't think I have to worry about letting him down, because I probably permanently scared him off."

"I doubt that," she scoffed.

I wasn't so sure. Especially since he'd smelled alcohol on my breath in the middle of the day. Then again, I'd had reason to be upset. I'd just connected the dots that my father had given J.R. Simmons access to Hugo Burton's office after the man had been declared missing so Simmons could clean it out before the police went through it. Not that Nate—or anyone besides Malcolm—knew those details. I'd given Nate no explanation. I'd dropped in, cried on his shoulder, and then ran. I was embarrassed, to tell the truth.

"When was the last time *you* talked to him?" I asked.

"I don't know … I guess after you found out about your mom."

"So, several days?"

"Yeah. But he was at the funeral, and he wouldn't be much of a friend if he wrote you off for being upset."

It was more than that, but I couldn't bring myself to admit it. And I was also eager to change the subject. "I went out to the river today."

"Oh," was her quiet reply.

We were both silent for a moment before I took a breath and said, "I wanted to see where my mom's car went into the water."

"Harper…"

"It's okay," I said firmly. "But after seeing it, I'm confused about what made them decide to dredge the river for her car. We hadn't reported her missing."

"I'm not really sure," she confessed. "But you could always call Detective Monahan and ask him."

"I don't want to bother him."

"You, of all people, should know you wouldn't be bothering him," she insisted. "That's part of his job."

"I don't want to make any unnecessary trouble," I said. And alerting my father to what I was up to by asking questions could definitely cause trouble. I released a short laugh. "I guess I have a whole new appreciation for the victim's side now. The need to know everything."

"I thought you would have gained that after your sister."

An unexpected pain stabbed my heart. "I think I was too young. Not to mention, I didn't *want* to know what she'd gone through. It was too much."

"I get that."

"Anyway…" I decided to make a confession, telling myself it would help sell my story—but I also had to admit that I needed to confide in someone who might understand. "I keep obsessing about what she was thinking when her car left the road and plunged into the water. How scared she must have been." My voice tightened. "I know it's morbid, but it's not unexpected, I guess. I met my fair share of families while working traffic fatalities who asked the same questions. They were desperate to know if their loved one died quickly, or if they suffered."

"Harper…"

"It's all part of the grieving process," I said, suddenly feeling like bugs were crawling all over my skin. "The need to know all the details, like having them will ease the pain. Like wondering what made the sheriff look for her car, and everything else."

"You should call Monahan, Harper. I know he'll share what he knows."

"Maybe not with the infamous Harper Adams." After I was disciplined for an on-the-job shooting last fall, most cops seemed to consider me a pariah. Like if it happened to me, it could happen to anyone.

Louise knew that better than most people, but she was willing to take professional risks to be my friend. "Monahan seems pretty fair minded, but how about this? If I'm around Monahan, then I'll ask some casual questions. I can do that without making it a big deal."

"Thanks. Whatever you find—*whenever* you find it—is fine. It's not like it's going to bring my mother back."

"True, but it fills in the pieces of her last moments," she said softly. "I get it. I've had cases like that too. It's stupid to think we wouldn't want the same answers when it happens to us."

"I suppose," I admitted. I sat with the phone in my hand for a moment before I said, "You've been a good friend, Louise. I don't know how I would've gotten through the last few months without you."

"You would've been even more of a mess," she said with a laugh. "But I know you'd do the same for me."

"Yes," I assured her. "Definitely."

"Well, I hope it goes well with your grandparents. If you need to talk afterward, you know how to reach me."

We hung up, and I couldn't stop the flood of guilt. I was lying to her, and you didn't lie to friends. Which meant I was a shitty friend to someone who'd been a great one.

Another sin to add to an already lengthy list, but I could pick it apart later. I needed to devote my time and attention to finding out who'd killed my mother.

Would my grandparents know anything that would help me solve the case? It seemed doubtful, but it was worth a try, not to mention, telling them in person about my mother's death was the right thing to do.

I couldn't imagine how they'd react—if they'd slam the door in my face or pull me into a hug. After Andi's death, they'd retreated into silence. Maybe they'd buried me too. Had they realized that I was the Little Rock police officer accused of killing a supposedly unarmed boy? If they did, would they turn me away before I could tell them why I was there?

I was sure it wouldn't help having James Malcolm in tow.

What would they think if they realized I'd brought a former crime boss to their doorstep?

I guessed I'd be finding out soon enough.

## Chapter 9

After my call with Louise, I took a few more bites of my food, then pushed my plate aside. I needed to get more work done. Breaking into my mom's pharmacy account had been a bust, and it would be next to impossible to look into my father's finances on Malcolm's computer. Perhaps some of his login information would be saved on my mother's computer, but I needed to go to her house to find out. Which left only one task on my to-do-right-now list: finding my grandparents' address.

I knew I could probably find the address in my mother's address book at her house. But doing nothing would feel like giving in to what was going on in my body, and sitting here twiddling my thumbs was unacceptable.

The light was too much, my eyes were photosensitive, so I turned off all the lights except for a table lamp next to the desk. I moved to the sofa, setting the laptop on my legs. What should have taken only a few minutes to search on the internet, took more like ten. My vision was getting blurry as my other symptoms progressively worsened. I was feverish, my body running hot then cold, and drenched with sweat. The few bites of chicken I'd eaten weren't sitting well in my stomach, and I found a trash can next to Malcolm's desk that I kept next to me … just in case. I felt so weak I wasn't sure I could make it to the bathroom if I succumbed to the nausea.

It took everything in me to find the address for Gary and Shirley Langford of Jonesboro, Arkansas, and plug it into the map app on my phone. The app showed the trip would take about three hours. If we left early enough, we could potentially be back in time for Malcolm to work the evening shift.

If I felt well enough to make the trip.

I *had* to feel better. I refused to let my own weakness halt finding justice for my mother.

I needed rest. I'd take a nap and then wake up feeling better. Maybe I'd even feel up to going to my mother's house after Malcolm's shift, although it seemed like a better idea to do it tomorrow before we left for Jonesboro.

I set the open laptop on the table next to the sofa, then laid down, closing my eyes against the pounding in my skull.

Even though I felt like I was dozing, I must have been out cold, because the next thing I heard was Malcolm softly swearing next to me. I hadn't heard him open the door.

I cracked open an eye, my head throbbing at the light. He stood on the other side of the coffee table. "Good thing your sofa is leather," I said through my chattering teeth. "Otherwise, I'd have to pay to have it dry cleaned."

He headed for his crystal decanter on the bar cart against the wall across from the door and picked it up. I'd had that whiskey. It was the best I'd ever tasted, and my mouth watered for another taste. "You need to take a drink, Harper,"

I wanted a drink more than I wanted my next breath, but I wasn't giving in. I was scared I wouldn't stop. "No."

"Goddammit," he muttered as he poured a finger of whiskey into a glass. He set the decanter down without replacing the stopper, then moved back over to me. He sat on the coffee table, his jaw set as he said in an icy tone, "You've got two choices: take a few sips or I'm taking you to the ER."

I glared up at him, but my hair was plastered to the side of my head and my shirt was sticking to my chest, so I wasn't sure I looked as threatening as I'd hoped. "If I go to the ER, there's a good chance my father will put me in rehab up in Little Rock."

He rocked the crystal whiskey, holding it between his fingers. "Your choice."

My gaze followed the swirl of the amber liquid, every nerve in my body begging me to reach for it. "If I go to rehab, then I won't be able to investigate my mother's murder, and we both know you want me to investigate it. That's why I'm here, ruining your sofa."

His face remained impassive. "You can't investigate if you're dead."

"This won't kill me." Then my body betrayed me, and my stomach rebelled. I leaned over and threw up what little I'd eaten a couple hours earlier.

Thankfully, Malcolm had quick reflexes and had the trash can in place. As I leaned over the can, I felt something lightly brush my cheeks. It took me a second to register that he had swept my hair back, holding it out of my face.

I started to glance up, wanting to see his reaction, but another wave hit me and I doubled over again, dry heaving.

When the nausea finally passed, my head felt like it was about to split in two. I collapsed on the sofa, but closing my eyes didn't make the room stop spinning.

I heard Malcolm cross the room, then return seconds later. His hand slipped behind my neck, and he pulled me upright as he held the small opening of a bottle up to my mouth.

"I'm not taking a drink," I mumbled, turning my head to the side as I tried to lift a hand to bat it away, but my aim was off.

"It's water." He tipped the bottle higher as he chased my lips and poured some of the liquid into my parched mouth. I swallowed greedily, then he gave me a little more before lowering my head back down.

Seconds later, he was lifting my head again and slipping a pillow under my upper body.

"Why are you doing this?" I rasped.

"Because you're right." he said, his voice rough. "I want you to investigate your mother's murder and the sooner we can get you over this, the sooner we can get on with it."

"You don't need me." I wished the sofa would swallow me whole and end my misery. "You can get any investigator you want."

"You have access to your grandparents that I can't get without you."

"I was the one who suggested it," I countered. "It never even occurred to you."

"And it never occurred to you until you talked to your father. As his *daughter*. You have a familiarity with your family that one of my guys wouldn't have."

He had a point, but it could be argued that I was the last person who should be investigating my own father.

"You need to take a drink," he said, quieter.

"No. This afternoon, I swore I wouldn't drink again." It was a better excuse than admitting I didn't trust myself to monitor my intake. And something told me Malcolm valued someone who gave their word.

"So, take one anyway. It's not like you're gonna burst into flames."

I opened my eyes to focus on him. Irritation flickered on his face.

"You're right," I said. "I won't burst into flames now. That'll happen when I end up in hell."

"So take a goddamn drink." His voice was sharp.

I shook my head, instantly regretting the movement as pain shot through my skull. I nearly told him I didn't trust myself, then doubled down. "I gave my word, Malcolm, and if I don't have my word, then what do I have?" But as I said the words, memories of the Little Rock shooting and its aftermath flooded my head, and I realized I meant it.

He remained silent, watching me.

I drew in a ragged breath. "I swore that kid in Little Rock had a gun. I swore over and over, despite the fact that they couldn't find it. It would have been *so* easy to recant my statement, and trust me they *wanted* me to. They told me that I'd imagined it, and people would understand if I just admitted I'd made a mistake. That these things happened. That *accidents* happened…" My voice broke and I realized I was close to tears. "They made it sound like shooting that boy was like spilling a glass of milk. Nothing worth crying over."

He just watched me with those intense brown eyes.

"I didn't accidentally shoot him," I said, my eyes burning with unshed tears. "I only had a split second to act when I saw his gun. I acted on instinct. Just like I'd been trained to do."

He waited.

"They told me it would all go away if I told them what they wanted. That I could keep my job, and it would all get swept under the rug. When I refused, the union attorneys told me the kid had a record, that he'd been arrested multiple times and had a history of trouble." My chest heaved as I remembered that meeting, the horror of it still there in my bones. "They said the world was better off without him. That I'd done the community a *favor*." My voice caught. "They called him vermin."

"Forget what they said," Malcolm grunted. "The fact remains that he *did* have a gun. The rest is superfluous."

"It cost me my job. I lost everything. That's not superfluous."

He lifted a brow. "There's the truth, and the lie. You live the truth. They pushed the lie."

I sighed, raw and exhausted of this conversation.

"There had to be a reason they wanted you to lie," he continued. "Why?"

I didn't have the energy to contemplate the why, but it wasn't lost on me that James Malcom—above practically everyone other than Nate and Louise—believed me. I wasn't even sure my father believed me. But Malcom never once doubted my side of the story. That was the why I was most interested in at the moment, not that I was likely to get an answer if I asked.

"Where is this little talk going, Malcolm?"

"You won't take a drink because you gave your word," he said, gentler.

"Yes!" I snapped. "Because my word is all I have left!"

But was it? I'd proven myself trustworthy during my career in the Little Rock police force, and they'd turned on me in the milliseconds it had taken to pull the trigger. My word wasn't worth a hill of beans.

"You still have your brain." He lightly tapped my forehead. "You're still alive." He glanced down at the glass of whiskey on the coffee table, then lifted his gaze back to me. "You realize you'd likely be dead if you hadn't shot him. He would have killed you."

"I'm very, very aware."

He studied me with cool detachment. "But you regret it. You wish you'd let him shoot you."

My anger surged. "I *never* said that."

"You didn't have to," he said evenly. "I could ask you why his life is worth more than yours, but we both know what you'd say."

"What the hell are you talking about?"

He released a sardonic laugh. "You and I, we're more alike than you'd care to admit."

He'd said it before, and I'd always denied it. Fought it. But now, caught in the haze of my withdrawal, I knew he was referring to the truth I'd buried down deep. That I wished I'd let that kid shoot me.

Had he wished he'd died in someone else's place?

Either way, I was facing hard truths, so I might as well face this one. The Harper Adams on Malcolm's office sofa was far more like the notorious crime boss than the police detective I'd been before last fall.

I *was* like him.

A monster.

Only when I looked up at him now, I didn't see a monster. I wasn't deluded enough to believe he was trying to help me for purely altruistic motives, but I didn't believe he was completely detached either.

"You think the wrong person died last October," he continued, his voice calm, like he was reading a bedtime story. "There's part of you that wishes it had been you lying in that alley, not him. But your sense of self-preservation is stronger than your desire to become a martyr."

"You're full of shit," I said, but it didn't carry enough heat to sound convincing, even to my ears.

His brow lifted. "Am I?"

"What's the point of all of this? Are you trying to drive me to drink? Wear down my defenses so I'll cave so we can get on with the investigation?"

"And have you back in the same position you were in last week?" he asked in disgust.

"Then what *do* you want, Malcolm?" I asked as I closed my eyes, weary to my bones.

"I want you to face the real reason you're drinkin'." If he'd said it in a fit of anger, it would have lit a fire in me, but he said it with so much compassion, it nearly stole my breath.

Why did he care why I drank? All he wanted was for me to quit drinking. I wanted that too now, which meant we were on the same page.

Besides, it was so fucking obvious why I drank. I'd lost my entire world, and drinking had helped me cope, or at least I thought it had. I could see now I hadn't really coped at all. I'd merely smothered the pain.

I knew he wasn't going to let this go without an answer, but I wasn't going to make it easy for him either.

"You know why," I said through gritted teeth as a wave of pain shot through my head.

"Because you killed a kid in self-defense?" he shot back. "You and I both know it's not that simple."

That pissed me off, and I sat up, intensifying the pain in my head. "Okay, asshole," I grunted, pressing the heel of my hand to my temple. "You think you're so goddamned smart? Then tell me why I drink. Because apparently, wanting to drown the nightmare of that boy bleeding out in an alley isn't enough."

"The real answer's so damn obvious, you should be embarrassed you haven't figured it out."

"Why the fuck do you even *care*?" I demanded.

He leaned forward, his eyes sharp. "Because if you're this good of an investigator as a drunk, I can only imagine how good you'd be if your head was clear."

I hadn't expected that and some of my anger bled out of me. His back-handed compliment made my face flush with embarrassment.

He shook his head, pity filling his eyes. "You could take a drink right now and ease your symptoms, take the slower, steadier path to sobriety, but you won't. Sure, you could say your refusal is because of your vow, but it goes deeper than that. You *want* to hurt."

His statement hit home, ripping a layer off my carefully shielded heart.

"You think you *deserve* it. Your mother treated you like shit. Your father wrote you off. You told yourself you didn't deserve love. Hell, you don't think you even deserve to be alive."

Tears stung my eyes.

But the look in his eyes told me I wasn't the only one who believed that about themselves.

He held the glass toward me. "Take a drink, Harper."

I eyed the glass in his hand, my body screaming to snatch the glass and gulp it, and yet…

I looked up at him, feeling pathetic as I whispered, "If I take that drink, who's to say I won't just keep drinking?"

His face hardened as his gaze held mine. "You won't because you're stubborn as a mule. You're not gettin' drunk. You're taking a medicinal dose. Before, you drank to ease your guilt. Now you're doing it to get sober."

I released a bitter laugh. "That sounds like something a drunk would say to justify their next drink."

"Good thing you're a stubborn bitch," he said, holding the glass out to me again. "Now drink."

I reached for the glass, feeling the ridges of the crystal press into the pads of my fingers and thumb, and slowly brought the glass to my lips.

Relief spread through me like wildfire as the whiskey hit my tongue. Malcolm might be convinced I was drinking to ease my symptoms, but my body thought otherwise.

I guessed it would learn soon enough.

"Take another sip," he said.

It took everything in me to not down the entire glass, but I took a small sip, letting it slide down my esophagus. Within seconds, my muscles uncoiled and my nausea eased.

"For what it's worth," he said, his voice surprisingly gentle. "There's no shame in admitting you have a problem. Especially now that you've decided to fix it."

I released a bitter scoff. There was plenty of shame in getting to this point.

A dark grin spread across his face but didn't reach his eyes. "It kills you that I'm the one helpin'."

A month ago, I would have hated every minute of him seeing me like this. But now?

Like me, Malcolm was a pariah. He'd confessed that the police and the sheriff's department harassed him. Other than

Carter Hale, his attorney, I was pretty sure he didn't have any close friends.

I wasn't sure how I'd define our relationship, but I couldn't deny I didn't want my friends knowing I was with him right now. Or that he'd helped me find Ava Peterman or solve Hugo Burton's murder. He was my dirty little secret, and he knew it. *Of course* he'd think I hated that he was the one helping me.

But surprisingly, he felt like the only person who understood.

"No. It feels right that it's you."

Surprise flashed in his eyes, before he recaptured his usual detachment. "Close your eyes and get some sleep. You'll feel better in the morning, and then we'll head to Jonesboro."

## Chapter 10

Around seven, I woke to light streaming through the window's wooden blinds. Malcolm was slumped in the armchair, asleep. His feet were propped on the coffee table, his ankles crossed, and his head leaned to the side.

The lines around his eyes seemed softer, and he looked less jaded.

Less dangerous.

It made me wonder what life choices he'd made to get to this point. You didn't wake up one day and decide to become a crime boss, or at least, I didn't think someone like Malcolm did. Most people did it for money or power, often both. Had that been his motivation? Fenton County was poor, one of the poorest in the state. Maybe he'd seen it as a way out of poverty.

When I sat up, my head swam, so I rested my elbows on my thighs and leaned my forehead into my hands. My head and muscles ached like I was recovering from an illness, but I was a hell of a lot better than I'd been last night.

I turned my head to look at Malcolm and saw his eyes had cracked open.

"She lives," he said with a tight smile.

I sent him a grim smile in return. "For another day."

"You feel up to drivin' to Jonesboro?" he asked, still slouched in his seat.

"I've felt better, but it doesn't change my plans. We need to go by my mother's house first. I can take a shower there and then we can head out of town."

He gave a slight nod and stood. "Let's not waste any time."

I felt a little queasy as we drove to my mother's house, but Malcolm snuck a glance at me and silently handed me his flask. I unscrewed the lid, then took a swig, the warmth of cheap whiskey sliding down my throat. Taking the sip still felt wrong, but I'd forced myself to accept that it was the only way I could make this trip, let alone investigate my mother's death.

When Malcolm pulled into my driveway, I headed for the back of the house and found the poorly hidden spare key in the fakest looking rock I'd ever seen.

"You don't have a key?" he asked in surprise.

"Not until a few weeks ago," I said as I walked over to the door and inserted the key. "And that one is up in my apartment. This was faster."

I pushed the door open and he followed me inside. I headed for the kitchen counter, where my mother kept her address book, then flipped it open to the L section. I'd already gotten the address from the internet, but it wasn't a bad idea to get confirmation. My grandparents were listed at the top, Gary and Shirley Langford, with the address I'd already found.

I closed the book and set it on the kitchen table. "We're bringing this with us. We might need it later."

"Okay," he said, still standing by the back door.

I gave him a long look. "I'm surprised you didn't just start searching the house."

"It seemed rude to barge in and start rifling through things."

I scoffed, realizing he was probably waiting for me because I knew where things were, not out of respect for me or my mother's house. Her laptop was on the kitchen table, but I bypassed it to head to my parents' bedroom. I'd already checked out my father's office last week, looking for anything that might link him to Hugo Burton and J.R. Simmons, but he'd cleared his things out. If he had a paper trail for his financial information, he'd likely kept it in his home office and taken it with him, but I knew Mom had kept some papers in her bedroom.

I walked into her room, catching the faint whiff of Estée Lauder perfume. She'd worn it as long as I could remember, and the scent stopped me in my tracks. My heart wrenched, and I wondered why losing her hurt so much. I'd spent most of my life without her, rarely giving her a second thought. How could you grieve someone you had mostly written off? Had she slipped through my defenses with her neediness over the last few weeks? Or was I mourning the mother I'd always wanted?

"You okay?" Malcolm asked in a hushed tone behind me.

"Yeah," I said, my voice gruff. I shoved my feelings down as I took a few more steps into the room. "Mom kept some papers in her dresser. She might have some of my father's financial documents there."

"You don't think he took them?"

I bent over to open the bottom drawer of her dresser. "The chances of them being here are fairly small, but it's worth a quick look."

There was a stack of documents, but a quick search through them revealed about five years' worth of electric and water bills, car and house insurance premiums, and their personal bank statements. I pulled out the entire stack, closed the drawer and stood upright. "I doubt anything useful is here, but I'll bring it with us and go through it on the drive."

"Could they have kept financial statements anywhere else?" Malcolm asked.

"It's possible, but this is where she always kept her bills and paperwork. If you want, feel free to search the rest of the house while I go check out her laptop."

His brow rose in surprise. "You don't want to keep an eye on me?"

I looked up at him. "Are you asking if I'm worried you'll steal something? You never struck me as a petty thief."

His mouth tipped into the hint of a grin. "Was that a compliment?"

"Take it as you will."

"You're not worried I'll hide something from you?"

I quirked a brow. "Should I be?"

"We both know that's how we've operated in the past," he said matter-of-factly. "We've had our secrets. Only shared what we must."

Was he warning me that he was still operating that way? But what could he possibly find that would only help him and not me? Was I willing to take the chance?

This man had shown multiple times now that he wouldn't hurt me—that he'd go to great lengths to protect me—but that didn't mean he wouldn't keep secrets. Maybe he should. There was no denying he'd been a criminal in his previous life. And while I suspected he'd gotten immunity with the feds prior to his release from federal prison three years ago, I didn't have confirmation of that. If I ever find out anything about his previous illegal activities, I'd be duty bound to report them. Then again, that had been Little Rock Detective Adams, not private citizen Harper Adams. Sure, I knew I was still oblig-ated to report such things, but unless he confessed to some-thing truly heinous, I wouldn't. I'd keep his secrets.

Last week, when I still hadn't fully trusted him, I'd done some research about Malcolm's connection to J.R. Simmons. I'd discovered he'd worked with a woman named Rose Gardner to get J.R. Simmons arrested in Fenton County over four years ago. At that time, Rose had been the girlfriend of the ADA of Fenton County, Mason Deveraux.

Malcolm and Rose's partnership had struck me as strange, especially since he'd been on law enforcement's radar. So, I'd made an impulsive call to Mason Deveraux, who was now the lead prosecuting attorney in the Arkansas Attorney General's office, to ask about it. His assistant had taken my message because he was in court.

Deveraux had called late the previous Friday, leaving me a message to call him on his personal phone, something that wasn't typically done. But I'd listened to the message a couple hours before I'd been kidnapped, and the next day I'd learned about my mother's death. I'd forgotten about calling him back, and now, I didn't want to.

I wanted Malcolm to explain the past to me himself, and it no longer seemed urgent for it to happen immediately. What I did need to know was what he was up to right now.

I tilted my head, studying him. "What are you really doing here in Lone County, Malcolm?"

He released a short laugh.

I shot him a smile. "Didn't expect that question?"

"I suppose I opened that door when I asked if you trusted me." When I didn't respond, he said, "I already told you I'm sniffing out Simmons's successor."

"And it's taken you this long?"

His eyes darkened. "I never said *when* I started looking."

"True." But if he'd only recently started looking, what had he been doing here before that? As far as I knew, Malcolm had no previous ties to Lone County, and it seemed like an odd place for him to suddenly decide to open a tavern. I'd presumed the feds had asked him to come here, but while they might have been playing the long game, three years seemed like a stretch.

Nevertheless, I had no doubt he was interested in the successor now. That was why he'd been so interested in Hugo Burton and his associates. And *that* made me wonder why he was so invested in unmasking my mother's murderer. "Do you think my mother's death has something to do with the successor?"

"Maybe. Maybe not."

"But you *do* think it has something to do with my father." We'd both agreed we believed it possible, but standing in my parents' bedroom, looking at my mother's neatly made bed, it seemed insane. How could you live with someone for forty years and have them killed? But that was a stupid question. The world was full of murderers who justified what they did. It was possible my father had done the same thing.

*Is it really?* my inner voice protested.

I knew I had to pretend my father wasn't my father, that he was just the husband of a murdered woman, and there was no denying the spouse of the deceased was always the number one suspect until proven otherwise. But he was still my father.

Malcolm's gaze found mine. "I honestly don't know if your father was involved, but it makes sense, doesn't it?"

It did, which was why I was suddenly feeling nauseous in a way that went beyond withdrawal sickness.

Walking past him, I paused in the doorway. "Search wherever you want. I trust you." Then I headed back toward the kitchen.

He didn't follow me, not that I expected him to. I didn't care what he found, because I *did* trust that he'd tell me if he found something related to my mother's murder.

Before doing anything else, I started a pot of coffee. I wasn't sure my stomach would be able to handle it, but my brain needed the caffeine boost.

While the coffee maker began to brew, I sat down at the

table and opened the laptop, entering the password Primrose to wake it up. At least I remembered that one.

While I'd planned to log on to her pharmacy first, I saw the phone icon at the bottom of the screen. My mother had connected her phone to her laptop, so the first thing I did was search her phone calls.

She hadn't made many, and most had names attached, which meant they were in her contact list. But my gaze narrowed in on the call she'd made after I'd phoned to cancel on her last Tuesday around noon.

It had been made ten minutes later after my call was recorded. There was only a number with no name attached. The interesting part was that it had a 327 area code, which was a relatively new area code. While Northwest Arkansas and Little Rock and the surrounding areas had their own area codes, the rest of the state had used 870. But recently, the FCC had added a second area code—327—since the 870 area was nearly out of numbers. Lone County and all the southern and northern parts of the state fell into the 870 and 327 areas. So did Jonesboro. Did the number belong to my grandparents? It didn't seem likely since the number had to be relatively new.

I pulled up the service I signed up for skip tracing after I'd passed my PI license test and entered the number. I expected to see a name and hopefully an address pop up, but there was nothing.

No name. No utilities or credit attached. No address. Just the carrier, a known burner phone service. And the most ominous part was that the phone had been activated a week ago Sunday, two days before my mother called the number.

Whoever my mother had called wanted to be untraceable.

What had my mother been up to?

## Chapter 11

Malcolm walked into the kitchen. "I smell coffee."

Still reeling from my discovery, it took me a moment to acknowledge what he'd said. I nodded toward the coffeemaker. "Help yourself." I nearly told him there was creamer in the fridge, but he already knew that. He'd made coffee here last week.

He opened the cabinet where my mother stored her mugs and grabbed two, then poured coffee into both.

"Find anything?" I asked, sitting back in my seat and watching him.

"Nope." He answered flippantly. I was tempted to question him, but mostly out of habit. He brought both cups to the table, setting one in front of me and the second on the other side of the table, then headed to the fridge.

I looked up at him. "*I* found something interesting."

When I didn't continue, he said, "Go on."

"I told you that I called my mother last Tuesday around noon to tell her I couldn't take her to her luncheon. I just looked up her calls on her laptop, and ten minutes after I placed that call, she made a call to a number that's not in her contacts."

He shut the fridge with his hip, grabbed a spoon from the drawer, and carried both to the table before he sat in the chair across from me. "I take it you already looked up who it belongs to."

I added creamer to my coffee. "It's a burner phone with no other information. No name or address. It's not linked to anything. And even more suspicious, it was activated two days before my mother called the number."

His brow shot up as he took the creamer from me. "What do you make of that?"

I picked up the spoon and stirred. "It's strange, that's for sure. She lived a small life. Sure, she was in all the women's clubs, but this town's pretty small. I can't see how she'd even know someone with a burner phone, let alone call one."

"Was she good with numbers, or would she have needed to write it down somewhere? Like on her phone or a notepad?"

I shook my head, then regretted it as the dull ache expanded. "She had a terrible memory. She must have stored it somewhere."

"But likely not on her phone," he mused, "otherwise she would have saved it as a contact, even if she'd used some kind of code for the name."

He was right.

"So where would she have kept it?" he asked before taking a sip of the coffee.

"I think she would have either written it down here somewhere in the house or kept it in her purse."

"If it was here in the house, where would it be?"

"Maybe her address book, but I doubt she'd put in a number for a phone that was only two days old. What I don't get is how she even had a chance to get someone's brand-new number sometime between Sunday and Tuesday at noon. As far as I knew, she mostly stayed home lately. But if it's here in the house, she might have kept it in the pen drawer. Or maybe a drawer in her dining room hutch."

"Maybe someone emailed it to her."

"It's possible."

"What's the number?"

I grabbed the notepad she kept on the table, then reached for a pencil she kept in a small vase for her crossword puzzle book. My hands were slightly shaky, so I gripped the pencil tightly, hoping Malcolm didn't notice, then started to lightly scribble over the paper. It revealed writing, but it was her grocery list of coffee, eggs, roast beef, potatoes, and carrots.

"Guess she didn't write the number there," he said.

"Agreed. This had to be her grocery list for Sunday lunch since she made a roast with potatoes and carrots, all on her list. She put it in the oven before she went to church, and we ate it after she came home."

"So, she went to church Sunday morning, did she go anywhere else the rest of the day after lunch?"

"I don't know when she left for church. I was still asleep." More like sleeping off my hangover. "But she usually left around 8:30. She always got to church early so she could help set out donuts, muffins, and coffee for people to eat during Sunday School. Last Sunday, she came home around noon, and I came over for lunch. That was her usual time for getting home, so I don't think she went anywhere between church and home."

"If she actually went to church," he said with a pointed look.

"True. Everything fits with her usual schedule, but it's easy enough to find out. I can call a couple of her friends to make sure she was there."

He gave a slight nod.

"I came over a few minutes after she got home and helped her finish getting lunch ready. We ate around one, then I watched a movie with her on the TV. Around three or a little after, I told her I was going to head to my apartment for a while. She wasn't happy about it, but she didn't fight me on it. I hung out in my apartment the rest of the afternoon, then came over around six-thirty to have sandwiches with her. We watched more TV, and then I left at around nine."

"You don't think she went anywhere when you were in your apartment?"

"No." But I couldn't be one-hundred-percent sure. I'd had a few drinks and napped a bit before my alarm went off, reminding me to go over. "Besides, it would have been out of character for her."

"So is calling a burner phone, so we can't rely on her doing things that are in character."

He was right and I felt foolish for suggesting it. We were looking for actions that weren't usual for her.

His jacket was slung over the back of his chair, and he reached behind him, into the jacket, then pulled out his flask. After he uncapped it, he handed it to me.

I took it without protest. Between my shaky hands and my comment about my mother's regular habits, it was clear my brain wasn't working on all cylinders.

I limited myself to a healthy sip, ignoring the voice in my brain that said I needed to take another one or two or ten. I hated myself for sinking so low that I couldn't control my drinking, but I'd deal with my self-recrimination later. Right now, I needed to focus.

It took everything in me to hand the metal flask back, but he took it without comment, even though he had to know about the inner battle I was waging.

I leaned back in my chair, letting the whiskey work its magic. The tight muscles of my back and neck began to relax before I focused on what we'd been discussing. "I don't think she left the house Sunday afternoon," I said, "but if I'm honest, I can't be totally sure."

Should I admit I'd been drinking? But a quick glance over at him suggested he already knew.

"But," I added, "I don't think she got the number for the burner during that time. That kind of thing would have made her nervous, and she didn't seem particularly on edge when I came back over."

"She might not have known it was a burner," he said, lifting his mug. "She might have thought it was just a number."

"True."

He nodded. "Someone could have given her the number on Monday. Do you know what she was up to that day?"

"Her car was in the driveway when I left for work around 7:45, and I could see a light on in her bathroom window. I have no idea what she did while I was gone, but I got home a little after five, ate dinner with her and watched more TV. She could have easily met someone during the day."

"And Tuesday?"

"I left for work around the same time, and there was a light on in the kitchen."

"Was it out of character for her to be up that early?"

I shook my head. "My mother wasn't a night owl. She was an early riser. If anything, it was unusual that the kitchen light wasn't on yet when I left for work on Monday."

"And you were at work on Tuesday morning, so you don't know what she did before you called her."

"Yeah."

He leaned back and took a sip of his coffee. "At least we have a rough timeline to work with. We should confirm she was at church on Sunday morning. You said she kept a calendar, but did she have a planner? She might have written her Monday and Tuesday activities in there."

"Good point. I'll check her email first. You can search the pen drawer and the buffet for the phone number while I pull it up."

He stood, taking his coffee cup with him as he headed to the kitchen drawer I pointed to.

I woke up the laptop, then clicked on the email icon. When the login page came up, the autosaved login and password filled in the fields. To my surprise, she only had twelve unread emails. That was a remarkably small number considering she'd been dead a week. Most of the emails were part of a historical society email chain. Another was a recipe newsletter, and there was a reminder for a dental appointment last Friday that had been sent out the day before. Late Friday afternoon, she'd received a follow-up email to reschedule her missed appointment.

That one struck me as odd.

Malcolm had already rifled through the pen drawer and moved into the dining room—I could hear him pulling out a squeaky drawer in the buffet.

"She missed an appointment with her dentist last Friday," I said, raising my voice so he could hear me. "And they sent an email for her to reschedule. She would *never* purposely miss an appointment, which makes me think she wasn't planning on leaving so quickly on Tuesday. That or she thought she'd be back by Friday."

"You think something spooked her?" he called back.

"Maybe." I took a sip of my coffee, hoping the mix of whiskey and coffee would work its magic soon, then rethought my answer. "She was upset when I said I couldn't go to the historical society luncheon on Tuesday. I'd just gotten the Hugo Burton case, and it was the only time his wife could meet with me. Those meetings are at least an hour to an hour and a half. I don't think she would have planned to go to the meeting if she was leaving town in a hurry."

"Who's to say she was in a hurry?" he asked, still in the dining room. "What if part of the reason she was upset you didn't take her was because she wanted to tell you about her plans?"

Guilt shot through me. I couldn't deny it was a possibility.

"You had no way of knowing," he said behind me, leaning into the door frame.

I twisted in my seat to face him.

"And you canceled for a legit reason."

Malcolm walked over to the coffee maker and refilled his cup. "The real question is, what made her decide to call a number she'd just received within the last two days?"

I pushed out a sigh. "Good question."

Malcolm returned to the table and poured more creamer into his cup without sitting. "You said she'd been anxious and safety conscious. Maybe she got mixed up in something dangerous or realized someone was out to get her."

Releasing a short laugh, I said, "She always wore her seat-belt, even if she was driving in a parking lot. She unplugged her appliances if she was leaving the house for more than four hours. She threw out milk the day before its sell-by-date. She was the epitome of careful."

She'd always been that way, but she'd become even more vigilant after Andi's death.

"Maybe so, but there's no denying she called a two-day-old burner after she talked to you. It's suspicious as hell. Especially for a woman like your mother."

He was right. So why had she called the number? And who did the number belong to?

I did another scan of her email, this time looking for anything threatening, but came up with nothing.

Unless she'd deleted it.

I pulled up her archived emails, but there was nothing there either.

I opened her text message icon, but there were only a few texts, all spam or from stores she'd likely signed up for. My mother hated text messaging and refused to use it.

I told Malcolm my findings.

"Do you think someone came to her house?" he asked.

"Maybe? But I don't know how we could verify that. She doesn't have a camera doorbell. It was too high tech for her. And I don't think the neighbors have one either."

A grin cracked his lips. "Are they busybodies?"

I considered it for a moment, then lifted a shoulder into a shrug. "Some are, some aren't."

"Maybe *they* saw something."

Did I really want to take the time to canvas the neighborhood right now? I needed a shower, and it was a three-hour drive to Jonesboro. Not to mention we still had to dig through my mother's waterlogged things to see if there was a note with the phone number.

"I can ask around," he said nonchalantly.

I nearly spat out my coffee. "*You?*"

He shrugged. "How likely are they to know who I am?" A grin spread across his face. "I can be charming when I want to be."

"You? Charming?' I snorted. "I'd *love* to see that." But even as I said, I knew he was right. I'd seen hints of it before.

He sat back and brought the coffee cup to his lips, a smirk filling his eyes.

I shook my head. "No way are you going through the neighborhood. If anyone puts together who you are, then we'll have a whole new mess to deal with. I think it can wait for now. We need to go through her suitcase, and I should do that before I take a shower since it's bound to stink to high heaven."

"Did you look up her pharmacy account?"

"Not yet."

"Pull that up first, then we'll tackle the suitcase."

It was easy to log in since her computer auto fed the login information. A couple of clicks showed her list of medications. Zoloft was the most recent one filled.

"She had a prescription of Zoloft for 50 mg," I said,

shaking my head. "I still find it difficult to believe she'd agree to take it."

"What if she didn't?"

I glanced up at him and narrowed my eyes. "What do you mean? Are you suggesting someone had it prescribed for her to make it look like she was on antidepressants?"

"It would sure help sell the suicide theory."

I pushed out a sigh. He was right, but the only person I could think of who could pull that off was my father. The prescription had been sent in three weeks ago, so if he was responsible for it, her death had been premeditated.

My heart began to pound, and I reminded myself that this was just another case. A random woman. *Of course* her husband was the number one suspect.

"We need to find out if she asked for the prescription," Malcolm said. "Who prescribed it? Her usual doctor?"

I checked the screen. "Yeah. Dr. Duncan."

"Is Dr. Duncan friends with your father?"

My stomach sank like a stone. "They're golf buddies."

He lifted a brow. "Say they're out on the course, and your father mentions how anxious your mother's been, only she's too embarrassed to call or make an appointment to ask for help. So, your dad's buddy offers to prescribe it and save her the visit."

"That would be illegal. She'd have to ask for it herself."

"You really think that kind of thing doesn't happen?" he scoffed. "Especially in a town like this?"

He had a point, but how could I find out?

I'd deal with it after we came back from Jonesboro.

I closed the laptop and plugged it into the charger at the table to make sure it was fully charged before I took it with us. Malcolm would be driving, which would give me plenty of time to search her computer using the hotspot on my phone.

I took a long sip from my mug before I stood. I couldn't put this off any longer. "Let's dig through her bag."

He nodded and drained his cup.

I was dreading this. Not only the smell but going through her things. It felt like an invasion of her privacy, even if the sheriff's department had done it before us.

We headed out the back door and walked over to the detached garage at the end of the driveway. My mother had never kept it locked, so it lifted easily, revealing the clear plastic bag containing a black, carry-on sized suitcase in the middle of the concrete floor. Her handbag was also in the bag. The smell of mildew was already strong, and we hadn't even opened it yet.

Malcolm approached the plastic bag first and began to work on the loose knot at the top. Once he had it open, the smell nearly knocked me over. I buried my nose in the crook of my arm.

"That's even worse than I expected," I said, my voice muffled by the sleeve of my sweatshirt. But burying my nose into my own rank shirt reminded me that I wasn't smelling like a rose myself.

"No denying it's ripe," he said, tugging down the side of the bag. "Got any gloves?"

"Not latex or nitrile."

He lifted his gaze to me, flashing a smile. "What kind of PI *are* you?"

"I just got my license," I said half-defensively. "I've barely gotten started."

He walked over to my father's work bench and began rifling around until he found a pair of grimy work gloves. I expected him to complain, but he just shoved his hand in the first glove and tugged it up to his wrist, then started tugging on the other. "I'll open the suitcase and spread it open, then we'll go through it, item by item."

"I have a pair of winter gloves upstairs. I'll get them so I can help."

"I think it will work better if I go through it, and you point out if anything's off."

I gave a short nod, my stomach starting to protest at the stench. It would be faster if I got my own set of gloves, but he was right—I really needed to look at everything since I was more likely to spot if something was off.

He pulled out her purse first and set it on the concrete, water still dripping from the bottom.

The image of my mother and her purse sinking into the river filled my head, sending a wave of panic through me. I drew in a sharp breath, then instantly regretted it as my nose filled with more of the putrid stench.

He glanced up at me as I coughed, repressing a gag. "You okay?"

"I'm fine," I said testily, pissed at myself for showing a reaction like a damn amateur. Sure, I hadn't examined submerged purses and suitcases before, but I'd seen a lengthy list of equally disgusting things. "Keep going."

He pulled out her wallet, then opened it, revealing her driver's license, a credit and debit card, and sixty-four dollars and fifty-three cents in cash.

"No receipts," he said. "A lot of people keep a receipt or two in their wallet. Like a recent gas purchase."

I wasn't sure if he knew that for a fact or was just guessing. "Not my mother. Her wallet was always neat and tidy."

"No paper with the burner phone number."

I couldn't stop my frown. "Yeah, not that we'd necessarily be able to read it anyway. The ink may have bled."

"True," he said, setting the wallet aside. "But we still don't know how she remembered the number, so even a blank piece of paper would have been worth our consideration."

He was right. I wasn't sure why I was being contrary, but I also wasn't going to apologize.

Next, he removed a compact with powder and a puff, two tubes of lipstick, her key fob for her car, and her slim planner.

I hadn't considered her planner, which I could only attribute to my brain working on half its cylinders.

"There might be clues in here about what she was up to before her death," Malcolm said.

My stomach knotted. Was it too much to hope she'd recorded where she was going or who she'd met with to get the burner? Could it be that easy?

Malcolm stood and walked over to me, carefully opening the cover. The printed ink was still slightly intact and readable, so I was hoping whatever she'd written was legible.

He started flipping pages, and once he hit January, my hopes were dashed. While I could see that something had been written on certain days, the words were mostly unreadable smears.

"We're looking for March," Malcolm said. "The interior pages might be more legible."

Possibly, but I wasn't going to risk getting my hopes up.

He carefully turned the page and February was the same, just ink smears on the page. Next was March, which was just as unreadable, but held more smears than the other pages.

"Maybe if we let it dry, it will reveal more," he said.

I narrowed my eyes as I glanced up at him. "Since when did you become delusional?"

He shrugged slightly. "You never know what's going to turn up. Maybe we'll be able to see indentations where she wrote."

I leaned closer, nearly gagging again. "The paper's wet, and the fibers are swollen. Any indentations are long gone." I couldn't keep the bitterness out of my voice. "Is there anything else in her purse?"

He walked back over to the purse and squatted next to it, then peered in, the calendar still in his hand. "Nothing." He looked up. "She was definitely a neat and tidy woman."

"Neat and tidy was her middle name," I said through gritted teeth. She'd hated clutter and threw out just about everything she considered no longer useful. Just like she'd done with me.

*Stop with the melodrama.*

If she hadn't been so fastidious about paper clutter, then maybe there'd be more clues about what had happened to her.

"You ready to move on to the suitcase?" he asked.

I nodded, not trusting myself to speak.

He put everything back in the purse, except for the planner, which he put on the work bench. He gave me a look as though expecting me to challenge his hopes for the planner, but I kept my mouth shut. If he wanted to venture to dreamland, I wasn't going to stop him. Let him crash and burn on his own.

He lifted the suitcase out of the bag, and I was either getting used to the smell or it wasn't as stinky. I suspected it was the former.

He moved it several feet toward the opening of the garage before laying it down and unzipping the case. The zipper stuck a few times, but he gave it a good tug and got it unfastened, then opened the lid. Her clothes were neatly folded and placed in neat stacks on one side. A makeup bag was on the other side, along with a pair of heels, a pair of flats, and carefully packed underwear and socks.

It was neat, just like my mother, but it shouldn't have been.

"The sheriff didn't go through this."

Malcolm was kneeling behind the top of the case. He glanced up with a questioning look.

"The sheriff's department should have gone through her personal items, and if they had, they wouldn't have repacked it so neatly. They never opened her suitcase."

"You're saying they broke protocol?" he asked sarcastically.

I ignored his tone. "Her car was in a river, which made her

death suspicious. It's why they did an autopsy. They *definitely* should have gone through her bags."

"Unless they already came up with their explanation and decided they didn't need to go through it. Presume the sheriff's detective isn't crooked. What would have stopped him from searching the bag?"

"If he found her bottle of Zoloft in her purse or the car—because this is too neat for them to have looked for it in her carry-on—but even that's a stretch. He wouldn't have the toxicology report likely for days. It's standard procedure to search."

"So they were sloppy?" he asked.

"Or they let my father sway their conclusion."

He gave me a pointed look. "Or they're crooked."

I had no problem believing the Jackson Creek police were lazy or crooked, but I'd gotten a different impression about the Lone County Sheriff's Department. Still, I had to admit it was a possibility. "Or if the detective on the case is crooked."

He started to reach for the first piece of clothing, but I stopped him.

I pulled my cell phone out of my pocket. "We should do this right." I took several photos, then opened a note taking app and prepared to start an inventory list. I should have done it for the contents of her purse. One more piece of evidence my brain was shit.

Should I even be investigating?

He carefully sorted through the sopping-wet clothes, unfolding each item to check for anything hidden. Then, to my surprise, instead of tossing the items into a pile, he refolded each one and set it on the floor. I was sure he was being this careful because they belonged to my mother. Part of me wanted to tell him to just drop them and move on to the next piece of clothing. It would be faster if he did, but I couldn't bring myself to do it. I felt like my mother deserved some shred of dignity. I couldn't help noticing the irony that

James Malcolm was the one giving it to her. I had no doubt she wouldn't have granted him the same consideration.

By the time Malcolm went through all the clothing, I'd counted two pairs of pajamas, five pairs of slacks, six long-sleeved and three short-sleeved shirts, a cardigan, and two business-style dresses.

"Your mother was a great packer," he said with a short laugh. "Not a lot of people could have gotten that much into one side of a carry-on suitcase."

"True." Funny how I'd never known that about her. Then again, she hated to travel, so I'd never seen her packing skills in use.

He started on the other side, searching inside each shoe before setting it beside the stacks of clothes. Next, he pulled out a trench coat and searched the pockets, which were completely empty. The makeup bag held her cosmetics, her toothbrush, and skin care bottles, but it was the two pill bottles that commanded our attention.

Malcolm held one up and read the label. "Zestril."

"Her blood pressure medication."

He shook the bottle, and the pills rattled inside of it. Then he opened the cap, showing me the contents. "Do you know if this is what they look like?"

I looked up the medication and compared the photo of the orange tablets to the ones in the bottle. "They look the same."

He set the bottle to the side and picked up the other one. "Lipitor." He looked up at me. "Cholesterol medication." He shook the bottle, then glanced at the white tablets. "Yep, that's what they look like."

I didn't ask how he knew.

"Her bottle of Zoloft isn't in there," I said.

"Nope." He set the bottle on the floor. "Seems like she would have kept all her medication together. It's not the kind of pill you pop when you get anxious. You take it once a day."

"Agreed." It seemed unlikely, but I suppose there was a chance it been in her purse and they'd removed it. But I wondered if she'd been taking it at all. Could I convince the pharmacy to tell me who'd picked up her prescription? Or maybe Malcolm could use his other questionable resources to find out?

"Can Carter have his mysterious helpers find out if my mother picked up the Zoloft or someone else did?" As soon as the words fell out of my mouth, I knew I should be horrified that I'd suggested it, but I couldn't muster up the self-disgust.

His brow lifted in surprise. "You don't want to question them yourself?"

"They're not going to tell me anything," I said. "It seems like it will be a more efficient use of our time if you get someone else on it." Then I realized the people working for him didn't do it out of the kindness of their hearts. "I'll pay for their time."

A frown creased his forehead. "Like hell you're gonna pay. Whatever we find out will likely benefit me too." He gave me a smarmy grin that didn't quite reach his eyes. "And if it doesn't benefit me in any way, I'll let you work it off."

His tone made it sound like an innuendo. I put a hand on my hip. "With a PI case?"

"Of course," he said like I was an idiot. "What else?"

What else indeed? After last night, there was no way in hell he'd ever want to sleep with me, and even though my wandering eyes were lustful, I knew better than to sleep with him.

What the hell was I thinking about anyway? I was investigating my mother's murder. Why was I imagining James Malcolm naked, pinning me against a wall?

I suddenly wished I had a fifth of whiskey—vow or no vow—to wash that image away.

His eyes narrowed in concern. "You okay? You need a drink?"

"I'm fine," I said gruffly. "Let's finish."

He gave me a lingering look before he searched the lining of the case. After he'd gone over it twice, he announced. "Nothing hidden in here."

Thankfully, my attention was back where it belonged. "She packed for multiple days. It wasn't just a day trip, which is weird because she didn't cancel her dentist appointment."

"Maybe she forgot."

I gave a slight shake of my head. "She wouldn't have forgotten."

"So if she didn't cancel before she left, she planned on cancelling later?" he asked.

I considered it. "Or she packed to be gone for a lengthy period of time just in case she needed to be gone longer, but hoped to be back before Friday."

We were both silent for a few moments, mulling over the various possibilities.

"You think she was going to her parents' house?" Malcolm asked breaking the silence.

I shook my head. "Not unless she was planning to surprise them. I didn't see their number in her call log."

So where had she been going? The navigational app on her phone might have been able to tell us her planned destination, but she had an older phone. One that wasn't waterproof.

"Wait," I said. "Her phone wasn't in her purse."

He stared at me for a moment. "You think the sheriff's office still has it?"

"Maybe. The phone would have been dead once it became submerged. They wouldn't have been able to get anything from it. They might try to see if they can get anything from the SIM card, but it's highly unlikely to give them much beyond the phone number and the carrier. That's if the river sediment didn't already corrode the metal." I glanced at the suitcase. "But if I were working the case, I'd take the phone anyway. You never know what you might get."

"If the sheriff's department didn't take the phone, then someone else did?"

"Maybe," I said. "Or they gave it to my father." I gestured to the suitcase and purse. "They gave him this."

"And if he kept the phone … if it's not waterproof, it's worthless." His face darkened. "That seems suspicious."

"Agreed."

We were silent again, me trying to come up with a logical explanation for why my father would keep my mother's phone and came up with nothing. It seemed far more likely the person who'd killed her took it. But why? What could she have on it that they would want?

"Harper," Malcolm said in a gentle tone. "Go take a shower."

I gaped at him in surprise.

"I'll repack all of this, you go shower so we can get on the road to Jonesboro." When I didn't move, he lifted a brow. "Fair warning, I'm taking a shower too. Let me know which one you plan to use so I can use the other."

"I'll shower in my apartment."

He gave me a curt nod, then I headed up the stairs to my apartment.

## Chapter 12

I emerged from the bathroom about fifteen minutes later—my partially blow-dried hair still damp—then headed into the house wearing a pair of jeans and a white button-down shirt. I'd spent several minutes deciding what to wear, which was unusual for me. Dress pants and a button down would have made me look too much like a cop. I could have worn a dress, but I didn't have anything casual. So, I'd decided to wear the jeans for a casual touch and dress them up a little with the button down. I grabbed a tweed blazer I'd only worn once before and headed to the house.

When I opened the kitchen door, Malcolm stood in front of the stove, his back to me, wearing jeans and a gray thermal shirt. The smell of bacon made my stomach growl, then churn with nausea.

"You're cooking breakfast?" I asked in disbelief.

"You think I'm incapable of frying bacon and making eggs?"

"I know you're perfectly capable; you made me breakfast last week. I just didn't expect you to do it today. I thought we were in a hurry."

"I'm hungry and I found bacon and eggs in your mother's fridge. She obviously won't be needing them."

My stomach dropped at the reminder. "True."

"Besides," he said, turning back to the stove, "you need to eat. It'll help with your withdrawal."

He had a point, but admitting I was going through withdrawal was a still sore subject. "How much longer until it's ready? If it's ten minutes or so, I could check in with a couple of neighbors." Then I added, "That is, if you trust me to talk to them without you."

"I trust you," he said without turning around. "And you've got about ten minutes, but I'll keep it warm if you take longer."

I gave him one last look, unable to ignore the way his shirt stretched across his shoulders and biceps, then practically ran out of the house.

The two next-door neighbors both offered their condolences before they said they hadn't heard or seen anything out of the ordinary other than some loud noises the week before. I thanked them and asked them to call me if they remembered anything.

I was about to head back, but my ten minutes weren't up, so I decided to try one more house. The neighbor across the street and slightly to the left had always held a grudge against my mother, long before Andi's murder. Becky Comstock was about my mother's age and had lived in her house as long I could remember. She'd kept track of our family's comings and goings back when we were kids and teenagers, complaining about a multitude of things, from Andi and I being too loud when we played basketball in the driveway to my father mowing the lawn before ten a.m. For all I knew, she'd stopped after Andi's death, but then again, maybe she'd seen it as reason to stalk us even more. She stopped complaining to my mother, or at least, my mother didn't mention her at our forced family dinners anymore.

When Becky opened the door, her eyes flew wide, and she cast a glance over my shoulder at the house. "Harper." Her voice was strained. I'd interviewed enough people to know when someone didn't want to talk to me. The question was why. Was it because of my notoriety or because of my mother?

"Hello, Mrs. Comstock," I said politely. "I'm sorry to disturb you so early this morning."

Her mouth puckered with disapproval. "I would hardly call nine in the morning *early*."

"True," I said, sweetly. "But *some* people do."

Her scoff made it clear what she thought of those people. "What can I do for you?" she asked, crossing her arms over her chest and glancing at the house again. Then I realized her gaze was focused on the car in the driveway.

Still a snoop. I hoped that would work to my advantage.

"I'm trying to piece together my mother's whereabouts last week," I said, attempting to sound conversational and not like a cop canvassing the neighborhood. "I was wondering if you'd noticed anything unusual."

She gave me a pointed look. "You mean unusual like the sounds of gunshots coming from your property last Thursday night?"

I played innocent. "I'm sorry? You heard *what*?"

"I know what gunshots sound like, Harper Adams," she said in disdain, "and I know they came from your mother's backyard."

I gave her a serious look. "Did you call the police?"

Her brow rose with an accusatory look. "Should I have?"

"Seems to me that someone as concerned about the safety of the neighborhood as you were when we were kids would call the police." Keeping the sarcasm out of my voice was a Herculean feat.

Her arms dropped and she looked momentarily chastised.

"Well, I figured you were there, and you *were* a police officer and all."

My car had been in the driveway, but it still didn't explain why she hadn't called 911. Maybe she'd thought I was target practicing? But who target practiced in their suburban backyard?

Her eyes narrowed again. "Why are you asking about your mother's whereabouts? They said her car skidded off the bridge in the rain last week."

"Well," I said, hunching my shoulders slightly to appear as unintimidating as possible. "We're not sure *when* exactly her car went into the river." I gave her a sad smile. "I know it's silly, but I'm trying to piece together her last days." When she didn't comment, I pressed on. "Do you remember the last time you saw her?"

She gave me a condescending look. "You're presuming I gave a flip about what your mother was doing."

"You're right," I said, taking a step back as though preparing to turn around and walk away. "I just remembered you were always so observant. I thought you might have picked up on something." I took another step back. "I'm sorry for bothering you. Thank you for your time."

I started to pivot when she called out, "Wait. I may remember something."

"Really?" I asked with genuine enthusiasm, even if I was amping it up for her ego. "Thank you."

"Don't thank me yet," she snapped. "I'm not sure how helpful it will be."

"Anything will help."

She stepped onto the porch, leaning into the open door. "The last time I saw her was last Tuesday. She came out of the back of the house with a small black suitcase."

Which meant she really did leave last Tuesday. It still killed me that I hadn't noticed. "Do you remember what time?"

Her lips twisted as a faraway look filled her eyes and she bit her bottom lip. "I want to say it was between two and three?"

A couple of *hours* after her call to the burner phone? That surprised me.

"Yeah," she continued, "it was after the black car stopped in front of her house and dropped off that woman."

I blinked, staring at her in shock. "A woman showed up at my mother's house?"

Was that who she'd called on the burner phone?

"Yep, she walked right up to the front door, and your mother opened it before she even had a chance to knock. Your mother let her into the house, and the black car drove off. Then a few minutes later, Sarah Jane and the woman walked out from the back of the house, your mother rolling a suitcase behind her. They got in your mother's car and left."

I still couldn't believe it. "Do you remember what this woman looked like?"

She shrugged. "I don't remember much."

"Anything would help. Maybe what she was wearing?"

Tapping her chin, she made a face and said, "Well, let's see." After two more taps, she dropped her hand. "She had on dark jeans and knee-high black boots. She was wearing a black T-shirt and a gray winter coat that hit her mid-thigh."

That was not remembering much? "Do you happen to remember her hair color?"

"It was salt and pepper colored. Shoulder length. One of those bob cuts everyone associates with a Karla."

Karla? I gave her a questioning look. "Do you mean a Karen?"

She waved her hand. "Karla, Karen. Whatever. Basically a bitch."

"Are you saying the woman was a bitch?"

"Shoot no," she said in irritation. "I never talked to her."

"Did you recognize her? Any idea who she might be?"

She shook her head. "Nope."

"How old do you think she was?"

"Well, she must have a great skin care routine, because her face looked like she was in her forties, but her hair made her look a little older. It was a lot more gray than dark."

That didn't necessarily mean anything. She could have been anywhere from thirties to sixties.

"Had you seen the woman at my mom's house before?"

She crossed her arms over her chest and looked down at me with plenty of attitude. "You think I pay attention to the comings and goings at your mother's house?"

That's exactly what I thought, but I wasn't about to admit it. I forced a smile. "Heavens, no, Mrs. Comstock, but I was hoping maybe you had noticed. You know, when you were gardening, or happened to see something when you left the house to go to the store."

"Nope, that's the only time I saw her, but I have to say, I was pretty surprised when I heard they pulled your mother out of the river and that woman wasn't with her. I mean, it was obvious Sarah Jane was leavin' town with her suitcase and all. I figured she and that woman were going on a trip together. It just seems odd Sarah Jane was in that car all alone."

She had a very good point.

"Yeah," I agreed. "It's very odd." It meant my mother hadn't headed straight out of town and off the bridge. At some point, the woman with her had gotten out of the car. Had the woman been part of her murder?

Or had she been in the car, and someone removed her body before the police found the car? That seemed highly unlikely.

"Do you remember anything else that might help me piece together what happened in the last few weeks of my mother's life?"

She gave me a scrutinizing look. "I thought you were trying to put together her last few days."

"I am," I said nonchalantly. "It's just that I don't know anything about the woman she left with, so I'm curious if she had any other new friends I didn't know about."

"Friends," she scoffed. "Sarah Jane Adams didn't have friends."

I couldn't argue with her there. The behavior of the people who'd shown up at her funeral only proved her point. "Then maybe not *friends*," I said, not feeling the need to protest my mother's lack of relationships. "Maybe people you hadn't seen at the house before?"

She pointed to Malcolm's car. "Seen him around, but I don't think he's here for your mother, now is he?" A smug look tipped up her lips.

"No, I suppose he's not," I admitted. I wasn't surprised she'd noticed his presence. I only hoped she didn't realize who he was.

"Got yourself a boyfriend, huh?" Her eyes twinkled. "Not bad lookin', although I bet your mother didn't approve. Too many tattoos."

How had she seen Malcolm's tattoos? I was pretty sure he'd always had a jacket or long sleeves on. Although some did peek above his shirt collars. But she must have been really looking at him to notice those. I decided not to correct her about our relationship, and instead said, "My mother hadn't met him yet."

She nodded, her smug look back. "Oh, I figured that, considering he usually came around late or when she was gone."

I needed to steer this conversation away from Malcolm. "Back to my mother and any new acquaintances she might have made…"

"That woman was the only one."

"Did you notify the sheriff about your concerns?"

"Heck no," she scoffed and waved a hand dismissively. "That wasn't any of my business. Sarah Jane can come and go with whoever she pleases." I started to ask another question, but she cut me off. "Look, I don't know what your mother was up to," Mrs. Comstock said curtly, "But I'm sure it had something to do with your father. In fact"—a delighted gleam filled her eyes—"I half wondered if the woman was your father's *mistress*."

"Did my father have a mistress?"

"Beats me," she said with a laugh. "But if she was his mistress, maybe she drove Sarah Jane off the bridge. Or," she added, looking even more gleeful, "maybe Sarah Jane invited her over and planned to kill her and leave town."

I was momentarily stunned. Was any part of that possible?

Becky Comstock could see I wasn't totally convinced. "Your mother wasn't one to sit still and let someone walk all over her. There's no way she would just let your father up and divorce her without some kind of fight or pay back, now would she? I'm sure she had some tricks up her sleeve to either get him back or make him pay."

None of that had been on my radar, but there was no denying my mother had possessed a vindictive streak. But she'd seemed too beaten down to be plotting my father's—or anyone else's—demise. But Mrs. Comstock seemed to be waiting for a response, and I found myself saying, "If she *was* up to something, I didn't know anything about it."

She released a barky laugh. "Well, I suspect you'd be the *last* person she'd tell. She never really liked you much, did she?"

I was surprised at the sudden stinging in my eyes.

Her expression softened. "Oh, Harper, it was no secret that your sister was the favorite. We all worried about you after Andi died."

"We?" I forced out.

"The neighbors. We were worried your mother would blame you and treat you like crap."

"She did," I said, feeling numb. "She very much blamed me. You were right to worry." They may have worried, but not a single one had invited me into their homes to give me a reprieve. Or asked how I was doing. Or told my mother to be grateful she hadn't lost both daughters.

"We thought so," she said, with a smug nod. "Especially after you left for college and rarely came back." She lowered her voice. "Not that I blame you."

I wasn't sure what else to ask her, and I sure wasn't going to keep discussing my dysfunctional relationship with my mother, although I guess I'd invited the discussion when I'd admitted their concerns were justified. "Thank you for your help."

"Any time," she said, her posture softening. Maybe she thought she'd gone too far. "Say, if you like, I can go through my security video and get some images of the woman. If nothin' else, you can ask your dad if she's his lover." She shrugged. "Who knows? Maybe she's missing too?"

I shot a glance to the doorbell, confirming she had a regular non-video doorbell.

She laughed. "That's too obvious. I have it pointing out my spare bedroom window." She pointed up, and sure enough, I could see the tiny lens in the bottom corner of a window on the second floor.

"Yeah," I said. "That would be great."

She pulled her phone out of her pocket. "Give me your number, and I'll send the video to you."

"Thanks," I said, still in shock she had video. If we could identify the woman, this might be easier to solve than I'd expected. "I'd really appreciate that."

"Yeah, sure." She cringed as though suddenly embarrassed. "Say, sorry if I was a bit abrupt when I answered the door. I wasn't sure about you—with all the rumors and such—

but it's obvious you're nothing like your mother. Then again, you never were."

Then she turned around and headed back into the house, shutting the door behind her. I stood on her doorstep with more answers than I'd bargained for and a heart I hadn't realized could still break.

## Chapter 13

When I walked through the back door, Malcolm was setting two plates with eggs, bacon, and buttered toast on the breakfast table.

"Any luck?"

I walked around him and sat down at the table, then picked up my coffee cup, which I noticed had been refilled. "More than I expected."

"Oh?" he asked as he took a seat.

"I talked to three neighbors. Two didn't know anything, but one saw my mother leave on Tuesday afternoon with her suitcase sometime between two and three."

His brow lifted. "So, she didn't leave right after her call to the burner phone."

"No, but I'm burying the lede. I might have a clue about who she called." I took a sip of my coffee, then lowered the cup. "The neighbor said a black sedan dropped off a woman who was anywhere from her thirties to her sixties in front of the house. My mom opened the door before the woman knocked and let her in, then the car drove away. A few minutes later, Mom and the woman came out of the back of the house and got into Mom's car and left. My mom had her suitcase with her."

"Any idea who the woman was?"

I shook my head. "I don't have a clue. Mrs. Comstock said she had salt and pepper hair that was more salt than pepper. She was wearing dark jeans, black knee-high boots, a gray winter coat, and a black T-shirt."

"Could it be one of her friends?"

"Maybe," I said, "but she didn't recognize her, and she made a suggestion that caught me off guard."

His face remained passive, waiting.

"She suggested the woman could have been my father's mistress."

His brow lifted. "Was he having an affair?"

"I never saw any sign of it, but that doesn't mean anything. Especially after he moved out. Mrs. Comstock didn't know if he was unfaithful. She claimed to be guessing. And then she said she wouldn't have been surprised if my mother had invited her over to murder her. Or if the mistress was the person who ran her off the bridge."

He looked momentarily stunned. "She thinks your mother was murdered?"

"Honestly, I don't think so. She didn't contact the police or the sheriff's department about any of it. I think she was just speculating for entertainment."

"Gossiping," he said dryly, then cut into one of his fried eggs and took a bite.

I picked up a piece of bacon, my stomach giving me mixed signals about what it wanted. "Same thing." I took a bite, hoping it would make me feel better, not worse.

"Do you think your mother was capable of murdering your father's mistress, if he even had one?"

"No," I said. "Maybe another time, but not last week. She was too broken. I've seen my mother vindictive more times than I can count, so believe me when I say she wasn't plotting anyone's demise, literal or figurative, over the last few weeks."

He nodded, accepting my answer as he cut off another piece of his eggs. "We obviously need to find out who this woman was."

"Thankfully, we might have help with that. I noticed her doorbell didn't have a recording device, so I was shocked when she told me she has a camera in her upstairs window. She said she'd get footage of the woman and send it to me."

He sat back in his chair. "I wonder what else she has on there."

I took another bite of bacon. "What do you mean?"

"What if Skip Martin's guys weren't the only people to show up at your mother's house looking for something?"

"Martin's guys were looking for the information I had on Hugo Burton's case. It didn't have anything to do with my mother."

"Maybe, maybe not, but I'm still not convinced they weren't looking for *you*."

I released a sigh. He wasn't wrong. Skip Martin had planned to kill me. There was every likelihood his goons would have kidnapped me that night if Malcolm hadn't shown up.

"But what if your mother *was* tied up in the Hugo Burton mess somehow? We have no guarantee your father told you everything. There's no denying *he* was involved with Hugo Burton."

I considered his suggestion. "Dad drew up Burton's contracts off company time, and while it wasn't technically illegal, it *was* unethical."

"I'm not talking about Hugo Burton."

"Simmons? He contacted my father to work on some contracts after Dad got mixed up with Burton."

"Are you sure?"

I started to say yes, then stopped. I was repeating what my father had told me, but I'd be stupid to take his word for it.

I was letting my personal bias affect my instincts again. There was a reason cops weren't involved in investigations dealing with themselves or family or close friends. They weren't neutral. They came in with preconceived ideas and opinions. Good investigations didn't start that way.

"I think I'm making a mistake," I said, barely above a whisper.

He set down his toast and placed both hands on the table. "What are you talking about, Harper?"

"I shouldn't be investigating this. I'm too close. I'm ignoring things I shouldn't." I reached for my coffee cup, then put my hand down, too anxious to take a sip.

He leaned closer, his face softening. "Do you or do you not want to be part of finding out who killed your mother?" When I hesitated, he said, "There's no shame if you decide it's too much. I had no right to back you into this."

"You didn't," I countered, but he cocked an eyebrow. "Okay, you strongly coerced me, but I readily jumped on board."

His question was fair. Did I want to find her murderer myself or would I be content letting someone else do it? The sheriff's department clearly wasn't interested in an investigation, but I suspected Malcolm would dig into it with or without me. The answer was easy. "I want to investigate. I needed you to push me. I was drowning."

The corner of his mouth tipped up slightly. "Bad pun."

I grimaced, then couldn't stop myself from laughing. "True, but not intended." I took a deep breath. "I want to investigate, but I'm gonna be brutally honest, Malcolm. I'm not sure I'm going to do this investigation justice. Hell, the things I've missed or overlooked within the last couple of hours are proof enough." I glanced down at the table, ashamed to look him in the eye. I realized how close our hands were on the table, our fingertips separated by mere inches.

He shocked me when he lifted his hand and covered mine. "That's what I'm here for."

I jerked my gaze up at him in confusion and shock. His touch was comforting but also tugged at something deep inside of me. The part that was desperate to be touched. Not just by anyone—but by someone who understood me. And after a little over one month in Malcolm's orbit, I realized no one had ever really seen me before. Not like he did.

And that scared the hell out of me.

I pulled my hand free and picked up my toast. "Does that mean you're going to tell me whenever I fuck up?" I asked, my voice shaky.

A grin lit up his eyes. "How is that any different than our other two investigations?"

"Asshole."

He reached into his coat pocket and pulled out his flask and handed it to me.

He'd mistaken my quiver for my detox tremors. Or maybe he hadn't. Maybe he knew he'd shaken me, and he was giving me an out to hide my embarrassment.

I took a longer swig than necessary and handed it back, waiting for my muscles to relax. But while I waited, I needed to get this back on track.

"So, we have two working theories," I said, picking up my fork and scooping up some eggs. "The first is my mother found out something about my father, and whoever killed her did it to protect their secrets. The other is that my father had a mistress and either he or she or both of them killed her."

Malcolm sat back in his chair. "If the woman was his mistress, she'd be stupid to show up at your mother's house in broad daylight, let alone go off with her." He cut off another piece of eggs and took a bite.

I snorted. "Trust me, most people who commit crimes

aren't all that bright." I shoot him a pointed look. "Present company excluded."

He choked on his egg and started coughing.

I laughed, surprised at how genuine it felt. "Just stating the facts."

He picked up his coffee cup and took a big swig and grimaced, presumably from the temperature.

"So," I said, "We'll wait for Mrs. Comstock to send the video, then I'll ask my mother's friends if they know who she is."

"I'm assumin' you don't want to ask your father?"

"No," I said automatically, then added, "At least, not right now. And if I show it to him, I want to do it in person. I need to see his face."

His gaze darkened, and he gave a short nod. "We should see if any other neighbors have video. Maybe we can capture a license plate on the car."

"That would be great," I said, "but we don't have time for more canvassing. It's going to be past ten by the time we get out of town as it is."

"I'll have Carter get someone on it."

I looked at him in disbelief. "Carter's going to have someone knock on doors asking for video footage?"

"He'll be more discreet than that," he scoffed.

"You mean he'll do something illegal?"

He shrugged. "He'll do what needs to be done."

Would his people hack into their video systems?

I picked up my fork and pushed out a sigh, more at my own lack of reaction than at his proposal. I really was turning to the dark side.

His gaze stayed on me for a couple seconds before he reached for a piece of bacon on his plate and took a bite.

I scooped up a forkful of scrambled eggs. "You expected me to protest?"

"I admit I thought I'd have to convince you."

I didn't answer, especially since I wasn't sure what to say. Fake a protest or admit I was okay with it? Neither seemed like great options.

My mind was reeling as I took a few more bites, telling myself to focus on the investigation and not on my changing moral compass. But everything was getting under my skin, and my symptoms felt like they were getting worse, too, a wash of nausea joining the shakiness of my hands. I put down my fork and took a few breaths through my mouth and out my nose.

Malcolm started to reach for his flask.

I shot him a glare. "I just had a drink a few minutes ago."

"Take another."

It pissed me off that he was ordering me around, but I still accepted the flask and took a sip. It took everything in me to lower it, then a full two seconds before I could bring myself to hand it back.

Panic swamped my head. I was terrified I couldn't stay sober, and the last two days had proven I had reason for concern. I pushed my feelings down, something that was much easier when I was under the influence. Looking back, I'd used alcohol to help numb how I felt, so how would I deal with all these feelings now?

But I couldn't waste energy on feeling sorry for myself.

And no, this wasn't sympathy. This was disgust and loathing. The therapist I'd been assigned by the police department would probably have had a field day with that—if he'd actually been interested in my psyche. Our meetings had been totally ineffectual. A way for the department to check an item off their list, no more, no less. Didn't matter. I couldn't let myself wallow right now. I'd do what I needed to do to find my mother's killer, then let myself implode later.

By the time Malcolm finished his plate, I'd only taken a

few more bites and pushed the plate away. He carried both to the sink, rinsed them off, then put them in the dishwasher before declaring it was time to go.

It was strange seeing Malcolm domesticated like this, but he was a forty-four-year-old man, and he didn't seem like the kind of guy who lived in filth. It made sense he cleaned up after himself. It just felt odd to see him do it here. In my mother's kitchen. And it didn't explain *why* he was cleaning. Sure, I knew he was interested in what I found out, but that didn't explain why he'd made breakfast and cleaned up after himself.

Regardless, it was nice of him, a word I didn't really associate with Malcolm, but there was no denying it fit. It made me want to do something nice for him, which made me uncomfortable.

I knew Malcolm liked my lattes, and it wouldn't hurt to make one for myself to take on the road. I could make him one too.

"I'll be right back," I said, then headed out the back door before he could pepper me with questions.

I made my latte first and put in a thermal mug, then made his, telling myself this didn't mean anything. There was nothing weird or wrong about doing something nice for someone. Hell, he'd been helping me with my withdrawal symptoms. Making him a damn latte seemed like the least I could do.

By the time I walked into the kitchen with the two mugs, he was wearing his jacket and pacing the kitchen with his phone pressed to his ear. His gaze shifted to me, and he said a quick, "Gotta go," then ended the call and slid his phone into his front jeans pocket.

"I made you a drink for the road," I said, holding it out to him. I felt awkward, although I had no idea why.

He took it from me and glanced down at the lid.

"It's a latte."

"I figured."

"I made one for myself. It's no big deal."

He grinned at me. "I didn't think it was."

I gave a short nod, wishing the ground would open and swallow me whole. Unfortunately for me, there were no reported sink holes anywhere near here.

He took a sip, then lowered his cup. "You want to take anything besides your mother's laptop and her address book with us? Maybe a notebook?"

Grateful we'd moved on, I said, "Yeah, that's a good idea." I headed into the dining room to look for one in my mother's stationary supply cabinet, kicking myself for forgetting the notepad I'd started making notes on in Malcolm's office. Not that there was much on it.

I really needed to get my shit together.

When I got back into the kitchen, Malcolm had a charging cord lying next to the laptop, along with a couple of pens and my mother's address book.

I scooped up the laptop and address book, while Malcolm grabbed the power cord, and we headed out the back door. Something caught my attention in my peripheral vision. Malcolm had brought the pocket planner in and placed it on the counter. Two glasses were on either side, holding it open while two pages stood up—presumably the March pages—air drying.

"That's not going to tell us anything," I grumbled as I headed out the door. "It's a waste of time."

"Then you can gloat and say *I told you* so later."

Malcolm locked up, then we headed to the car. I knew I should give it more thought, but a sudden weariness had slammed into me, and all I could think about was reaching the car.

Once we were inside, he turned to look at me. "How are you doin'?"

"I'm fine," I snapped as I buckled my seatbelt, only it took three attempts to make it click.

"There's no shame in what you're goin' through." His tone was unexpectedly sweet, and my gaze jerked up to his.

"You seemed to heap plenty of shame on me last week."

He paused, resting his hand on the steering wheel, as though trying to figure out what to say.

"Stop before you say something you'll regret," I said through gritted teeth. I had no idea what he was about to say, but the resignation on his face looked like he was dangerously close to apologizing. I wasn't sure I could handle it if he did.

He started the car and backed out of the driveway. "I was going to say, I need your grandparents' address to put into my GPS."

He was full of shit and we both knew it. But I pulled up the address on my phone and sent it to him. He pulled to the side of the road and programmed it into his car's navigation system. The map popped up on his screen, telling us it would take us three hours and fifteen minutes to reach our destination.

My hand was noticeably shaky as I set my phone down, but I suspected it wasn't from my detox. Malcolm was unnerving me. If I didn't trust him, I'd be highly suspicious of his niceness, and the small, desperate part of me was scared to believe it could be anything else.

"Do you need another sip?" I could hear the worry in his voice. I'd already had two sips in less than a half hour. If I was needing them more frequently, then I might be in real trouble.

"If I didn't know better," I said in a snotty tone, "I'd think you were trying to keep me a drunk."

He didn't respond, just pulled his car away from the curb and started driving down the street.

I felt like an ass. Of course he wasn't trying to keep me drunk. He was the only person who'd even noticed my drinking. The only one who'd tried to convince me to stop. He'd stayed up a good portion of the night to help me through my

DTs, and we both knew it wasn't because he needed me for this investigation.

And this was how I repaid him?

"I'm sorry," I said, sinking back into the seat and staring out the windshield. "I know you're not trying to keep me drunk. That was an asshole thing to say."

"It's not easy gettin' sober." He shot me a glance. "It's not easy *stayin'* sober. Soon, you'll take it one day at a time, but right now, you're takin' it one minute at a time. Maybe even one second. Yeah, you're gonna need shots to get through this, maybe more than you feel comfortable with, but think about how much you were drinking before. We both know it was a lot. Your body's addicted to it, so you'll just have to baby yourself until it's ready to give it up."

I slowly shook my head, silently berating myself for putting myself in this position.

"You sure you don't need a drink?" he asked quietly.

"No. I know my hand was shaking, but I promise it was because of something else. See?" I held out my hand, relieved when it held still.

He shot a quick glance in my direction, then turned back to road. "You slept like shit last night and you look exhausted. The cell phone coverage sucks for the next hour, so it's not like you can get much work done on your mother's laptop. I'll wake you up when the coverage is better."

I nearly protested, but he was right. I felt like I could sleep for a week, and I knew from firsthand experience how shitty the cell phone coverage was, so I settled back in the seat.

"That was easier than expected," he said with a chuckle.

"While I may have gone along with your orders this morning, don't get used to it," I said in a firm tone. "I'm not one of your employees you can just boss around."

"I never said you were," he said, but without the bite I'd expected. "But we both know sleep's the best thing for you right now. It'll help clear your head, so you'll be ready to see your grandparents."

I chose to ignore that it was another order and closed my eyes. As I drifted off to sleep, I tried to remember a single time my old boyfriend Keith—or any other man—had taken care of me. I couldn't come up with a single instance. It used to make me feel independent.

Now it just made me feel sad.

—————————

## Chapter 14

—————————

I wasn't sure how long it took me to wake up, but I stirred a few times, only to fall back asleep. Finally, I opened my eyes and took a moment to orient myself to my new reality. To being here with Malcolm, on our way to see my grandparents after all those years.

"How're you feeling?" he asked softly.

I took a second to assess. "I have a headache, and my stomach feels gross, but … better?"

He grinned. "I told you that you needed sleep."

He was right, but I didn't want to admit it.

I glanced out the window, seeing nothing but countryside. "Where are we?"

"We're about an hour out of Jonesboro."

Anger surged me. I jerked upright and the throbbing in my head intensified. "You said you'd wake me after an hour! I could have been working!"

His brow lifted slightly, and he jerked a gaze toward me for half a second before focusing back on the road. "And how do you feel?"

I gritted my teeth. "That's beside the point."

He smirked. "What's done is done. You're awake now, and

we have decent coverage to connect the laptop to a hotspot on one of our phones."

It wasn't worth a fight, especially since I did feel better. With a sigh, I reached for the laptop at my feet, then placed it on my lap.

"You missed a couple of calls and a few texts," he said, pointing to my phone in the console.

I picked it up and checked the screen, wondering who would be calling me. Either Louise or my dad, because there really wasn't anyone else. Only the calls weren't from either of them. Both were from the same phone number. It looked familiar, and it took a moment to recognize it as the cell number Mason Deveraux had called me from last week.

His calls were an hour apart. Dread burrowed in my gut. Why was a man as busy as the lead prosecutor for the attorney general of Arkansas putting so much effort into calling me when I was the one who'd contacted him?

I flipped over to my messages and saw that Becky Comstock had sent me several texts, each one with a video clip, only the thumbnails were gray images that had the videos' numeric labels rather than images.

"My neighbor came through," I said.

"She sent the video?"

"About ten of them."

He shot me another glance. "Ten? Didn't the neighbor say the woman only came over once?"

"Yeah. Maybe she went through the video files and found some other visits."

She didn't send any messages with the videos, but if she'd sent something helpful, I'd be happy to ignore the lack of niceties.

I opened the first video. My mother's house was centered in the frame, which meant she'd been flat out spying on her. But I immediately forgave her once a black sedan pulled up in front of the house. The back passenger side door opened, and a woman got out. She shut the door and started heading up the front walk, as the car drove off. I kept my eyes glued to the screen, disappointed, but not surprised when I didn't see a license plate. The woman reeked of confidence, from her perfect posture to her lifted chin and brisk stride. The front door opened and my mother appeared in the opening. Once the woman reached the porch, my mother stepped to the side and let her in. The video stopped seconds after that.

"*Shit.*"

"What?"

"I can't see her face."

"Can you see the driveway?"

"A little." Hopefully one of the videos would show my mom and the mystery woman walking out to her car.

I pulled up the next video. After a couple of seconds, I could see the lower half of my mother's body and her suitcase as she rolled it down the driveway alongside her car and then brought it to the back. She stood behind it for several seconds while she lifted her suitcase, presumably to put the bag in the trunk, then she walked along the side of the car again, opened the door, and got in. Seconds later the car backed up, out of the frame, and the video ended.

I told Malcolm what I'd seen. "The woman wasn't in this one."

He nodded to the side of the road. "There's a rest stop up ahead. I'm gonna pull over so we can watch the rest of them together."

I set my phone in my lap, trying to temper my disappointment. While the two videos I'd watched corroborated Becky Comstock's version of events, there wasn't a good enough image the mystery woman for me to show to my mother's friends. There were plenty of other videos, but I had no idea what they showed. Mrs. Comstock claimed she'd only seen the woman that one time.

Malcolm pulled into the parking lot and pulled into a space in the back. "Show me."

I started with the first video, then moved on to the second when he didn't make a comment. After it played, I said, "At least we know Mrs. Comstock was telling the truth, but the woman's not even in the second video. The first video is helpful, but not enough."

"Play the next one," he said, his gaze still on the phone.

I closed the second video, then returned to the text string and clicked on the third. The video began to play, and I immediately recognized that this one was from different a camera, aimed at my mother's driveway and the neighbor to her left. It showed my mother walking down the driveway, pulling her suitcase behind her. The woman was walking in front of her, moving around to the passenger side of the car, only a tree branch from the across-the-street-neighbor's tree blocked the view of the top of her body. My mother walked to the back of the car and put her case in the trunk, then got in and backed it up into the street. But when she pulled into the street, I could see the mystery woman's face in the passenger seat. She'd rolled down the window, making the view as perfect as it could be from such a distance. She looked to be in her fifties or early sixties. The car pulled out of the frame as my mother drove down the street.

"Recognize her?" Malcolm asked.

"No," I said as I pushed out a heavy breath. I looked over at him. "Do you?"

He looked slightly surprised, then said, "No."

His reaction caught me off guard, not because he was surprised but because he'd let that surprise show. He was the master at covering his reactions, so if he'd wanted to hide his reaction, he would have. Did this mean he was letting me see the real him?

"Let's look at the other videos and see if there's anything else there," he said.

I didn't respond, simply loaded the fourth video. I cringed when it showed two dark figures slinking through the shadows as they crept down my mother's driveway and to the back of her house.

"Is that Pinky and his dimwit Brain?" Malcolm asked. I knew he was talking about the men who'd broken into my mother's house the previous week.

"No," I said as the video kept playing, even though nothing was happening. "They came to the front door."

Seconds later, a light flashed on in the living room window. It was covered in sheer curtains, so we could only make out vague shapes. Then the light turned off, and a bedroom light flipped on.

"They're looking for something," Malcolm said. "When was this recorded?"

I stopped the video and looked at the name, which included the date and time stamp. "Two Wednesday nights ago, at 9:11 p.m."

"Your mother's car's not in the driveway," he said. "Where was she?"

I released a short laugh. "Mine's not there either. Are you gonna ask where I was?"

"You were at the tavern with Louise and the bookseller. He was watching you like a lost puppy."

I cringed. "First of all, don't say that about Nate."

"Why not? It's true."

"Second," I said, refusing to admit he was right, "how do you know I was there that night?" I looked over at him and he gave me a look I was learning was his obstinate *I'm not going to answer you* expression.

"Seriously, Malcolm." Sure, he'd been working behind the bar that night and had seen me. We'd even had a short conversation about nothing while I'd ordered a beer, but the fact he knew immediately that I'd been there that night threw me off.

It wasn't outside the realm of possibility that he'd been keeping track of me. I knew some of his dangerous secrets. Maybe he'd worried I would rat him out.

And yet…

I didn't think that was it.

"Let's watch the rest of the video," he said, gesturing to the phone.

"You were watching me," I said without any hint of anger. "Did you have someone trailing me?" If so, I'd missed it, which made me feel like an idiot, but there was no doubt I'd been impaired.

"No," he said softly, sitting back in his seat as though he realized this was about to become a discussion.

"Then how did you remember I was there two weeks ago on a Wednesday night?"

He turned and looked out his side window, remaining silent for several seconds. I was about to restart the video when he said, "I was keeping an eye on you."

"Why?"

He was silent again, and I realized this was his way of answering difficult questions. Was he coming up with a fabricated response or was he finding the nerve to answer?

I nearly laughed at the idea. Finding the nerve? James Malcolm was composed of nothing but granite and steel.

Finally, he answered, sounding resigned, "I was worried about you."

He was worried about *me*? That nearly shocked the shit out of me.

"Because of my drinking?" It was the only reason I could come up with. I hadn't started working the Burton case yet, and the man who'd kidnapped Ava Peterman was dead.

He turned back to face me. "Press play."

I studied him for a moment. This man was a confusing mess, and the closer I got, the more of a conundrum he became. But I did as he said, because if he was worried about me for some reason other than my drinking, I wasn't sure I wanted to know. At least not right now. Not until after we found who was behind my mother's death.

We watched the rest of the video, which lasted several minutes. Different lights went on and off in the house, and then my mother's car pulled into the driveway. She got out and walked to the back of the house, but we didn't see the men come out.

"She's in the house with them," I said.

Malcolm grunted his acknowledgment.

A few seconds later, a faint light appeared in the dining room, faint enough that I was sure it was from the kitchen. There was still no sign of the men leaving the house, and I wondered if they'd escaped out a back window and slunk off through the backyard. But why was the clip still playing?

Nearly a minute later, the front door opened, and the two men walked out the door. Their faces were shadowed, but I could make out a few of their features.

"That isn't Pinky and Mike," I said, the hair on my neck standing on end. "And I'd bet money they made contact with my mother."

"Agreed," he said with a tight voice.

I glanced over at him. "Do you recognize them?

He shook his head. "No, but as soon as we're done, we're sending these to Hale to see what he can find."

I gave a short nod as I turned back to the phone, but I didn't start the next video. I needed a moment to let this sink in. Two men had broken into my mother's house, remained in the house after she came home, and very likely confronted her, and she'd never breathed a word of it. Had she called the police? I reached for my laptop and connected it to the hotspot on my phone.

"What are you lookin' for?" he asked.

"To see if she called the police."

"It wasn't on her phone records," he said.

He was right, but I looked anyway and came up with nothing.

"Why wouldn't she call the police?" I asked as I closed the laptop lid.

"Maybe she was scared," he said. "What if they made some kind of threat?"

"They were obviously looking for something," I said. "And when she came home while they were still there, they must have decided to be more direct."

"Give them what they were looking for or something bad would happen," Malcolm said.

"I guess *you'd* know," I said, my irritation rising out of nowhere.

He was silent for a second, then calmly said, "You're referring to my previous life?"

"What else?" I snapped. "Or are you still threatening people now?"

"I don't think you really want me to answer that," he said, his voice calm—but not the scary calm he exuded when he was being threatening. "You're lookin' for someone to blame, and I happen to be the closest target."

He had a point. He hadn't threatened my mother or had her killed. He was on my side, but he was sitting beside me. A convenient scapegoat.

"Sorry," I said, although I wasn't sure why. He'd undoubtedly employed the same tactics on other people in the past.

"We're gonna find out who did this," he said, his usual hardness gone. "The lot of 'em were sloppy when they showed up at your mother's house. We have three faces to look up. We're gonna find them, Harper."

I nodded, trying to breathe normally despite the fact it felt like a vise was wrapped around my chest.

"Do you need a minute before we watch the next video?"

I was about to say no, but I kept thinking about how scared my mother had been over the last month. She knew I was a former detective but hadn't told me about any of it. Why?

Malcolm waited patiently until I took a breath and reached for my phone with shaking fingers.

He pulled his flask out of the side pocket of his door and handed it to me.

I wasn't sure if my shaking was from withdrawal or my nerves, but I took it, struggling to remove the cap. He gently took it back from me and unscrewed it before handing it back.

"Just a sip," he said. "You're gonna be tempted to take more to ease the pain you're feelin', but drag that stubborn bitch out and show it who's boss."

I laughed despite myself, then took a tiny sip. He was right. I wanted to drink the rest of the contents, then drive to a liquor store and get more. But I *was* a stubborn bitch, and I wasn't giving in. Not now that I'd allowed myself to acknowledge the problem.

He took back the flask and screwed the cap back on.

"Are you sure you weren't an alcoholic?" I asked with a scoff. "You seem to know a lot about it."

"My brother was a drunk for a while," he said, surprising me with his willingness to share something personal.

"I'm sorry."

He shrugged. "It's not hard to understand why he took to it. Sure, he saw the evils of drinkin' with our father, but you can't live through something like our childhood and escape it unscathed."

"Then how did you escape unscathed?" I asked, genuinely curious.

His brow lifted. "Who said I escaped unscathed?"

"So, then what's your vice?" I asked, turning in my seat to face him. "Because you say you didn't drink to excess, and I don't think you'd use drugs."

"You're right," he said, turning to face me. "How did you deal with your trauma?"

"You already know," I said with a hint of incredulity. "I started drinking."

"You didn't start drinking until after you shot that kid last fall. I'm talking about your sister's death. And the only reason you finally succumbed to alcohol was because you'd been through so much already it was either drink to smother your pain or you were gonna lose your fucking mind." Then he quietly added, "Or worse."

I started to respond, then stopped, unsure of what to say. He'd accused me of having a death wish, wishing that I'd been killed last fall instead of the boy I'd shot. I suspected he was right. But I'd never outright considered actually ending it myself.

"After your sister, you buried the pain and let it simmer."

"What else was I supposed to do?"

He released a short laugh. "Believe it or not, I've learned it helps to talk about it."

"What if you don't have someone to talk to?" I asked in a huff. "And don't you dare say I should talk to a therapist. I've been down that road with the department's quack. He was more worried about getting through the required number of meetings than making sure I was okay."

"You're basing your opinion of therapy on a LRPD-assigned therapist?" he shook his head. "You need to find another."

"Wait," I said, sitting upright. "Are you suggesting that *you've* seen a therapist?"

"Yes," he said with no hesitation.

It took me a second or two to process that piece of information. "When?"

He paused, then said, "Recently, and we'll leave it at that."

I gave one slow nod, still chewing on his admission, which I was sure hadn't been easy. A guy like him needed to keep up appearances, and if word got out he was talking to a therapist it could make him look weak, something he couldn't afford.

And yet he'd told me.

I couldn't wrap my head around it.

"And you think I need to see one too," I said in a whisper.

"It sure as hell wouldn't hurt, but until you make that decision for yourself, you need to find someone you trust who you can talk to."

Who was that? While I trusted Louise, I wasn't sure I felt comfortable unloading my trauma on her. She didn't deserve it, for one thing, and for another, that would mean opening up about Malcolm and there was no way I could do that. In my apartment, he'd suggested I could talk to him, but I'd never considered it a real possibility.

Then why was part of me yearning for that very thing?

"Okay, enough armchair psychiatrist," I grumped, picking up my phone. "We have work to do." I started playing the next video, which showed the night Pinky and Mike broke into my mother's house. They knocked, then picked the lock and went inside. Similar to the video of the previous break-in, lights went on and off in the house. Then the video ended. The next video was of Malcolm showing up shortly afterward and finding me in the garage. We disappeared into the back of the house. The next video was of Malcolm leaving to get his car, then me getting inside. The last video was of him bringing me back to my mother's house.

"Why do you think she sent these last videos of you?" I asked.

"Hard to say," he said, staring out the windshield. "Maybe she knows who I am."

"But you didn't do anything wrong or illegal. And besides, she thinks you're my boyfriend, which means you'd have a reason for coming over."

He didn't seem disgusted that she'd thought we were a couple, but he didn't acknowledge it either. "Maybe this is her way of showing you she's watching."

"Maybe." But I didn't like it. "That's the last video."

"You gonna take screenshots of the woman and the guys who broke in the first time?" he asked.

"Yeah, I'll send a screenshot of the woman to my mother's friends, and I'll send all the videos to Carter."

"Good." He nodded to the concrete block building across the lot. "I suggest we go to the bathroom since we're so close to your grandparents' house."

I drew a breath to settle my nerves. "Good idea."

"You hungry?"

I lifted a brow in surprise. "Are you?"

"No, just checking on you. We can stop and get something to eat. We got delayed with construction traffic when we went through Little Rock so it's later than I expected it would be."

I glanced at the clock on his screen, surprised to see it was already a little after two. "I'm not hungry."

"Let me know if you change your mind."

I got out and strode to the restroom, unnerved by the way he was considering my needs, but the thought of Big Bad James Malcolm going to therapy quickly took over. How did that work? Was it like *The Sopranos*? Or more like *Ozark*, where the therapist didn't know what the patient did, and when she found out…

But if Malcolm could not only go to therapy but recommend it, it made me wonder if I should give it serious consideration.

I quickly squashed the thought. This wasn't a self-help mission. I was on the hunt for a killer.

But something in the back of my head whispered, "Why can't it be both?"

---

# Chapter 15

---

Unsurprisingly, Malcolm was already in the car by the time I came out. He must have raided a vending machine, because he had a couple of bottled waters, multiple bags of assorted chips, and some Oreo and Nutter Butter cookies.

"Oh," I said, picking up the package of Nutter Butters. "I haven't had these in years."

"Maybe I wanted those," he said with a laugh as he started the car and headed toward the highway.

"Then you should have hidden them." I picked up the laptop again and put in my mother's password to wake it up. While I nibbled on the cookies, I transferred the videos to the laptop, then worked on isolating still images of the mystery woman and the two men. When I was done, I sent the pictures and the videos to Carter in a text with an explanation of what they were. He quickly responded that he'd get on it.

I was in the process of trying to determine which of my mother's friends to send the woman's image to when my phone rang. I picked it up and my heart skipped a beat when I saw the number on the screen.

Mason Deveraux really wanted to talk to me.

That was not a good sign.

I silenced the call and let it ring, not wanting to let Deveraux know I'd screened his call.

"Not gonna take that?" Malcolm asked, his hand draped over the steering wheel.

Opening the laptop, I started to connect it to my phone hotspot. "I'm sure it was spam."

He tapped his thumb on the steering wheel, and I wondered if he'd seen the number on my screen when Deveraux had called earlier. The caller ID didn't give his name away, but all he'd have to do was give the number to Carter. He'd probably find out who the caller was in a matter of seconds.

What would Malcolm do if he knew I'd called Deveraux for information about him? Would he be mad enough to leave me on the side of the road? Would he kill me? How well did I really know him? I knew he valued loyalty, and he would see calling Deveraux as the epitome of disloyalty.

But strangely, I was less worried for my safety and more worried about losing his respect and his friendship.

Dear Lord. Did I have Stockholm Syndrome?

I kept my gaze on the computer screen, resting on my fingers on the track pad. "I asked you before how many people you'd killed," I said, trying to sound nonchalant. "But you didn't answer."

"You think I *have* an answer." He gave me a devilish grin. "Maybe I lost count."

I turned to look at him. "No. I don't think you did."

"You think I remember every person I've killed?" he said in a stiff tone.

I considered it for a moment. "Maybe not every one of them, but I think you remember the ones that mattered. Like the Sylvester brothers."

His brow rose and he turned to face me, studying me for a full second before turning back to the road. "They don't deserve to be remembered."

He had a point. But I suspected we'd both remember them until our last breath anyway.

"Why ask me now?" he asked. "Last time you asked me, you quickly changed your mind and said didn't want to know."

"Maybe I realized that you know a whole hell of a lot about my past, but I know very little about yours."

His laugh was a short bark. "That's bullshit if I ever heard it. You know plenty about me."

"I know what everyone else knows. That you were the Fenton County crime boss until you were arrested. You worked for J.R. Simmons before that, as one of his Twelve." One of the twelve crime bosses he'd sent out around the state to run their own empires, all while still offering fealty and likely a share of their profits to Simmons.

"See? Not many people know I was one of the Twelve, so you already know more than everyone else."

"A little more, maybe, but not much."

He tapped his thumb on the steering wheel a couple of times before he said, "I wasn't one of the Twelve until I went to Fenton County. After Simmons sent me back there from El Dorado and a short stint in Little Rock." He shot me another glance, his eyes hard. I was momentarily taken back, but I knew he wasn't mad at me. He just didn't like talking about his past.

"You grew up in Fenton County?"

"Yep." Was his bitter reply.

He obviously hadn't been happy about returning. "Did he send you back as punishment?"

"No, I was still one of his prize protégées, although I didn't feel like it when I found out where I was going. But he wasn't happy with who was runnin' it, and he expected me to make a power move at some point and take over. He thought the fact I was familiar with the county would help," he said, some of his roughness gone. "But I was under his thrall, so I didn't question it. I wasn't happy to go, but I went none-theless."

"Because you wanted to run a crime syndicate? Was that your ultimate goal?"

He released a short laugh. "Hell, no. I went because I didn't want to be dirt poor."

"You were raised dirt poor?"

"As poor as you can get."

I didn't know anything about his childhood other than the bits and pieces he'd told me. That his father was a drunk, and he and his younger brother, Scooter, had been through hell—so much so, it had driven his brother to drinking. Malcolm had said he'd spent his life trying to protect him and some-times he'd been successful and other times not. Was he refer-ring to their beatings? Or the fact that Scooter had become an alcoholic? It seemed kind of ironic he'd named his tavern after his alcoholic brother.

Ultimately, despite caring deeply for his brother, Malcolm had left him behind. I'd inferred that this was his exile.

I wasn't going to press the matter, so he surprised me when he said, "I met Simmons when I was fourteen years old. He pulled into the gas station I was workin' at. I saw his fancy car and suit, and I told him I wanted to be just like him someday. He got a chuckle out of that and handed me a business card and told me to come hit him up for a job when I turned eighteen."

"And you did."

"I didn't know what he did back then, just that he had a lot of money, and as far as I was concerned, if I could get money, my troubles will be over." He released a self-depre-cating laugh. "Little did I know."

"Did your parents disapprove?"

"My father was long gone, not that I gave a shit about what that bastard thought."

"He was a mean drunk." It wasn't a question, more of an acknowledgement.

"The meanest. He used to beat my brother and me for the fun of it. He'd beat my mother because of any imagined wrong." He shot me another long glance before he turned back to road, saying, "He was the first man I killed."

If he'd meant to shock me, he was about to be disappointed. "Because he'd pushed you too far," I said. "He'd hurt your mother or brother one too many times."

"You really want me to be noble," he said in disgust. "It would help the narrative you're trying to build in order to justify working with me."

Maybe he had a point, but this wasn't one of those times. "That has nothing to do with the fact that you killed him to protect someone you loved. I've seen it before. I know what it looks like."

He was quiet, the only sound was the creaking of leather as he wrung the steering wheel as if he were strangling it.

"Did they arrest you?"

"No."

"Did they know you did it?"

He laughed. "No. They thought it was an accident. We told them he fell in a drunken stupor and hit his head. Nobody questioned it. Everyone knew he was a drunk and a mean one at that. Good riddance to bad rubbish." He turned to look at me again, his face devoid of any emotion. "You plannin' to turn me in?"

"Sounds to me like justice was served. Besides," I said flippantly. "I'm sure you have some kind of immunity deal with the feds."

He didn't confirm or deny my statement. Instead, he looked lost in memories.

"Are you close to your mother?"

"She's long dead."

"Any cousins? Aunts or uncles?"

"Nope. My brother's the only one left."

"After you started working for Simmons, and especially after you became one of the Twelve, it must have been hard to form attachments to people. Anyone you were close to could be used against you."

Releasing a sigh, he said, "Like I said, little did I know."

"But you must have been close to *someone*. You told me you betrayed someone back in Fenton County. It was someone you cared about."

He was quiet for a long moment, and I didn't think he was going to answer when he practically whispered, "His name is Jed." He hesitated as though unsure he should continue, then said, "We grew up in the same poor neighborhood, if you could call where we lived a neighborhood. We went through some dark times." He paused, wearing a haunted look. "When I came back to Fenton County after workin' for Simmons for several years, I hired Jed to work for me. He became my right-hand man. He took care of my business, and I took care of him financially."

"And you betrayed him?" My stomach twisted, but this time it had nothing to do with my withdrawal. Maybe I couldn't trust him after all.

"Not how you're thinkin'," he said, sounding exhausted. "I made sure he was out of reach when the whole deal with the Hardshaw Group went down. I didn't want Hardshaw messin' with him, and I wasn't about to hand him to the feds on a silver platter either. I made damn sure they wouldn't try to charge him with anything."

Malcolm had made a deal with the Feds to help deliver the international crime ring to them, but something had gone wrong.

He sighed. "It didn't stop them from threatening to renege on their offer after I didn't follow their guidelines for the Hardshaw bust to the T." He paused again, his jaw setting as a dark look crossed over his face. "But they soon realized it was in their best interest to see our original agreement through."

What did Malcolm have that the feds wanted so badly?

Or maybe the question was what did Malcolm have on *them*?

"You protected Jed," I said. "So how did you betray him?"

"He would have followed me to the ends of the earth, but he finally had a chance at a real life with someone who could make him happy. Give him the kind of future I knew he wanted. So, I cut him loose."

"What does that mean? You fired him?"

"Let's just say I saw an opportunity to help him leave."

"He doesn't know about your deal with the feds?"

"Nope. At least not then."

"Why didn't you tell him?"

"Because he wouldn't have trusted them—with just cause. And I didn't trust them to treat him fairly. Not to mention, he would have gotten an ulcer trying to protect me from both sides. I didn't see any reason to drag him into it, so I found an excuse to fire him and used it."

"And he wouldn't have quit?"

"No fuckin' way." He shrugged as if it meant nothing. "He saw it as a betrayal, and if you look at it, it *was* a betrayal. I'd made him choose between helping the woman he loved and dropping everything to do my bidding. I knew he'd choose her, or at least I hoped to God he'd chose her, and when he did, I knew I'd made the right call." He tapped the steering wheel, his jaw tight. "It was the only way to protect him."

"How long did he work for you?"

"About fifteen years."

"That's a long time, Malcolm, not to mention you grew up together." I tilted my head trying to study his reaction. "Sounds like he was your best friend."

His face hardened. "He was my *employee*."

"He was more than your employee and we both know it,"

I countered. I hesitated before asking the next question, but he'd already told me far more than I'd expected. I might as well take the leap. "Did you have anyone else in your life? A girlfriend?"

His mouth twisted. "As you pointed out, I couldn't afford to have a significant. It would have made them a target. A liability. Couldn't risk it."

"So, Jed was the one constant in your life, loyal enough that you were worried he'd put his own happiness on hold to support you." I shrugged. "Sounds like a best friend to me." When he started to protest, I held up a hand. "Count yourself lucky. I've never had a best friend."

His brow furrowed. "What about that deputy sheriff you hang out with?"

"Louise?" I asked with a short laugh. "And don't pretend you don't know her name. You said it earlier." I shook my head. "No. We're friends, and maybe we *could* become best friends, but I don't let people get close to me. And I've heard you need to let people get close to you to become best friends."

"What about your detective boyfriend?"

"Keith?" I snorted. "Definitely *not* my best friend. Even in the best of times." I made a face. "See? Never had one. Count yourself lucky."

After we were silent for several long seconds, I decided our conversation had come to an end. I'd admitted I was a loser, and he'd refused to admit it had hurt to cut off his friend. So why was I tempted to push him?

I reached for my mother's address book, trying to shake off the impulse, then stopped. "You had to have fired Jed … what? Three or four years ago?"

"Four.

"Did you ever tell him the truth?"

"About what?"

"About why you fired him, you fool."

He scowled. "No."

"Why not tell him now? Why let him suffer thinking you didn't care about him?"

"It's not a good idea."

"Why?"

"Because," he said, getting irritated. "It could go one of two ways. The first, he'd tell me to fuck off, because I was a selfish bastard for lying and hurting him like that. Or two, he'd forgive me and want to renew our friendship. Both options are bad."

"Why would it be bad if he forgives you and wants to be your friend again?"

"It just would be."

That didn't make sense. He'd been released from the feds. He'd gotten immunity for Jed. As far as I could tell, Malcolm wasn't working with any crime groups. What harm could come out of rekindling his friendship? Did he still have enemies in the wings, waiting to hurt him? He'd been worried Jed would talk him out of working with the feds and Hardshaw. Maybe he was worried Jed would interfere with his plan to root out and destroy Simmons's successor. But even if he reopened the friendship, he wouldn't need to share everything that was going on in his life. I suspected only two people in Malcolm's orbit knew what he was up to —me and Carter Hale. And possibly some federal agents, but I had the impression he was doing this for himself. Not someone else.

So why wouldn't Malcolm reach out to his friend?

"Is Jed still in Fenton County?"

"Yep."

"You're still afraid someone might hurt him."

"I'm *always* afraid someone will hurt him. All the more reason to stay away."

"But if Jed was your second in command, then he knows how to protect himself."

"He has more than himself to think about, and I refuse to put any of them in danger for my own selfish needs."

"Shouldn't that be Jed's decision?"

He gave me a murderous glare. "Just because you're making me privy to your personal life doesn't mean you get access to mine."

"I never said I did, and frankly, you told me a lot more than I expected." I hesitated. "Thanks for trusting me."

"I don't trust you worth shit," he spat out, still pissed. "What I told you isn't some deep dark secret. It's public knowledge Jed worked for me."

I'd done some snooping into Malcolm's life and hadn't seen Jed's name mentioned, but I didn't correct him. We both knew damn well he'd told me more than he'd intended.

But he and I both had acknowledged we were a lot alike. Maybe he was drawn to that. Maybe he thought I'd understand, the same way he'd understood me.

His change in demeanor wasn't surprising. I'd struck a nerve, a deep one. Why couldn't he admit that he'd protected his best friend, not just a loyal employee? Maybe the same reason I'd never let anyone reach the best friend status. At least he had an excuse for keeping people distant—I had none.

My mind drifted back to his childhood. He'd been enthralled by J.R. Simmons's money and power. Sure, Malcolm hadn't admitted to being drawn to the latter, but you didn't become a crime boss if you didn't want the power that came with it. And it was easy to see that Malcolm had felt powerless being raised by his abusive, drunkard father. Until he'd taken the power and killed him.

Malcolm had made bad decisions—by his own admission—but from what he'd said, he hadn't known what he was getting into when he'd taken that first job with Simmons. Maybe it was like boiling a frog—you made small decisions and found yourself in a place you never thought you'd be.

Hadn't the same thing happened to me? I'd shot a boy and lost my job, and it had hurt so badly I'd numbed the pain with a drink. It had worked, temporarily. But then I'd taken another the next day, until I couldn't get through an hour, let alone a day, without a drink.

Then I'd realized I was a raging alcoholic.

Had Malcolm worked with the feds because he'd wanted out of his life of crime?

I shot him a glance, considering asking him how he'd found his way into that deal, but the sharp angle of his jaw told me he was done with story time.

If he'd wanted out, what had prompted it? Something told me it went back to his deal with Rose Gardner to bring Simmons down. Had he fallen on the authorities' radar then? Or was busting Simmons the original deal that started the whole Hardshaw Group arrangement rolling?

I wasn't sure if he'd ever willingly tell me, and I'd told myself I didn't care. Or shouldn't. There was no denying I'd made a lot of bad decisions over the last six months. Taking a road trip with James Malcolm to visit my grandparents was definitely one of them. What did it say about me that I didn't regret it? Then again, we hadn't gotten there yet. There was plenty of time for regret later.

## Chapter 16

I opened the address book and considered who to call first. My mother's so-called friends had no problem gossiping about her, but I didn't want the mystery woman's visit spread all over town. It would be better if no one knew we were looking into her death. Besides, I wasn't sure how forthright her friends would be after my confrontation with them at the funeral. So, who was most likely to give me something and keep it quiet?

Then it hit me. Lisa Murphy.

She was the one who'd alerted my mother to Ava Peterman's kidnapping less than an hour after the police showed up. I'd talked to her during my investigation into the girl's disappearance. She'd been both insightful and blunt, so it seemed likely she wouldn't hold back.

I looked up her number in the address book. After the third ring, I was sure she wasn't going to answer, so she surprised me when she picked up and said, "What are you doin' callin' my landline, Harper Adams?"

"Sorry," I said, slightly taken back. "It was the only number I had."

"Let me guess, you got it from your mother's address

book." She made a tutting sound. "She wasn't fond of cell phones."

"Guilty on all counts," I admitted.

"What can I do for you, Harper?" she asked in a no-nonsense tone. "I assume this is about your mother."

"You're practically clairvoyant, Mrs. Murphy."

"I told you last time we talked to call me Lisa. Mrs. Murphy makes me feel old. And there's nothing clairvoyant about it," she scoffed. "It's plain common sense, something most people in this town lack. Your mother died mysteriously, and you know I know things other people don't."

She had me there. "Right again, although most people don't think her death was mysterious."

"Most people are imbeciles."

Again, no arguing with that.

"*Of course* it was mysterious," she said, sounding annoyed. "I heard she had a suitcase in her car, and it was common knowledge that your mother practically refused to leave Jackson Creek, let alone go on an overnight trip."

"You heard she had a suitcase?"

"I believe you announced it to a small group of women at her funeral," she said. "Rather loudly, I might add."

Not my finest moment. "I suppose I did."

"The real question is where she was going."

"That's what I'm trying to figure out," I said. "If you have any insight, it would be helpful."

"I'm afraid I can't help you there."

"I'm sure you knew that my father had left my mother."

"*Everyone* knew that," she said wryly. "Much to your mother's chagrin."

"What were the rumors about their situation?"

"There were multiple theories. One was that your father got tired of her nonsense and moved out. But it can't be coincidental that it happened right after you returned, and the fact that you remained in the apartment made some people think he moved out because he wasn't happy you were back. They think your mother was the one who wanted you there. And then, of course, there was her recent behavior."

"What recent behavior?"

"Why, just two weeks ago, she heard Donna Wheaten bad-mouthing you at church. Sarah Jane told Donna to hush her mouth before she told the whole town what Donna had planted in her backyard."

While I would have loved to think my mother was defending me out of devotion, I was sure it had been for selfish purposes. "That doesn't prove anything," I said dismissively. "She wouldn't want people gossiping about me because it made her look bad. If she'd had her way, no one would ever have mentioned my name again."

"She might have felt that way when you first came back," she said, "but she told Donna you were caught up in a bad situation and doing the best you could. And then she made the threat about disclosing what Donna was growing in her backyard if she wouldn't quit."

I was momentarily speechless. "Wow." I finally said.

"Exactly," she said in a smug tone. "Total turnabout. So some people thought your father didn't like you here in town and left to preserve his good name."

"Except I work at his firm," I said.

"Like I said," she said with a sniff. "Most people in these parts lack common sense."

"Have you heard any rumors that my father was having an affair?"

She was quiet for a moment. "Interesting," she said, sounding intrigued. "I haven't."

"My neighbor across the street insinuated that he might have had a mistress."

"Anything's possible," she said, as though still considering the idea. "But tongues haven't been wagging about it. I suppose you would know better than most."

I wasn't going to confirm or deny why he'd really left. That was up to him. As far as I knew, he didn't want to give people an explanation. He was letting them come up with theories of their own.

"Do you know if my mother made any new friends over the past month or so?"

"New friends? She knew everyone in town and had long since decided whether they were worth her time or not. And as we both know, new people in town are a rare occurrence." She paused and lowered her voice. "Why, do you think your mother had made a new friend?"

"I didn't say I did," I countered. "I was merely asking."

"Do *not* mistake me for a fool, Harper Adams." She enunciated each word, each one icier then the last. "Either be honest with me or end this call now."

Lisa Murphy lived for gossip. But the last time we'd spoken, she'd told me she was capable of keeping secrets, especially important ones. Still, I suspected she used most of what she learned as currency—which meant she couldn't be relied upon.

I hesitated to tell her about the woman who had been dropped off at my mother's house, but there was a chance she might know something about her. And that *was* why I'd called. "I would like to ask you to keep this information to yourself."

"I believe I previously told you I'm capable of keeping secrets."

"You did," I conceded, "but you never specified which secrets you keep and which ones you share."

"If you want me to keep a secret, Detective, quit dilly-dallying and ask me."

"And what will it cost me for you to keep this secret? Because I get the impression that anything you know can be gained by someone else for a price."

She released a chuckle. "Well, you have me there, but I'll

insist on quite a high one for what you're about to tell me. One most people wouldn't be willing to pay."

I considered pushing her, but if she could keep the information to herself until I solved this, then it wouldn't really matter. "All I ask is that you don't sell it for a week. Then it's fair game."

Malcolm shot me a long look, but I ignored him.

"Confident you'll have this all wrapped up in a week, huh?" she asked with a laugh.

"It sounds like you think there's something to investigate."

"I never pretended otherwise."

"What do you think happened to my mother?" I asked.

She was silent for a moment. "I'm not sure," she finally said, not sounding as haughty as before. "My best guess is she was leaving town, and in her haste, she drove off the bridge in the rain. Everyone knew she hated driving in any kind of bad weather. But when you get down to it, the *real* question is *why* she was leaving."

"That's what I'm trying to figure out." If I could discover what had driven her to pack a suitcase for multiple days, I suspected it would either point me toward the killer or at least in their direction. "I had no idea she was going anywhere. She didn't tell me, and she wasn't answering her cell phone when I tried to call her last week."

"She didn't have one of those apps that tell you where somebody is? Like Life 360?"

"My mother barely used her cell phone." Although if she'd known about that app, she might have used it to track my father. "One of the neighbors said a woman showed up at my mother's house last Tuesday and then she and my mother got into my mother's car a few minutes later and drove off."

"And you're trying to find out who this woman was?"

"Yes. I don't recognize her, but then again, I don't know everyone in town."

"Let me guess who told you about her," Lisa said slyly. "Becky Comstock."

I saw no reason to hide it. "Yes."

"Well, if she didn't know who she was, I likely won't either. Becky's a snoop and a gossip."

A surge of disappointment washed through me. "And a spy. She has multiple video cameras pointed at my mother's house."

She released a short laugh. "Don't go feeling all that special. I suspect she has cameras pointed at all her neighbors. I wouldn't be surprised if she has game cameras set up all over town."

"If I send you a photo of the woman, would you take a look and tell me if you've seen her or not?"

"Of course, but don't get your hopes up."

"Thank you."

"Of course. If something untoward happened to Sarah Jane, then of course I'll help however I can."

My head was beginning to throb, so I pressed the heel of my hand to my temple. "Lisa, other than my father leaving, have you heard any other rumors about my mother?"

"No. I didn't even know she was taking an antidepressant."

I blinked in surprise. "How did you find out she was?"

"Dr. Duncan's nurse, Zoe, told her cousin, who told Linda Gill."

"And Linda told you?"

"Not exactly." She was silent for a moment. "It came out at the funeral luncheon."

Of course it did. "And what was my father's reaction?"

"He didn't look pleased, but he also didn't contradict her."

My mother was probably rolling in her barely covered grave, and I felt a strange surge of protectiveness. But if Dr. Duncan's nurse was spreading the information, I could use it to my advantage to get information. I could threaten to press charges for breaking HIPAA if she didn't tell me how my mother had gotten her prescription.

"What's Zoe's last name?"

"She's a sweet girl, Harper," Lisa cajoled. "Don't be bringin' trouble on her head. She's a bit naïve, but she meant well."

If she was a nurse, she should have known better, no matter what her age. "I don't plan to cause any trouble for her. I just want to ask some questions."

Lisa didn't answer for several seconds.

"I *am* going to talk to her," I said in a stiff tone. "It would be far less embarrassing for her if I don't have to call Dr. Duncan's office to reach her."

"I'll give you her last name, but you have to promise to go easy on her."

Lisa had some kind of attachment to Zoe, but what could it be? She said she was young and naïve, so that meant she was probably in her twenties. I took a shot in the dark. "How are you related to Zoe?"

"How did you—" she asked in shock, then turned sober. "She's my niece."

"I'm surprised Zoe didn't come directly to *you* with the information. Seems like it would be a hot commodity."

"Her mother and I aren't speaking. She's a loyal girl."

"I see." I took a beat. "I'll be kind to her, and I promise I won't get her in trouble." That didn't mean I wouldn't threaten her with legal action if she didn't tell me what I wanted to know.

"So what's her last name?"

"St. Martin. Zoe St. Martin."

"What's her phone number?"

"I can't do *everything* for you, Harper Adams!" she snapped, then hung up, and I realized I hadn't gotten her cell phone number or email address to send the photo.

Damn it.

"Interesting call?" Malcolm asked.

"Yeah. Give me a second." I tried calling her again, but it rang until it went to her answering machine. I'd really fucked this up. Now I'd need to find someone else to call.

But when I reached for the address book, my phone pinged with a text.

My stomach clenched, worried Mason Deveraux had resorted to texting me, but a number I didn't recognize appeared on the screen.

*Send me the photo via text and I'll tell you what I know. But only if you PROMISE you won't get her in trouble.*

Relief swamped my head. Lisa Murphy was still going to help me.

Since I'd already decided that my goal was answers, not reporting her, I had no problem with that. Nevertheless, I waited a couple of seconds, not wanting to appear too eager or disingenuous.

*I promise.*

I texted the photo, and Lisa responded within seconds.

*I don't know who she is, BUT she looks familiar. Let me ponder on it a bit and maybe it will come to me.*

Her response was better than nothing, but it also made it clear that the woman wasn't one of my mother's regular friends.

Then who was she? How did my mother meet her and why would my mother trust her enough to leave town with her?

All questions I didn't have the answers to, but I'd find out. One way or the other.

"So?" Malcolm prodded.

I told him what she said while he kept his stoic gaze on the road.

"Do you think she really looked familiar or was she just saying that so you'll keep your word to protect her niece?"

"Well, damn. I hadn't considered that."

He lifted his shoulder into a half shrug.

"What do you plan to do next?"

"Find Zoe's number and give her a call."

"Sounds like a good next step."

After I opened my Skip Trace app, I looked up Zoe St. Martin in Jackson Creek. Information about her popped up within seconds. Only one phone was listed—unsurprisingly, a cell phone—and I called it. It went to voicemail. I hadn't expected her to answer, given it was closing in on three and she worked in a doctor's office. I was pretty sure they couldn't carry their cell phones around and answer every call that came in. Still, I'd hoped to get ahold of her before Lisa warned her I was calling. I was more likely to get honest answers if I could catch her off guard.

Her voicemail message popped up, and a sweet, young voice said, "Hey! This is Zoe. I can't chat right now, but I'll get back to you as soon as I can. Bye!"

I considered leaving a message, but I wasn't sure she'd call me back, and I really didn't want her calling me while I was talking to my grandparents.

"You didn't leave a message."

I glanced over at Malcom. "I don't want to leave it up to her to call me. I need to be on the offensive." I looked at the road and realized he was exiting the highway. The map app said we were about five minutes from my grandparents' house.

I swallowed the bile rising in my throat. I considered telling him I needed a drink, but I took a deep breath, held it for several seconds, then let it go, trying to ignore the voice in the back of my head that kept telling me over and over, the voice growing more and more insistent, that I really *did* need a drink.

A sudden wave of fear made me seize up. Would the voice eventually go away? I wasn't sure I could live with it. What if I couldn't do this?

He must have noticed how I'd stilled. "Do you know what you plan to say?"

"Why? Are you afraid I'll screw it up?" I asked, but it lacked the heat to come across as accusatory.

"You won't screw it up. I trust you."

My heart tightened, and my irritation flared. "Less than a half hour ago you told me you *didn't* trust me."

He pushed out a heavy breath and ran a hand through his hair. "You have to understand, Harper. Some secrets aren't mine to tell."

Lisa Murphy had pretty much said the same thing. Which meant he was protecting someone or some*ones.* I tried to remember what had prompted him to snap that he didn't trust me—I'd asked him about contacting Jed, saying it should be his decision too.

But I quickly slid the thought to the back of my head as Malcolm switched on his blinker and turned down a tree-lined street with homes that looked like they'd been built nearly a century ago and hadn't been updated since.

"I don't have a plan," I admitted. "I'm torn between treating it like a death notification or telling them who I am first."

He snorted as he tucked the flask into his jacket pocket. "You're their granddaughter. Tell them who you are first."

"And if they kick me off their property, then what?"

"Then you shout at them from the street that their daughter is dead, but I doubt that's gonna happen."

"If only I can get so lucky," I grumbled.

"Seems to me your luck has been holding out pretty well." He pulled up to the curb in front of their home, which was so weatherworn the dingy gray had probably been white once upon a time. The bushes were wildly overgrown and the concrete driveway and sidewalk to the front porch had large cracks in them and sections that had been pushed up by large tree roots. "Let's hope it continues to hold on."

I had vague memories of this place. I was pretty sure we hadn't visited since I was a little kid, but I remembered it being neat and tidy. The multiple landscape beds in the front of the house had been bursting with flowers. My mother had gotten her love of gardening from *her* mother. She'd been forlorn when neither Andi nor I had shown any interest. Every spring, she'd renewed her efforts, but she'd given up after Andi died.

I stared at the rundown house in disbelief. Had my grand-parents moved, or were they so old they couldn't take care of the property anymore?

"This the place?" Malcolm asked.

"There's only one way to find out."

## Chapter 17

As I reached for my door handle, Malcolm held a metal tin toward me. "You might want this."

Breath mints.

He had a point.

I took the tin and shook a couple of them into my mouth, then took a moment to steady my frazzled nerves. I desperately craved a stiff drink, but I wasn't going to get one. I could do this without a drink, despite the voice in my head insisting otherwise.

I got out of the car.

There was no denying I was scared to knock on their door. Scared they'd either recognize me from my notoriety or blame me for ignoring them for twenty years. And if I were honest with myself, there was a part of me that was terrified about what I might find out about my parents.

I gave myself a mental shake. None of that mattered. The main reason for my visit was to tell my grandparents that their oldest daughter had died. They didn't owe me anything.

Despite my rising dread, I strode up to their front door, burying the feelings. A fleeting thought flashed through my head that maybe Malcolm was right. Maybe all this emotion burying was what had gotten me where I was in life—thirty-six years old, mostly friendless, and without having had any meaningful romantic relationships. But this wasn't the time to analyze my life choices—that was a problem for Future Harper.

Malcolm stopped behind me, thankfully giving me space while I stared at the door for several seconds.

This wasn't like me. I was decisive, unafraid to face the hard truths, but then again, that wasn't exactly true. I just had a habit of glossing over them.

*Enough.*

I lifted my hand and knocked, then took a step back, so it wouldn't look like I was crowding whoever answered. My heartbeat sped up, and I took a deep breath to settle my nerves.

How many families had I broken bad news to? Logically, I knew I had to keep trying to treat this like any other case I'd worked on—but this wasn't any other case. These were *my* estranged grandparents. This was about *my* mother.

More than a few seconds passed. I was considering knocking again when the door slowly creaked open. A short older woman with snow-white hair appeared in the opening. She wore a pink knit top and black pants. She was slightly stooped over and her left hand rested on the handle of a three-footed metal cane. The last time I'd seen my grandmother, over two decades ago, her hair had been darker and longer, but this woman was definitely her.

Her face darkened with irritation. "We already go to church so we don't need savin' and we ain't got two nickels to rub together, so don't waste your time tryin' to sell us anything,"

"I'm not here to sell you anything," I said with a half-smile, "and I don't go to church myself, so I won't be doing any proselytizing either." I took a breath, then said, "I'm your granddaughter, Harper."

Her jaw dropped as she stared up at me, tears flooding her eyes. "Harper?"

"It's me," I said, my voice tight.

She lifted her free hand to her mouth and started shaking. "I can't believe it."

"Harper," Malcolm said quietly behind me. "Maybe she should sit down."

He was right, and I was kicking myself for not pushing for that myself. "Grandma, he's right. You should probably sit down. Can my friend and I come in?"

Her head bobbed up and down, and she made a sound as though she was trying to say something, but it came out garbled. I suddenly worried the shock had given her a stroke, but when I walked over the threshold, she wrapped her arms around my body and held tight as she started to cry.

I hugged her back, surprised at the burning lump in my throat. My visits with my grandmother had been infrequent when I was growing up, but she'd always been warm and loving. It made me wonder even more what had really caused the rift with my parents.

I realized she was still shaking, so I released her, lowering my face to hers. "Let's get you to that chair."

She nodded, and Malcolm walked in around me and tucked my grandmother's right hand into the crook of his arm. "Where should we go, Mrs. Langford?"

It took me a second to realize he'd jumped in next to her in case she collapsed.

The entry was so small that they took three steps and were at the threshold to the living room. My grandmother pointed her cane. "That recliner over there."

Malcolm guided her across the small living room to one of two threadbare recliners against the wall left of the sofa. "You have a lovely home," he said, patting her hand.

I blinked hard, shocked at how sweet he was being to her.

While he'd said he could be charming, this wasn't what I'd expected.

Malcolm helped her turn and remained next to her as she sat in her recliner. Knitting needles with a square of knitted baby blue yarn rested on the overstuffed arm of her chair. The TV was on and tuned to a black and white movie, the sound surprisingly low given my grandmother's age.

My gaze swept over the room, and I was amazed that that décor was exactly as I remembered, down to the landscape painting over the sofa. I was pretty certain they hadn't redecorated in thirty years or more. I remembered she'd had a small ceramic rabbit that I'd been fascinated with when I was in preschool, and after another sweep of the room, I saw it sitting on a shelf on the wall over the television.

My grandmother stared up at me, tears streaming down her face, still mute. I worried the shock was too much for her, so I knelt in front of her, placing a hand on her knee.

She patted my hand, then leaned forward, pressing her forehead to mine. The smell of Estée Lauder perfume filled my nose, reminding me of my mother and why I was here.

"Grandma," I said, my voice catching. "Is Grandpa home?"

She pulled back, nodding, then pointed toward the kitchen, but I knew he wasn't in there. Memories of wood shavings and the scent of pine flooded my memories. He was in his workshop out back.

"I can go get him," Malcolm said, still standing to the side.

"No. He doesn't know you," I said, studying my grandmother's face, still worried about her. "Grandma, will you be okay if I go out and get him?"

"Yes, of course," she said, reaching for a tissue from the box on the table next to her chair. "He'll be thrilled to see you."

I shot a glance to Malcolm, who gave me a reassuring look. "I'll make sure she's okay. You go see him."

I nodded, nervous all over again. Grandma thought he'd be happy to see me, but what if he wasn't?

It didn't matter. I still had a job to do.

The door to the backyard was through the small kitchen with its avocado green appliances. Nothing had changed in here either.

Once I was out the back door, I took in the yard, from the lilac bushes planted against the house, the bird bath and feeder in the center of the yard, and the single bay, detached garage at the end of the cracked concrete driveway. The garage door was open, and I could hear the hum of an engine and the familiar whine of wood giving way to a blade.

My heart skipped a beat as I saw my grandfather through the open garage door. He was turning a piece of wood on his lathe, his gnarled hands holding the end while he wore safely goggles. He was shorter and more stooped than I remembered him, but he still had a full head of grey hair.

I took several steps closer and stopped, not wanting to startle him while he was working with a power tool, but he must have caught my movement out of his peripheral vision because his head turned to face me, surprise filling his eyes. He stood upright and stared at me for a moment before reaching down and blindly flipping the switch to kill his machine. The motor slowed down then stopped as he took off his safety goggles and set them on his work bench.

"*Harper?*" he asked, his eyes wide. "Is that you?"

I nodded, my eyes burning as I closed the distant between us.

He engulfed me in a massive hug, nearly squeezing the breath out of me. "I can't believe it's you," he choked out.

I hugged him back, fighting the tightness in my chest. I felt dangerously close to crying, something I hadn't even done after finding out about my mother's death. But I couldn't fall apart, especially now. I had a job to do. I had to tell them their daughter was dead.

After several seconds, he released me and grabbed my shoulders, leaning me back. "Let me look at you." His sharp eyes scanned my face, then he lifted a hand to my cheek. "I can't believe you're here."

"How did you know it was me? Grandma didn't recognize me."

"I'd know you anywhere," he said, his eyes filling with tears. "My little Harper all grown up."

I hated that I was about to kill their joy with the news about Mom. I wasn't ready to tell them, not when they were both so happy to see me, but they'd be justifiably angry if I spent time talking to them, then half an hour later said, "Oh, by the way. Your daughter is dead."

My stomach felt heavy, but I forced myself to say, "Grandma's inside, maybe we should go in so I can talk to you both at the same time."

He nodded and put a hand at the small of my back and ushered me to the back door.

"Shirley!" he called out as we entered through the back. "Can you believe it? Harper's here!" He stopped short when he saw Malcolm sitting on the sofa next to my grandmother's chair, but then he winked at me, a cheesy grin stretching across his face. "You brought a young man with you."

I nearly laughed at him calling Malcolm a young man, but I supposed he was compared to my grandparents. "Grandpa, this is my friend—"

Malcolm stood and took a step toward us, extending his hand. "James Malcolm, sir. I'd like to thank you and your wife for having me in your home."

My grandfather shook his hand and looked pleased. "I like a man with a firm handshake," he said when he dropped his grip on Malcolm's hand. "If you're a friend of Harper's, you're welcome here."

Malcolm gave me an honest-to-God grin, and I wondered

who the hell this man was and where the James Malcolm I knew had gone.

"Thank you, Mr. Langford."

"You can call me Gary, James," my grandfather said as he moved across the living room to sit in his recliner on the opposite side of the room. He sat down but didn't recline back, watching me in amazement instead. "We always hoped one day you'd change your mind, but I confess, I'd decided years ago that it wasn't likely to happen."

I took a seat next to Malcolm on the sofa and gave my grandfather a confused look. "Change my mind?"

"About seeing us." When I still looked puzzled, pain flashed in his eyes. "Your mother made it clear you didn't want to see us. We'd hoped it was just a phase, but when she told us we weren't welcome at your high school graduation because you didn't want us there…" He took a breath to compose himself. "It broke our hearts, and right or wrong, we just couldn't bring ourselves to try again."

I slowly shook my head. "Grandpa, I never said that." When he still looked hurt, I said, "I *never* said I didn't want you there. Mom said she invited you, but you and grandma said you couldn't come. That you had other plans. She told me you didn't want to see me."

His face reddened and his jaw clenched. "That's not true."

My mother had purposely kept us apart. Why?

Grandma sniffed and I turned to see that she'd started to cry.

"Grandma, I swear. I never, ever said I didn't want to see you. I know you and Dad had some kind of falling out, and that you made Mom choose between you and him, and she chose him. I figured I was just collateral damage."

"Falling out with your father?" Grandma said, shaking her head. "What falling out?"

I stared at her in disbelief, then swung my attention to my grandfather. He didn't look confused. He looked angry.

Had everything been a lie?

"Mom and Dad said you blamed Dad for Andi's death, and you all stopped speaking because Mom was furious at you."

He clenched his jaw. "I think I'm gonna need something to drink to continue this conversation." Then he got up and walked into the kitchen.

I looked over at Malcolm who was watching me with concern, which caught me off guard as much as the conversation I'd just had. Malcolm had never shown concern for me. Irritation, condescension, understanding, but never concern. Not even the night before, when he'd helped nurse me through my withdrawal. I'd known he was worried given the way he'd nursed me, but he hadn't shown it. His lack of concern seemed like a cornerstone to our relationship. He never treated me like I was fragile.

The hard truth was that I *was* fragile, as hard as that was for me to accept. I'd always prided myself on being strong, no matter what, but if I were honest with myself, I'd been fragile for a hell of a lot longer than a couple of days.

My grandfather returned a half second later, carrying a tray with three juice glasses and a bottle of whiskey.

My stomach dropped with dread, while another part of me lit up in anticipation of the warmth sliding down my throat and spreading through my body.

Grandpa set the tray on the coffee table and then grabbed the whiskey bottle and twisted off the cap. He poured a finger of liquid into the cup closest to Malcolm, but when he turned it toward the cup in front of me, somehow, I managed to reach up and cover the opening. "None for me." Everything in me screamed to grab the bottle from his hand and fill my glass half full, but the stubborn part of me held strong.

Grandpa didn't question it, just skipped me and poured a finger into his own glass, then picked it up and took a healthy sip. Malcolm did the same, then set the glass on the table, out of my reach.

"We've all been lied to, child," Grandpa said, his voice breaking.

"I realize that now," I said, holding my hands in my lap, trying to keep them from grabbing the whiskey bottle.

He took another sip, then shook his head. "We weren't happy when Sarah Jane said she was cutting contact with us, but she'd been distant for years, so we weren't surprised. It was losing you that broke us." He took another sip. "Especially after what happened to your sister. We knew you had to be devastated, but your mother said she'd have us physically removed if we came to her funeral. And when we tried to reach out to you later, Sarah Jane said you didn't want to speak to us either."

I had a million questions, and unfortunately, the one person who might have the answers wasn't here to give them. Guilt flooded me as I realized I *still* hadn't done what I came here to do.

"Grandpa." I glanced over at my grandmother. "Grandma. There's something I need to tell you about Mom."

My grandmother grabbed another tissue from the box and dabbed her eyes. "We know about Sarah Jane."

My eyes widened. "You know?"

"We know you buried her yesterday," Grandpa said. "And that your father didn't tell us about the service."

"We wouldn't have gone anyway," Grandma said. "Sarah Jane made it clear we weren't welcome in her life, so it seemed wrong to show up after she was dead."

Her hand rested on the arm of her chair, and I reached over and placed my hand on hers. "I'm *so* sorry."

She shook her head, tears flooding her eyes again. "There's no need to be sorry that we missed her funeral. We mourned her long ago."

We were all silent for a moment. I was still trying to figure out what could possibly make my mother cut off her parents at the very moment she probably needed them most. I suspected my grandparents were reconciling that my mother had lied about my desire to see them and all the years we'd wasted.

Grandpa took another drink, then lowered the glass so it rested on the arm of his chair. "We're sorry, Harper. We should have tried harder."

"We *did* send you cards and letters," Grandma said. "But they always went unanswered, and after a while, they started coming back with 'return to sender' written on the envelope. A part of me always wondered if it was you or your mother keeping us apart, but deep down I knew it was her. She just seemed too daunting to cross."

"I could have reached out too," I said. "Especially after I left home for college. But by that time…"

By that time, I'd shut everyone out. The last thing I'd wanted to do was let someone in.

But my grandmother misinterpreted my meaning, and fresh tears filled her eyes. "By that time, you thought we'd turned our backs on you too."

I had, but I still could have tried.

"I don't understand why she cut you out of our lives," I said. "Why then?" The whiskey bottle was in my peripheral vision and my mouth began to water.

Grandpa shook his head. "I don't know, but we weren't necessarily surprised it happened. More by the timing of it."

I sat back a little on the sofa cushion, trying to put distance between myself and the bottle. "You said Mom grew distant several years before she cut off contact. Do you know why?"

Grandma dabbed her eyes again. "Sarah Jane never thought much of us, even growin' up. She was friends with girls who had parents with means, and she resented that we couldn't give her what their families could. When she set off for college, she did so with the ambition to marry a rich man."

"She was after her MRS Degree," Grandpa said, staring down at the dregs of his drink and shaking his head.

Grandma gave him a dirty look, then turned back to me. "I suppose she didn't do too poorly with your father."

We hadn't been rich, but we'd been very comfortable. Either they were wrong about her objective to marry rich, or her goal had changed. From what I'd seen, she'd been more obsessed with power and being in control than with money, and living in a small town gave her plenty of opportunity to rule with her iron will.

"So she was already distant before she left home for college?" I asked.

My grandfather cleared his throat. "She wasn't as close to us as her sister Hannah is, but Sarah Jane always came home for holidays and over summer break while she was at school. She seemed pleased to see us when we were together. Especially after she started dating Paul."

"And things got better after we agreed to give her the weddin' she wanted," Grandma said. "Of course weddings weren't the expensive affairs they are nowadays, but we still had to come up with more money than we had to pay for it."

"Had to get a second mortgage," Grandpa grumbled.

I grimaced. I suspected my mother had known that and hadn't felt an ounce of guilt. I was sure she'd thought it was no less than what she deserved.

"So, we were in her good graces for a while after that," Grandma said with a sigh. "And then she had you, and she went through a terrible postpartum depression. She could hardly function, so the two of you came and stayed with us for a couple of months. Your grandpa and I took care of you while she recovered."

My mother had suffered from depression before? If my mother had suffered from depression before, it might be totally possible that she had asked for an anti-depressant from Dr. Duncan. "Was she treated for it?"

Grandma scoffed. "She refused therapy and wouldn't even consider medication. Said she didn't believe in it, but I suspect she didn't want the *stigma* of going to therapy or takin' medication." She gave me a sympathetic look. "There was a bit of shame attached to it back then. Some people, especially around here, thought it meant you were weak, and your mother hated to appear weak."

That was the mother I'd known, at least until my father left.

Grandpa finished the last of his drink, then said, "She likely would have recovered faster if she had agreed to the medicine, but we didn't push it."

My grandmother cringed. "Your grandpa's right. We didn't, but we should have."

"Did she breast feed?" Malcolm asked, catching me by surprise. "Maybe she was worried it would hurt Harper."

"Heavens no," Grandma said. "She refused to breast feed because she said formula was better for babies. Scientific research and nutrition and some nonsense." She shrugged. "We never bought it for a minute. I suspect the real reason was she wanted help gettin' up in the middle of the night, and if she wasn't breast feedin', she could have someone else do it. I know your father got up with you quite a bit when you were in Jackson Creek, and I did it when your mother brought you here."

If my mother had been depressed, she might not have had the energy to get up in the middle of the night. Or she could have just not wanted to. Either was possible.

Grandma gestured to my grandfather. "He helped with the middle-of-the-night feedin's too." Tears filled her eyes. "I think that's why we felt so much closer to you than any of the other grandkids. Because we took care of you for nearly two months."

"I didn't know any of that," I said. "No one ever told me. Did she suffer a postpartum depression after Andi was born?"

"No, thank goodness, but she knew she didn't want to have any more kids after her. I think your father would have liked to have tried for a boy, but he seemed thrilled with his two daughters. Doted on you whenever we were around y'all."

"You got along with Harper's father?" Malcolm asked, looking at my grandmother and then my grandfather.

"Loved him," Grandma said fondly. "He seemed like a genuinely good guy, and he mellowed her some. She wasn't too pleased when he moved to Jackson Creek, but one of his partners was from there and his father gave them the money to start the firm."

"But you were part of her life until she cut you off after Andi died?" I asked.

Grandma made a face. "Oh, no. When you were about ten or so she started to call less. That would have made Andi about eight."

"What happened? Did you guys have a fight, or did Mom perceive some kind of slight that made her mad?" The latter was entirely possible.

"Not in that instance. I know she and her sister weren't getting along at the time, but everything seemed fine at Christmas—well, normal for her—and then we came for Andi's ninth birthday, and she seemed withdrawn."

"Was she like that with just you and Gary or with everyone?" Malcolm asked.

Grandma looked lost in thought for a moment. "Well, now that I think about it, I guess she was just quiet in general. She *did* lose her temper with Hannah, but that was nothing new. Those two were like piss and vinegar. One minute they were sweet to each other, the next they were fighting. They almost always made up, but they never did after that last time. As far as I know, they only saw each other at our house for holidays. Then when you were twelve, your mom said your family wasn't coming to see us during Christmas break, that it wasn't fair on you girls to have to travel. We offered to come visit y'all in Jackson Creek and she agreed, but didn't seem thrilled about it. Then the day before we were supposed to drive to Jackson Creek—the day before Christmas Eve—she called and said Andi had strep throat and the doctor said they couldn't have anyone in the house."

I distinctly remembered the Christmas I was twelve, because I'd gotten the bike I'd seen in the window at Milton's Hardware after talking about it for months. I also distinctly remembered that Andi hadn't been sick. She'd gotten a bike too, and we'd spent all afternoon on Christmas Day riding our new bikes all over the neighborhood.

My mother had lied.

Turned out she'd lied about quite a few things.

# Chapter 18

We were all quiet for a moment. I had no idea what my grandparents were thinking, but my mind was in turmoil. Had my mother up and decided she had no further use for her parents? How could she just write off her family for no reason?

A little voice in the back of my head reminded me I'd pretty much written off my own parents, but then again, my mother had made that decision for me. She'd spent her life cutting people off.

Hadn't I done the same thing? Sure, I hadn't ghosted people, but I hadn't let them get close either.

At least I was in good company.

A hollowness opened deep inside me, revealing a void that had always been there. A typical black hole pulls everything in —planets, stars, even light. But mine did the opposite. It repelled relationships like two magnets forced together at the same pole.

My palms began to itch, and my throat went dry. I needed a drink. I was *desperate* for a drink, and a whiskey bottle was three feet away from me.

As though reading my mind, Malcolm grabbed the bottle

and poured a tiny amount into the empty glass and handed it to me. I took it with a shaky hand, then gulped the contents down.

"Oh, Harper," my grandmother said, reaching over and patting my arm. "I'm so sorry. Here I am talkin' badly about your mother and you just lost her."

I took another gulp, finishing what he'd poured for me, but I still wanted more. I put the glass on the table and put my hand back in my lap, hoping the burn would settle my nerves any second now.

Then Malcolm put his hand on my leg, and a surprising calm washed over me. Some of my anxiety dissipated, but I refused to let myself dwell on why.

"Is that why you came here?" my grandfather asked. "To tell us that your mother had died?"

"Dad said he didn't tell you, and I felt like you needed to know." I drew in a shaky breath. "How *did* you find out?"

My grandmother shot a look at my grandfather, then gave me a grim smile. "Hannah. She saw it online."

I knew Mom's accident had made the local news, so it wasn't outside the realm of possibility for my aunt to have heard about it. The last I'd heard, she lived in Jonesboro too.

"I can't believe you came all the way up here to tell us," my grandfather said. "Even though you thought we might turn you away."

"I hoped that you wouldn't, but if you did, I would have understood. I thought you wrote me off with my mother, but there was actually another reason." I suspected they knew about my shooting incident in Little Rock, but there was a chance they didn't. I hated to bring it up, but they deserved to know everything about me before wholeheartedly welcoming me back into their lives. I paused, preparing myself for the rejection I'd expected. "I was a detective in Little Rock and last fall … something bad happened." I drew a breath. "I shot and killed a teenager."

My grandmother and grandfather exchanged a glance, then they both gave me sympathetic looks.

"We know about that too, Harper," Grandma said. "We saw it on the news."

I grimaced. "I guess you'd have to live under a rock to have missed it."

"For what it's worth," my grandmother said with a look of determination, "I never believed you lied. You said you saw a gun, so you must have seen a gun."

I stared at her in disbelief. "How can you say that? You haven't seen me since I was fourteen, and you'd barely seen me for a few years before that. How could you be so certain?"

"We know who you are, Harper," my grandfather said. "You always had a good heart. You wouldn't have shot the boy if he hadn't had a gun."

"I'm not sure if you realize it," Malcolm said, "but other than me and her friend Louise, you two are the only people who believe her."

My head swiveled as I gaped at him. I'd told him my story two months ago, and he'd believed me, but this was something different. It felt like he was declaring he was on my side.

My grandmother's face lit up with adoration as she pressed her hand to her chest. "I'm so glad she has you and her friend in her corner." A tear slid down her cheek. "Thank you."

"You're a good man," Grandpa said with a nod.

My deceit about Malcolm's true identity was eating at me. What would my grandparents say if they knew James Malcolm was a notorious ex-crime boss? I couldn't imagine my grandfather would call him a good man if he knew about his past.

"I'm not surprised about Sarah Jane turning her back on you," Grandma said. "She never could abide bein' in the center of a scandal. She much preferred to be the one doin' the judgin', not bein' judged."

That fit with my own assessment of my mother.

"But your father," my grandmother continued, "he didn't stand by you either?"

"No," Malcolm said before I attempted to sugar coat it, "not until she lost everything and his conscience got the better of him. When she lost her house, he came to Little Rock and offered to let her move into their garage apartment."

My grandmother tsked. "I don't understand that. He always doted on you and your sister. I would have thought he'd move heaven and earth to protect you." She stopped short, her eyes widening slightly. "Then again, I guess he couldn't keep your sister safe from that kidnapper."

I bit my tongue to keep from telling her that my mother had blamed me for not keeping my sister safe. I'd already dragged her memory over the coals. No need to roast her anymore.

"He changed after Andi," I said. "He became more quiet. More distant from all of us. He didn't handle it well."

My grandmother pressed her knuckles to her mouth. "We should have reached out to you, Harper," Grandma said, shame washing over her face. "Especially after you graduated from high school and went to college. Little Rock isn't that far away. We could have tried to visit you."

"You knew I went to college in Little Rock?" I asked in surprise.

She grimaced. "Hannah found that out too. At the end of your first semester, she saw your name on the Dean's List."

Did Hannah have an alert set up to notify her every time my or my mother's name appeared on the internet? Or had she just searched online in an attempt to find me?

I realized I needed to speak to my aunt before I left town … provided she was still living in the area.

"That was very resourceful of her," I said. "But there's another reason I'm here."

My grandfather looked surprised. "Oh?"

How did I admit my mother had been missing for days and we hadn't noticed? "My mother's death wasn't——"

"It took everyone by surprise," Malcolm said. "Especially when we learned she'd packed a suitcase and was going on a trip without telling anyone."

Had he thought I was going to tell them she was murdered? Or was he trying to play the part of the supportive friend? Why wasn't I more annoyed that he'd interrupted me?

And why was I letting him keep his hand on my knee?

But I left his hand in place as I said, "We're confused about why she was leaving and where she was going. After Andi died, she pretty much refused to spend the night away from home. In fact, I can't think of the last time she went on an overnight trip, let alone packed a bag for multiple days. We have no idea where she might have been going and why she left."

My grandfather frowned. "She didn't tell your father she was leaving?"

"They were separated," I said. "My father left her about a month ago, so they weren't speaking to each other much."

Grandma slowly shook her head in disbelief. "I can't believe he left."

"What happened?" Grandpa asked.

I saw no reason to lie. "Because my mother was mad that he'd asked me to come home. He hated how she treated me."

"Oh," she said, her face turning pale, then she seemed to come to her senses enough to reach over the arm of her chair and take my hand. "I'm so sorry you had to go through all of this, Harper. I'm so, so sorry she turned her back on you."

"It's funny," I said with a short laugh. "After he left, she was more interested in spending time with me than she ever had been, even before Andi's death."

Based on the horror in her eyes, my statement didn't seem to make her feel better. My grandfather turned away, looking like he was about to cry.

"You have us," Grandma said, squeezing my arm. "Isn't that right, Gary?"

My grandfather nodded, then turned to face me, his eyes glassy. "That's right." His words were rough with emotion. "You have us."

While I appreciated their love and support, I couldn't let myself bask in it. Especially not right then. I had a job to do. They didn't seem to have any information that would help me find out who killed my mother, but I wondered if my Aunt Hannah might.

"Does Hannah still live in Jonesboro?" I asked.

"Yeah," Grandpa said. "She's a second-grade teacher at the elementary school down the street. It's where she and your mother went to school."

"That's sweet," I said, glancing at the clock on the wall. It was close to four, which meant she might have already gotten out of school. "Do you think she'd be open to seeing me while I'm here?"

Grandma clasped her hands together as her eyes turned glassy. "She'd be thrilled. How about I ask her over for dinner? You and your friend James can stay, and I'll roast a chicken."

"No need to make dinner," I said. "We don't want to be any trouble."

"Nonsense!" she protested. "We would love to have you eat with us. It'll give us a chance to catch up more."

"We really need to—" I started to say before Malcolm interrupted.

"We'd love to stay." He squeezed my knee slightly. "Thank you for your generous offer, Shirley."

I smothered down my irritation. We needed to get back to Lone County and keep digging into my mother's death. Sure, I would love to continue this stroll down memory lane, but if my aunt came over soon, we could have a short, contained conversation. Not a possibly hours' long event.

"Do you think it would be okay if Harper and I looked at any old photos you might have?" Malcolm asked. "I'd love to see some from when Sarah Jane and Hannah were younger."

My grandmother excitedly pushed herself to her feet, then grabbed her cane, bobbing a bit before she gained her balance. Malcolm tensed beside me as though preparing to spring from his seat to prevent her from falling.

"I have a bunch of photo albums in my room." She beamed as she turned her attention to Malcolm. "Can you help me bring them out, James?"

He got to his feet. "I'd be honored."

Grandma glanced over at my grandfather. "Can you text Hannah and ask her over to come over for dinner? Don't tell her that Harper's here. Just say we have two special guests."

My grandfather lifted his butt as he reached into his front jeans pocket. "On it."

"How long have you been with my granddaughter?" Grandma asked as they disappeared down the hall.

"A couple of months," he said.

"We're just friends!" I shouted after them. The last thing I needed was for my grandparents to get the wrong idea.

Grandpa chuckled. "Just friends, you say?"

"Yes," I countered, trying to soften the automatic attitude that rose up. "Just friends."

He shook his head. "Why would a man drive three hours with a woman if they weren't in a relationship?"

I wasn't about to explain the true nature of our relationship, not that I could if I tried. "It's possible for a man to be friends with a woman and offer her moral support while she tells her grandparents their oldest daughter died."

"I suppose that's true," he conceded sheepishly before adding, "But I saw the way he was watching you when you were upset. It was the look of man who cares for a woman."

I nearly laughed. Malcolm was doing one hell of a job selling my grandparents on our friendship, but I needed to tell him to tone it down since they'd both gotten the wrong idea. "I can assure you, we're not romantic at all. We've both been very clear with each other that our relationship is platonic."

He wore an amused expression as he kept his gaze on his phone and tapped the screen. "Friend or more, he's a fine young man. I'm glad you have him. As a friend."

I silently groaned then couldn't help laughing. I'd forgotten the way he used to tease me when I was a kid. He and my grandmother had always been so lighthearted. It was hard to believe they'd raised my mother, who was the exact opposite. Would things have been different for me if they'd still been part of my life after Andi's death? Would I have been less damaged? Our family of three had become so solemn and depressed, which was understandable, but we'd never found our way out of it.

My grandfather spent the next minute composing his text, stabbing the phone screen with his right index finger. By the time he'd finished, Malcolm appeared at the edge of the living room with an armload of photo albums.

I stared at the stack in surprise. "You guys have a lot of photos."

Malcolm dropped them on the coffee table, then picked up the whiskey bottle and carried it into the kitchen, calling out as he went, "There's even more back there, but they were from before your mother was born."

"I've got photos all the way back to the late 1800s," my grandmother said. "Some of random things, but a lot of them are of my grandparents and their families."

"I keep telling her she needs to turn them over to a historical society," Grandpa grumbled, balancing his phone on the arm of his chair. "But she's not ready to part with 'em yet."

She groaned in exasperation. "I've told you a *million times*, Gary, that you can give 'em to whoever you want once I'm dead. Right now, they aren't hurtin' a doggone thing back in the closet."

"They're takin' up valuable space," he countered.

Malcolm walked out of the kitchen and stopped in the doorway holding a glass of ice water. "I hope it's okay that I helped myself to a glass of ice water for Harper. I thought she might need it after our drive."

"Oh, my heavens," Grandma said in horror. "I never offered either of y'all refreshments."

"Gary gave us whiskey," Malcolm said, handing me the glass before he sat down next to me. "That seemed more fitting at the time."

"I suppose you're right." Grandma said, then turned her attention to the albums. "But I've still forgotten my manners."

"You had a few other things on your mind," Malcolm said, then put a hand on the photo album at the top that stack. "Where should we start?"

"It seems like the logical place to start is back when Sarah Jane was a baby," Grandma said, pulling the top album off, then nearly dropping it onto the coffee table. She pointed to one that was two albums deep. "This one."

Malcolm moved the other albums and set the book on my lap. "Would you point things out? I'm sure Harper would appreciate hearing the stories behind the photos."

"Oh course," she said, beaming with happiness, then reached over to open the cover.

What was Malcolm up to? Was he hoping the photos would give us some clues? That seemed doubtful, but then again, you never knew where you might find a breadcrumb and where it might lead.

I took a sip of the water, my eyes widening at the slight taste of vodka on my tongue.

Malcolm wasn't looking at me to confirm what he'd done —given me a glass of water with what tasted like a half shot of vodka. Enough alcohol to keep the edge off and keep me from looking sketchy from taking shots from his flask.

He scooted a few feet away from me, then patted the seat

cushion. "Why don't you sit between us, Shirley? That way we'll all be able to see."

She gave the book a longing look. "I want to, but I need to figure out what we're havin' for dinner."

"I thought you said you were gonna roast a chicken," Grandpa said.

"And I plan to," she shot back, "but I might need to go to the store and get one, not to mention anything else we need."

"No," Malcolm said insistently. "I refuse to let us put you out. I'll take you all out to dinner. I'll pay."

My grandfather looked startled. "We can't let you do that."

"I insist," Malcolm said. "If Shirley is making dinner, then she's not spending time with her long-lost granddaughter, which I think we can all agree is more important. So respectfully, let me handle dinner. Y'all have been so kind to Harper, it's the least I can do."

My grandfather shot me a smug grin, making it clear he saw this as further proof Malcolm wanted more than friendship with me, but I knew better. Turned out that Malcolm had a secret soft side, and it was currently on full display. It had nothing to do with his feelings—or lack thereof—for me.

But for better or worse, it endeared him to me even more.

# Chapter 19

As I'd suspected, the photos didn't reveal any clues, but I enjoyed hearing about my mother's childhood. Her sister was two years younger, just like me and Andi, so she was in plenty of them too. My grandmother had photographs of my mother up through college, which I found surprising. Most parents took more photos of their kids when they were cute and adorable, and less when their angels became surly teens. But my grandmother's stuffed albums proved her to be the exception.

It was surreal to see images of my mother as she grew from a baby to her high school graduation. She was smiling and happy in most, especially in her younger years. My aunt Hannah, whom I'd barely known, was with her in many of them.

There were plenty of candid shots as well as posed, but I was amazed there were so many of my mother and aunt taken inside their elementary school.

I touched the edge of a photo of a school Halloween party. Most of the kids were wearing cheap store-bought costumes and a good portion of them had plastic masks covering their faces, the kind secured with cheap elastic strings. "Were you a room mother?"

"Oh heavens, no," she said with a wave of her hand. "They didn't have those at their school, but I volunteered now and again." She winked. "I liked to do it on the days they had parties. And since the other parents weren't there, I made sure to take lots of photos so they could get copies too."

"That was very thoughtful of you," Malcolm said.

She shrugged as though it was no big deal, but she seemed pleased by his compliment. "They seemed to appreciate it."

I struggled to mesh the woman who'd raised me with the young girl and then teen who'd looked so happy. There were images of her with friends at school and at home at every grade level. She had photos taken with quite a few kids in her younger years, but by the time she reached junior high school, her friends had changed. They looked more polished, and I was fairly sure they were in the popular crowd. My grandmother confirmed it.

Studying a photo of my mother and her friends dressed for a cotillion and obviously loving it, I had a new understanding for why my mother had preferred Andi. I favored jeans and T-shirts, while Andi had loved dresses and skirts and bows in her hair. I'd been quiet and reserved, but my sister had been larger than life and popular. And the few friends I'd had had quickly disappeared after Andi's death. My mother must have seen my sister as a replica of herself.

The photos dwindled by the time my mother went to college, but during her sophomore year, she'd brought Dad home to meet her parents. Younger versions of them, barely looking like adults, sat on the very sofa we were sitting on now, my dad wearing a nervous smile.

"He was so anxious about meeting us," my grandmother said, pointing to the photo I'd been studying. "But we loved him immediately."

"Did Mom love him?" Then I realized how that sounded.

"I mean, obviously she loved him. I guess I'm asking if she was head over heels for him?"

"I'd say she loved him, but I don't think she was head over heels. At least from what I saw," she said as she stared pensively at the photo. "But then she seemed much more mellow, sedate, after they started dating. I asked her once if she was happy, and as expected, she didn't take it well. She said she'd grown up, but the grown-up version of her didn't laugh much. Your father didn't cut up much either, so I always wondered if she'd tempered herself for him."

That wasn't something I'd considered, but I supposed it could be true. If she'd thought my father could give her the life she wanted, I could see her toning down her personality to be more appealing to him. How ironic that stiff, snobby person she'd become had ultimately turned him away.

There were photos of their wedding, and then of my mother pregnant. Images of my father putting a crib together and of a baby shower where my mother was surrounded by at least forty women.

"The church in Jackson Creek gave her a shower," Grandma said, pointing to photo of a rectangular table covered with a white tablecloth and loaded with gifts. "Your father's law firm gave her one too, but we didn't make it for that."

Many of the photographs showed my mother sitting in a rocking chair in varying stages of opening gifts. She was smiling in the images, but they weren't the wide, bright-eyed smiles of her youth and teen years. These smiles looked cultivated and slightly fake.

Had my father expected that of her or had she determined that was what he wanted?

Next were tons of photos of me as a baby, starting with my mother and me in the hospital after my birth. There were only a few photos of my mother holding me. Instead, I was held by my father and grandparents. The photographs continued both at our Jackson Creek house and here in my grandparent's home when Mom and I had stayed for a few months. They captured Halloween—I was dressed as a pumpkin—Christmas, my first birthday, and then my mother pregnant with Andi. There were fewer photos of baby Andi than me, and while it was often true that second children were photographed less, these photos had been taken by my grandparents. This could be proof my mother had begun distancing herself from her parents even earlier than they'd suggested.

The photos dwindled until the year I turned thirteen and had a roller-skating party. My grandparents had come, but my mother hadn't. She'd wanted a tea party theme at home with frilly dresses and tiny cakes, not roller skating, but my father had insisted it was *my* birthday, not hers, and she had to let me do what I wanted. She'd gotten pissed and told him if I was having a party at a dirty roller rink, he could plan it himself. To his credit, he had, not that it was anything fancy. I'd invited half a dozen friends, and Andi had brought some of her own. My father had gotten what my mother called a tacky store-bought cake, and it had been one of the best parties I could remember having. Several parents had asked where my mother was, and my dad had said she'd been suffering from a killer migraine.

It was the last birthday party I ever had. My mother refused to plan one the next year, then after Andi's death, I'd never wanted one.

All these memories were like a heavy weight on my shoulders, and an ache filled my chest. What had happened to my mother to make her turn out the way she had? And did it have anything to do with what had ultimately killed her?

I didn't realize my breathing had become labored until Malcolm gave me a concerned look.

"Harper, why don't we go outside and get some air?"

As he asked, he was already getting to his feet and offering me his hand.

I took it without thinking, mostly because I wasn't sure I had the presence of mind to find the exit on my own, but once our hands connected, it felt right, like we'd always held hands. Still, I didn't give it much thought other than I wanted him to hold my hand, no, *needed* him to hold my hand. His touch was the one thing keeping me from losing it.

He led me out the front door and across the yard to the back of his car, then released my hand. It felt wrong to not be connected to him anymore, but I couldn't very well protest.

What would he do if I asked him to hold it longer?

What would he do if I asked him to hold *me*?

But obviously, I couldn't do either of those things. Even though I suspected he'd give me both if I asked.

He rested his butt against the trunk, and I did the same, my heart beating wildly. I recognized this for what it was—a panic attack. I'd had them after Andi had died, and thought I was having a heart attack. (My mother had accused me of creating unnecessary drama.) Then I'd started having them again after I'd shot the boy in Little Rock. Alcohol had helped hold them at bay. Did that mean they'd become more common again?

We stood side by side for a few minutes while I struggled to breathe, Malcolm giving me quick glances every so often. By the time it began to subside, my anxiety was replaced with anger. What the hell was wrong with me? Millions of people had lost their mothers. Millions of people had shitty childhoods, and the majority of them weren't drunks who fell apart without their alcohol crutch.

This wasn't me. I was strong, goddamn it. I didn't fall apart.

*Liar*, a little voice in my head said mockingly. *You've been unraveling for years, you've just tried to outrun it. But you can't outrun it forever.*

I ignored the stupid voice because that wasn't true at all. I'd had a tough-as-nails reputation in the police department.

I'd held my shit together for years, but one trip to my grandparents had me on the edge of a nervous breakdown.

"What the hell are we even doing here?" I spat, my voice breaking.

"We're looking at photos with your grandmother," he said evenly, his hands jammed in his front jeans pockets as he stared down the street.

"We told them my mother was dead, found out what little we could, so we should be on our way back to Jackson Creek. Going through ten million photos isn't helping find out who killed her."

"You're right," he admitted in that frustratingly reasonable voice. "I doubt we'll find anything in those photos that will lead to who killed her, but you need this."

I turned on him, so angry I had to clench my hands into tight fists. "Who the hell are you to tell me what I need?"

He didn't move, didn't flinch. He just stood there, close enough that the heat from his body tangled with my anger in ways I didn't want to name. When he turned to me, his face neutral, but his eyes—quiet, intimate—cut through me.

Dangerous.

My breath hitched. The heat rising in me had nothing to do with withdrawal.

But he was the picture of calm, and it pissed me off even more.

"Is this a *game* to you?" I demanded.

Irritation flickered in his eyes.

*Ah, a reaction.* Smug satisfaction filled my chest. I was spoiling for a fight, and it wouldn't work if he didn't participate. But I couldn't ignore a different tension that sent a tightening to my core. It had nothing to do with anger. It was the kind of tension that made my skin heat up and my pulse go wild. The kind that made me want to close the distance between us and make a very bad decision.

"What the hell does that mean?" he asked.

I took a step back and gestured to the house, trying to ignore the way my body felt alive. It only made me more pissed. "You must be *loving* the *Harper meets her grandparents* show. Plenty of fodder to use against me later."

He shook his head, his jaw tightening. He took a step closer, trapping me between the car and his body. The air between us felt charged, making it hard to remember why I was supposed to be angry with him.

"Is *that* what you think this is all about?" he demanded. "You think I suggested we look at photo albums so I could watch you squirm and rub it in later?"

"Why else would you convince her to drag them out?" I countered, trying not to shout.

"That's what you think of me?" he asked, his cheeks flushing. "You think I'd have you look at photos of your mother to torture you?"

Torture was too strong a word, but if he didn't think we'd learn anything from them, what was the point? What could have been a five-minute trip down memory lane had dragged out for a good forty-five minutes.

He studied me for a moment, shaking his head. "You must think I'm an absolute monster. Of course you do. You've called me that before." Only he'd worn the title proudly then. Now he looked affronted. No, not affronted. He looked hurt. But that couldn't be right. There was no world in which I was capable of hurting James Malcolm's feelings.

Still, my heart lurched. What if I was wrong?

"I'll admit I was a bastard when we worked on our first case together," he said in a tone that sounded reasonable but had a hint of danger under the surface. "But I thought we'd made progress on our last investigation. And after last night, I thought you'd begun to trust me."

"You're an ex-crime boss, Malcolm," I countered. "That in and of itself makes you untrustworthy."

He nodded once slowly. "Yeah. You're right. Thanks for

the reminder." He took a step back. "You know what? Do whatever the fuck you want with the photos," he said, his voice so icy it made me shiver. "But maybe ask yourself this: what would *I* get out of torturing you? If I wanted to torture you, I would have let you fumble your way through the DTs last night. I would have been the monster you think I am to your grandparents."

He was right, and I knew it, but there was only one logical explanation, and it didn't make sense. "Then why, Malcolm?" I demanded, the pain in my heart so sharp I could hardly breathe. "Why help me last night? Why make me look at photos of my mother?"

He drew a breath. His face had morphed into the steely blankness I was all too familiar with. "Why do you *think* I helped you?" he asked in a snide tone. "I did it because I need your help with this investigation. If your mother's murder has any ties to what I'm lookin' into, then it's a win/win for both of us." He gestured to the house. "And as for the photos?" He stopped, quiet for several seconds as though weighing his words. "I thought there was a slight chance we'd find something useful, and since we had to kill time until your aunt shows up for dinner, I figured we might as well do it looking at photos of you and your mother."

Two weeks ago, I might have believed him, but now I knew he was lying. The ease with which I could read him caught me by surprise. But I'd gotten to know him over the past few weeks, and I recognized that a lot of his bravado with me was a front.

Just like mine was with him.

Taking a step backward, he pulled his phone from his pocket and checked the screen. "While I've been busy babysitting you and your family, I've missed some important calls."

"Malcolm." It came out as a plea.

"I know we suggested goin' out to eat, but I think it might be a better idea to eat in. Especially given the questions we plan to ask your aunt." He tugged his key fob out of his jeans pocket. "Tell them I'll be back in an hour with dinner."

"You're leaving me here?" I asked, feeling slightly panicked, although I wasn't sure why. Was it because I'd have no way out if I became too overwhelmed by the family reunion? Or because I was worried he'd head back to Lone County without me, leaving me to find my own way home?

He scoffed in disgust. "You make it sound like you're a puppy abandoned on a country road." He shook his head, then pointed to the house. "This is your *family*, Harper, and unlike your parents, they actually give a shit about you. I would have *killed* to have grandparents like yours, but mine were too goddamned drunk to give a shit about me, let alone spend time with me."

Something cracked in his voice, a rawness I'd never heard before, and it hit me square in the chest. The vulnerability in his tone made me want to step closer, not away. This was dangerous territory—not just because of his pain, but because of my sudden, fierce urge to comfort him.

"Those people—" He cut himself off and drew in a deep breath. "I'll be back in an hour."

Before I could respond, he was already walking to the driver's side of the car.

I couldn't let him leave like this. While I'd been going through my own emotional crisis, apparently, he'd been going through one too. Like recognized like, and I realized he was lashing out to keep his emotions locked up. Still, me being nice to him was the last thing he wanted right now.

So I did the only thing I knew how to do, because habits die hard. I lashed out at him too. "Aren't you afraid I'll find out something from my aunt and keep it from you?"

He turned to look at me, his jaw clenched so tight it would be a wonder if he didn't crack a molar. Then he just shook his head, got in the car, and drove away.

What the hell just happened?

And why did it feel like I'd just lost my best friend?

I stood there, staring at the empty street, my chest tight with more than just anxiety. My body still buzzed with leftover adrenaline and something else I didn't want to name. Something that pulsed low in my belly, equal parts heat and regret.

The distance between us felt like a thread ready to snap, stretched taut with all the things we hadn't said.

Now he was gone, the thread snipped, making me feel untethered.

## Chapter 20

I was about to go back inside when my phone rang. I pulled it out of my jeans pocket and glanced at the screen, hoping that Malcolm had already calmed down and was calling me. That theory was shot to hell when I saw the number on the screen.

Mason Deveraux.

He'd already called me three times today, so it was apparent he was going to keep calling until I answered. His persistence was ringing alarm bells in my head. Deveraux had to be a busy man. Why was he putting so much energy into contacting me?

I wasn't ready to go inside and come up with some lame explanation for running out of the house and coming back without Malcolm, so I decided to answer.

"Harper Adams," I said as I answered gruffly, just like I had when I was a cop. I needed to be the professional PI who had called him last week.

"You're a hard woman to get ahold of, Ms. Adams," Deveraux said in a genteel drawl. I suspected his opening and closing statements in court charmed the juries.

"Yeah," I said with a hint of attitude. "My apologies. I just buried my mother yesterday, so I've been a little busy."

He paused and I was sure he was going to apologize, but he surprised me by saying, "I read about her accident online. I'm sorry for your loss."

I doubted my mother's accident had made it past local news, which meant Mason Deveraux had probably researched me. Not that I was surprised. His assistant had warned me it might be over a week before I heard from him, but he'd returned my call right away, and on his personal cell at that. I hadn't called him back, even after I'd stressed how important it was I talked to him, so he must have wondered why. But if he'd researched me, then he knew about the shooting last October—that is, if he hadn't already known. His department would have been paying attention to Pulaski County's investigation and the indictment in the shooting.

Shit. I really should have thought through that initial call before placing it.

I should have been grateful he'd called me back, but I felt slimy, like I was laying a trap for Malcolm. I needed to end this call as quickly as possible without causing any more problems.

"Thank you for your condolences, Mr. Deveraux. And thank you for being so persistent in returning my call from last week, but thankfully, the case I was working on got wrapped up soon after I tried to contact you. Sorry to have bothered you for nothing."

"Hold on," he said, sensing I was about to hang up on him. "You said you were investigating the disappearance of a businessman named Hugo Burton?"

Any other prosecutor would have probably been thankful for the reprieve, but then again, most of them wouldn't have been so persistent trying to reach me. This was a very bad sign. Obviously he had a personal connection to the case I'd called about—hell, I'd pointed out the connection myself when I'd mentioned Rose Gardner had been his girlfriend at the time—

so it wasn't his persistence that made me wary, it was an undercurrent I couldn't quite name. I needed to give him enough information to satisfy him, then get off the call as quickly as possible. "That's correct. Mr. Burton's body was found after a man came forward offering to take the police to his grave. He said a man named Pinky confessed that he and their boss, Skip Martin, a local car dealership owner, killed Mr. Burton."

"Have Skip Martin and Pinky been arrested?"

I cringed. While the Lone County's Sheriff Department had bought the story, I suspected Mason Deveraux was going to poke it full of so many holes you could see daylight through it. "No, Martin and Pinky are dead."

"That's convenient," he said dryly.

I ignored his comment. "The sheriff's working theory is that I made Martin nervous by asking so many questions about Burton. In fact, I'd questioned the man twice. Maybe it made Martin's employee nervous. There was some kind of confrontation, and Pinky killed his boss, then himself."

"And this all came from… what did you say the man's name was?"

"I didn't, and you *do* know that I'm not a detective with the sheriff's department, right? My job was to find Hugo Burton, one way or the other, and I did."

"I'm guessing a sharp detective like yourself would have dotted all the Is and crossed all the Ts." He paused. "You have a reputation of being very, very good. Very thorough."

"Past tense," I said, trying to keep the bitterness out of my voice. I knew I'd been good. He wasn't going to butter me up by telling me so. "I'm no longer with the Little Rock police or any other law enforcement agency, Mr. Deveraux. I'm a private detective, available for hire. I was hired to find Hugo. My client was happy. And…" I added, hoping my next statement would end this conversation. "My mother's car was pulled out of a river around the same time Hugo Burton's body was found. My job was done, and I moved on to mourning my mother."

"Yes, of course," he said sympathetically. "I'm very close to my own mother. I would be devastated if something like that happened to her, but it sounds like you and I are a lot alike, Detective Adams. We're both workaholics. So if my mother passed, I'd probably jump into work and bury my feelings."

"I'm sure I'll find another case," I said, my voice hard, "but the sheriff's department is taking over Hugo Burton's murder, and I doubt they'd appreciate my interference, even if I felt inclined to give it."

"Sorry for all my questions," he said good-naturedly. "I'm just trying to figure out if Simmons came into play in the case or not."

"I never found any evidence to suggest he had any ties to Skip Martin."

"When you called, you said you believed there might be a connection," he said, "Even if Simmons had nothing to do with Mr. Burton's murder, he still could have investments with Hugo Burton."

"Whether Simmons invested or not is a moot point for me now that my investigation was closed."

He paused a second before adding, "I've been looking into Burton's missing person case file."

Of course he was. I was a fucking idiot.

"Seeing how I never saw the actual sheriff's file," I said, "I have no idea what's in it. The case was still considered open, so Detective Jones, one of the original detectives, only shared things he thought might be useful to my investigation."

"You had his cooperation?"

"I did. I told him if I could find Mr. Burton it was a win for both of us."

"I see." He paused. "And what about James Malcolm?"

He'd sounded congenial up to this point, but Malcolm's

name sounded a little bitter on his tongue. Definitely bad feelings there. Did Deveraux still blame Malcolm for involving his girlfriend in taking down Simmons? "What about him?"

"When you called, you said J.R. Simmons might be involved and then you mentioned James Malcolm. Did you think Malcolm was tied to Burton's disappearance-turned-murder?"

I needed to handle this with kid gloves. "No. I was merely turning over rocks, trying to see what crawled out."

"So why mention him at all?"

"When I heard Simmons's name mentioned, I put his name into Google, and Malcolm turned up in the search. Malcolm was involved with Simmons's arrest for the kidnapping of a Fenton County woman, and it seemed a coincidence that he was living here now. But again, I found no evidence that either man had anything to do with Burton's disappearance."

"You mentioned the Fenton County woman by name when you called, Detective," Deveraux said, his voice like honey, but I heard the edge. "Why not say it now?"

I didn't know much about Mason Deveraux, but I suspected he was a man I didn't want as an enemy. "Obviously, I jumped the gun in calling you. Afterward, I learned she was your ex-girlfriend. I didn't want to bring up any bad blood."

"No bad blood on my end," he said smoothly. "And from what I know about you, you're not one to jump the gun."

I really, really hated that he found me so predictable. I'd really fucked up by calling him. How much had I had to drink before dialing his number? But at the time, I'd jumped in deep with Malcolm, who was keeping more secrets than a priest in a confessional, and I'd needed to know if I could trust him.

"From what I've learned about you," he continued, "you wouldn't have called me if something hadn't convinced you Simmons's involvement was a strong possibility."

I released a short laugh. "Shows what you know. I never hesitated to call my ADA contact at the Pulaski County prosecutor's office if I was working a case and wanted information."

"But you wouldn't have called the Attorney General's office."

"Mr. Deveraux," I said, not trying to hide my impatience. "You were the ADA on Simmons's murder charges. You had more information than anyone. I'm terribly sorry I bothered you, and in hindsight, I obviously should have waited until I had something more concrete."

"And you found absolutely no evidence tying Simmons to Lone County?"

I sure as hell wasn't about to tell him my own father had worked for Simmons.

It wasn't lost on me, that I would have told him everything six months ago. Sure, I would have felt guilty turning on my father, but I would have done it because it would have been the "right thing to do." I'd also trusted the people above me to have my back. Look how that had turned out. Deveraux would be looking out for his best interest, just like I'd started looking out for mine. And I didn't see any scenario in which it served me to tell him anything about Simmons's involvement in Lone County.

"Sorry to disappoint you, Mr. Deveraux, but my call was nothing more than a fishing expedition, hoping to get information that would point me down another avenue to investigate."

"And you're *not* looking into James Malcolm?"

"Why would I be looking into him?" I asked innocently. "I only mentioned him because of Simmons."

"So why mention Rose Gardner?"

What was up with Rose Gardner?

It was obvious I found her connection to the whole thing strange, as anyone would. Maybe their breakup had been amicable and he still felt protective of her, but Malcolm had said that working with him had cost Rose her relationship with Deveraux. Had Deveraux been jealous? I'd seen a few photos of Rose, and she'd looked more wholesome than a corn-fed virgin at Bible camp. There was no way Malcolm would get involved with someone like her, and even less of a chance that she'd go for him. The break-up was likely due to the fact she'd worked with Malcolm behind Deveraux's back. It had probably cast a shadow over his integrity and left a grudge.

"Yeah," I said, running a hand over my head as I swung my gaze toward the house. No one was staring out the window watching me, which meant my grandparents had probably found a more secure stake-out spot. We were family, after all. I suspected curiosity was embedded in our DNA. "Her name was in the internet search. Nothing more, nothing less."

"I see."

I was quickly learning that his *I see* meant a hell of a lot more than it sounded.

My head was throbbing, and my hands were beginning to shake again. I wasn't thinking clearly when I said, "It seems odd to me that you keep mentioning Rose Gardner's name when I only mentioned her as the tie between Malcolm and Simmons. Was there more to her involvement than that?" I regretted it the moment the words left my mouth, but there was no reeling them back in.

He was quiet for several seconds, and my heart began to race. I really didn't want to make an enemy of this man, and I suspected I'd just driven the wrong way down a one-way street straight onto his shit list.

"Of course not," he said with a laugh. "Rose was merely in the wrong place at the wrong time."

"So her kidnapping didn't have anything to do with you?"

"No."

He was lying. Of course he was probably doing it to protect her. According to Malcolm, she'd joined forces with him to help Deveraux. Sure, they'd broken up, but Deveraux probably felt like he owed it to her after she'd saved his life. Only I wasn't sure it was that simple. I didn't have anything to base my theory on but a hunch, but my hunches had always served me well in the past.

The question was what did this mean? Did this change anything regarding Malcolm?

"Thank you for indulging my repetitive questions, Detective," he said, his congenial tone back. "If there's anything I can ever do for you—anything at all—don't hesitate to get in contact." Then he ended the call, and I couldn't help wondering if I'd just made a friend or a powerful enemy.

## Chapter 21

I'd been outside far longer than I'd planned, and I still had to go in and not only explain why I'd run off outside, but why Malcolm had left.

Malcolm.

Shit. I had to tell him about my call with Deveraux—to warn him in case Deveraux decided to go after him. The AD's interest had seemed more than just general curiosity. If he blamed Malcolm for his breakup with Rose Gardner, maybe he was looking for something to put him away. And I'd practically invited him to our backyard.

Fuck.

I took several deep breaths, then marched for the door, wishing I could pour a glass of my grandfather's whiskey and down it, but I wasn't giving into my ghosts.

When I walked into the living room, my grandparents were where I'd left them, but based on the guilty looks on their faces, they'd spied on us.

"I'm sorry I walked out so abruptly," I said, forcing a smile. "I just needed some air."

My grandmother frowned. "There's no need to apologize. I was worried this all might be too much for you. But James thought looking at the photos might help you work through some of your grief over your mother's passin'."

My jaw dropped. "He said that?"

"Well, yes," she said in confusion, glancing at my grandfather then back to me. "He said it might help for you to see her as a kid. He said something about people being complicated."

Pot meet kettle. James Malcolm was one of the most complicated men I'd ever met. Had he told her that as a cover, or had he really meant it?

But I already knew the answer—I just didn't understand it.

My eyes burned, but I swallowed the lump in my throat. Now wasn't the time to lose it. Not again.

"Where'd he go?" my grandfather asked.

"He thought it might be better to eat here at your house, but he didn't want you to cook, so he's picking up dinner for us."

My grandmother clutched her hands to her chest over her heart. "Isn't he the sweetest?"

I nearly laughed. I was pretty sure very few people—if any —had ever called James Malcolm the sweetest.

"What's he gettin'?" my grandfather asked.

"I don't know," I said. "But I'm sure it will be delicious."

"That's a thoughtful young man you have there," Grandpa said. "You're lucky to have him."

He was right on both counts. Malcolm had been a good friend, and I'd repaid him by verbally attacking him and then calling the man who probably wanted to put him back behind bars.

With friends like me, who needed enemies?

I felt like I was going to be sick.

What exactly had happened outside? Why had he been so … kind? Understanding? He'd let down his guard, dropped his usual armor, but I couldn't figure out why. Was it my grandparent's influence? His wish that he'd had grandparents like mine?

To my horror, I realized I'd caught a glimpse of *James*—not Malcolm—the real him, and I'd thrown it in his face with insults and accusations.

I felt like I was going to be sick.

"You don't look like you're feeling well," my grandmother said, starting to get to her feet.

I patted my hand toward her. "I'm fine. Just tired. It's been a long week." I gestured to the hall. "Is it okay if I use your bathroom?"

"Of course," she said, her forehead pinched with concern. "Do you remember where it is?"

My grandfather laughed. "Even if she doesn't, it's not like we live in a mansion. It's easy enough to find."

I shot him a smile, then headed down the hall to the bathroom, which was exactly where I remembered it. I shut the door behind me and leaned my back against it, squeezing my eyes shut.

As impossible as it seemed, I'd hurt Malcolm. His persona was made of steel. He came off as someone who didn't *have* feelings, but in reality, he was a human being who had *massive* feelings. I'd never bought his assertion that he was good to his employees because happy employees were better workers. He felt responsible for them, so he wanted them to be cared for and protected.

I was taking too long, so I did my business, then moved to the sink to wash my hands. I glanced at my reflection, mulling over our conversation and Malcolm's reaction. The more I thought about it, the more unsettled I became.

Why did I care so much about what he thought? It was easy to say we were just friends, but the part of me that was forcing me to face the truth about my addiction refused to lie about how I felt about him. I'd been admiring his good looks from a safe distance, but I had to admit I was drawn to him. The more he revealed himself, the deeper my attraction became.

I wanted more than friendship with him, and for the first time, my reasons for keeping my distance didn't seem as insurmountable as when we'd first met.

But I wasn't the only person in this non-existent relationship.

*Is it possible Malcolm is interested in something more than friendship?*

I turned off the water and tried to study my face objectively. I had big brown eyes and long lashes—which were undoubtedly my best features. The rest of me was passible. Not beautiful but not hideous. Average. I'd never attracted the attention of men the way my friends in college had. Men had become interested in me after they got to know me, not because they glimpsed me across the room and thought I was gorgeous. Even then, I was fairly sure they were drawn in because I seemed unavailable—a mystery to unlock. Only they never could, because I would never let them get close enough to see beneath the surface. Still, I'd never had a problem with my looks, or lack thereof, but now I felt a tinge of… what? Jealousy?

It was ridiculous to even think of something with Malcolm. He'd made it clear he didn't want to sleep with me, and frankly, why would he? He was a *very* attractive man and could have just about any woman he wanted—as long as she was willing to overlook his past. But it wasn't like he was looking for a long-term relationship. Besides, should he ever decide he wanted to settle down, I had no doubt there were plenty beautiful women he could choose from.

Besides, even if he got past my average features, it wasn't like he would be drawn in by my sparkling personality. I'd been nothing but confrontational and rude. I'd been a downright bitch. Who would want a woman like that?

James Malcolm probably found me vile. And I'd given him plenty of reason to feel that way. And if he wasn't done with me after what happened outside, he definitely would be after I told him about Deveraux. He wouldn't want to be my lover, my friend, my anything.

The thought of losing him filled me with a profound sadness that made my lungs thick and difficult to breath. But the thought of putting him in legal danger scared the shit out of me even more. I'd find a way to protect him. I didn't know how, but I prayed it would come to me. And if by the grace of God he didn't turn his back on me…

I shook myself out of my reverie. What the hell was I doing in my grandparents' bathroom, pining for James Malcolm?

I had a shitload of problems, and wanting to sleep with him couldn't be one of them.

I spent the next half hour talking to my grandparents about their lives—their jobs, their friends, their hobbies. I was starting to wonder if Malcolm was coming back, when the front door creaked opened. I expected to see his large frame filling the entryway to the living room, but instead a small, slightly round woman entered the room. The sprinkles of gray in her light brown hair and the wrinkles around her eyes and lining her forehead suggested she was in her fifties or her early sixties. She stopped in her tracks as her gaze landed on me. Her eyes went wide, and her face paled as if she'd seen a ghost. Lifting her knuckles to her bottom lip, she turned to my grandmother. "Is this real?"

"She's real," Grandma said, starting to cry again.

I hadn't seen my aunt in years, but I recognized her instantly. She looked older but was still mostly the same. I, on the other hand, had been a preteen the last time she'd seen me. Had she Googled me to know what I looked like?

I got to my feet, feeling uncomfortable and wishing Malcolm were here to help ease me through this. It only made me appreciate how he'd helped me when I met my grandparents. And I felt even more ashamed for lashing out.

I extended a hand. "Hi, I'm—"

I didn't get my name out before she rushed over and wrapped her arms around me, pulling me into a bear hug.

"Harper. I'd know you anywhere, girl. I can't believe you're here."

"I can't believe I'm here either," I said.

She released me and placed her hands on my cheeks. "I'm so sorry to hear about your mother.'

"Thank you. I'm sorry for your loss too."

She made a face. "I grieved losing your mother years ago." She shot a glance at my grandfather, then back to me. "Dad said two someones were here." She looked around. "Where is he?"

"Who said the other someone was a he?" Grandpa asked with a chuckle.

"*Please*," Hannah said. "Who else would she bring?"

"My father's not here," I said, in case she thought he was the mysterious he.

She waved a hand in disgust. "He's the *last* person I would expect to show up."

My grandparents had told me they didn't have any issues with my father, so I was surprised by her response. They might not have bad blood with Paul Adams, but it was obvious she did.

Hannah continued, "And if you brought someone, I would think they'd be close to you." Her brow lifted mischievously. "Like a boyfriend or fiancé?"

"He's picking up dinner," my grandmother said.

"And they're just friends," my grandfather added.

Hannah frowned. "Dad said we were going out to eat."

"James thought we might be more comfortable eating here," I said, making sure to use his first name since that was how he'd introduced himself. "He figured we'd have more privacy this way."

"And also," Malcolm said, walking up behind my aunt through the still open front door, "so we don't feel pressured to leave if we get into a lengthy conversation." He was carrying two large brown paper bags by the handles. "I hope the change of plans is okay."

Relief swamped my head, making me lightheaded. I never seriously thought he'd desert me, but seeing him loosened the tightness around my heart. He didn't appear angry, but he hadn't looked at me yet either.

Hannah spun around and gasped. "You picked up food from Viva Italiana? You can change plans *anytime* if you're feeding me food from there." She gasped again, then cocked her head, turning serious. "Please tell me you got the ravioli."

He raised a brow, the left corner of his lip lifting, giving him a mischievous look. "I got the ravioli."

Her face lit up like she'd woken up to a house full of presents on Christmas morning. "I'll get the plates!" She sprinted toward the kitchen, then stopped and turned around. "I'm Hannah by the way. Harper's aunt."

He nodded in acknowledgment. "James. Harper's friend."

Hannah waggled her eyebrows. "*Friend,* huh?"

"So they insist," my grandmother said, but she wore a big smile that said she didn't believe it for a minute.

I rolled my eyes and then tried to make eye contact with Malcolm, but he'd already headed to the dining room.

I tried to swallow my disappointment. He was putting on a show for my family, but I was guessing he was still pissed at me. And if he wasn't, the peace wouldn't last after I told him about Deveraux.

He pulled a container out of the bag and started to put it on the table, then stopped, asking my grandmother if he needed to put something underneath it to protect the table.

"The table's covered in scorch marks from decades of too

many hot pans, so you just set everything down," she said with a laugh. "The damage has already been done."

After he set the rectangular aluminum pan with a shiny silver lid on the table, he reached into the bag and brought out several more, then started on the next bag. He'd gotten enough food to feed at least ten people.

When my grandmother commented on it, he said he hadn't known what everyone liked so he was covering his bases. But I suspected he wanted leftovers for my grandparents. The state of their house made it clear they weren't rolling in money. A month ago, this would have surprised me about him, but not now. He'd noticed they were in need and done what he could to help. Just like he'd helped his brother, Jed, Misti, and probably countless other people.

The irony wasn't lost on me. My parents—social pillars in their community, who certainly had the means to help—had cut off their own family. Yet here was James Malcolm, criminal and social pariah, stepping in to take care of people who meant nothing to him.

Hannah brought out plates and silverware, and Malcolm served everyone, giving them a little of just about everything. When I handed him my plate, I held my breath, hoping to catch his gaze. He focused on the plate as he filled it, but when he handed it back, his eyes finally latched onto mine for a second. Instead of anger or contempt, I saw concern and a hint of warmth.

I sucked in a breath as I took the food. He was a man who was capable of holding grudges. Why wasn't he holding one against me now?

After he filled his own plate, my grandfather said grace. I snuck another glance at Malcolm, who was seated next to me. His head was bowed, his hands folded together at the edge of the table. Had he been raised going to church? The more I learned about him, the more questions I had.

As soon as my grandfather said, "Amen," Hannah began

to pepper me with questions about my life. Thankfully, she skipped over my childhood, instead focusing on my college years and why I'd decided to join the police department. I glossed over my answer, saying I'd felt drawn to serve my community. She asked questions about my career as a beat cop, then a detective, but stopped short of asking anything about the shooting.

Any time there was a lull in the conversation, she came up with another question, but she was so effervescent it never occurred to me to not answer. I began to realize she reminded me of someone I missed terribly.

"You're a lot like Andi," I blurted out before I could stop myself.

Hannah's mouth dropped open and then quickly closed. My sister was one of two elephants in the room, and up until this point, she hadn't been mentioned or even hinted at since Hannah had arrived.

"That is the highest compliment you could pay me," she said, tears filling her eyes. "Your sister was a blessing, Harper. The world lost a beautiful soul when she died."

"Agreed," I said, the familiar pang of regret and sorrow flooding my veins. "My mom felt the same way." That was one of the few things we'd agreed upon.

Hannah looked down at her plate and stabbed a piece of penne pasta, likely shocked into silence. I'd brought up both unspoken taboo subjects in practically the same sentence.

And as much as I hated to change the conversation, I realized I'd accidentally shifted it where we needed it to go. "Aunt Hannah," I said softly. "Tell me about growing up with my mother."

She cast a cautious glance to my grandmother, who nodded. Hannah took a deep breath and then started spilling stories of their childhood. I'd already heard some of the stories from my grandmother, but some were new, and I realized that their relationship reminded me of my own connection with my sister.

"It sounds like you were close when you were younger," I said. "When did you two drift apart?"

She hesitated for a moment, then stuffed a forkful of salad into her mouth, probably to buy herself more time. But I waited her out, and once she swallowed, she reluctantly said, "Junior high. She decided it wasn't cool to hang out with her little sister anymore. Part of it was understandable." She shrugged. "There's a big difference in the maturity of a twelve-year-old versus a ten-year-old. But it was ultimately her new friends who drove us apart. They thought I was uncool, so she did too."

"I'm so sorry," I said. "She shouldn't have done that to you." I could only imagine how I would have felt if Andi had turned on me.

Hannah shrugged. "It's the way of the world. Of course, some siblings grow out of it, but Sarah Jane just seemed to get worse. Especially when we were older. We still fought like cats and dogs. We always seemed to get over it. Until our last fight."

"What did you fight about?"

"Stupid shit." She sighed. "I admit, in hindsight, I kind of deserved it. We were there for Andi's ninth birthday party, and your mother didn't do anything by halves, so it was no surprise the party looked like something on a TV show. I told her that the whole thing was a desperate attempt to impress people." She made a face. "Well, *that* pissed her off, and she said I didn't understand her life. And of course, I didn't help matters when I told her in a not-so-quiet voice that I'd rather take a bullet to the head then give my nine-year-old a birthday party with a petting zoo."

I cringed. My mother wouldn't have reacted well to that in private, let alone in front of her friends. Somehow I'd missed it. "And you never spoke again?"

"Oh no, we spoke a few times after that, although it was terribly strained. I apologized. I admit, I saw things a little differently when I got married a few years later and had kids of my own."

"I have cousins?" I blurted out. The Aunt Hannah I remembered hadn't been married, but she'd been in her thirties. She'd still had plenty of time to get married and have kids.

She grinned. "Yep. Two of 'em. Although they're a whole lot younger than you. Amelia's twenty and Becca is sixteen."

"I'd like to meet them sometime," I said.

Her grin softened into a warm smile. "They'd like that too. They know about you"—she held up a hand—"none of the bad stuff, just that they have a cousin who used to be a police detective and now lives in Jackson Creek. When they ask why they can't see you, I tell them you're really busy."

"You could have made me look like a bad person," I said, my voice tight. "My mother told you all that I didn't want anything to do with you."

She shrugged. "You were a kid when it all went down. I'm sure she stuffed your head with her side of everything."

I shook my head. "She didn't tell me anything, really, other than you and your parents didn't want to see me."

She gasped, clearly caught off guard, but then she shook her head, sorrow filling her eyes. "That damn Sarah Jane. Of course she did."

I was sure this had to come as a shock, but then again, it sounded like my aunt knew my mother was manipulative. Just maybe not to this extent.

"Not only that," my grandmother said in righteous anger, "Sarah Jane told her we didn't want anything to do with her because we blamed her father for Andi's death."

Hannah didn't look as outraged as I'd expected.

Did she think my father had something to do with Andi's kidnapping, or did she just hold a tight grudge? I wanted to know but didn't want to offend her. So I stuck with a response that was not only true, but hopefully reconciliatory.

"I'm sorry."

"Honey," she said, her back stiffening. "You have *nothin'* to say you're sorry for. This is all your mother's doin'."

She had a point, but I was sorry nonetheless.

"You said you only spoke with her a few times after the birthday party," I said. "Did she cut you off when she cut off Grandma and Grandpa or before?"

She released a bitter laugh. "Before. I saw her here at Mom and Dad's a few times after the party, but soon she stopped coming back at all. Mom and Dad went down there, but I got married, and well, I knew I wasn't wanted, so I just didn't go."

I nodded. I couldn't say I blamed her.

"Plus, she showed no interest in my kids, so that was definitely the end of that. I felt sorry for her after everything that happened to Andi, but after an animal repeatedly bites you, you learn to leave it alone."

I couldn't blame her for that either.

She made a face and picked up a piece of bread off her plate, then smushed it together as though considering something. After she took a deep breath, she said in a rush, "Which is why I was so surprised when she called me a few weeks ago."

My heart skipped a beat. "She called you?"

"She did *what?*" my grandmother screeched.

"Do you remember exactly what day?" Malcolm asked, his body tense.

Hannah paused and seemed to consider it. "Two weeks ago. It was a Wednesday night."

The night the two men broke in and confronted my mother.

My grandmother was still upset. "Why didn't you tell me?"

Hannah ignored my grandmother's questions and kept her focus on me. "Her call was totally out of the blue, like late on a weeknight. Very unusual for her."

"When you say late," I said. "How late?"

"Dang near close to midnight," Hannah said. "Your uncle Buster was dead to the world, but I was bakin' cookies for my Becca's school fundraiser, which, of course, she didn't tell me about until about nine o'clock that night." She leaned her head toward me and lowered her voice. "I should have made her stay up and bake 'em herself, but she had a chemistry test the next day, and she's basically bombing chemistry." She stopped, realizing she was getting off topic. "Anyway, it startled me when the home phone rang. I mean, who uses landlines anymore? But Buster *insists* we keep it. So I answered, ready to give the person a piece of my mind for nearly wakin' up my husband, who gets cranky if he doesn't get a quality eight hours of sleep, when I heard her voice on the line, saying, 'Hannah, I'm sorry to be callin' so late. Please don't hang up.'"

"She didn't identify herself?" I asked.

She chuckled. "Listen to you, sounding like a cop."

"Hannah," my grandfather gently admonished.

"Oh, sorry," she said with a sheepish look. "I tend to get off track like that. In any case, no, she did *not* identify herself." She snickered. "But I'd know her voice anywhere. If she'd called in the daytime when I had more wits about me, I might have hung up, but I admit I was curious."

"What did she say?" I asked.

"She said she was going to send me something in the mail and asked me to please hang onto to it. She said she knew she had no right to ask, but the thing she was sending was for you."

"For *me*?"

She nodded, then got up from the table and walked into the living room. A few seconds later, she came back in with her purse and sat down again. She reached inside and pulled out a cream-colored envelope, which she handed to me. "I've been carryin' it around in my purse, scared I was gonna lose it."

The first thing I noticed was it was heavier than a standard letter. It was addressed to my aunt, and my mother's name and address were handwritten in the upper left corner. I went to lift the envelope flap but realized it was still sealed. "You didn't open it?"

Her face stretched with indignation. "It may have my name on it, but it wasn't mine to open. Your mother made it clear it was yours."

I picked up my unused butter knife and slid the top open, then pulled out a cream stationary card with gold foil initials —SJA. While the card was thick, it didn't account for the weight of the envelope. I opened the card and found a small silver key attached to the inside with clear tape. *Box 172* was handwritten underneath it.

Perplexed, I turned the card so Malcolm could read it.

"Safe deposit box?" he murmured.

"That's what I'm thinking. It's the right shape and the number fits."

Malcolm turned to my aunt. "Did she say why she was sending this?"

"No. I asked her why she couldn't just give it to you herself, but she claimed she had her reasons. She said not to give it to you unless you came to see me."

I shot Malcolm a look of confusion. How could she have known I'd come see her sister?

"I confess," she said, "when I saw that she'd died, I nearly came to the funeral, but I wasn't sure your father would want me there. The last time he and I spoke, we didn't end on good terms." She grimaced. "In fact, it got pretty heated."

"You and *my father* argued?" I asked in surprise. I could understand why she'd argue with my mother, but my father made it his business to be agreeable. I could count on one hand the number of people I'd heard him raise his voice to.

She hesitated, glancing at my grandmother before turning back to me. "Your mother's the only person I told about this, and she definitely didn't appreciate what I had to say." She grimaced again. "The saying *don't shoot the messenger* obviously came from truth."

She told my mother something bad about my father? Had she discovered my father was up to something shady?

After she drew in a deep breath, she shook out her hands, then set them on the table. "After your mother and I had our argument at Andi's party, I knew I needed to cool down, so I headed to your father's office to hide until everyone left." She shrugged with a resigned look. "I mean, let's be honest. I didn't fit in with your mother's friends. I was only there because I loved you girls, and I came with Mom and Dad. I figured the best thing I could do was to get out of her hair."

"My father was mad you were in his office?" That seemed strange given his office had never been off-limits.

"Not exactly." Her cheeks flushed. "Like I said, I'd planned to hide out, so I brought a bottle of wine with me, and I drank quite a bit of it. I sat in the chair in the corner and fell asleep." She squeezed her eyes shut for a second. "When I woke up, I heard sounds that could have come from a porno movie." She made a face at my grandparents. "Sorry."

My grandmother looked too mesmerized by the story to be offended that her daughter had obviously watched porn. "Don't stop there," she said. "What happened?"

"It had gotten dark outside, so the room was really dark. When I opened my eyes, I could see two people hovering over the desk. It took me all of two seconds to realize your dad was screwing Sarah Jane from behind on the desk. Only..." Her cheeks pinkened. "It wasn't Sarah Jane."

"My father was having an affair," I said, my heart sinking.

If he had a history of affairs, then he very well could have been having one with the woman who showed up at my mother's door.

She nodded with an apologetic look. "I wasn't sure what to do. They obviously didn't know I was there, and I hated to interrupt them. Anyway, by the time I had sorted out how to let them know I was there, they'd already finished—she wasn't very quiet, by the way. I almost think she wanted your mother to find them, but your father slapped his hand over her mouth to quiet her, not that it slowed them down any."

"Hannah Nicole," my grandmother admonished.

"What?" Her eyes widened with feigned innocence. "It's all true."

"Did they ever see you?" Malcolm asked.

She turned to him. "When they finished, they lingered for a few seconds before Paul slapped her ass—"

"Hannah!" my grandmother cried out. "We don't need all the details!"

"And then pulled her skirt down. They kissed and they agreed they needed to go out separately. So she left first and your father cleaned himself off with some tissues. It was while he had his dick hanging out of his pants—"

"Hannah!"

She ignored her mother. "—I said, 'Not bad, although the conclusion seemed a little rushed. Four out of five.' He spun around, shoving himself back into his pants, and accused me of being a voyeur. I told him I was there first, and it wasn't my fault they were so horny they hadn't noticed the drunk woman sleeping in the corner."

I expected my grandmother to get onto her case again, but she just hung her head.

"I suspect he was pretty mad," Malcolm said.

"Furious, but he also knew I had him. He wanted to know whether I was gonna tell Sarah Jane, and I asked him how long it had been goin' on. He told me it was none of my business, and I got up, a bit wobbly, and asked if he knew where his wife was. Well, he sure surprised me with what he did next." She paused. "He pushed me back down in the chair. Hard. Just put a hand on my chest and shoved me down. Then he leaned over my face, veins popping on his forehead, and told me that if I said anything to her, he'd make sure I regretted it."

I stared at her in shock. Was she telling the truth? Or an exaggerated version of the truth? I'd never seen my father violent like that.

"Did you tell her?" I asked.

"Not at first, but it wasn't because I was scared of your father. Not yet." She drew a breath. "When he threatened me, I asked him what he thought he could possibly do to me, and he said that I had no idea what he as capable of. I laughed in his face and told him that if he ever touched me again, I'd have him arrested for assault. He laughed too and said he had the cops in his pocket. It ended in a standoff, and I stormed out."

"You said you were scared of him later," Malcolm said. "What happened?"

She gave him a tight smile. "We were there for that whole weekend, and I kept a close eye on him after I caught him in the act. I was pretty pissed that he'd shoved me like that, not to mention he was cheating on my sister. Sure, I was pissed at her too, but I was tryin' to look out for her. We had dinner together later that night, and right after we finished, I saw him sneak off into the backyard with his phone. I followed him. I thought maybe he was gonna call his lover, and I was hopin' to catch her name. But he wasn't talkin' to his girl-friend. He was talkin' to someone named Richard, and he mentioned a guy named Ambrose, saying Ambrose was getting out of control. He told Richard he needed to rein him in. I thought that sounded kind of dangerous. I never would have thought that Paul was capable of hurting someone or paying someone else to do it, but after the way he'd shoved me…"

She took a breath and shook her head, then gave me a pleading look before continuing. "I was worried about Sarah Jane and you girls. So I got a subscription to the Lone County paper and started scouring the news, looking for anything to do with a Richard or an Ambrose. I knew it was a long shot, and I hoped I didn't see anything, but then…" She took a breath. "About a month later, there was a story about a man named Dale Ambrose driving his car off a bridge into the Red River. They ruled it an accident, but I knew in my gut that your father and that Richard guy had"—her eyes suddenly grew large with realization—"drove his car into the river," she finished, barely above a whisper.

Two things became apparent. The first, Aunt Hannah had figured out my mother's accident had been anything but, and second, my father had done this before.

It was looking like my father really had killed my mother. Now I needed to prove it.

# Chapter 22

Chaos erupted as my grandparents started shouting that my mother had been murdered, then demanding why Hannah had never told them.

"At least you could have warned Sarah Jane!" Grandma said, her voice shaking. "You could have saved her!"

"I did," Hannah said quietly. "I *did* warn her."

My grandmother's face fell and she slumped back in her seat.

"How soon after you saw the article did you tell her?" Malcolm asked, his voice tight.

"That very day," she said, tears filling her eyes as she glanced at me. "I told her everything—about your father screwin' that woman in his office, how Paul shoved and threatened me, hearin' his conversation outside, and then what I saw in the paper. She was quiet through the whole thing, and when I finished, she said, 'Are you done?' I expected her to be pissed, if not at Paul, then at me for keeping it to myself for so long. But she wasn't pissed. Her voice was quiet and calm, like she was a Stepford Wife or something."

That sounded like my mother. I'd heard her use that tone on my father and me multiple times.

"Well," Hannah continued, "When she asked if I was done, I said, no, I *wasn't* done. I told her to take the girls and get away from him. I even offered to help her. That's when she accused me of making up lies and exaggerating, and I told her that in this case, it was one or the other—either I was lying about the whole thing or part of it was true and I was exaggerating the truth. Which one did she pick?"

"I'm sure she didn't take that well," I said under my breath.

She tilted her head, still full of attitude from her story-telling. "You're right on the money. It was no surprise when she said she picked her husband, then she hung up on me. After that, the only time we saw each other was when she came to see Mom and Dad, and she barely spoke to me. But then Andi disappeared…"

Her face twisted into an apologetic look, like she knew bringing up my sister's kidnapping would hurt me. "It's okay," I said, my voice barely above a whisper. "Go on."

"After your sister…" Aunt Hannah's voice faltered, the sharp edge of her anger dulling. "I was worried sick about Andi. About your mother. About *you*. I didn't know how she'd take it, but I had to try. I called her, and when she answered the phone, I asked her if Paul had something to do with it."

I blinked. "You asked if she thought my father had something to do with Andi's kidnapping?"

She gave a tight nod. "I braced myself for her to tear into me—call me delusional, vindictive. But she didn't. I'll never forget her answer. Or how she said it."

The room tilted, and I gripped the table, my knuckles growing white as her words hit me like a physical blow. A cold weight dropped into my stomach, spreading through my chest like ice water. "What did she say?"

Aunt Hannah's eyes met mine, her jaw tightening. "She said, 'I don't know.'"

I felt like the floor had vanished beneath me. My chest

constricted, each breath coming shallow and fast. I opened my mouth, but nothing came out—the air seemed too thin, like I was drowning. I didn't even realize Malcolm had reached over until his fingers closed around mine, firm and steady.

Never—never in my life—had I considered that my father could have hurt his own daughter. Even if he'd gotten mixed up with bad people. He'd loved us. He'd *adored* us. I could still see him squatting in front of Andi when she was six years old and had just found a dead bird in the backyard. His voice had been so soft, so patient, as he gently wiped her tears with his thumb and told her that death was a part of life, but it was okay to be sad. His hands had looked so large and safe around her small ones as he'd helped her choose the perfect spot for the burial. Those same hands had pushed my aunt in anger. The thought made my stomach lurch.

It was hard to believe he would have caused her harm, even unintentionally. But, hadn't he hurt me? Not physically. But after Andi's murder, he had withdrawn. Left me alone in a house full of grief and silence. Ignored me like I was too painful to look at.

It wasn't the same thing. Not even close. Or was it? Doubt slipped into me like a draft under a locked door.

"She really thought he might have made her disappear?" My voice cracked on the last word.

Aunt Hannah winced. "I needed her to tell me I was wrong. That I was being paranoid. But she didn't."

"You wanted reassurance," I said, needing reassurance of my own.

"And she didn't give it," Hannah said, "So I asked what she thought had happened to Andi. Had she overheard something about your dad's business dealings? There was a long pause. Then she said it again. 'I don't know.'"

My mother hadn't said no.

She hadn't said no.

My entire life began to unravel like a loose thread tugged

too far. We'd each played our roles to perfection: my mother, the brittle socialite of a small town; my father, the gentle Atticus Finch type. Andi, the golden child. And me? I was the pancake child. The one you practice on. You flip too soon and she's uncooked in the middle, flip too late and she's burned around the edges.

I'd always believed my father's kindness was the steadiness that ran beneath our dysfunction.

Now I wasn't so sure.

"She sounded so broken," Aunt Hannah whispered. Tears streamed down her face and she swiped at them, as though embarrassed. "I asked if she'd told the police. She said Paul had them in his pocket—that they'd never believe her. I told her to go higher, to the FBI. To someone who could actually do something. But she said she had it handled." My aunt drew in a shaky breath. "I pushed her. Asked how she had it handled, but I could tell she was close to the edge. So I backed off and offered to come down and be with her. But she said Paul wouldn't want me there, and it would only make things worse." Her voice cracked. "So, I stayed away, and then… after they found Andi…" She stopped again, wiping furiously at her reddened cheeks. "She called me, sounding like that conversation had never happened. Back to her usual stiff upper lip. She said I had a lot of nerve to doubt her husband. And as far as she was concerned, her family was dead to her."

I felt like I was watching a horror movie.

"She cut Mom and Dad off after that," Aunt Hannah added softly.

"Why do you think she cut your parents off?" Malcolm asked, voice pitched low.

Hannah turned to face him. "Because I told her I was going to tell them everything."

"But you didn't," my grandfather growled.

She turned to face him with guilt-filled eyes. "No, because

I hoped she'd change her mind. And if I told you, you would have never forgiven Paul."

"As we shouldn't!" he exploded, slamming a palm on the table. The silverware rattled, and I instinctively jumped.

Malcolm tensed next to me but didn't let go of my hand.

"I know," she whispered, dropping her gaze to the table. "I know."

Silence fell over the room, heavy and aching. The kind that follows a natural disaster, when the dust hasn't settled yet and you're checking for damage.

The silence roared in my ears.

I stared at my half-full plate on the table, but my vision was fuzzy, like I was about to pass out or I was waking up from a bad dream.

My mother had cut off her parents.

She'd defended my father.

She'd chosen him. Even when she'd thought he was capable of being a monster.

But she'd been cold to me my entire life, even before Andi's death. Every sharp word, every time she'd looked through me like I wasn't there—it all made some kind of sick sense now. She hadn't been just *distant*. She'd been protecting my father's dirty secrets. She'd picked him over her daughters. Over her family. Over me. Even knowing what he might be capable of, she'd chosen to share a bed with him, share a life. She'd let him tuck us in at night and pretend we were a normal family, all while suspecting he was capable of murder.

I felt a wail rising inside me, begging for release, but I clamped it down. I was not going to lose it now. Not when I finally had some answers. Still, I couldn't get past her choice.

"She said you were dead to her," I stated, not feeling the words. "But she cut me off that day too, and she let me believe…" I stopped. I wasn't going to confess what she'd done to me, and how it had filled me with a deep well of guilt and pain that nothing had been able to quench.

"She let you believe what?" my grandmother asked, her eyes red with tears.

I turned to her and offered her a tender smile. "She stole us from each other, Grandma. But no more."

She sat up straighter and shook her head. "No, Harper. No more."

"She knew," I said, looking up at Hannah. "She knew what he might've done, and she still let him stay in that house. With her. With me." I shook my head, my voice breaking. "How do we live with that?"

Aunt Hannah's composure crumpled.

"*I* don't," she said, starting to cry.

My grandfather leaned his forearms on the table, like the weight of reality had settled on his shoulders. "Harper. We should have checked on you. We had no idea."

"If only I'd told you," Aunt Hannah whispered through her tears.

Secrets were the currency my mother had dealt in—held tightly and fiercely protected. They'd made her bitter, paranoid, and miserable. And they hadn't just hurt her. They'd harmed all of us.

They'd destroyed me.

But they weren't just *her* secrets.

They were the ones she'd died protecting. The ones no one had dared to name. The rot at the center of our family wasn't just the silence that had overtaken us after Andi's death.

It was my father.

And I was going to crucify him.

My anger was back, and I nearly collapsed with relief. It felt like I was putting on armor I'd forgotten I owned, familiar and protective. My entire life had been fueled by anger, and I couldn't lose it now. Not when it was the only thing standing between me and the devastating truth that my mother had chosen a monster over her children.

Malcolm leaned into my ear, so close I could smell his masculine scent. "What do you want to do?" he asked.

I leaned back and turned to face him, surprised at the fire burning in his eyes. "She said she had it handled. We need to figure out what that meant."

"Do you have any idea where to look?"

Not really. My mother wasn't the type to share her feelings. I was shocked she shared that much with her sister. But I knew someone who had known her back then, someone observant enough to see the cracks in her façade. She might not have the answers, but it was a place to start. "Lisa Murphy."

He gave me a slow, sharp nod of approval, then turned to my family. "We're sorry for the abrupt departure, but there are a few pressing matters we need to attend to."

My aunt reached across the table to me, and I lifted my hand to take hers. "You're gonna find out who did this, aren't you?"

"Yes."

She nodded her approval.

"*But*," Malcolm interjected. "As difficult at this might be, we need you to keep it to yourselves until we get this solved."

"I've kept this secret for twenty-some odd years," Aunt Hannah said, squeezing my hand then releasing it. "I can keep it longer."

Malcolm turned to my grandparents.

"It was secrets that got Sarah Jane into this mess," my grandfather said, shooting a dark look to Hannah before shifting his attention back to James. "But I can see that you still need the secrecy so the people who did this to Sarah Jane won't know you're comin'. We'll keep our mouths shut."

"Not that we have anyone to tell," Grandma said, giving me a weak smile. "People around here forgot about Sarah Jane long ago."

They may have forgotten her, but any juicy gossip would

be sure to stoke their memories. I'd seen it happen often enough.

"We'll let you know when we have things resolved," I said.

"One way or the other." Malcolm's jaw was as hard as granite, and the tone of his voice matched.

If my grandparents and aunt caught the unspoken promise of violence in his tone, they didn't let on.

I stood and started to back up toward the door when my grandmother pointed to me and called out, "You stop right there."

I froze, taken back by her strict tone, but then she hurried around the table, her hobble even more pronounced by her pace. When she reached me, she threw her arms around me. "If you think you're gettin' out of here without a hug, then you've got another think comin'."

I wasn't a hugger, maybe because hugs hadn't been a ritual in our nuclear family. Usually, they made me feel awkward, but this one felt like coming home. The hunger for a family who actually wanted to hold me nearly brought me to my knees. I hugged her back, holding on tighter than I'd intended. "Thank you for everything."

"Girl, I'd give you the moon and more, you only have to ask," she said, her voice thick with twenty years of regret. "We should have fought harder to reach you. We failed you when you needed us most." She held on tighter, as if making up for every lost embrace.

When she let me go, she turned to Malcolm and hugged him next. "Thank you for bringing her here."

He went rigid, then, when she didn't let go, his body softened a bit, finally accepting he wasn't getting out of it. "I didn't bring her here," he finally said, his voice sounding hoarse. "*She* brought *me*."

"I don't care who brought who," she said with a chuckle, then dropped her arms and took a step back. She lifted a hand and cupped his cheek, staring intently into his eyes, scanning his soul. "You're a good man, James Malcolm, and you're always welcome in our home."

They were just words, because obviously they didn't know him, not like the rest of the world did. But the way his throat worked like he was trying to swallow something too big, it was like watching someone hear that they were an elephant after being told they were a giraffe their entire life.

I thought about how he'd said he'd give anything to have grandparents like mine, because his hadn't given a crap about him. Standing there, watching this hardened man who'd killed without hesitation melt under my grandmother's fierce affection, I understood something fundamental: we were both orphans. The difference was I'd found my way home, and he was still learning what home could feel like.

My grandfather was behind her, and he hugged me even tighter, as though he was afraid to let me go.

"I'll come back," I whispered huskily into his ear.

"Promise?" he asked, his voice cracking.

"Promise."

He gave me a kiss on the cheek, then released me. And when he moved aside, Aunt Hannah was standing in front of me, her face tear-streaked and red.

She clasped her hands in front of her, twisting them nervously. "I understand if you never forgive me."

I shook my head. "There's nothing to forgive."

"If I'd told Mom and Dad—"

"It wouldn't have changed a thing," I said, as certain of that as I was that the sun would rise tomorrow. "Mom would have still kept you away."

"But you—"

I shook my head again. "No regrets, Aunt Hannah. We found each other again, and I think that's the best possible outcome."

Her eyes darkened. "Other than making your father pay for killing her."

"Right now, we have no proof that he did," I said. "But James and I will do our damnedest to find it." I shot him a quick glance. The dark glint in his eyes confirmed he was still on board, then I turned back to her. "And we're a damn good team. If anyone can find proof, it's the two of us."

"Is James a detective too?" she asked, giving him her full attention. "I never asked what you do."

"I'm a tavern owner," he said, looking more than a little dangerous, but it was clear no one in this room had anything to fear. "I'm good at unburdening people of their troubles, and secrets are a part of that."

Little did she know that he didn't do it by plying them with alcohol, but I saw no need to fill her in.

"I'm glad Harper has you," she said, giving him a quick hug. When she pulled away, she looked him in the eye. "You watch over our girl. I'm sure she's good at takin' care of herself, but we didn't just get her back to lose her again."

"I won't let anything happen to her," he said, shocking me with the sincerity of his tone. "I promise."

## Chapter 23

We left moments later and got into Malcolm's car, the weight of what we'd just learned heavy on my shoulders. The silence stretched between us as he pulled away from the curb.

We were still silent by the time we reached the highway. Everything in me screamed for a drink. Something to take the edge off the raw nerves Aunt Hannah's revelations had scraped wide open. But I reminded myself I was a stubborn bitch, and I was going to beat this demon. Even if my life was burning down around me.

But there was no denying my withdrawal symptoms were hitting me full force. The back of my neck was damp with sweat and the ache in my head felt like a jackhammer was splitting my skull open. What little food I'd had at the table was spinning in my gut.

I lifted a hand to rub my temple to ease the pain. Malcolm caught the way my hand shook, and reached for the flask. "You need a drink."

"No," I forced out through gritted teeth.

"I know you want one," he said, his voice a low growl. "Hell, you'd probably kill for one, so I appreciate the effort you're goin' through to refuse it, but you're not through your withdrawal yet. If you don't take a drink, it's only gonna get worse."

Tears burned my eyes, and a knot clogged my throat, but self-disgust quickly followed. I only had myself to blame for being in this situation. Self-pity would get me nowhere.

I held out my shaking hand, biting back tears nonetheless, because even though I was a stubborn bitch, I felt like I'd left some of that strength back in my grandparents' dining room.

He handed me the flask. It took some effort to unscrew the cap, but I got it off and forced myself to only take a sip.

The sweet relief that washed through me nearly made me cry with gratitude as some of the pain started to ease. My hand trembled as I held the flask, every cell in my body begging for more. One more sip—just enough to stop the screaming in my head. My hand tightened on the metal, and for one terrifying moment, I wasn't sure I had the strength to let go.

I shoved the flask at him, and once he took it, I pressed my hands between my legs, willing them to stop betraying me.

Malcolm's tension radiated from the driver's seat. The same coiled energy of someone who'd shown too much, revealed a crack in the armor they'd spent years perfecting. His hands gripped the steering wheel like it was the only thing keeping him anchored.

I recognized it for what it was—the same reaction I had when someone started to see the person I kept buried beneath the tough persona I projected to the world.

Today had stripped away our defenses, leaving us both raw and exposed in ways that terrified us.

After a few moments, the silence became suffocating. We were both drowning in our own thoughts, and someone had to throw a lifeline before we both went under. I decided he'd carried me this far on our journey. It was time for me to pull the weight.

"I'm sorry about the way I treated you when we went outside earlier," I said. "I got mad for absolutely no reason, and … I'm sorry."

"Yeah," he grunted, keeping his gaze on the road ahead of us. "It's fine."

"No," I insisted. "It's not fine. You've been nothing but nice to me since you showed up on my doorstep yesterday, and I was a first-class bitch."

His jaw tightened. "Maybe you had the right to be."

I studied him for several seconds. "No. I didn't."

He focused on the road, wearing a solemn expression, but some of his fierceness had faded a bit. "Carter got back to me while I was out. He got video from some of the neighbors, but none of it proved helpful."

I sighed. "It was a long shot anyway. At least we have the images of the two guys and the woman Mrs. Comstock sent us."

"Carter's still running them, but he hasn't come up with anything yet."

I pulled out my phone and checked for messages. Lisa had sent a text saying she didn't recognize the woman, and she'd shown it to several other women who didn't recognize her either. I relayed the information to Malcolm, and he gave a silent nod, still lost in his emotional stew.

I decided to address the new elephant in the room. "My grandmother liked you."

He released a snort. "She doesn't know me."

"I think she's a good judge of character."

He snorted again. "You hardly know her either."

"Is it so hard to believe you're capable of being good?"

"Being capable doesn't mean I *am*."

The way he said it made me realize this was an internal battle he'd had for some time. Obviously, he'd done some bad shit in his life, but maybe he *wanted* to be a good person.

Maybe he just thought he'd sunk too deep to crawl out of the pit he'd dug himself into.

"Then tell me this," I countered, "why are you helping me?" When he didn't answer, I added, "Why help me last night? Why come with me today? Why be so nice to my grandparents?"

"I'm not a *total* dick," he said in disgust.

"Maybe you're not a dick at all."

He tilted his head toward me and gave me the side-eye. "How many drinks did you have while I was gone?"

I nearly told him I'd had none, then caught myself—he was deflecting. "You said you helped me because you needed me to uncover who took over Simmons's operation. But you could have hired someone to babysit me. You must have other people at your disposal, like the woman who stitched me up."

He shifted in his seat, irritation etched on his face. "What is it you want me to say, Harper?"

"You said it before, and you're right—you and I are a lot alike. If someone gets too close, we go on the offensive." When he didn't contradict me, I continued. "It's this dance we do: I lash out. You lash out. But what if we tried to stop? What if we both accepted that there's something about the other person that makes us feel safe opening up? Letting the other person see the parts we hide from everyone else?"

I took it as a small victory when he didn't immediately tell me to go fuck myself.

"I think we have bigger issues to address," he said matter-of-factly. "Like the fact your mother knew your father was capable of murdering someone but let him keep living at home with her two little girls."

"I wasn't a little girl when Andi was kidnapped," I countered.

"But you were still a minor. And your aunt confronted your mother about your father being potentially dangerous when you were eleven, Harper—yeah, I'm capable of doing math. The way your mother completely dismissed her warning makes me think she already knew something was up with him." He turned to look at me for a long moment before turning back to the road. "She put you in danger, and for what? To fucking save face? To protect her Queen Bee of Jackson Creek status?"

"I don't know," I admitted, something inside me crumpling. "She loved Andi. I think she would have done anything to protect her."

"And *yet*," he said, his tone harsh, "when Hannah called your mother after she was kidnapped, she said she didn't know whether your father was responsible."

"He wasn't," I said. "He had nothing to do with it. We both know John Michael Stevens was the one who kidnapped and murdered my sister."

"True, but until they caught the bastard, she wasn't sure."

He was right and I took a moment to let that sink in. She'd been so insistent we come straight home that day. Had something been brewing outside of my sister's kidnapping? "Do you know anything about a Richard or a Dale Ambrose?"

"Nope. Ambrose should be easy enough to look into, but Richard? The name's too common." He tapped the steering wheel with his thumb. "We can't overlook that your father was screwing someone back when you and your sister were younger. Which means the woman who came to your mother's house last week could have been his mistress after all."

I nodded, because the thought had occurred to me too. "She must not be from the area. Lisa and her friends would have recognized her otherwise."

He made a face as though considering whether he should say what he was thinking. Finally, he said, "When you asked if I had girlfriends, I told you that I don't do relationships, but when I'm lookin' to get laid, I don't shit in my front yard." He shot me a look. "If your father had a lick of sense in his head, he wouldn't either."

"Yeah," I said. "While my father has done some stupid shit, in this instance, I think he'd be smart. Especially after getting caught when we were younger."

He gave a nod. "So if the woman was your father's mistress, why would she show up at your mother's house?"

I shook my head. "I don't know. Dad already left Mom, so it's not likely the woman was there to confront her." I turned in my seat to face him better. "And then there's the fact that someone dropped her off. I don't think the woman would show up unannounced and have her ride drive off."

"True."

"We can't forget my mother called that burner phone a few hours before the woman showed up. I think my mother called her and she came."

He pursed his lips. "You think your mother would call your father's mistress and invite her to her house for a chat?"

"It wasn't a chat, though, was it?" I said. "They left minutes later."

"Does your mother seem like the kind of woman to leave with a suitcase and take her husband's mistress with her?" he asked pointedly.

"No," I admitted. "I can't even imagine that happening. Unless…" I said as a new thought hit me. "Unless the mistress had information about my father too. What if they both knew something, and they were both afraid?"

"That seems like a stretch," he said. "How would they know the other felt threatened?"

"I don't know," I said, exhaustion washing over me. "It's all hypothetical right now."

"Yeah," he said, sounding distracted. "If she wasn't a mistress, then who was she?"

"I have no idea."

"Okay," he said, his forehead creasing as he considered the possibilities. "Mistress or not, how did your mother get to know her? Especially since her friends don't recognize her."

"That's the question, right? My mother lived a small life. She didn't meet new people. She rarely left her bubble."

He nodded slowly. "Regardless of who she was, it seems like they must have connected through your father. Agree?" He gave me a questioning look.

I considered it. "While it seems likely, I don't want to declare it as fact."

"Agreed, but if they are connected by association to your father, how did it occur? Could she be one of your father's clients?"

I considered this for a moment, then said, "Or the wife of a client. What if she had information about her own husband and approached my mother? Like what if she was married to the Richard Aunt Hannah overheard him talking to?"

"And if not Richard, then some other underhanded partner or client."

"Yeah."

"So, what if you show the photo to the people in his office and see if any of them recognize her? That way we can figure out if she knows your father through his profession."

It was a good place to start—with one problem. "They might tell my father."

"Would they?' he asked. "Or would they just gossip about it?"

I only took a second to come up with the answer. "Gossip. But I'll have to come up with an excuse to show up at the office. I can't just come in and show them the photo and take off, or their tongues will really be wagging."

"You could say you're checking on your father. Is he back at work?"

The thought of seeing my father felt like a punch to the gut. It took me a second to respond. "He is, but I'm not sure I can face him right now."

He gave me a quick glance, then nodded. "We'll hold off on that one for now." He took a beat, then softened his tone.

"You're gonna have to face him at some point. You think you can get yourself ready for that?"

"I *want* to face him," I said, the anger in my belly beginning to smolder. "But when I look at him, I want to be ready to nail him to the wall."

"I can wait for that." A slow smile spread across his face. It was terrifyingly menacing, and some part of me soaked it in.

I had a partner in this. A real partner, and not the self-indulgent, back-stabbing partner Keith Kemper had turned out to be. I knew in my gut that Malcolm had my back. Just like I had his.

I knew I should question that feeling, but I didn't want to. I was going with my instincts, just like I used to before I'd lost everything last fall, and right now, my instincts told me that I could trust him. Hell, if I was honest, I never felt this sure about Keith, even in our best moments.

"There's one thing I can't quite wrap my head around though," I said. "When I asked my father if he'd told my grandparents about my mother's accident, he told *me* to do it. He practically sent me to them. I can't believe that he'd send me here, knowing Aunt Hannah might tell me everything. It makes me wonder if my mother ever confronted him about Hannah's accusations."

"Maybe she didn't."

I tried to put myself in my mother's head over twenty years ago. "You're probably right. If she liked her life as it was, then I don't think she would have confronted him and risked losing it all. Even if she had proof. I think she'd keep it to herself."

I took a second to let that revelation sink in. Further proof that she didn't give a damn about our safety.

As if reading my mind, he said, "Just because he was involved with bad people didn't mean he didn't care about you and your sister."

The way he said it sounded like he was trying to convince himself as much as he was trying to convince me.

But that didn't make sense. Malcolm had said his own father was a piece of shit. So, who had he been thinking about? His friend Jed? But that still didn't fit, because from what he'd said, Jed had left the criminal world behind to raise a family.

Still … his statement had sounded personal.

Did Malcolm have any secret children? It didn't seem like any of my business. If he did, then I'd leave it up to him to tell me.

He glanced at me, and I realized I'd left him hanging.

"You're right," I said. "Just because he was involved with murderous people didn't mean he would hurt us himself. Just because someone kills another person, doesn't mean they would hurt the people they love. Especially if they thought they were killing to protect their loved ones."

He drew in a deep breath, his shoulders drawing up. "You think your father had Ambrose killed to protect you and your sister?"

"No," I said, running a hand over my head. "I don't know." My brain was sluggish, as though it had worked too much today and it was calling it quitting time.

*Focus.*

"I have to believe he loved us," I said, my voice breaking slightly as the nostalgia of my childhood flooded my head. So many memories, and now I was looking at them through a new lens. "You can't fake that kind of affection. Not for as long as he showed it. And yeah, he stopped showing me affection after Andi died, but I think that's because he was grieving for her so hard."

"Or distancing himself from you."

My brow shot up.

"We don't know what he was doin' or thinkin'," he said. "But what if there was something goin' on with him when your sister was kidnapped? What if he—and your mother—suspected he was the reason your sister was taken? Sure, it turned out she was taken by a sick pervert, but what if your father pissed someone off and he thought they took his daughter as retribution? It hurt like hell, so he distanced himself from you. That way it wouldn't hurt him as much if they took you."

Horror rushed through my head, stealing my breath. "That…" I didn't know how to finish the sentence.

"That's sick. Twisted," he said, punctuating each word. "Again, we don't know what happened, but we *do* know he turned his back on you." His gaze turned to me, a challenge on his face. "There's no disputing that."

He was right, so I didn't even try.

He shifted in his seat. "Another question is why your mother sent that key to her estranged sister. Especially when you hadn't spoken to her since you were a kid."

"Whatever is in that safe deposit box is something she either didn't want my father to see or was holding it as blackmail. But why would she wait until after she died to tell me she had evidence against him? Why not tell me while she was alive, when I could have tried to save her?"

"I suspect she thought she could handle it on her own," he said. "It sounds like she was used to things going her way. She thought she could control this too."

"Maybe," I said, still turning it over in my head. "But maybe not. She wasn't acting confident after he left. She was paranoid and scared."

"What if—" He held up a hand to preemptively stop any protest. "What if she was trying to protect you?"

He was right to hold me off, because my first instinct was to tell him he was crazy. But this was why investigators didn't work on personal cases. You were too familiar with the involved parties, prejudices and all. It made it difficult to look at things objectively.

"Okay," I said slowly, truly considering the possibility. "For argument's sake, let's say she *was* trying to protect me. Wouldn't hiding the information put me in more danger?"

"Not necessarily. If you thought her death was an accident, you'd never have to find out otherwise. That would have been the end of it. And it makes sense that she would have assumed it would be made to look like an accident. She knew about Dale Ambrose. Her sister told her. If she thought she was in danger, she'd presume her death would be staged too."

"She was scared to drive alone." I gasped as the truth slammed into me. "That's why she wanted me to take her everywhere."

"Which brings us back to the mystery woman. If she was scared to drive alone, maybe she called that woman to be with her."

"My mother thought that woman would protect her?"

"Depending on who the woman was to your mother, it's a possibility."

"You're right," I said. "We have to look at all possibilities. All the angles. Let's say my mother thought she might be murdered, so she sent the literal key to why she was murdered to her estranged sister and told her not to come to me. To let me go to *her*. Why would she think I'd reach out to her?"

"Maybe she didn't," Malcolm said. "But what if your mother was dotting her I's—she figured you'd get suspicious, and if you did, it would be better for you to get the information from her rather than poking around in the wrong places. And she figured if you started looking into things you'd probably go to her sister and ask questions."

I tried to wrap my head around my mother's scheming.

"You were only in danger if you started poking. Still, there's no arguing that if your mother wanted you to solve her murder, it seems she would have made it easier."

I released a bitter laugh. "My mother never made anything easy for me."

He paused before he said, "She told Hannah that you had to come to her, that she couldn't go to you." He gave me a pointed look. "What if that was your mother's way of entrusting the key with Hannah but protecting your aunt at the same time?"

"You could be right," I said, mulling it over. "My dad and Hannah's last words were harsh. If my mother thought my father was capable of murder, she might have been worried about what he would do if he saw her, especially if he thought she was stirring up trouble." I shuddered. I still couldn't mesh the monster my aunt had described with the man I'd known. He'd fallen to pieces after Andi's kidnapping. My mother had been the strong one.

Further evidence my father may have thought he was responsible. What would I do if I thought someone I loved had been murdered because of my bad choices?

I supposed I'd have to let myself love someone before I could understand the true depth of those feelings.

I ran a hand over my face, my brain numb with exhaustion. I felt like we had more pieces to the puzzle, but none of them seemed to fit anything we knew.

"We're gonna find out who did this," Malcolm said in a firm tone. "We're gonna get justice."

I wanted to believe that, but at the moment it felt hopeless. I knew exhaustion was clouding my emotions, because I'd solved cases with less evidence than we had right now. We just had to follow the breadcrumbs, and that usually took time. I needed patience, something I was fresh out of.

"You need to rest," Malcolm said. "All of this is a lot, and you're still recovering."

"Still recovering is a kind way to say detoxing," I said bitterly.

He cast me a glance. "You want me to be blunt?"

"No," I said with a sigh. "But you could have called me on

my bullshit. Further proof you're taking my feelings into consideration." I gave him a tepid grin. "That you're *nice*."

He snorted again, but he didn't contradict me.

"You said you're seeing a therapist. I suspect she'd want you to own up to being nice."

"You have no idea what we talk about," he scoffed.

"True, but I doubt your therapist is encouraging you to be mean."

"Maybe we're talking about setting boundaries, which some people would see as mean." After a second, he shrugged as though even he thought the suggestion was bullshit. "If I admit to being nice, will you try to take a nap?"

"You want a moment of peace and quiet?" I teased.

His lips tipped into the hint of a grin. "If I get to drive in silence for an hour or two, I won't complain."

I released a genuine laugh, then leaned back in my seat. "Fine."

I closed my eyes, knowing there was more we needed to discuss, but I was too tired to dig through my brain to figure it out. Malcolm was right. I needed sleep, and when I woke, I'd be refreshed and ready to tackle this with a fresh perspective.

Despite the multiple thoughts racing through my head, exhaustion pulled me under, and the hum of the tires on the road lulled me to sleep.

# Chapter 24

When I woke, it took me a few seconds to figure out why I was in a dark car, parked in front of a small, warmly lit modern cabin with cedar planks and large glass windows trimmed in black. A full porch ran the length of the house. The front door was on the left side of the porch, and a set of rocking chairs sat in front of the bank of windows.

Confused, I turned to see James sitting behind his steering wheel, staring at the house with a look of indecision.

"Where are we?" I asked, sitting up. Obviously somewhere he was having second thoughts about visiting.

"My house."

My heart sunk. "You look like you're not sold on me being here." He'd said we were going to stay at his house last night, but I'd gotten too sick for us to go. It was obvious he was reconsidering. "We don't have to stay here. We can go to your office or a hotel." I tried to smile, but it was weak at best. "I'll even pay."

He turned and gave me a tight smile, the lights from the porch cast shadows across his face. "It's just been a rough day."

Guilt hit me like a freight train. "Sorry I dragged you into this."

"No," he said, shaking his head. "That's not what I meant. Come on." He opened the car door and got out.

I was too tired to figure out what he meant by that, so I got out too and waited by the passenger door as he opened the trunk and pulled out my bag.

I followed him as he climbed the two steps to the porch and then punched a series of numbers into the digital keypad under his handle. There was an audible click, and he pushed the door open, motioning for me to enter.

I gave him a last look. If he still seemed hesitant, I'd insist on leaving, but the indecision had been wiped off his face. He still didn't look happy about it, though.

"We can go somewhere else," I offered again.

"Don't be stupid," he grunted. "I've been to your place multiple times. It's no big deal."

It wasn't the same and we both knew it. James was private, even more so than I was. I couldn't help wondering how many other people he'd invited here.

I walked inside. The décor was a mix of modern and rustic, with a stone fireplace, leather sofa, and wrought iron and glass coffee and end tables. It was open to his kitchen, a modern looking space with maple cabinets and dark stone countertops.

"Wow," I said, "This is nice … really nice."

He walked in behind me and shut the door. "You sound surprised."

"I'm not sure why I am," I said. "Your office in the tavern sort of has the same feel. I had no idea something like this existed in Lone County."

He headed into the kitchen. "It didn't start out this way. It was a dump when Carter found it, but he got to work redoing it so it was ready when I could move in."

My brow shot up. "You never saw it before you moved in?"

He opened a cabinet and pulled out two glasses, then headed to the fridge, casting a glance at a pill bottle on the counter. "I was a bit *detained*."

Oh. "Carter bought it while you were in prison."

He didn't answer, instead focused on filling both glasses with ice.

I wanted to ask why he'd moved to Lone County, but I'd asked before and he hadn't given me a straight answer. There was a better chance he'd tell me now, but I didn't want to push. Especially since I hadn't told him about the situation with Devereaux yet.

"So Carter was in charge of all the renovations? How did he know you'd like it?"

"He knows my taste," he said over the clink of the ice cubes. "He showed me some plans though, and I gave my approval."

The renovations must have taken months, all while James was in prison waiting a trial for charges that could have kept him in prison for life. It seemed risky that he'd have Carter renovate a house he wasn't sure he'd ever move into. Unless he'd spent part of his time in prison working out a new deal with the Feds.

"I renovated my house in Little Rock," I said, walking over to him as he filled one of the glasses with water. "It was a hundred-plus-year-old craftsman. I hired out a lot of the work, but I also did some of it myself."

He looked at me as he handed me the glass he'd finished filling. "You sold it, right?"

"Yeah," I said, trying to keep the bitterness out of my voice. "My legal bills were exorbitant."

"The police union didn't pay for any of it?"

"In the beginning, but then I didn't do what they wanted." I took a sip of water to soothe my parched mouth. "It became apparent they weren't going to put their best efforts into my case. So I got my own attorney." I'd told him this before, but it didn't feel redundant. The first time had been contentious. This time it felt … right.

He picked up the pill bottle, read the label, then unscrewed the cap. "This'll help with the detox. No more tapering off alcohol. You'll taper off these instead." He shook two tablets into his palm and held them out to me.

I eyed them cautiously, not taking them. "What is it?"

"Lorazepam."

My eyes flew wide. "What … where did you get those?"

He gave me a look that said, *really?*

I could have pointed out that Lorazepam was a Schedule IV controlled substance—illegal to possess without a prescription. A misdemeanor for me, but a felony for him if caught distributing.

But I'd already crossed so many lines, this seemed like nothing. That wasn't the part that stopped me.

"So, I'm trading one vice for another," I said bitterly.

He gave me an impatient look. "If you were in rehab, you'd be doin' the exact same thing. This way, you're on a schedule. You'll stop taking them in less than a week."

He was right, and it meant no more temptation with his flask.

I held out my hand and he dropped the tablets into my palm, then went back to fridge to fill his own glass.

I popped both pills in my mouth and took a sip of water, only realizing as I swallowed that they could have been anything. I'd just taken his word for it. But the panic I expected never came. For better or worse, I trusted him.

"You'll take them three times a day—morning, noon, and night. The dosage is on the bottle."

"Thanks."

He didn't respond, just finished filling his glass, his shoulders stiff. He looked like he was about to say something, then stopped.

"Are you hungry?" he asked at last, meeting my gaze. "I don't have much food here, but we can dig up something."

The air between us felt charged again—just like it had outside my grandparents' house. Even if I'd been hungry, I wouldn't be now. My stomach buzzed with anticipation, a feeling I wasn't used to.

He cleared his throat, his hand tightening around his glass, and deliberately looked away.

What was I doing? Had I imagined the tension or was it one-sided? Could I actually trust my insights right now?

Taking my cue that I was making him uncomfortable, I said, "I'm good," and headed to the living room, needing to put some space between us.

I was about to sit on the sofa, but a framed photograph on the fireplace mantel caught my attention. I walked closer, surprised to see two little girls sitting on a tree branch with their arms around each other. There was a creek and trees behind them. Both girls looked to be about four years old and had big smiles. The one on the left was blond with bright blue eyes. She had a pink bow in her hair and wore a pink shirt and black leggings with sparkles. The other girl was brunette with shoulder-length hair. Her dark brown eyes had an inquisitive look. She was wearing a gray long-sleeve shirt with a Bluey graphic, and a pair of jeans. There was something familiar about her I couldn't place.

Why did James have a photo of two little girls on his mantel? At first, I'd thought they might be from his child-hood, but the Bluey graphic definitely suggested it was more recent.

"The blond one is Jed's little girl," James said, his voice strained.

I turned to stare at him, feeling guilty, although I wasn't sure why. "Does Jed send you photos?" I asked before I thought better of it. "Sorry. Of course not. You said you're not in contact."

"His wife sends me letters with photos from time to time," he said, glancing out the front window.

"Oh." I had a million more questions, but I didn't want him to reveal anything he wasn't ready to share.

"You'd like Neely Kate," he said with a grin, although there was a strain of longing in his voice. "Although you too are nothin' alike except for your penchant for callin' out bullshit."

"It's a gift not everyone is blessed with," I teased.

Chuckling, he sat down in one of the side chairs and took a sip of his water. "True enough." He looked guarded. "I suppose you're wondering why Neely Kate sends me letters," he mused, finally looking at me.

I still stood by the fireplace. This photograph was important, otherwise he wouldn't have displayed it so prominently. I wanted to understand why, but I still didn't want to push. "You're right. I'm wondering," I said, turning back to the image. "But I suspect Neely Kate is hoping you and Jed will change your minds about talking to one another."

He lifted his glass in salute, then took a drink. As he lowered it, he said, "Not at first, she wasn't. She was glad to have me out of his life."

I walked over to the sofa and took a seat. If he was going to share part of his personal life with me, I was going to be at his level, not staring down at him. "I take it she hated him working for you."

He paused, then inhaled sharply. As he exhaled, he said, "Especially at the end, but Neely Kate and I got along. I helped her out of a few scrapes, and she helped me with a few of mine."

A streak of jealousy shot through me, catching me off guard. I had no right to feel jealous of a woman he'd known before our paths had crossed, but the sentiment was there, nonetheless. "Like me," I said, trying my damnedest to sound nonchalant.

He grinned. "Nothin' like you." A fondness covered his face as he said, "She's sweetness and sass all rolled up into one."

I couldn't help laughing. "No one's ever accused me of being sweetness and sass."

"I know what you're thinkin'," he said, resting his glass on his knee, "but there was never anything between us. She was a friend of a friend, and while I confess that, in the beginning, I helped her because of her friend, in the end, I helped her because she's a genuinely good person who deserves good things."

Further proof he had a good heart, but I was smart enough not to say what I was thinking.

"Neely Kate is perfect for Jed," he said, his face glowing with fond memories. "It took me a while to realize it, but to be fair, she was married to her deadbeat husband when she walked into our lives. Then, later, her husband left her high and dry, practically days after she'd nearly died miscarryin' their twins, so when she asked me to help find him so she could serve him divorce papers, I readily agreed. She deserved better. Carter drew up the divorce papers."

"He left her after she almost died?" The guy sounded like a complete jackass.

"And he was a polygamist." He added dryly, "But he got his in the end."

"Neely Kate got her divorce and took him to the cleaners?"

"It's a long, complicated story, but basically, no. Her no-good husband was murdered." He took a sip of his water.

Had James killed him? The question hung in my head, but I realized I wasn't as horrified by the possibility as I would have been a month ago.

As he lowered his glass, he made a face, then added, "I

suppose I should add he wasn't murdered by me, nor did I have anything to do with it." His gaze lifted to mine, and for a second it felt like time froze. He was only a few feet away, but it felt too far. I wanted to be next to him, hell, I wanted to be on his lap. The heat in his eyes suggested he wouldn't push me off.

But the fact he felt the need to clarify reminded me I had a secret of my own. And I couldn't follow through on my need to be closer to him until I made my confession.

But I wasn't ready. Not yet. So, I forced myself to focus on what he said. "Wow. That had to mess Neely Kate up."

"It was rough, but she had Jed to help her through it."

"Did you cut Jed loose before or after Neely Kate's wayward husband was murdered?"

"Before." He took a breath, then said, "Neely Kate had gotten into some trouble in Oklahoma after she graduated from high school, and she caught wind that someone was digging into it. Jed knew how hard it was for her and wanted to go with her. So I told him he had to choose—Neely Kate or me. I'd hoped to God he'd choose Neely Kate, and he did." A sad smile tugged at his lips. "Smart man."

Was the sadness because he'd lost his best friend in the process? Or was there a small part of him that had hoped Jed would choose him?

How many people had chosen him? Or maybe a better question was how many people *hadn't*? He'd spent most of his life pushing people away, partly to protect them, mostly to protect himself.

I understood that well enough. I'd lived most of my life that way too.

"I should add," he said, his gaze fixed on his water glass. "In full disclosure, Neely Kate is J.R. Simmons' illegitimate daughter."

My mouth dropped open.

He finally looked up, his expression carefully guarded. "I

didn't know when I first met her. Hell, she didn't know either. It all came out during the whole Simmons mess. And none of this has anything to do with her."

I nodded. "Thanks for telling me."

But if he was sharing things to earn my trust, it was time for me to come clean with him too.

"There's something I need to tell you," I said, summoning the courage. He'd just opened up to me—trusted me—and I was about to blow it to hell. But I couldn't let him confide in me without telling him about my call with Deveraux.

His face shifted from open to closed, like a door slamming. "Go on."

"Last week, while we were working the Hugo Burton case, I made a call." I grimaced. "J.R. Simmons's name popped up, and you weren't totally forthcoming with information. I'd searched the internet for clues that might clue me into why Simmons might have been in Lone County, and his name lit up like bonfire with links to Fenton County."

"Go on," he said, his tone still chilly. Not that I blamed him.

"Your name came up too, which seemed odd, and again, you weren't forthcoming, so I decided to talk to someone who might have more insight." I gave him a pleading look. "I was hoping to get something that would help me solve the case."

His eyes were so cold, it felt like the temperature of the room dropped ten degrees.

"I figured who else would know the facts better than the man who brought charges against him?" I paused, realizing this confession would probably change everything between us. James would likely kick me out of his house and tell me to go fuck myself.

He'd have every right to do it, but I had to tell him anyway.

I held his gaze, hoping he saw how much I regretted my decision. "I called Mason Deveraux."

He swallowed, then said, "I see." The betrayal in his eyes was nearly my undoing. "And did you talk to him?"

"He called me back right before I found out about my mother," I said. "I didn't call him back. And I didn't hear from him again." I paused. "Until today."

His silence was deafening.

"He was the one who kept calling while I was sleeping."

"Did you call him back?"

"No, but I was concerned, because he shouldn't have been so persistent. He called me this afternoon after you left, after our fight." I took a breath. "I knew I had to answer and try to appease him, so I took the call."

"And…?"

"I told him I was sorry for bothering him, but the case was closed, and I didn't need any information. He said I'd mentioned Simmons, and he was curious about whether I'd found a connection. I told him no. I didn't want him to know."

"I see."

For the first time since we'd started this conversation, heat filled my voice. "Actually, I don't think you *do*. You think I did it to protect my father, but I did it to protect *you*."

For someone used to schooling his emotion, he had a rare lapse. Surprise covered his face, but then he quickly covered it with a mask of indifference. "How does that protect me?"

"Because, if I told him about Simmons investing in Burton's property, I was afraid he'd start digging." I pushed out a breath of frustration. "Any other prosecutor would have let this go the moment I said the case was closed, but Deveraux was on this like a dog on a bone. He kept asking me questions about how the case was resolved and stating how convenient it was that the men responsible for Burton's death were dead, and he's right," I said. "But it was a cold case and Matt Jones was glad to clear it off his desk, so he took everything that happened at face value."

His mask didn't waver. "Again, how did you protect me by covering up Simmons's involvement?"

"I'm getting to it. It didn't make sense that Deveraux was so invested in finding out if Simmons was involved. Simmons has been dead for years. Deveraux's the lead prosecutor for the state. He doesn't have time to fuck around, and he couldn't bring charges against a dead man. Which means he wanted to know for another reason. The more I tried to dodge him, the cagier he got." I narrowed my eyes. "I don't trust him. I suspect he's after you."

He sat back in his chair, giving the impression that he'd relaxed, but I knew better. "You're right. He has a vendetta against me, so once he heard Simmons's name, he probably started salivating like one of Pavlov's dogs." He took a beat, then his tone lowered. "What did you tell him about Simmons when you made the original call?"

"I left a message with his assistant and said Simmons's name had come up in regard to a case I was working, then asked him to call me back."

"And when did my name come up?"

I swallowed. If I ever wanted him to trust me, I had to be honest. The irony was my honesty would probably break my ties with him forever. "When I left my message, I said I'd seen your name associated with Simmons's arrest for murder and kidnapping. That's the only thing I said."

"What about Rose Gardner?" he asked, his face a blank.

"I mentioned her name too," I said. "I thought he might return my call if I made the connection, given their history."

"Go on."

"But when he called me back today, I avoided using her name, worried in hindsight that it might be a touchy subject. He was the one to bring her up. In fact, he called me out for purposely not mentioning her by name."

He just watched me, waiting for me to finish.

"When I took his call, I was polite and professional, but as the call went on, I realized he was interrogating me. So, I was short and told him my only job had been to find Hugo Burton's body, and once he was found, I'd let the sheriff's department take over. He said he'd asked around about me, and he found it surprising I'd let it go so easily, but I reminded him I no longer work for law enforcement and that the sheriff's department wouldn't have welcomed my interference." I released a breath I'd been holding in. "In any case, I don't trust the man."

He gave me a cold look. "You could have asked me, and I would have told you he's a bulldog when he gets set on something."

"Really, James?" I asked with plenty of attitude. "And you would have told me? Because when I asked you about the case last week, you told me jack shit." When he remained silent, I let out a bitter laugh. "Exactly. Look, I understand you have your secrets, and believe it or not, I respect most of them. But I needed answers about Simmons that very few people had, and when you refused to confide in me, I went to what I saw as the next best source." I shook my head. "I never considered the fact that the man might have a vendetta against you."

James's countenance seemed to soften, but his eyes were still closed off. "You're right. I should have shared more."

"I regretted calling him almost immediately after I placed that original call." I leaned forward, my tone insistent. "I know you're after the person who took Simmons's place, and if Deveraux starts sniffing around, it will make it harder."

His brow shot up in mock surprise. "You expect me to believe you prefer my way of handling it to Deveraux's by-the-books approach?"

"Were either of the two cases we worked together by the books?" I countered. "I could have turned you in for the Sylvester brothers' murders and I wouldn't have been held accountable." I drew a breath. "I'll be honest, at the time, I didn't understand why I *didn't* turn you in, but I was never tempted to report you. And you and I both know we violated quite a few rules while investigating Hugo Burton's disappearance."

He cocked his head, his face still a mask of indifference. "Much to your reluctance."

"But I stayed anyway," I said, then my tone softened as the truth sunk in. "I stayed."

At the time, I'd told myself I was cutting corners to solve the case, but if I were totally honest, that wasn't the only reason.

Something flashed in his eyes that looked remarkably like panic, but it was gone just as quickly. He stood. "It's been a long-ass day. I'm goin' to bed. The guest bedroom is the one in the front."

I stood too. "Do you believe me?"

"Do I have reason not to?" he countered, one brow cocked.

"I have no intention of betraying you, James," I said solemnly.

He gave me a sad smile, then shook his head. "That's what I'm afraid of." And with that, he turned and walked down the short hall.

I stayed in place until I heard the soft click of his door, wondering what he'd meant and why it scared him.

## Chapter 25

The guest bedroom was nice but sparsely furnished. After I went into the bathroom to get ready for bed, I refilled my glass of water and saw the pill bottle on the counter.

I hadn't properly thanked him for getting it, and I *was* grateful. Monitoring the pills would hopefully be safer than sneaking swigs of alcohol. The temptation to drink would probably never go away. If I could get through withdrawal without caving, then maybe I had a shot at sobriety.

One thing was certain: I didn't want to go back to the place where I'd been. Even if James tossed me out on my ass in the morning.

Despite the remarkably comfortable mattress, I didn't sleep well. Partly because I'd slept so much in the car, but mostly because of how James and I had left things. He hadn't kicked me out or turned his back on me, but I almost wished he had. My guilt might be easier to deal with. Maybe he was only putting up with me because he wanted to see this case through, and once we were done, we were *done*.

If so, I'd brought it upon myself.

I had a million excuses for why I'd called Deveraux, but

the bottom line was I hadn't trusted James. He'd told me *not* to trust him, and I'd taken him at his word.

While I regretted what I'd done, I couldn't change it. All I could do was own it. If James couldn't forgive me, then I'd have to find a way to accept it.

Since I was up at the crack of dawn, I got up and made a pot of coffee, then took a cup onto James's porch and enjoyed the view of the woods surrounding the house. A single lane asphalt road cut through the trees and curved out of sight. I had no idea how far we were from a road, but it was obvious James enjoyed his privacy.

The thought cut deep.

I wondered again how many people he'd brought here. I suspected not many, and after what he likely saw as my betrayal, I doubted I'd ever be here again.

I brought my mother's laptop onto the porch and looked up Dale Ambrose. The accident had happened long enough ago that it took some digging to find it, and even then, there was nothing but a quick mention in the Jackson Creek newspaper. The report said he'd lost control of his car and driven off the bridge into the river. There was no mention of witnesses, so I opened my PI websites and did some digging to find the police report. It had been a cursory investigation. The report said a witness had seen the back end of the car sticking out of the river, but no one had seen the vehicle go in. There hadn't been an autopsy, and the case had quickly been closed. It was a very tidy way to get rid of someone. Especially since the Jackson Creek police were known for their laziness.

The question was why the Jackson Creek police had investigated the case given it was outside of their jurisdiction. I considered asking Louise, but she likely hadn't been in the department long enough to know. Detective Jones, who'd met with me about the Burton case, was next on my list. While he'd likely been around long enough to know the history of the Lone County Sheriff's Department's history with the Jackson Creek police, there was a good chance he hadn't been employed by them that far back. Still, it was possible. The accident had happened about twenty-four years ago, and I'd pegged him to be in his early forties.

A quick glance at the clock on the laptop confirmed it was too early to call him without looking suspicious, so I put it on my mental list to follow up on later.

Next, I searched my father's name, but there were multiple pages of listings to sort through. He'd been mayor of Jackson Creek for several years, and he'd been active in the community before that. After searching for nearly an hour, I didn't find anything suspicious. If he'd been involved in something shady, he'd covered his tracks. However, Google searches rarely provided evidence in an investigation. At most, it might point to a door to open. The best sources were people closest to the suspect, but it would be a challenge to talk to his friends and business associates without raising red flags.

I looked up the hours of my mother's bank, but it occurred to me there was a good chance the safe deposit box wasn't at her regular bank. That would make it harder for me to track down, but if my father was really after the information, it would make it harder for him too.

I tried to put myself in my mother's head. If James and I were right, she hadn't wanted me to know anything unless I started asking questions about her death or disappearance. Somehow, she'd intuited I would go to her sister, which meant she must have had a plan for me to access the box.

Safe deposit boxes had signature cards—the signature of the people who were allowed access to the box, and I knew I hadn't signed one. But if she'd left me a key, she must have made some kind of arrangement for me to get in it. The only legal way I could get in was if she'd changed her will.

James and I hadn't found anything about the will or the

box in her house, and there hadn't been anything on her computer. Where would she have kept that information?

Who would she have used to draw up the new will?

I logged into her bank account and went through her transactions, looking for anything that could have been a payment to an attorney. When I didn't see anything from the past six months, I wondered if she used one of Dad's partners. They wouldn't have charged her.

But that would have been dumb. If she'd used one of my father's friends, there was a good chance they would have told him. Had he already found her will? Had he already accessed the box?

Cold dread stole my breath, but I forced myself to take several deep breaths, in and out. I had to tackle one problem at a time. First, I needed to find out if there even *was* a will.

I checked the time on the laptop, sighing with frustration when I saw it was 7:48. Dad's partners usually got to the office around eight, but I was anxious and impatient. My father knew I'd planned to talk to my grandparents. Had he suspected I'd talk to Aunt Hannah too? Had he used my day out of town to cover his tracks?

I decided this was important enough that I could go against convention and call the other attorneys on their personal cell phones. Being a partner's daughter came with *some* perks.

I called Mitch Morgan first even though I doubted my mother would have used him. She'd found his womanizing distasteful, but I was the most familiar with him now. Since he'd asked me to take Hugo Burton's case, and I'd solved it, I hoped he'd be more likely to give me answers.

I pulled up his name on my phone and placed the call.

"Harper," Mitch said, his voice full of sympathy. "Once again, I'm *so* sorry about your mother. How are you doing?"

"I'm hanging in there," I said. "And that's actually why I'm calling."

"Oh? Don't worry about your job. You take off as much time as you need."

"Thank you, I really appreciate it, but that's not why I'm calling either." I paused. "It occurred to me that since my parents were separated, my mother might have updated her will."

"Oh," he said, sounding surprised. "I suppose she might have."

"I take it you didn't update it for her."

He chuckled softly. "No, Sarah Jane's never been too fond of me, but I can look her up in the system and see if I find something."

"Thank you," I said. "I haven't found a will in her house, but if she changed it recently, she might not have a copy here. Do you want me to call you back once you get to the office?"

"No need," he said good-naturedly. "I came in early. I'm looking it up right now." The sound of the clicking filled the silence for several seconds before he said, "I'm not seeing anything. Only the will she created with your father about fifteen years ago."

Disappointment hit me hard. "Okay. Thanks for checking, Mitch."

"Although…" he said, drawing out the word.

"Yeah?"

"It's no secret your mother wasn't my biggest fan, so it stands to reason she wouldn't have asked me to draw up a new will, but she might have asked John David. They were much friendlier. And if he changed it, he probably did it on his own time, which would explain why it's not in the system."

"Do you do that often?" I asked, thinking about my father's off-the-books deals. "Create contracts on your own time?"

"We try not to, but for simple things like this, we can and do. John David probably didn't even bill her, especially since he and your father haven't been seeing eye to eye lately."

That caught my attention. "Why aren't they getting along?" I sure hadn't caught wind of it, but then again, I hadn't been working in the office long.

"I have no idea," he said with a sigh. "But your father can be mercurial, and John David is as steady as they come. I think he gets tired of the drama."

I never would have described my father as mercurial and dramatic. Turned out I didn't know him at all. Then again, my entire view of him came from my childhood, and what child truly knows their parent?

"Thanks, Mitch. I'll call John David."

"No problem," he said. "And I know this pales in comparison to everything you're dealing with, but you did a great job with the Hugo Burton case. I never expected you'd get it wrapped up so quickly. I'll have more cases for you once you get back to work."

"Thanks." While I was eager for the work, I had no idea whether that offer would still stand if things went south with my father. I hung up and decided to call John David on his cell too. While I didn't have his number in my phone, it was easily accessible with my mother's address book.

"John David Hightower," he answered, sounding professional.

"John David," I said, "This is Harper Adams."

"Oh. Harper." He sounded surprised, then lowered his voice. "I suppose I know why you're calling."

"About my mother's will?"

He exhaled an exaggerated sigh. "Yes, thank God you came to me. Your mother asked me to change her will, but I could only give you a copy if you asked for it."

That fit what I suspected was my mother's agenda.

"And I was hoping you'd ask me for it before your father files probate. We'd contest the first will, of course, but it would get messy and with your father and me in the same firm…"

"It would put you in an awkward situation," I finished.

"Exactly. Sarah Jane knew it might be a possibility. She offered to see someone else if I was uncomfortable, but I assured her I'd take Paul on." His voice hardened as he finished the sentence.

"I take it you and my father haven't been getting along?"

"That's an understatement."

"Funny," I said. "I never picked up on it in the office. Or even when you came over for dinner at my parent's house back in February."

"We've tried to keep things civil in the office, and we didn't have a problem in February."

"If it's not too personal to ask, why were you two having problems now?"

"Let's just say I didn't approve of some of the company he kept," he said, his words tight and clipped.

"Was he having an affair?" I asked.

He hesitated. "I have no proof, but I saw him with another woman, and it was clear he was trying to be secretive."

My stomach dropped. "Can I ask where you saw them?"

"I went fishing in the city park early one Sunday morning. When I pulled into the parking lot in front of the lake, I saw two cars parked side by side, about a space apart. I parked a few spaces away. As I was getting my gear out of the trunk, I saw your father getting out of one of the cars and into the other. It was his car. Then the first car left, and as it drove past, I saw that the driver was an attractive woman. He must have seen me, because he confronted me the next day in the office. He told me it wasn't how it looked, but a few days later, I heard he'd left your mother, and about a week after that, Sarah Jane came to me, asking me to create a new will for her. She said I had to keep it from Paul, and if I couldn't, she'd go somewhere else." His voice hardened. "I told her I had no problem at all. But it was the contents of her will that took me by surprise."

"Is there something about a safe deposit box?" I asked, then held my breath.

"Actually … yes."

"Thank God," I muttered. "She left me a key without any information on how to access it."

"It's all in her will," he said. "I'm pulling into the office right now. I can email it to you as soon I get settled at my desk. I suspect the copy she signed is in the box."

"Thanks, John David. That would be great. But, before you go"—I drew a breath—"do you know the identity of the woman my father is having an affair with?"

"No," he said, "and while she was attractive, she didn't fit the stereotypical mid-life crisis affair partner. She looked like she was in her fifties."

So far, she fit the description of the woman who'd shown up at my mother's house. "I know this is a lot to ask, but if I text you a photo of a woman, can you tell me if it's the woman who met my father?"

"You have a photo?" A hard edge filled his voice. "I'd be happy to."

We hung up, and I texted the photo. Seconds later, he texted back.

*That's her.*

The mix of emotions caught me off guard. At least we knew she had a connection to my father, but I realized I'd still been hoping he hadn't been having an affair. Funny, after all the other crap I'd learned about him—including the fact he'd slept with a woman years ago—I was still disappointed in him.

Of course, there was a chance he didn't have a romantic relationship with her, but the evidence wasn't looking good for his innocence.

I signed into my law office account on the laptop, and a few minutes later, the email pinged. I opened it, then opened the attached document titled "Sarah Jane Adams Last Will and Testament." I started scanning the pages, holding my breath. She hadn't left me much, not that she had much of her own to give. She gave me her personal bank account, her jewelry … and access to a safe deposit box at a bank in Wolford.

But that was all I needed.

## Chapter 26

I went inside to see if James was up yet. The house was quiet, and his bedroom door was closed. I was starting to get hungry, so I checked the fridge and the cabinets for breakfast food, finding eggs, bacon, and bread. I spread some aluminum foil on a cookie sheet and spread out six pieces of bacon, then set the pan in the oven and turned it on. I didn't want to start the eggs or toast until James was up, so I freshened up my coffee and walked over to the photo on the mantel. There was something about the other girl in it that pinged my memories, but I couldn't figure out why. Then it hit me.

Neely Kate was J.R. Simmons's daughter, albeit illegitimate.

Which meant Joe Simmons was her half-brother.

And Joe had a four-year-old daughter with Rose Gardner. I pulled out my phone and searched for Rose Gardner, then pulled up the article about her nursery I'd found last week, scrolling down until I found the photo of Rose, Joe and their two children.

The girl in the photo was Hope Simmons.

I wasn't sure what to do with that information. It made sense that the two cousins would have their photo taken together, but why would Neely Kate send him a photo of both girls? Why not just her daughter?

Or maybe I was just reading too much into it.

I walked to the window and looked outside, thinking to myself that James had the right idea. He spent most of his life at the tavern, but when he wasn't at work, he had the perfect place to relax and escape from everything.

"Enjoyin' the view?" James said from behind me.

I turned to look at him, wondering whether I'd see contempt in his eyes. Instead, he seemed open and relaxed.

The tension in my shoulders eased. "I am. I've been sitting on the porch getting some work done. My father's law partner saw my dad get out of a car about a month ago, and it was driven by the woman who showed up at my mother's house last week. He suspected my dad was having an affair."

"Does he know who she is?"

I shook my head. "No, but he also created a new will for my mother about three weeks ago. In the will, she granted me access to her safe deposit box."

"That's good news," he said, walking into the kitchen and pulling a coffee cup out of the cabinet.

My stomach twisted as I watched him fill it with coffee. "James, about last night…"

He held up a hand. "What's done is done."

"I don't like how we left things."

He took the cup over the peninsula and put his hand on the counter. "You were right. I was keeping secrets, and you were tryin' to solve a case. Of course you'd call Deveraux."

"I don't want you to think I'm using you or setting you up."

He held my gaze. "I don't."

I watched him, not sure I believed him. If our roles were reversed, I'd be watching my back. How could he forget it had happened? He *shouldn't* forget. There was a good chance Deveraux might start breathing down his neck.

"But Deveraux…"

He gave me a grim smile. "There's a reason Deveraux is breathing down my neck. I can tell you part of it but not everything. The fact is, I can't tell you everything about my life, because some of my secrets protect other people. I refuse to put them at risk."

"I'd never ask you to."

"And that's part of the reason I've decided to be more open. If I tell you something that could end up hurting someone, I believe you'd keep it to yourself."

"How can you be so sure?" I asked. "I called Mason Deveraux."

"I'd already suspected you did," he said. "Even before you told me."

"*What?*"

"I checked the number on your phone yesterday afternoon and had Carter look into it. It's Deveraux's personal cell."

My mouth dropped open. "You snooped on my phone?"

He grimaced. "I didn't snoop, but I checked the number when it vibrated while you were asleep. I thought it might be your father or your friend Louise. I made note of it. I sent it to Carter after our fight, but it took him a few hours to get back to me last night." He grimaced. "Right before we pulled up to my house. I admit, when he told me who it belonged to, I was furious, but I decided to see if you'd tell me." He shrugged. "Of course, at that point, I only knew that he'd called you and you hadn't answered. I didn't know you'd been the one to initiate the call, or that you'd talked to him after I left. Now I know both."

"So you trust me because I confessed?"

"You had no reason to confess, other than to prove I can trust you."

"What if I only confessed because I thought you'd find out and I wanted to get in front of the situation?"

"Is that why you did it?"

I flinched. "It occurred to me that you'd probably think I betrayed you if you found out. But mostly I wanted to warn you that Deveraux might be sniffing around so you can watch your back."

He gestured toward me with his cup. "I believe you."

It felt too easy, which set me on edge. We both had trouble trusting—would we always be suspicious of one another?

"So why is Deveraux out to get you?" I asked.

"He blames me for losing his fiancée."

"Rose Gardner?"

"Yep."

"*Are* you to blame?"

He hesitated as though considering his answer. "If I'm honest, yes, I'm completely to blame. She had a skill set I could use to my advantage, and in return, I agreed to help find out who was trying to kill Deveraux."

"That doesn't sound like it was your fault."

"It depends on how you spin it," he said stoically. "But the truth is, when I first started using her skill set, I forced her into it."

"You blackmailed her?"

"I was in a precarious situation, and she came to me asking for help with something. The first instance was a fair trade of services, but I contacted her again and, in that instance … let's just say I forced her hand."

I let that sink in. He'd been a crime boss. A little ruthlessness shouldn't surprise me. "But she ultimately decided to work with you?"

He was silent for a moment. "Turned out she was very good at it and part of her liked it."

"You both took down J.R. Simmons?"

"Simmons wanted Deveraux taken out, and I wanted Simmons taken out. It benefitted us both."

"Simmons had Rose kidnapped?"

"Yeah, but we used it to our advantage." Something about

the way he said that told me he wouldn't be expanding on the subject.

While I wanted to ask more questions, I decided to accept what he'd told me.

"You haven't asked what her skill set was," he said, eyeing me carefully.

"If you wanted me to know, you'd tell me," I said. "You mentioned that some of your secrets are to protect people. I can't imagine it would help Rose's public image if it was widely known she'd worked with a crime boss. I suspect you're protecting her because she helped you."

He was silent for a moment, then said, "You're right. There's no reason for her involvement to get out. It would only hurt her."

There was fondness in his voice, and I wondered if he had the photo of Rose's daughter on his mantel out of sentiment.

Did James regret not having a family of his own? Was he living vicariously through the people he'd grown fond of?

"Are you still in contact with Rose?" I asked.

He coughed, then said derisively, "No."

"For the same reason you're not in contact with Jed? To protect her?"

"That and her husband's not too fond of me." He sighed. "I've found it's better to leave the past in the past."

I wasn't so sure he was right, but I didn't feel like calling him on it. Not that I was one to talk. I'd put my own past in the rearview mirror when I'd left Little Rock.

I made breakfast while I told him everything I'd found before he'd gotten up. He sat on the other side of the peninsula, working his way through two cups of coffee while I talked, his gaze tracking my movements around the kitchen.

I deliberately avoided looking at him, though I couldn't help noticing the way his long-sleeve T-shirt clung to his shoulders and hugged his biceps. Or the way he leaned back in his stool, all casual confidence. Like he owned every space he occupied.

Yesterday, in front of my grandparents' house, I'd come dangerously close to doing something I'd probably regret. Or maybe not regret at all, which made it even more dangerous. The more distance I kept between us, the better.

"So, you're going to the bank after we finish here?" he asked as I set his plate on the peninsula. I placed mine on the opposite side, still needing space. Sitting next to him didn't feel like the wisest idea.

But he must have read my mind—or thought the same thing—because he picked up both plates and moved them to the table, placing us directly across from each other.

He scooped up the silverware on the counter while I freshened my coffee, trying not to read into the fact he wanted me to sit down.

Oh, wait. He'd asked me a question.

*Get it together, Harper. You're acting like a horny teenager.*

"That's my plan," I said, sitting at the table, across from him. "I think I might also call Detective Jones, the guy I worked with on Burton's case, and ask him if he knows why the Jackson Creek police investigated Ambrose's death and not the sheriff's department."

"You're not worried it'll get back to your father?" he asked. We were sitting closer than we'd been at the peninsula, and I caught a hint of cedar.

"I'll say my aunt mentioned hearing about someone else going off that bridge, so I looked it up. It might come across as suspicious, but I'll try to spin like I'm just curious. Maybe along the lines of I was relieved the Jackson Creek Police Department hadn't investigated."

He nodded his approval. "Then what?"

I made the mistake of looking into his dark brown eyes, and I found myself mesmerized for a moment. Something flickered in his gaze—something I wasn't ready to name—

before I jerked my eyes back down to my plate, my pulse unsteady. "I suppose it depends on what I find in the box," I said, my voice a little too tight. "I need to figure out if I want to confront my father."

He was about to say something when my phone rang. I picked it up from the table and turned it over. The name on the screen made my breath catch.

*Keith.*

My ex-partner, both professional and personal.

I felt like what little I'd eaten was about to make a reappearance. I couldn't imagine why he was calling. I hadn't heard from Keith since November, after his last attempt to coerce me into lying about the shooting. To say things hadn't ended well would be an understatement.

So why was he calling me now?

I considered ignoring him, then I remembered Mason Deveraux had asked around about me. Going to my old partner was the best way to get information.

*Dammit.*

I answered the call, squaring my shoulders as I prepared myself to deal with his gaslighting. At the last second, I turned on the speaker and set the phone on the table. Whatever he was calling about, I wanted James to hear.

"Hello, Keith," I said, my voice cold.

James shifted in his chair. His brow rose, but he said nothing.

"Harper," Keith said, his voice full of forced warmth. "How are you?"

A year ago, I would have fallen for it. Hell, I *had*. But we were way past that now. "Cut the bullshit, Keith. You don't give a single fuck how I am. Why are you calling?"

Keith paused, probably surprised by my tone. "I can't believe you're saying I don't care. After everything we've been through?"

James's jaw tightened, his fingers tightening around his mug.

I shook my head, my anger rising. "I'm not wasting my time going through our history, so once again, why did you call?"

"I heard about your mother."

"Did you now?" I countered, not bothering to hide the venom in my voice.

"I know you two weren't close," he continued, ignoring my sarcasm. "But I can only imagine what you're going through."

I rolled my eyes. James shifted again, now bracing his forearms on the table, his body tense.

"You care what I'm going through *now*?" I asked, pissed that I'd taken the bait.

"You know that I cared," Keith said in that soft, manipulative tone he'd always used when he wanted something. "We can't have shared what we did without it leaving a mark."

James released a low growl, barely audible, but unmistakable.

"That's funny," I said. "Since narcissists usually only care about themselves." I forced myself to calm down. I needed to regain control. "Which means you're calling for another reason, so again, stop wasting my time and tell me why you're calling me after five months."

"You're wrong, Harper," he said in the sultry tone he'd used when he was trying to seduce me. "I do care about you. I miss you."

Once upon a time, it had worked. Now it filled me with disgust. I just rolled my eyes.

Across the table, James's knuckles whitened around his mug.

I stayed silent, refusing to fall into whatever trap he was laying out.

"Like I said," he continued when he realized I wasn't

going to respond. "I heard about your mother, and I was checking on you."

"I'm fine. Thank you for calling," I said in a professional tone. "So if that's all, I'll let you go."

"Wait."

A grim smile of satisfaction spread across my face. He knew how to play me, but I knew how to play him too. "Was there something else?"

James leaned in slightly, posture alert, like he was waiting for the first sign of a threat.

"I got a call yesterday."

"I'm sure you got a dozen calls yesterday."

"Fair enough," he conceded, his tone shifting back to business. "But the caller was asking about you specifically."

"Who was it?" I knew who had called, but I was curious to get his take on it.

"Someone from the Attorney General's office. He was asking about your performance as a detective."

I felt the tension in the room shift—tight, electric—but I kept my eyes on my phone, my expression neutral.

"Really?" I asked. "And did you tell him I was reckless and … how did you put it? Prone to flights of fancy?"

"That was wrong of me," he said, his tone shifting into something almost apologetic. "I was upset that you were so adamant and wouldn't take the union lawyer's advice. I was trying to save your career."

"How magnanimous of you."

Across the table, James shifted again, his expression unreadable, but his jaw flexed.

"Harper," he said with a heavy sigh. "Why is it so hard for you to believe I care about you?"

"Stop."

"No," he said, becoming more insistent. "I love you. You know that."

A lump filled my throat, not because I loved him, but

because I'd been stupid enough to believe him. I'd learned the hard way that Keith Kemper only loved one person—himself.

I shoved my emotions aside and focused on the fact that his declaration had very odd timing. "Why tell me this now? After five months?"

"I never made a secret of the way I feel about you, but you cut me out of your life. That was your choice, not mine."

"We both know it happened because you refused to accept my decision to stand by my word."

James released a low grunt, almost like he was biting back a comment.

"Look," Keith said, adopting his *I know better than you* tone. "That's all water under the bridge."

James's coffee cup hit the table with a loud thunk.

"And you're right," Keith continued, "I called for a reason other than your mother. I was worried after the prosecutor called about you. Are you in trouble?"

"Nope," I said tightly. "And he was likely calling you as a reference since I was the one who contacted him about a case last week."

"A case?" he asked in surprise. "Are you working for the police department there? You always claimed the Jackson Creek police were corrupt."

*Claimed.* How had I never realized how much he belittled my insights?

"No," I said, ignoring his jab. "I'm a private investigator, and I was working a case for a law firm and thought Mr. Deveraux might have information about a possible suspect. But it turned out to be a dead end. I solved the case last Saturday. He returned my call right after I found out about my mother's death, so I didn't answer. I suspect he was following up."

"So you're not in trouble?"

"Why would I be in trouble?"

James snorted, shaking his head with a muttered curse under his breath, unmistakably aimed at Keith.

Keith was silent for a moment, as though trying to figure out what to say next. "I miss you, Harper," he finally said, using the warm tone that had often convinced me to go along with what he'd wanted. "If you're a private detective now, then you'd have more business in Little Rock. I can even throw some cases your way."

"You're suggesting I move back to Little Rock?" I asked, my voice sharp with disbelief.

"I know you're hurt by everything that happened last year, but yeah. I miss you. I'd like to start over."

Keith knew how much I hated Jackson Creek, and that I'd loved living in Little Rock. But there was no way I was going back to be with him. He was delusional. Not after how things ended.

"Thanks for your *generous* offer," I said in a tight voice, "but I'm happy where I am. Was there anything else you wanted? Because I need to get back to my case."

"You're working another case?" he asked, clearly surprised.

"I'll take that as a no." I ended the call and stared at my plate, trying to figure out what had just happened.

"Your ex, obviously," James said in a dry tone, lifting his coffee to his lips. He held his mug in a death grip.

"No need to tell me I was an idiot to fall for his shit. I figured it out eventually."

"Narcissists know the right things to say."

"True enough," I said, swallowing a wave of self-disgust.

"Do you think he really wants you back?"

I considered it. "Maybe there's a small part of him that wants me back, but no, I don't think he really does."

"So why suggest it?" His tone was casual, but his posture was rigid.

"I have no idea. Obviously, Deveraux's call triggered it,

but why?" I shook my head. "It doesn't matter right now. I need to focus on my mother's case."

He set his mug down then looked me in the eyes. "Are you okay?"

My neck bristled at his question. "Because an asshole from my past called me? I'm fine."

"He said he loves you." His face was guarded, his eyes hard.

"He doesn't love me," I scoffed. "And I doubt he ever did. He only loves himself." I picked up a triangle of buttered toast and took a bite. "Our breakfast is getting cold."

I could see the question on James's face, the one he didn't want to ask.

Did I still love Keith?

Because you could realize someone was terrible to and for you and still love them. I knew that too well.

"I didn't love him either," I said quietly, my voice breaking. "I'm not sure what I felt, but it wasn't love."

James looked like he wanted to say more but wisely picked up his fork and started to eat.

Keith Kemper was the last person I wanted to think about, but I couldn't ignore the creeping unease.

Why was he calling now, and why did he want me back in Little Rock?

# Chapter 27

After we finished breakfast and cleaned up, James helped me print my mother's will and we discussed how to work out the rest of the day. I didn't have a car, but it didn't seem smart for us to be seen together in town.

"You can drop me off at the tavern, then let me know what you find," he said. "We're short staffed for the lunch rush today, so Misti'll appreciate the help."

"Are you sure?" I asked.

"You're askin' if I think you're gonna keep things from me?" He met my gaze. "I trust you."

I half-expected him to look pained, but his expression was sincere. Could I trust this change of sentiment? I hated that I questioned his motives, but if I couldn't trust my ex-partner-- then I'd be stupid not to wonder about an ex-crime boss who'd admitted to using an innocent woman because of her unique skill set.

He must have seen the questions in my eyes, because he looked like he wanted to say something. But after the brutal beatings of the past few two days, my heart was too raw to deal with anything else.

I snatched up my bag. "Let's go."

We were silent as he drove to the tavern. I found myself studying the lines of his profile when he wasn't looking.

His driveway was about a quarter of a mile long, and it twisted multiple times, so it was hidden from the county road. It took us less than ten minutes to get to the tavern, and when I commented on it, he said, "I work a lot of late nights, so I appreciate the short commute."

"If someone looks up the property records, they wouldn't see your name, would they?" I asked.

He grinned. "What good are multiple businesses if not to help create a paper trail?"

I wanted to ask what else he owned, but all in good time.

He pulled into the parking lot and put the car in park, leaving it running. "If you need anything, give me a call. And if you need a gun, there's one in the glove box. It has a fully loaded clip, and there's a spare one in there too."

I cocked a brow. "Is it registered?"

"Of course," he said with a mischievous grin. "Can you imagine how long the multiple law enforcement officers who pull me over would lock me up for if they found unregistered guns in my car?"

Guns. Plural. But I didn't ask about the others. If this one was registered, the others were too. As for why he might need more than a single handgun? That seemed like a question for later too.

"Thanks."

He gave me a long look, and for a moment, the air felt heavier. "Be careful, Harper. I can't help thinking your call to Deveraux may have stirred up some shit."

"I know," I said, apologetically. "And you know I'm sorry."

"I didn't mean for me." He gave me another long look then got out and walked into the back door of the building without a backward glance.

I watched him walk away, noticing the set of his shoulders. I felt an unexpected pang of something I didn't understand. I told myself it was because I was stunned by his suggestion that my call to Deveraux could come back to bite *me*. Maybe Deveraux might think I was guilty by association to James, but I was pretty sure that wasn't what he'd meant.

Keith's call must have spooked us both.

I was still sitting in the passenger seat, so I walked around the car and got behind the wheel, then headed to Wolford.

Once I got to the bank, I carried my papers inside and walked up to a teller. "I'm here to access a safe deposit box."

"What's the box number?" she asked.

"One-seventy-two." Thank God for the will.

"Okay, follow me," she said, walking toward an open vault. A metal box was on the table, and she used a key to open it and flip through small, index-sized cards. She pulled one out and looked it over. Recognition filled her eyes. "This belongs to Sarah Jane Adams."

"I'm her daughter," I said. "Her will states that I get access. And I have a key." I held out the papers toward her.

"I don't know…" she said, looking leery. "I'll need to get my manager."

"That's okay, Megan," a woman said from behind me. "I'll take care of this. You head on back to the counter." The woman took the teller's place and lowered her voice. "Harper?"

Given my reputation, it wasn't unusual for people to know who I was, and they usually weren't happy to be in my presence. But I'd hoped to escape that attitude in Wolford. I steeled my back. "Yes."

She moved closer and lowered her voice. "I'm Jill, the bank's assistant manager. Sarah Jane was in about three weeks ago and opened a bank account and a safe deposit box. She put your name on both and said she'd get you to sign the signature card. She asked that I keep everything hush-hush. Something about going through a divorce, although I warned her that even though your name was on the checking account she opened, her husband might be entitled to half until the divorce was final. She said she was okay with that, but then she never brought your signature card back. You said you have a will granting access?"

"It's a copy," I said. "I think the original might be in her box."

She took the papers, gave them a cursory glance, then handed them back. "Good enough for me." She centered the signature card the other woman had pulled out on the table. "I'll just have you sign on the line below your mother's."

I signed under the two times my mother had accessed the box.

"I will warn you," she said as she picked up the card. "Your father was in here a few days ago, trying to access the safe deposit box."

My mouth dropped open. How did he know about it?

"He said he had a key, but Sarah Jane had been so adamant about keeping the contents away from him. All he had was a copy of her old will, so I told him he was out of luck. He said he'd be back with an injunction, but so far, he hasn't returned."

So, he knew about the new box and really wanted the contents, but how had he found out? I know John David hadn't told him. Had he known about my mother's new will? Had he purposely sent me to my grandparents, thinking they might have a copy of the new will or a means to get into the box?

Unaware of my inner turmoil, she gave me a grim smile. "Okay. Let's open your box."

I followed her into the vault and watched as she inserted her key, then she took my key and inserted it into the second lock before turning both keys. She pulled the box from the wall and set it on a table in the center of the small space.

"I'll give you some privacy," she said as she walked out of the room.

My heart hammered in my chest as I opened the lid, trying to prepare myself for whatever I might find.

The box revealed a manila envelope with my name written in my mother's neat handwriting in the center. I pulled it out and opened the flap, revealing a thick stack of documents. I removed the stack, not surprised to see the original copy of her new will on top. I turned it over onto the table, about to examine the next page when the teller I'd met walked over to the table outside the vault with an older woman following close behind her.

I stared in shock as I realized it was the woman my father was possibly having an affair with.

The woman was staring openly at me, and when she saw recognition on my face, she abruptly turned and hurried for the exit.

I snatched up the stack of papers and started to go after her, but the teller blocked my path. "You can't just go. We need to place your box back in the vault and return your key."

"That's okay," I said, trying to get dodge around her. "I don't need it anymore."

She blocked me again. "Maybe so, but we need to follow the rules."

The woman was already out the door, and I was desperate to catch up to her, so I shoved the teller aside and ran for the double glass doors. But I stopped abruptly outside the bank, because there was no sign of her. Not even a car pulling out of the parking lot.

How could I get this close and lose her?

I ran my hand over my head as I scanned the area again, forcing myself to accept she was gone.

I went back inside and came face to face with the fuming teller.

"Who was that woman?" I asked.

"What woman?" she snapped.

"The woman who was just here and ran out."

"I'm sorry," she said, her eyes blazing as she shot me a glare. "I'm not allowed to divulge confidential information."

"I'm not asking you to show me the contents of her box," I said, getting pissed. "I just want to know who she was."

"And as I told you—" the teller spat.

"Is there a problem?" Jill, the assistant manager, asked.

The teller flung her hand toward me in disgust. "This woman is demanding to know personal and confidential information about a customer. And *of course*, I refused to tell her. Then she threw a fit."

I adamantly shook my head. "That's not what happened, but the woman who was just here might have information about my mother's death."

The teller's eyes widened.

"Why do you think she has information about her death?" Jill asked in a guarded tone.

"I can't tell you much," I said, then gestured to the teller. "Just as you can't tell me much, but that woman was likely the last person to see my mother alive, and we have some questions. If you could give me any information that might help me locate her, it would be greatly beneficial."

The teller gave her manager a questioning look.

"Frannie's right," Jill said regretfully. "We can't give you any identifying information, but Frannie can tell you anything else she said."

I quickly nodded.

Frannie made a face. "She didn't even give her name. Just told me she needed in box one-seventy-two. She had a key."

"That's my mother's box," I said. "Did you remember that when she asked to get into the box?"

"I don't memorize the box numbers," Frannie said.

"Did she show you ID?" I asked.

Frannie's upper lip curled. "*You* didn't show ID."

She had a point. "Is there anything else you can tell me?" I asked, feeling desperate. I'd been so close to her and I still had nothing. "If she didn't give her name, then I'm worried she was going to forge my mother's signature to get to the box."

Which meant she and my father were working together.

I felt like I was going to be sick.

"That's a very serious accusation," Jill said solemnly.

"Why else would she have given you my mother's box number?" I asked. "Especially after my father tried to get in a few days ago, and you turned him away. He threatened an injunction, with takes time and money. If he could send someone else in…" I let the accusation hang in the air.

The manager nodded slowly. "I assure you that we will be extra diligent with your mother's box from here on out." Her gaze dropped to my chest.

I was still clutching the papers and envelope to my chest like I was in the middle of the ocean and they were my life preserver.

I shook my head. "No need. I'm taking it all with me."

Jill looked like she wanted to argue, but then her face softened. "I'm sorry you lost your mother. I hope you find what you're looking for in whatever she left you."

I hoped I found it too, but knowing my mother, I doubted it would be that easy.

# Chapter 28

Unsure of what to do next, I headed back to the tavern. I still hadn't looked at the papers, although every thirty seconds or so, I asked myself why. I could pull over and go through them, looking for anything that would justify murdering my mother.

But I realized I didn't want to do it alone. I wanted to do it with Malcolm.

So, I drove, my hands tense on the wheel while my mind raced over the implications of Dad's potential mistress showing up at the bank. It was possible she'd followed me, but my first theory still seemed the most likely—that she'd shown up intending to impersonate my mother. While the assistant manager knew my mother was dead, it was possible the teller wouldn't have made the connection.

What would have happened if I'd showed up half an hour later?

I pulled into the tavern parking lot, scooped up the paperwork, clutching it to my chest with one hand, then headed to the unlocked back door. I peeked in James's office, and when I saw it was empty, I headed into the dining room. It was still several hours until they opened, but I knew they had plenty of prep work to get ready for the day.

I found him sitting in a booth with his open laptop, staring at the screen with a look of concentration. When I walked in, his face lifted, his eyes widening in surprise.

"You're back already." His gaze dropped to the papers in my hand. "I take it you got in. What did you find?"

"I haven't looked yet. I wanted to do it with you. Especially after my father's mistress showed up at the bank, asking to open my mother's safe deposit box." My fingers curled into a fist at my side. "She said she had a key."

James's gaze caught the movement, then lifted to my face. "Your mother's copy?" His voice was low. Not soft, just careful, like he knew the last thing I wanted was to feel weak.

Funny, I hadn't stopped to consider how I *felt* about it. "Yeah. Maybe? I don't know."

"What happened?"

I filled him in on everything, including my theory about her presence.

"Maybe she got the key from your father," he said.

"Maybe not." I gave a slow shake of my head. "What if she got it from my mother? She was in the house, and we don't know what happened after they left together. The key could've been in my mother's purse or her car. The woman might've taken it before the car was dumped into the river."

"Then why didn't she try to get in the box sooner?"

"If she wasn't working with my father, then maybe she didn't know which bank to go to."

He frowned. "Then how'd she figure it out now? Because if she followed you, you're right that it would've made more sense to wait until you came outside and take the papers then."

"Yeah." I sat across from him in the booth. "I don't know."

He drummed his fingers on the table. "If she disappeared after she left the bank, someone must've been waiting for her.

They probably drove off before you made it outside. Did you ask the bank manager to see video footage?"

"No. She was sympathetic about the box, but I doubt she'd pull surveillance footage without a warrant."

He nodded, his jaw tightening. I could see he was processing this, trying to put it together.

Silence settled between us. We were getting close to piecing everything together—I could feel it. But I couldn't shake the sense that my father was one step ahead of us.

"You could report it to the sheriff's department," he said, slowly, like he didn't like the idea but felt obligated to suggest it. "Impersonating your mother has to be a crime."

"But *did* she impersonate my mother?" I countered. "The teller said she never gave her name, just asked to get into box one-seventy-two. Even if they find her, she could say she got the box number wrong."

"They still might be able to find out who she is."

I narrowed my eyes. "And if something happens to her, I'd be their prime suspect."

He gave me a pointed look. "What would happen to her?"

I met his unwavering gaze. "If I bring the sheriff into this, we lose all control of the investigation."

"True," he said, thinking. "But they might be able to find her faster. Carter still hasn't turned up anything."

I shook my head. "No. We're doing this ourselves."

His eyes turned dark and serious. "Why?"

I swallowed hard, unsure how to answer. I knew what he was really asking: *What are you going to do when you find her?*

The truth was, I didn't know.

And that scared the hell out of me.

"No sheriff," I said, my voice low. My mouth had gone dry.

He held my gaze and said quietly, "Okay. No sheriff."

I nodded, the weight of my decision settling in my chest. I

wasn't committing to vigilante justice. Not yet. But I wasn't turning this over to the authorities either.

I had to see this through. And I wanted to do it with James.

"Well, you've got a stack of papers that could take down your father and we haven't even gone through them yet." James closed his laptop, the soft click of the lid punctuating his words. He slid out of his seat and sat next to me, close enough that the heat from his body brushed mine. "Let's take a look."

My breath caught, not just from fear of what we might find, but because James's thigh was a mere three inches from mine. Solid. Still. I caught the faint scent of cedar and leather.

The room felt too warm. Too confined.

I cleared my throat, worried the quiver in my voice would give me away. I needed to focus, not lust after a man I could never have. "The original, signed copy of my mother's will." I flipped the first stapled stack over on the table.

"You'll want to keep that safe," he murmured, his voice low and rough. "We'll lock it up in my safe when we're done here. Along with anything else that proves he's shady."

I nodded, then slid the stack of papers between us so we could read them at the same time. It was hard to concentrate with him so close, his shoulder brushing mine, but I reminded myself that I was trying to solve my mother's murder, not get laid.

I closed my eyes and took a deep breath, forcing myself to refocus—to find my mother's killer. Once I felt grounded, I opened my eyes and realized part of me wasn't ready to face what might be in those papers.

But I couldn't turn away either.

The top paper was a contract for the purchase of a company two years ago. The company, Copper Ridge, was sold to a corporation James and I had first heard about while investigating Hugo Burton's murder—Larkspur, LLC.

I sucked in a breath, lightheaded. "Larkspur."

Larkspur had purchased Hugo Burton's residential property when it went into foreclosure shortly after his disappearance. The land had sat vacant since Burton's disappearance five years ago. We'd tried to discover who was behind it, but Larkspur had been incorporated in New Mexico, a state that helped hide the true owners.

"Obviously your father had something to do with Larkspur," James said. "The question is whether he was working for them, or if he *is* Larkspur."

I didn't respond, unable to find the words.

"Never heard of Copper Ridge," James said, reaching across the table for his laptop. "Have you?"

I shook my head. "No." But the word came out in a croak.

He entered the name of the business, but nothing came up in a simple Google search. I swung the laptop in my direction and pulled up a PI site to repeat the search. A few seconds later, the name popped up.

"Copper Ridge was created five years ago, then sold to Larkspur two years ago," I said. Unlike Larkspur, it had been incorporated in Arkansas. Two names were listed as principals: but one name was familiar from our investigation of Hugo Burton's disappearance.

"Brett Colter," James said with a tone of satisfaction. "Fuckin' liar."

Colter was a local land developer, and his name had kept coming up during our investigation. At the time, he'd denied knowing anything about Larkspur.

"Do you recognize the other one?" I asked.

"Clive Norwood." He studied the screen for a moment, thinking. "He's from Little Rock. I'm pretty sure he had ties to J.R. Simmons."

"Wow," I said. Another thread tying my father to Simmons. "Simmons died several years before this sale."

"Your father drew up the paperwork," James said as he

started a search for Clive Norwood. "Maybe Simmons gave his name to a few friends."

The results showed Norwood owned a small chain of furniture stores in Little Rock, Bentonville, and El Dorado.

"A land developer and a furniture store owner own a consulting firm," I said, mulling it over. "What would they consult on?"

"Good question," James said with a grim smile. "Since they don't have a website and there's no mention of them on LinkedIn, I suspect it was a shell corporation."

"A shell corporation for what?"

"Anything," James said. "Drugs, money laundering, arms dealing. We'd need to see more, like their financials, to know for sure."

The next document in my mother's stack was a copy of the sale of a building in north Jackson Creek seven years prior. The contract had been drawn up by my father, and the purchaser had been one of my early suspects in Ava Peterman's kidnapping.

"Ricky Morris," I said, my stomach dropping. "This is for the laundromat, isn't it?"

"Suds and Duds," James said. "Yep."

The laundromat was a suspected drug front, and Ava Peterman's father, who was on the city council, had been trying to shut it down.

"Was Morris known for criminal activity before he opened the laundromat?" I asked.

"I wasn't here seven years ago."

I gave him a pointed look. There was no way he didn't know the man's history.

A smug look lit up his eyes. "He's been dabbling in drug dealing for a good twenty years. It's no secret."

"Then my father must have known."

"Unless he lived under a rock."

The next set of pages showed contracts for land and business purchases going back over twenty years. James said most of the people involved had ties to criminal activity.

We were down to the last few pages in the pile when we found paperwork for the formation of an LLC, Hollow Ridge Development, with three partners—my father, a man named Richard Bell, and Dale Ambrose.

I drew in a sharp breath. "Here's our connection to Ambrose."

"And a surname for the mysterious Richard."

A search for Hollow Ridge Development showed they had bought and sold multiple properties, and the accompanying sales spreadsheet showed that the properties had been sold for excessive profit. The corporation had been formed about thirty years ago, which meant my father had already been in deep while Andi and I thought he was Father of the Year.

"The question," I said carefully, letting it all sink in, "is whether Hollow Ridge started out clean and turned dirty later."

"And if it started out clean, was it turning corrupt that made them get rid of their partner, Ambrose?" James asked.

"Ambrose was killed twenty-five years ago," I said. "Let's see when it first started to look shady."

We examined the spreadsheet. The first suspicious sale was twenty-six years ago, and it had closed two weeks after Ambrose's "accident."

"This doesn't prove anything," I said with a groan. "The timing sure as hell is suspicious, but it's not enough to prove beyond a shadow of a doubt."

"Who says you need a jury?" James asked, his tone low and dangerous.

My blood turned cold. "We're talking about my father, James."

He held my gaze. "It's not just your father. This goes deeper than him. I know it in my gut."

I suspected his gut was right most of the time. He couldn't

have gotten so far in the criminal world otherwise. Especially with a ruthless, international organization like the Hardshaw Group.

The next page was a folded newspaper page, the paper yellowed and the print slightly faded. At the top left was a newspaper article about Dale Ambrose's car accident. In the margin, my mother had written *Hannah heard P talking to R two weeks prior.*

My mother had believed her sister and *still* cut her out of her life? Had she done it because she didn't want her sister judging her, or had she done it to protect her?

Had she been trying to protect all of us?

There were still a few more papers, so I moved on and studied the next contract. Everything else had been in chronological order, but this one was more recent. It was dated last September, and it recorded the purchase of a building in Little Rock. The seller's name was Black Claw, LLC.

James tensed but didn't say anything. I shot him a questioning glance. Obviously the transaction meant something to him, but he kept it to himself as he turned the page.

Documentation for the creation of Black Claw was next, and of course it had been filed in New Mexico. I scrolled through the paperwork until I came to the names of the principal, Gerald Knox.

"Do you know who that is?" I turned to look at James. My heart skipped a beat when I saw the look on his face. His shoulders were locked, and every muscle in his body had gone rigid. "Malcolm?"

The corner of his mouth hitched up ever so slightly. "I think we just found J.R. Simmons's replacement."

Malcolm's reaction told me what I'd already suspected.

Gerald Knox was a hell of a lot worse.

## Chapter 29

I rolled the name around in my head for a few seconds. "I've never heard of him. It seems like I would have when I was a cop if he's that powerful."

"Not necessarily," James said, leaning back in his seat. "He likes to keep a low profile. He uses shell corporations and acts as a silent partner in a lot of businesses. I guarantee you Black Claw isn't his only secret LLC."

"So what makes you think he's taken over for Simmons?"

He tapped the address on the contract. "Simmons used to own this place. It's one hell of a coincidence that Knox is selling a property Simmons once owned."

"You think he bought it after Simmons died?"

"Or he was already a silent partner."

"What did Simmons do with it?"

Malcolm tilted his head, his eyes distant. "Last I heard, he was using it as a drop site. No one really knew what for, and most people knew better than to ask."

I raised an eyebrow. "Even you?"

He gave a dry laugh. "I had other issues to deal with."

"Such as?" I prodded.

He studied me for a moment. "I quit Simmons's years

before we busted him. By then, he was hell bent on destroyin' me, and I was hell bent on gettin' him out of my county. I kept tabs on what he was doing in other places, but I didn't have the bandwidth to dig into that one. The way I saw it, if I took him out, it all fell down." His face hardened. "Turns out I was naïve."

I scoffed. "That's not a word I'd use to describe you."

"And yet it fits."

I waited for him to elaborate, but instead he said, "After Simmons toppled, whoever took over has been a lot more careful to keep it all on the down low. But what's happening now is worse than what Simmons did."

"You've said that before but never elaborated why."

His voice dropped a notch. "I suspect Simmons's replacement is involved in human trafficking."

I couldn't hide my surprise. While I knew human trafficking took place in Little Rock, I'd never even heard whispers of something like that going on while I was on the force. "You think Gerald Knox is involved in trafficking people?"

"I have no proof, but he's been on my short list. Knox is third or fourth generation in the family business. His grandfather was a bootlegger."

"There are records of that?"

The corner of his mouth lifted. "My grandmother was a moonshiner. She knew the man, and said he was as ruthless as they come. I've heard his son was just as bad. Stands to reason the next in line would follow suit."

I tried to picture Malcolm's grandmother running moonshine and came up short. "Did she teach you how to make it?"

"Let's just say moonshine wasn't needed by the time I came around, but she taught me other things."

"Like what?"

He met my gaze. "Survival."

I wanted to ask where she'd been when his father was beating the shit out of him and his family, but the fondness in his voice stopped me. He'd told me that his grandparents didn't give two shits about him. Was she a maternal grandmother he rarely saw?

Now didn't seem the time to ask him about it.

"You said Gerald Knox's father was ruthless," I said. "Where is he now?"

"Rutherford Knox was killed about fifteen years ago, and Gerald—Gerry—took his place. I know Gerry worked with Simmons."

I looked at the stack of papers. "So, either my mother's been collecting evidence for years … or she found it recently. If it weren't for the newspaper clipping, I'd assume the latter. There's no way my father would have kept something this incriminating."

"Even he wouldn't be that stupid," James muttered.

His insult stung, but I kept my mouth shut. My father didn't deserve my loyalty.

"But where does the probable mistress fit in?" I asked.

"Good question. Maybe it's time for you to confront your father."

The thought of talking to him made me physically ill, but James was right. It was time to tell my father what I knew and see what he had to say for himself.

"And after you talk to him?" James asked. "What then?"

I tried to imagine what came next and drew a blank. "I don't know. I need to talk to him first."

His jaw hardened. "I'll be with you when you do."

"You don't trust me?" I asked, discouraged. I thought we'd come further than that.

"I don't trust *him*," he said, his eyes glittering with danger. "If he killed your mother, what's to stop him from trying to do the same to you?"

I tried to picture a world in which my father physically harmed me and just couldn't see it. He'd disappointed me. Betrayed me. But he'd never physically hurt me, not even spankings when we were kids. But I also knew emotions were blinding me.

I had to treat this like any other case. If the victim's husband killed his wife, then it wasn't out of the realm of possibility that he'd hurt his daughter to protect his secrets. Or have someone else do it.

A well of despair bubbled up, but I shoved it down. We were too close to the truth for me to lose it now.

Still, I'd have to go to this meeting as his daughter, not as an impossible-to-remain-impartial investigator.

"He won't open up if you're there," I said, keeping my voice steady. "I need to talk to him alone."

His jaw set and something fierce sparked in his eyes. "Then I'll hide, but you're not meeting him alone."

My stubborn side wanted to argue, but deep down I wanted him there. And not just as backup.

We were partners in this. He deserved to be there too.

"I'm torn between setting up a meeting and surprising him," I said.

"His potential mistress saw you at the bank," he said. "If they're working together, then he knows you gained access to whatever your mother left behind. If you set up a meeting, he'll come on the offensive. But if you tell him to meet you somewhere *you* choose, we can be ready for him."

"We shouldn't give him much notice."

"Agreed. And you need to dangle a threat. Give him a reason to show up."

My stomach twisted into a knot. "We should do it tonight. He'll be at the office all day, and this will give us time to prepare. Where, though?"

The door to the backroom opened, and Misti called out, "Hey, James! You plannin' to work today or you just gonna leave me high and dry again?"

James grimaced and his voice dropped as he turned to me. "Let me think on it. In the meantime, see what you can dig up on the people in those documents." He nodded to the laptop.

"Okay."

As he slid out of the booth, he called out to Misti, "I'm here. Quit your complainin'."

She laughed, obviously unfazed by his tone. "Whatever." She saw me and her face lit up. "Harper. You're here."

I gave her a little wave. "James and I are working on something."

She winked. "Yeah. Okay…"

I started to tell her she had the wrong idea, but she turned away. I decided protesting too much might make her think she was right.

After I grabbed my notebook from the office, I returned to the dining room and slid into a corner booth. I preferred to be close to James and his staff as they prepared to open, though I told myself it was for convenience, not because I liked being near him.

A few minutes after I made a list of things to research, my phone rang, and I saw Carter's name on the screen. I stared at his name for a second, caught off guard. Why was he calling me?

I glanced at James behind the bar with Misti, then answered before I could overthink why he was calling.

"Hey, Carter," I said keeping my voice low.

"Got a minute for some updates?"

I blinked in surprise. "You're calling *me*?"

"It's your case," he said matter-of-factly. "Skeeter's just assisting. Anyway, I found out who picked up your mother's prescription, and if you bet on her being the one to pick it up, you would have lost. It was your mystery woman."

I sucked in a breath in shock. "But my mother's doctor prescribed it."

"Correct. An inside source says the doctor just sent it without her coming in. There's a chance your mother called him personally—he *is* friends with your father—but we don't know for certain."

"I found out my mother refused antidepressants years ago, so it stands to reason she wouldn't take them now." But if my father called in a favor to get them filled, then he had to have told the mystery woman, so she would've known to pick them up. Which was more evidence that they were working together.

Carter continued, "Skeeter mentioned he had a suspicion your father might be in some financial trouble. But when I looked his financials up, he seems to be fine. In fact, better than fine. If you're lookin' for motivation to kill her, you can add his finances to the pot. He's worth about six million."

I was dumbfounded. "Six million *dollars*?"

"Yep, and half of it would have gone to your mother in a divorce."

I couldn't see him having her murdered for money, but at this point, I wasn't ruling anything out.

He hesitated, then said tentatively, "I also have more information about your mother's head wound."

"To the back of her head?" I asked, my chest constricting.

"Yeah. It looks like it was made with something long and cylindrical. Like a pipe."

"So, they whacked her in the head, drugged her up with Zoloft, and then put her in the car, and pushed it into the river," I said like I was reading a recipe.

"Perhaps the first two were reversed, but, yeah. It's definitely possible."

"Thanks," I said. "This is helpful."

"Sure," he said with a warmth in his voice that caught me off guard. "Let me know if I can help with anything else."

I released a chuckle. "With you and your sleuthing, I'm not sure James needs me for his own cases."

He was quiet for a moment then said, "He needs you, all

right. Whether he knows it or not yet. I hope you'll stay on board."

My heart skipped a beat at him saying James needed me, but I told myself that he meant something entirely different than my stupid heart took it as. "I don't work for him," I said. "There's no *staying* on board. I've never been on board."

"Okay. If you say so." A soft laugh filled my ear. "But again, let me know if you need anything else. I'm at your disposal."

I started to respond but I realized he'd hung up.

My heart fluttered in my chest like I was a teenage girl with a crush. What the hell was wrong with me?

I'd dated more than handful of men and never had a reaction to them like I had with James. Was it because my grief made me vulnerable?

Or had my heart found someone worthy of my attention?

I shook my head, trying to clear out the ridiculous thoughts. I needed to get a grip and get to work. And then once we'd wrapped this case up, I needed to put distance between me and James Malcolm before I lost my mind and did something impulsive.

Something we'd both regret.

The rest of the day, I searched all the names on the documents. Some had criminal records. The rest appeared to be clean, but I knew better. Just like my father, they'd just evaded investigations or arrests.

Maybe we could change that.

Misti brought me a plate of food around lunch time, but I was so deep in my work, I barely touched the roast beef, mashed potatoes, and cooked carrots. About a half hour later, James came to check on me.

"Makin' progress?"

"Some. Not enough." I tilted my head to get a better look at him as he stood next to the table, heat blooming in my lower belly before I could shut it down. "You figured out a place yet?"

"I'm thinkin' the factory where we met Drew Sylvester."

It was an abandoned site, so there were plenty of places to hide. "I'm not sure he'll meet me there. It's creepy as fuck."

"He will if you give him the right incentive."

I shook my head. "I still haven't uncovered anything that outright incriminates him."

His brow lifted. "*He* doesn't know that."

He had a point. "Okay, when should we ask him to meet us?"

"Let's wait until dusk. Then I can hide in the shadows."

I still had my doubts that my father would agree, but all I could do was try. "Okay. How about we wait until after the dinner rush so you're not leaving your staff in a bind?"

He gave a stiff nod. "Sounds like a plan." Then he gestured to my mostly untouched food. "Eat, especially the roast beef. Your body needs protein to fight this." He lowered his voice. "Did you take your pills yet?"

"Not yet."

He gave me a pointed look, and I grabbed the bottle out of my bag, shook out the pill, then washed it down with water. I took a bite of the beef, exaggerated and theatrical. His grin told me he was on to me before he turned and walked away.

My eyes were drawn to him—the spread of his shoulders and his waist tapering in a way that made my pulse quicken. I was an idiot to think someone like him would be attracted to someone like me. Not after the mess I made of my life. Not after everything he knew about me. Sure, we were getting along, but he saw me as a partner in our investigations, and he was smart enough to know you didn't mix business with plea-sure. A message I should have heeded before I'd gone to bed with Keith.

I was smarter now.

Even if my hormones weren't.

I continued working the rest of the day. My booth was tucked away so very few people noticed what I was doing, and those who did didn't seem to care. I gathered pages and pages of information, making new connections. Several times, irritation washed over me. My mother hadn't even left me a note explaining what all of this was about. She'd just dumped a pile of documents in my lap, and I could practically hear her saying, "You think you're so smart. You figure it out."

Just as the dinner rush started, my phone rang. I saw Louise's name on the screen, but I let it go to voicemail. I didn't feel like telling her about my trip to Jonesboro, and I didn't want to lie. I'd talk to her tomorrow—after I confronted my father.

But as I watched the call go to voicemail, it struck me that my father hadn't tried to contact me all day. If he knew about what had happened at the bank, wouldn't he have attempted some kind of damage control? And if he was clueless, he should have called to check on me. Then again, he'd gone years without checking on me.

Which begged a new question: what had motivated him to come to Little Rock and insist I move back home?

I shook my head, feeling the dull pounding of a headache at the back of my skull. I needed to focus on the facts and keep my personal shit out of this.

Another employee brought me a plate of baked chicken and roasted potatoes for dinner. I took several bites, hoping it would help my headache. So far, the Lorazepam was helping with my detox symptoms, and I wasn't feeling drugged up.

A while later, my phone rang again, and I was startled to see my father's name on the screen. It was a little after eight, and I realized I'd lost track of time. I should have already called him to set up a meeting.

Steeling my back, I accepted the call but didn't respond. I didn't know what to say.

"Harper?" he asked tentatively.

"Yeah," I said past the lump in my throat. "Hi, Dad. Sorry. Almost dropped the phone," I lied.

"It's okay. How're you doing today?" The kindness in his voice nearly killed me.

I shook my head, tears stinging my eyes, but I couldn't think of how to answer.

"Did you talk to your grandparents?" he asked softly.

His behavior was confusing me. He wasn't acting like a guy who knew he was guilty, but then again, he'd been this way my entire childhood. Maybe he was an amazing actor.

"I know about your mistress," I said flatly. While I didn't have absolute proof, there was plenty of evidence stacked against him.

I should have given more thought into how I was going to handle this call, but I was in it now. I needed to keep my shit together.

He was quiet for several seconds, before he said in a nonconfrontational tone, "Is that what your grandparents told you?"

Not a confirmation but not a denial either.

"They had a lot of things to say."

"I bet." The bitterness in his voice was unmistakable. "They hated me after Andi died."

"Funny," I said, sounding anything but amused. "They said they never blamed you for any of it."

"But your mother—" he said in protest, then stopped. "Why would your mother say they did?"

"Cut the shit, Dad." My tone was harsh, but I was holding back the worst of my anger.

"You don't believe me?" he asked as though it was incomprehensible.

"How long have you been having an affair?"

He released a short laugh. "Who told you that I was?"

"I saw her, Dad. She was at the bank this morning." I was screwing this up, yet I couldn't seem to stop myself.

"What are you talking about? What bank?"

"The bank with mom's safe deposit box. I know about it, and I know you tried to access it. While I was there this morning, your mistress tried to access it too."

He sucked in an audible breath, then said in a rush, "Harper. You need to stay *far* away from that woman."

"She was near *me*, not the other way around," I said. "And you're evading the question."

"That I'm having an affair with her? I'm not."

"Please," I sniped. "I know you had one when I was younger."

He hesitated. "Yes, I admit to an indiscretion, but that was a moment of weakness."

"*Indiscretion*," I scoffed.

"I'm human, Harper," he said, sounding exhausted. "And you know how your mother was."

"Then you should have divorced her, not cheated."

"I didn't want to divorce her." His voice broke. "I loved you girls too much to lose you."

I started to confront him on what I'd found in the box, but this wasn't the time or place. I needed to set up our meeting and do this in person.

As though reading my mind, he asked, "What did your mother have in the box?" He sounded fearful.

I had him on the defensive. I could still gain control of this conversation. "Some very interesting things."

He paused. "Some of it might be damaging to people who highly guard their privacy."

"You don't say," I said flippantly. Then I realized I had my hook. "You want the papers." It wasn't a question. It was so obvious.

"You'd just give them to me?" he asked in disbelief.

"I think we should discuss it."

His relief was palpable through the connection. "Why don't you come to my house?" he said in a rush as though he was trying to placate me. "Or I can come to your apartment. Whatever you like, but Harper"—his voice tightened—"you need to stay away from that woman."

Was this like a *Fatal Attraction* situation? Or was the woman not his mistress at all? The latter was starting to seem more likely. "I'll wait until after we talk before I make a decision."

"Okay," he said, "That's okay. Do you want me to come to you?"

There was no way I could suggest the factory. After the tone of our conversation, it would make him suspicious enough to cut and run. I needed him to think I was behaving as his daughter, not as—what? An ex-officer of the law?

A vigilante?

I shoved the last thought down, knowing I needed to trust my gut, but the question was where we could meet and still have James hiding in the shadows.

"Neither of those places," I said as it came to me. "Meet me at Mulberry Park in thirty minutes." Then I added, "At the playground."

He paused. "Why there?"

"Because if you're so worried about your non-mistress, then we should meet somewhere more discreet."

"And because…" His voice broke off. He recognized the real reason.

"Just meet me there," I said. "I won't wait long."

I hung up and slid out of the booth, rushing over to the bar. James was pulling a draft beer, and his eyes jerked up in surprise when he saw me.

"We need to go," I said. "I just talked to my dad and told him to meet me in thirty minutes."

He nodded slightly. "Okay."

"There's something else." A wary look crossed his face, and I braced myself for the fight I knew was coming. "We're meeting at Mulberry Park."

His entire body stiffened, and he leaned in, lowering his

voice to a growl. "The fuck we are. Call him back and tell him there's been a change of plans."

"No," I said firmly. "You can either go with me to Mulberry Park, or you can stay here."

His eyes burned, his fury barely contained. "I can keep you from goin'."

The promise held an edge of danger, and I had no doubt he could do just that. But I wasn't going down without a fight.

I steeled my back. "I'd like to see you try."

His jaw tensed and a vein in his temple began to pulse. James Malcolm wasn't used to people defying his orders, and when they did, I was sure they often paid dearly for it.

But as I studied his chiseled face, I wasn't the least bit afraid of him. Pissed, sure. Frustrated? Definitely. But not afraid.

"Look," I said evenly, "we can fight about this, or we can move forward with the new plan and work it out as we go." When he didn't respond, I took a different tactic.

"James," I said softly. "I need you to trust me on this."

A war waged in his eyes, but his face softened a little, even though it was obvious he was still pissed. "Then I guess we should get goin'."

## Chapter 30

Malcolm handed the beer he was pulling to the other bartender and told him he was leaving while I scooped up all the papers and laptop. I took them back to the office, unsure what to do with the paperwork.

"Where's your safe?" I asked when he appeared in the doorway.

He stalked toward a painting of a landscape on the wall and swung it open to reveal a safe. After he entered the combination, the safe door swung open, and he reached out his hand.

I started to hand him the paperwork, then hesitated. "Are you going to give this back to me?"

His eyes darkened, and his hands clenched at his sides. "You think I'd keep it from you?"

"In the past, I would've made you swear in blood you'd return it."

"So now I just swear without the blood?" The question wasn't lighthearted, making it obvious he was still furious.

"Malcom," I countered in frustration. "You just threatened to keep me from meeting my father."

We didn't have time for this, but I didn't want to bring the documents with me, and I needed reassurance. Sure, he could lie, but call me a fool, I trusted him to keep his word.

He took a deep breath, then let it out. Some of his anger faded, but he was obviously still unhappy about the location change. "When you ask for them, I'll give them to you. Now put the damn papers inside so we can beat your father there and come up with a goddamn plan."

Instead of handing paperwork over, I walked over to the safe and put the paperwork in myself. I'd half expected to see thick stacks of hundred-dollar bills, but all I saw was a short stack of twenties.

James stood directly behind me, so close I could feel the heat radiating off him.

My breath caught. A single step back and I'd be pressed against him. Every nerve in my body begged me to do it.

I squeezed my eyes shut. *Get it together, Harper.*

Was the Lorazepam messing with my head? It would be so easy to dismiss that as the reason, but there was no denying I'd felt this way before I'd started taking the pills. My feelings had been there, simmering below the carefully guarded surface of my heart.

His hand came to rest on my shoulder, warm and reassuring. He gave a gentle squeeze, and I nearly leaned into it, desperate for more.

Then the pressure disappeared, and he stepped back. I realized I was blocking the safe. He'd only meant to move me, not comfort me—or whatever my imagination had come up with.

My cheeks burned with humiliation. God, how many women threw themselves at him? Probably more than he could count. I was just another fool to add to the long list.

I stepped aside, and he closed the safe, locking it with practiced ease before swinging the painting into place.

"Let's go," he said, his tone clipped.

He walked out of the office and through the back door

without looking at me, not bothering to wait. I trailed behind, shaking my head muttering a curse under my breath.

Once I climbed into the passenger seat of the car, I turned to face him. "What's the big deal about changing locations? It's not like there'll be anyone at the park at this time of night. And even if there were, it could work in our favor."

He pulled out of the parking lot and headed for the county road. "A whole host of reasons. Did you ever confront a dangerous criminal without a well-thought-out plan?"

"You're right," I admitted. "It's not the best idea, but after talking to him, I don't think he did. He seemed surprised my grandparents didn't blame him for Andi's death."

"Harper…" he said, the first time I'd ever heard a shred of pity in his voice.

"I know you think I'm being delusional, but he seemed surprised. He also claims that woman's not his mistress, and he seemed surprised to hear she was at the bank this morning."

He shot me a look that made it clear he thought I'd just taken a trip to the Land of Delusion.

"Look," I said. "I didn't say I believed him, but right now, he thinks I'm open to hearing what he has to say. If I asked him to meet at the factory, he would have shown up on the defensive. The park is a neutral location, and he'll be more likely to talk. Especially if it's Mulberry Park."

"What's so fuckin' special about Mulberry Park?"

"It was my sister's favorite playground." The burning lump in my throat caught me by surprise. "He took us there a couple of times a month when we were little."

"You think some happy memories of pushin' you on a swing are gonna keep him from killin' you?" He grunted in disgust.

"I don't know," I said. "I'm the first to admit that I don't know him as well as I wish I did, but this seemed like the way to go."

He was quiet for a moment as though considering my words, then his shoulders stiffened again. "A million things could go wrong with this plan. In the first place, I'm not familiar with that location." He got more worked up with each word. "I need be somewhere close enough to hear what's going on but also stay hidden."

"I told him to meet me by the playground," I said. "There's a section that has a playhouse with a slide. I figured you could hide up there."

"What?" he barked. "You expect me to come down the goddamn slide with my gun blazin'? This isn't some goddamn action movie!"

I stared at him, confused. "It's not that big of a deal, Malcolm. I'll stand next to the slide, and you'll be able to hear everything." Then like a fool, I added, "If you like, I'll position my father at the bottom of the slide, so all you'll have to do is come down and knock him over like a bowling pin."

"This isn't a goddamn joke!" he shouted, giving me a look of frustration.

That was a lot of goddamns, even for him. But I had to admit he had a right to be pissed. I'd changed the plan last minute and now I was treating it like it was a trip to the grocery store. "I'm sorry. I don't know why I said that other than I was trying to make you realize it's not as dangerous as you think it will be. Besides," I said, lowering my voice and hoping it would help calm him down. "You have the paper-work. If something happens to me, you'll still be able to use it."

That only seemed to make him angrier. The veins on his neck bulged and throbbed. "You think I'm worried about—" He cut himself off, then shook his head.

"All I can tell you is that my gut says it's a better location, and I'm going with my gut."

He wrung the steering wheel with his clenched hand, his knuckles white. I suspected he wished it was my neck he was wringing. "It's too damn late to change plans now, so we'll go with it." He turned and shot me a dark look. "But I'm fuckin' not happy."

"Really?" I countered before I could stop myself, because this man brought out my ornery side. "I couldn't tell."

Something in him loosened, not much, but enough that the line of his shoulders eased. He was still wrapped up tight, but if he was a boa constrictor wrapped around me, I would have gone from being strangled to being able to take shallow breaths.

His gaze jerked to the rearview mirror. "Someone's following us."

I turned around in my seat to see the headlights of a car, gaining on us.

"Did your father know you were at the tavern?" he asked.

I kept my eyes on the car, which looked like a large SUV. "No. I didn't tell him where I was, and he didn't ask. If anything, I think he thought I was at my apartment."

Malcolm sped up, and the car sped up too, tailing us at a distance of about twenty feet.

"They're probably after the papers," James said, sitting up straighter as he maneuvered around a curve.

"Why would my father send someone after us to get the papers when he thinks I'm bringing them to show him?" I countered, then I realized I'd been stupid. "It's the woman."

"His mistress?"

"He said she wasn't his mistress. I'm starting to think he wasn't lying." I groaned at how closed-minded I'd been. "What if she's one of the people listed in those documents?"

"We didn't see any women in those documents."

"She doesn't know that. Maybe she thinks she is," I countered, the pieces starting to fall into place. "What if she showed up at my mother's house, offering to help her, but she wanted the papers? Maybe she tried to get my mother to open the safe deposit box for her—the woman had the key—and my mother refused, so she killed her?"

"You think that older woman pushed your mother's car into the river?" he asked derisively.

"You think that woman is driving that SUV that's gaining on us?" I snapped. "She's obviously got help. Those are pros, Malcolm, and you of all people know that only takes money."

"Fuck," he grunted, then activated the AI on his phone, telling it to call Carter.

"Hey, Skeeter."

"I need a photo of Rutherford Knox's wife."

Carter must have heard the urgency in his voice. "I don't know that I've ever seen a photo of her. Knox was always careful about keeping his family out of public view."

"See if you can find something," James said, glancing up at the rearview mirror. "Because I think she's sent someone to run us off the road."

"His son Gerald took over after Rutherford was killed."

"Maybe so, but I think his wife might be involved in the family business too. Get a name, an age, a photo if you can. Anything, and make it fast. I'm gonna try to lose them up ahead."

"On it." Carter disconnected the call, and I glanced at the road in front of us. "Where do you plan to lose them? There are no turn-offs for at least a couple of miles."

He made a face. "If he thinks I have a plan, he'll be less worried."

James Malcolm didn't want to worry his attorney? I wasn't sure why that surprised me, especially after everything else I'd learned about him. I'd seen them together, and I was guessing they were friends.

"So what's the plan?"

He sent me a quick glance. "How do you feel about firing on them?"

"They haven't shot at us yet," I said. "And they're definitely close enough to take some shots and expect to hit us. Which means they don't want us dead."

But why didn't they want us dead? In case we didn't have the papers with us? So why not ambush us somewhere else?

Or maybe this was how they operated.

"Did my mother's car have paint marks or dents on the side panels?"

His brow furrowed as though wondering why I was asking about my mother, but then I saw the realization hit his face. "There was a dent, but the report says it likely happened when she ran off the road.

Red-hot anger burned in my chest. "Ten to one those fuckers ran her off the bridge."

He made a face. "You might be right."

My gut told me I was. "My father met with that woman either to warn her my mother was collecting evidence, or maybe the woman found out and told my father to control her."

"That makes sense."

We drove for another minute, our speed hitting eighty. Thankfully, the road was empty, but if we encountered another car, we'd be putting innocent people in danger.

James's phone rang and I pressed answer on the screen.

"What did you find?" James barked.

"Nicole Knox, age fifty-nine. She's a bit reclusive, but I found a photo. I'm sending it to your phone."

The phone pinged, and I picked it up and realized it was locked. James grabbed my hand and held it up to his face to unlock it, then released me. I pulled up his messages, and gasped when I saw the photo. It was a surveillance shot of a woman in a parking lot, and she was very clearly the woman who'd shown up at the bank and my mother's house.

My gaze jerked up to Malcolm. "It's her."

Which meant we likely had the mob on our tail.

"Get a team together," James said, "because even if I lose them, they'll be back."

"It'll take at least an hour," Carter said, his voice tight. "Maybe longer."

"Do what you can." He reached up and tapped the screen to end the call. He was silent as he gripped the steering wheel. "We have two choices. One, we keep heading into town and try to lose them in a public place."

"If we lose them, that means they get away," I said. "What's the other?"

"We take a side road that's about a hundred feet ahead, then turn the tables on them and get them to pull over."

The second option sounded like the more dangerous one, but the only one that meant we'd get answers. "Take the side road."

"You sure?" he asked, his voice softening. "It'll likely involve a shootout."

"If we lose them, you're right. They'll be back."

"We can wait for backup and hunt them down ourselves," he said. "I highly doubt Nicole Knox is in that car."

"She was at the bank this morning, so she might still be in the area," I said. "We can get them to take us to her."

His brow lifted as he considered my suggestion. "And then what?"

Something in my chest hardened. "I guess we'll find out once we get there."

He accepted my answer without further questions. The side road appeared ahead, and he positioned his hands on the steering wheel, preparing to make the sharp turn.

He whipped the wheel, the back fishtailing as he turned and then he punched the engine, shooting down the road. I watched out the back window as the SUV slid past us, tires squealing as it stopped and then reversed before turning and following us.

"Now what?" I asked.

"We let them catch up," he said as he decelerated.

"Shouldn't we try to get ahead of them so we can be in a better position?" I countered.

"We could, but I want them to think they're on the offensive."

I didn't have time to argue with him, because another SUV appeared out of nowhere, pulling in front of us from the shoulder.

Had they planned on us turning onto this road? Had we just driven into a trap?

Malcolm cursed and swerved into the oncoming traffic lane, which was thankfully clear, with no cars in sight on the deserted-looking road.

The car fishtailed, and he punched the gas, trying to shoot past the new SUV, but it rammed into the side of our car, sending us toward the shoulder on the opposite side of the road. The car behind us had caught up. It rammed into the back bumper, and our car went off the side of the road, rolling down the embankment.

## Chapter 31

Raw panic slammed into me, my vision tunneling as the metallic taste of fear flooded my mouth. For a heartbeat, I was dazed. The headlights shone on a copse of trees in front of us, and it took me a few seconds to remember what had happened. Glass glittered across the dashboard from the shattered windshield. The car released an ominous groan, and I realized we'd been in a rollover accident.

Car chase.

We were run off the road.

We were in danger.

James.

I turned to face him, fear nearly paralyzing me when I saw him slumped in the driver's seat.

*Oh God.*

Finally, my instincts kicked in, and I quickly unfastened my seatbelt and turned, getting on my knees so I could lean over him. I placed shaking fingers on his neck and held my breath until I felt the steady thrum of his pulse against my fingertips.

The relief nearly broke me.

I hadn't realized how terrified I was of finding nothing there. I gently cupped his right cheek, my fingers sticky with blood, and searched his face, trying to figure out where the blood was coming from. A gash ran from close to his temple into his hairline. The cracked glass in the driver's door told me he must have hit his head when we flipped. He likely had a nasty concussion.

"James," I said, my fear making me sound breathless. I glanced down his body, looking for visible signs of other injuries, thankfully finding none. His seatbelt had done its job too.

But for how long? I doubted they were satisfied by running us off the road. Once they got turned around, they'd be back to finish the job. I pulled out my cellphone, but I didn't have any service.

"James," I said, my voice cracking despite my efforts to stay calm. I lightly patted his cheek. "I need you to wake up. *Please*."

He grimaced and his eyes squinted open. "Fuck. What happened?"

"We were in an accident."

He looked dazed, as though trying to piece it together. "Are you okay?"

"I'm fine. You're the one who's hurt."

He studied my face, which was inches from his, and gave me a wicked grin. "Were you plannin' to kiss me awake like Sleeping Beauty?"

I realized that not only were my lips inches from his, but my chest was pressed firmly against him, my heart hammering so hard I was sure he could feel it. My instinct was to jerk away, but I liked the feeling of his body pressed against mine, and something deep inside me said to stay, especially since he wasn't complaining.

*Not the time, Harper.*

"That wasn't the first thought that came to mind," I said, reaching down to release his seatbelt. "But I hadn't ruled out all my options."

His grin spread, but his eyes were unfocused, further proof he was suffering from a concussion. "You plannin' to kiss me somewhere other than my lips?"

It took me a second to realize he was talking about my hand resting on his thigh. "Not right now. We need to go."

Movement out of the corner of my eye through the driver's side back window caught my attention, and I turned to see a man in dark clothing walking down the hill toward us, about thirty feet away.

I doubted he was a good Samaritan coming to help us.

"Where's your gun?" I hissed, shoving James down so he was lying across the console.

"What the fuck?" he grunted, but he didn't resist.

"James! *Gun?*" I demanded, my voice barely above a whisper but sharp with panic. Then I remembered he'd told me his handgun was in the glove compartment. My hands shook as I fumbled with the glove compartment latch, offering a silent prayer of thanks when I saw it was loaded with a full magazine. I saw the spare magazine and pulled it out, then stuffed it in my front jeans pocket.

"What's goin' on?" he growled, trying to rise but swaying like he was fighting vertigo. His movements were sluggish and uncoordinated.

"*Stay down!*" I grunted as I practically threw myself on top of him while searching for the button to turn off the interior lights.

"What do you think you're doin'?" he asked, but the weakness in his voice made it less threatening.

"Taking care of a problem."

"Takin' care of problems is my job," he mumbled.

"Not this time." I found the button for the interior lights under the rearview mirror and pressed it, hoping I'd actually turned them off. I lifted my head slightly, hoping the gunman wasn't about to peer through the window. I could see him moving with predatory caution. He was taking his time, probably assuming we were either dead or too injured to fight back.

He was wrong on both counts.

I slunk down in the passenger seat and put my face in front of James's. "James," I said sternly. "Listen to me. We were run off the road and we rolled over a few times down a hill. A man with a gun is headed this way, probably to finish us off."

"Let me take care of it," he growled, as he tried to lift up again.

I tugged him back down. "Stop!" I hissed. "You've suffered a concussion. You're probably seeing double, so you're not in any position to take care of anything right now. I found your gun in the glove compartment, and I'm going out the passenger door to try to draw him away from you."

His eyes widened. "You're gonna do *what?*"

"James!" I shook his arm. "Listen. Stay down and let me handle this." I flashed him a tight grin. "I'm actually a pretty damn good shot." I cracked open the passenger door just enough for me to slip out, the hinges groaning softly in protest. I froze, listening for any change in the gunman's approach. My heart was hammering so loudly I was sure it would give me away.

Thankfully, the interior light stayed off, so James wasn't a sitting duck. "Stay down!" I whispered to him one last time.

For a split second, our eyes met in the darkness. I saw something that looked almost like fear in his eyes, and I knew he wasn't afraid for himself.

I gave him a tight smile. "I've got this."

I slipped out the door feet first, staying low to the ground. Once I was out, I carefully pushed the door closed but not enough for the latch to click. Hopefully, the gunman hadn't seen me slip out, and if my luck held up, he was still a good distance from the driver's window.

Crouching low, I crawled to the back of the car and peered around the side. The man was about ten feet away, close enough that I could hear his boots crunching on broken glass. Each step was deliberate, calculated.

"Freeze where you are," I called out. "Put your hands in the air."

He turned toward my voice, and two shots cracked through the night air. I threw myself sideways as one bullet whined over my head and the other punched into the back panel with a *thunk*.

I had every right to defend myself now that he'd shot at me, but I was going to do everything I could to keep him alive. I needed answers, and dead men didn't talk.

"Just tell me what you want and maybe we can work out some kind of deal," I called out, my back pressed to the side of the car. I strained to listen, hoping I could hear his footsteps in the quiet.

"We just want to have a little talk," he said.

*We.* Was he talking about a partner or Nicole Knox?

"Okay," I said. "Start talking."

"Where's Malcolm?" he asked. "Why're *you* doin' all the talkin'?"

"He's dead," I said bitterly, hoping he believed me. I also hoped James wouldn't hear him and try to come out. "Broke his neck in the accident."

"Well, that's a pity," the guy said. "He's the one she really wants."

That caught me by surprise. We'd been under the assumption they were after the papers from my mother's safe deposit box. Was this the person who'd taken over Simmons's operations? Or one of James's enemies from his past? How many had he faced since he'd been released from prison? But if this guy was Nicole Knox's hired gun, then we were probably looking at a cross of both possibilities. He did say *she*.

I peered around the back of the car again. "This is your last chance to stop."

"Or what?" he said with a laugh, walking toward me.

What a fool. Did this guy really think James Malcolm drove around unarmed? Did he not realize I was an ex-cop who was more than comfortable using firearms?

I lifted my gun, hoping I was hidden in the shadows. He was on full display, the nearly full moon making him more visible than expected. I aimed for his leg, then noticed the tremor in my hand. Was it withdrawal or nerves? I hadn't taken my evening dosage yet. Either way, I needed to make this shot. I drew a breath, willing my hand to be still, then slowly exhaled and squeezed the trigger.

The man grunted then howled as he crumpled to his knees. "You fucking cunt! You shot me!" A dark stain bloomed across the jeans over his left thigh.

I leaned over the trunk of the car, my gun trained on him. "Throw your gun to the side or next time I'll aim higher."

I couldn't make out the features of his face, but I recognized the rage making his body shake. "I dropped it when you shot me!"

"Bullshit. You have three seconds to toss it or I'm pulling the trigger. And unlike you, I'm an excellent shot." When he didn't move, I started counting. "One…two…"

"All right!" he shouted, his voice tight with pain. A dark object flew through the air, landing with a heavy thud in the grass several feet away. I could only presume it was his gun given the size and the shadows.

I swept my gaze across the top of the incline, then along the tree line on both sides. There had been a second SUV, so even if there had only been one person in each vehicle, there was at least one more person coming for us. Probably more. I didn't see anyone, but my ears strained for any sound that didn't belong. "Why did you run us off the road?"

He released a throaty laugh. "I thought you were supposed to be smart."

"The consensus is out," I said, "so humor me."

"I'm gonna bleed to death," he grunted, pressing his hand to his leg. "I need help."

"Your hand is working just fine. Where's your partner?"

He hesitated, inclining his head slightly to the side before he said, "What partner?"

"The other driver, and the people in both your vehicles."

"The other car left," he said. "His job was to jump in front of you, then let us finish the job."

*Us.* Even if the other SUV had actually left, there was at least one other gunman above us.

"We both know you're not gonna kill me," the guy said, sounding more confident than someone in his situation had any right to.

"What makes you so certain I won't?" I asked with a laugh.

He lifted his chin, then sneered, "Once a cop, always a cop."

"Haven't you heard? I'm the cop who shot an unarmed kid. You think I have any moral boundaries left to cross?"

I saw his body tense, but then he said, "I've tossed my gun away, so why don't you come out here so we can talk face to face. Or better yet, you can help me up the hill."

"I think I'm fine where I am," I said. I had no plans to let his partner shoot me. "But let's say I agreed to go with you, where would we be going?"

"You've made someone nervous," he said, sounding uncertain about sharing information, but he was putting more pressure on his wound.

"That much is obvious," I said. "*Who* did I make nervous?"

He looked up the hill, as though looking for help from his partner, then turned back to face the car. "Fine," the guy said, "but if I tell you, you have to help me up the hill."

"Agreed."

Before he had a chance to speak, a rifle crack split the

night air, a flash coming from the top of the hill. The injured man's head snapped back, and he slumped sideways.

"Fuck," I grunted, seeing a dark figure where the flash had come from before it streaked to my left.

That confirmed he had a partner. And that he was ruthless.

Our car wasn't perfectly parallel to the road, and I was worried if he went far enough, he might see me at the back of the car. I scooted more toward the center, then nearly jumped out of my skin when James's head appeared in the back passenger window like a concussed jack-in-the-box.

"That didn't go well," he whispered.

"What the fuck, James?" I grunted under my breath. "I could have shot you."

I drew a breath to get a hold of myself. My heart had already been racing, but now it was going double time. "Glad to see you're getting your wits back," I said sarcastically.

"Right now, I'm seeing two of you, so I doubt I could hit the broadside of a barn. Hell, I'm not sure which of you is real, but I'm not sitting in this car and waitin' for the jackass at the top of the hill to come down and finish us off."

The door crept open, and he tried to slip out with his usual predatory grace. Instead, he misjudged the distance to the ground and half-fell, half stumbled out of the car, hitting the ground with a thud that had to further rattle his already injured head. "Fuck."

"I don't have any cell service so I can't call for help."

He leaned the back of his head against the car, closing his eyes. "Get my sat phone out of the back."

"You have a sat phone?" I hissed, torn between relief and the urge to smack his concussed head. "That would have been helpful information about five minutes ago."

He leaned his head against the side panel of the passenger door and closed his eyes. "Never know when you might need one. It's behind the driver's seat."

I gave him a worried look. "How bad's your head?"

"I've been worse," he said, but the tight lines around his eyes and the way he kept blinking slowly suggested his "worse" had probably involved life support.

There was nothing I could do about his concussion at the moment, other than getting help. I swept my gaze across the hilltop one more time. Still no movement. Moving quickly, I opened the back door and leaned across the floor, feeling for the sat phone. I wasn't sure what to expect, so when my hand connected with a plastic rectangular box, I grabbed it and backed out of the car. "This it?"

He pried his eyes open into slits. "Yep."

"Are you hurt anywhere else other than your head?" I asked, trying to hide my worry. James struck me as the type who'd walk around with a compound fracture of his femur before admitting weakness, which meant if he was showing discomfort at all, he was in serious pain.

"Doesn't really matter right now," he said, gritting his teeth. "Call Carter."

I didn't argue about not calling 911. If we kept law enforcement out of this, then maybe we could still stay under the radar.

Who was I kidding? The fact that a professional sniper had just executed our only lead meant we were definitely targets. But calling the cops would mean handing over evidence, answering questions, and watching our investigation disappear into bureaucratic limbo. They'd take over and we'd be forced to stand back and let them.

I wasn't handing this over to anyone. Not when we were this close to answers about my mother's murder. And not when someone was willing to kill to keep those answers buried.

I was handling this myself. Consequences be damned.

I opened the phone case, and James told me how to turn it

on, then how to call Carter with his preprogrammed speed dial.

"Skeeter," Carter said, sounding tense when he answered. "Give me an update."

"It's Harper," I said, keeping my voice down as I scanned the hill again. The sniper up there was making my skin crawl.

"Where's Skeeter?" Carter asked, barely disguising his panic.

"We were run off the road, and he's got a concussion. He's talking, but his head is killing him."

"We have more pressing concerns," James grunted, one hand pressed against his temple like he was trying to keep his skull from splitting open.

"There's a gunman at the top of the hill," I said, "and he's already killed the buddy he sent down to pick us off. I'm worried he's called for backup. Supposedly, the SUV that jumped in front of us took off, but they couldn't have gotten far enough away that it would take long for them to come back."

"Where are you?"

I shot James a questioning look.

He grimaced. "County Road 82."

"But we're down a hill," I said, "so I doubt anyone driving on the road would be able to see us." I heard the sound of a car engine in the distance, coming closer.

"I've put out word you need help," Carter said, "and while it'll be faster than I originally thought, they're still at least a half hour away."

I highly doubted we had a half hour. Especially when I saw headlights sweep the incline above. The car engine, which was now near us, shut off. I pressed myself flatter against the car, hoping the shadows would hide us. We were sitting ducks.

"Well, tell them to hurry," I said, my heart beginning to race. "Because backup just arrived, and I don't think they're on our side."

---

# Chapter 32

---

"Okay," I told James, as I lowered the phone. "We have two choices—make a stand or make a run for it. This morning you said you had multiple guns in the car. Where are they?"

He grimaced. "In the trunk."

"Shit." I'd be shot if I tried to open the trunk.

"There's a nice high-powered rifle back there." He opened his eyes a slit. "I'm sure you've got some experience with one."

"I do."

He grinned. "That's my girl."

His words made my chest tighten. I told myself I didn't have time to dissect what he'd just said or the way he'd sounded proud when he'd said it. He'd just suffered a head injury, and for all I knew, he was hallucinating.

"Can you access the trunk through the back seat?" I asked, peering up the hill again. I didn't see any movement, but the calm felt like the eye of a storm. They were probably coordinating their approach, deciding whether to come down shooting or flush us out. What if they brought enough firepower to turn our cover into scrap metal? I took small comfort from knowing they wanted at least one of us alive, which meant I needed to hide James somewhere and draw them away from him.

"Center console folds down," he murmured, his voice strained. "Should be a release latch on the back of it."

"Okay." I opened the back door again and climbed into the backseat, making sure to stay as low as possible. The console opened easily, and a long, padded case sat right next to the console opening. I maneuvered the case around, pulled it out, and exited the car. Setting the case between us, I knelt in front of it.

The zipper had a combination lock, which meant he probably didn't use it on the regular and had it for backup in situations like this. "What's the code?"

He squeezed his eyes tight, then opened them, looking up at me. "Um… four, nine, two, six, zero."

I pressed in the numbers, thankful my fingers were steady, and the lock opened with a satisfying pop. As I got to work unzipping, I glanced up at him. "How much ammunition do you have in here?"

He struggled to focus on my face. "I'm not sure. I haven't checked in a while."

I took that as a promising sign that it had been a while since he hadn't used it. After I got the case open, I pulled the rifle out and looked it over. A loaded magazine had already been inserted. I spotted two more strapped inside the case, each holding ten rounds.

Thirty shots total.

Would it be enough? I had no idea how many people with guns were up there, how many bullets they had, or how long we could last down here. There was no way we had thirty minutes. Hell, I wasn't sure we had thirty seconds before they decided to end this standoff.

It was dark, an advantage for hiding, but it also meant I'd have a hard time spotting them unless they moved. And then, they'd probably be firing their weapons.

He turned his head slightly and stared hard at me. "You should make a run for the trees. I'll hold them off while you go."

Outrage raced through me. "What the fuck are you talking about? I'm not leaving you here."

"Look," he said, blinking as he tried to focus. "I suspect if I try to run, I'll fall flat on my face. I feel like I'm on a high-speed merry-go-round, and I already want to puke from just sitting here. I'll slow you down if we both try to go. You can run into the trees and bide your time until backup arrives."

"Fuck you," I spat out, good and pissed. "You think I'd just leave you here?"

"You can take the rifle," he said, ignoring my protest. "Leave me the handgun. I'll distract them with some shots."

"Apparently that hit to your head affected your hearing too." I leaned closer, my anger flaring. "I'm. Not. Leaving. You. James," I said through gritted teeth. "So, if this is your weird way of trying to prove you're a good person, stop wasting our time. We need a plan to hold them off, and I suspect you have more experience with this than I do."

His mouth stretched into a pained grin. "You really are a stubborn bitch."

"That's right," I said, the muscles in my back beginning to unknot. I already had a battle to deal with without having to fight him too. "I heard a car pull up. It sounded loud, so I think it's the second SUV that jumped out in front of us. I have no idea what we're up against, but there's at least two gunmen up there, probably more. The fact they haven't started shooting is a bad sign. They're probably planning something. Maybe coming through the trees to surround us?"

"That's what I'd do."

"So, we hope they're not as smart as you?" I said, half-teasing, but I was already scanning the trees. The headlights of James's car were still shining in the woods, so at least we knew they weren't there.

"They're never as smart as me," he scoffed, "but I'm not running on all cylinders, so there's a chance they could get the jump on us."

"Dammit," I muttered under my breath, trying to figure out our options. Instinctively, I wanted to put us both back in the car, but if they had high-powered rifles, James's car wouldn't provide much protection.

I needed to think like James—ruthless, calculating, always two steps ahead. What would he do if he wasn't seeing double?

I scanned him over again, reassessing our situation. We couldn't stay here, and I couldn't carry him. He probably had eighty pounds on me. And if we ran for the trees, they'd pick us off like we were target practice. Sure, they might not kill us. They might take a lesson from my book and shoot us in the legs.

I needed a distraction, and I'd be damned if James staying behind was it.

"Where's the flask?" I asked as an idea hit me.

He snorted. "I guess now's as good a time for a drink as any. Maybe even more so."

"James. Focus. Where is it?"

He patted around on his chest, but he wasn't wearing his jacket. "In the car. Side pocket."

Which meant it could be anywhere since the car had rolled over multiple times. It could have even fallen out the partially open driver's window. But I didn't have any other ideas, so I opened the back door again.

"What're you doin'?" he asked, his voice sounding fainter.

I leaned over and patted his cheek. "Stay with me, James. I'm looking for the flask."

"I'll take a drink when you get it."

"You can have the first one," I said as I crawled into the back of the car. I didn't dare turn my flashlight on, so I patted the seat, then the floor, reaching under the seats and sweeping my hand around so I didn't miss it. I was about to try to crawl into the front when the tip of my finger brushed against cold metal. I stretched my arm out farther, my already sore shoulder grinding painfully against the seat frame, but I ignored the spike of pain as I wrapped my fingers around the canister. I tugged it free, relief swamping me as I realized it felt at least half full.

I quickly scooted out backward and softly pushed the door closed.

James reached out a hand in an uncoordinated movement. "I'll take that drink now."

"Sorry," I said, still formulating a plan. "I think I'm going to need all of it." The idea was to make a Molotov cocktail, but a metal flask wouldn't exactly pull that off.

"This is payback for all the times I cut you off, isn't it?" he said with a smile, his eyes half closed.

"Yep." But he was too out of it to notice I was distracted.

*Think, Harper. Think.* Time was running out, and James wasn't in great shape. I could hear muffled voices above us.

I glanced over my shoulder and saw the gas cap on Malcolm's car. I'd considered soaking a rag in alcohol and lighting it, but that might not create the bang I needed. I had no guarantee the gas fumes would catch.

Then a better idea came to me. I could pour some whiskey into the trunk and hope the fire burned hot enough to reach the tank and set off an explosion. But for that plan to work, we needed to be at least twenty feet away. The problem was, James could hardly sit upright, let alone sprint twenty feet through rough terrain in the dark.

Which meant I needed a second distraction.

I rose up to peek over the trunk. No sign of movement, which was worse than if I'd seen them. Were they waiting us out, hoping we'd make a desperate move? Or were they sneaking through the trees, closing in around us?

I climbed into the backseat again and found Malcolm's

jacket on the driver's seat, but I quickly realized it probably wouldn't work. The lining felt like it might be flammable, but the leather shell would melt. I hadn't brought a jacket, but then I remembered the clothes in the trunk.

Reaching through the pass-through, I felt around until my fingers found denim—a pair of jeans. I positioned them near the opening, then kept digging until I found a loose T-shirt—James's—and my bag. I pulled my own jeans out of the bag and added them to the pile, then tossed the T-shirt and the rest of the bag out of the car.

I followed, dropping to the ground after it, but as soon as I landed, I realized the fatal flaw in my plan.

"Fuck," I whispered in frustration. All of this planning didn't mean shit without something to ignite it. How could I make such a basic mistake?

"James," I said, moving over to him. A fresh wave of panic hit me when he didn't answer. "James." I grabbed his arm and shook.

His eyes fluttered open. "What?"

"Do you have a lighter somewhere in the car?"

He frowned. "No."

I fell back onto my butt, my eyes closing in defeat.

"But I have one in my pocket."

I bounced up like a jackrabbit, leaning over him. "*Which* pocket?"

He patted his left hip, and I glanced down, noticing the slight lump on his outer thigh. "I'm going to reach into your pocket and grab it." I straddled his legs, then dropped to the ground on his left side, before I slid my hand into his pocket, angling my hand at the junction of his leg.

"If you wanted to grab my dick, you just had to say so," he murmured, his eyes still half-closed.

"You told me you weren't interested in sleeping with me," I said, trying to sound flippant while I dug my fingers deeper into his pocket. "Lift up your hips so I can reach."

He obeyed and turned his head toward me. "You're not searching in the right direction. My dick's the other way."

I couldn't stop the chuckle bubbling up in my throat. Sure, we were about to die, but James was giving me dick directions. My fingertip bumped into the lighter, and I leaned in and pushed deeper. Once I had my fingers wrapped around the warm metal, I tugged it out, then pushed his leg down.

I straddled him again, planning to move to the other side to start the fire, but his large hands spanned my waist. His thumbs pressed against my hip bones, pinning me in place with surprising strength.

He tried to stare into my eyes, but his focus was off. "I wasn't lyin'."

I drew in a sharp breath, my entire body freezing at his touch. A jolt of electric awareness shot straight through my core, making me acutely conscious of every point where our bodies connected. "Lying about what?" I asked, irritated when it came out low and breathy.

"When I said I didn't want to sleep with you," he said, his mouth twitching into a half-smile.

"Okay," I said in annoyance. "You've made that abundantly clear." I tried to move off his legs, but his hands dug in, holding me in place. For someone whose brain was scrambled, he was amazingly strong.

He made a face. "I meant at *first*," he said and paused. "I didn't want to sleep with you *at first*. But somewhere along the way, that changed."

My breath caught in my throat, but now wasn't the time for this discussion. Not while we were possibly minutes from being gunned down. I tried to pull free from his grasp, but it was like trying to escape a vise. "James. You have to let me go so I can get us out of this."

"Not yet," he said, licking his bottom lip, and damned if my heart didn't skip a beat watching him do it, my brain promptly conjuring up all the places that tongue could go.

*Not the time, Harper!*

I twisted again, but his fingers dug in tighter.

"If we're gonna die," he said, his voice softening. "I don't want you thinkin' I didn't want you. Because I did." He grimaced. "I *do*."

I sucked in a breath, my thoughts splintering. Because I wanted him too, more than I'd ever wanted any man. The acknowledgment equally thrilled me and scared the shit out of me. This wasn't just lust. It was something deeper.

Something dangerous.

Then his hand grabbed the back of my head and pulled my mouth to his. The suddenness of it caught me off guard. His hand fisted in my hair, holding my head in place as he coaxed my lips open, his tongue sweeping deep with expert intent.

Heat surged through me. I cupped both sides of his face as I kissed him back, hard and hungry, like I'd been waiting forever for this—for him.

He was desperate, like he was drinking me in.

Like this was our last kiss, not our first.

The thought cut through the haze, and I broke away, breathless. His grip on my hair eased, but he didn't let go.

But now wasn't the time to unpack what had just happened. For all I knew, fifty men with guns were advancing down the hill, and we'd be shot dead with me sitting on Malcolm's lap while he devoured me.

But of all the ways to go, I supposed it wasn't the worst.

Still, I wasn't dying today. Not when I'd finally found someone worth fighting for.

I brushed my thumb across his bottom lip, my voice low. "In case you haven't figured it out, I want you too." I leaned in close, my forehead nearly touching his. "But I'd actually like this mutual wanting to last more than five minutes, so you have to let me go so I can get us out of here."

He slightly shook his head, resignation in his eyes.

"There's no gettin' us out of this. You can't do this on your own."

I sat back. "Fuck you," I said, a half snarl/half laugh. Then kissed him again—hard and fierce—to show him I wasn't giving up. That we weren't done. When I pulled back, I narrowed my eyes. "Don't tell me what I can and can't do. Now you need to let me go so I can prove you wrong."

I pushed up, and this time, he let me. The loss of his touch left me cold, but it cleared my head and sharpened my focus.

"I take it you have a plan?" he asked, one brow lifting, amusement edging into his voice.

"Of course I have a plan," I said in a huff, with more confidence than I felt. "It might be crazy, but it's better than sitting here waiting to die."

I rifled through the bag, pulling out a cotton button-down shirt, two pairs of cotton underwear then picked up James's T-shirt next to the bag. I grabbed the lighter, then dropped to my belly and crawled under the car.

"What the hell are you doin' under there?" he asked, then added, "I guess it's not a bad place to hide if they ambush us."

"We're not hiding under here. We're putting on a show."

My plan was simple. Tires made thick black smoke. Once the smoke was dense enough to cover us, I'd light the jeans in the trunk on fire and pray the heat set off the gas tank. If we were lucky, the explosion would provide enough chaos for us to make a run for it. Or a wobble, in James's case.

I soaked the underwear with alcohol, rubbed it on the front driver's side tire, then wedged Malcolm's T-shirt under it. I lit the rubber first, relieved when the flames caught. The acrid scent made my nostrils sting.

I lit the underwear next and dropped them on the shirt, relieved when it caught fast.

I scooted to the back tire next and repeated the process, this time using the button-down shirt. It went up quicker.

By the time I backed out from under the car, thick black

smoke was billowing up, choking the air. My eyes watered and my lungs burned. I sat up, coughing, then quickly laid out the rest of the plan to Malcolm.

"It'll never work," he said, his voice flat. "We're at least twenty yards from the tree line, and I'm not sure I can walk straight. We'll be shot the second we break cover."

"What have we got to lose?" I said, heading for the trunk. "Staying here is a guaranteed death sentence. At least this gives us a chance."

I rose up and peered over the trunk just in time to see dark silhouettes moving against the skyline—at least three of them, probably searching for the source of the smoke.

I picked up the rifle and raised it over the top of the trunk, scanning for movement. I found a figure in the scope, my nerves buzzing. My mind raced with everything that could go wrong, but if I could thin out the herd, we'd have a better chance of surviving the night.

I inhaled slowly, let it out steady, then squeezed the trigger.

The rifle kicked against my shoulder, lighter than I'd expected. I didn't wait to see if he dropped: instead, I shifted targets and fired again. A second figure crumbled. Then the third. I swept the scope across the hill, but the smoke was thicker now, swallowing everything in its path.

A rain of bullets showered down on us. I ducked down, pressing my back to the car, waiting for the attack to stop.

Malcolm turned to me, his gaze steadier. "How many'd you take out?"

"Three, but that obviously wasn't all of them."

His jaw tightened. "You can count on it."

The attack began to slow, maybe because the smoke was getting thicker. The chemical fumes were definitely getting stronger.

It was time to go.

I set the rifle on the ground and scrambled back into the car. I dumped the rest of the whiskey onto the jeans, then struck the lighter. The cloth flared with a whoosh, heat licking up my arm. I backed out, heart pounding, and shut the door behind me.

"Okay," I said, breathing hard. "Let's get you into a squat so we can be ready to move. Then, if the hill looks clear, we'll make a break for the trees."

He gave a sharp nod, then grimaced as he pushed forward, bracing himself with his palms on the ground. His balance wavered, but he held it.

"Do you think you can walk by yourself if I cover you?"

He let out a grunt—annoyed, not at me, but at the situation. He was used to calling the shots, not being the one bleeding on the ground.

"I'll get there," he muttered.

I picked up the handgun and ejected the magazine, counting the bullets. Six rounds left. Not enough for a real firefight, but that was what the rifle was for.

"There are six shots left," I said, handing over the weapon. "I know you can't aim it, but if someone gets the jump on you, squeeze the trigger."

Still in a squat, he took it and swayed, his hand darting out to brace against the car. Definitely not a good omen for a twenty-yard sprint under fire. Fighting for balance, he managed to shove the weapon into the back waistband of his jeans.

I grabbed the extra magazines for the rifle and shoved them into my pockets, then tried to scan the hill again. The smoke was so thick I couldn't see past the hood, but I could feel the heat radiating from the trunk. The fire was spreading exactly as I'd hoped.

"Time to go," I said, hefting the rifle. "Don't stop running, no matter what happens."

I took one last look at Malcolm—concussed, unsteady, but determined—and prayed we'd both make it to the trees alive.

## Chapter 33

Carrying the rifle under my right arm, I grabbed Malcolm's upper arm and hauled him upright.

He swayed but stayed on his feet.

"Good," I said, my relief palpable. "You take off for the trees, and I'll cover you."

He grunted, clearly pissed, but didn't argue. He staggered forward, nearly face-planting, then managed a few more steps.

I moved behind him, walking backward with the rifle raised, ready to fire.

We made it about ten yards before I spotted a bright orange glow in the backseat of the car. If it blew, I wasn't sure we were far enough away.

More shots cracked through the night, ricocheting off metal and earth. I doubted they could see us—just like I couldn't see them through the thick smoke.

So much for the take-them-alive plan.

I glanced over my shoulder, terrified I'd see James crumpled on the ground, either because he'd lost his balance or he'd been hit. But he was still upright, staggering like a drunk man.

I turned back toward the hill, making sure no one had

flanked the car, then checked on James again. He'd made it to the trees, bracing himself with both hands on a trunk to stay upright. We'd only taken a few more steps when an explosion ripped through the night, slamming me into a tree.

The impact crushed the air from my lungs, pain radiating through my chest and stomach. I dropped the rifle and hit the ground hard, landing on my ass. Dazed, I scanned wildly for Malcolm.

Panic surged when I didn't see him, but then I spotted him, lying on the ground a few yards away, deathly still.

I tried to call his name but couldn't find the breath. I crawled to him, terror rising with every inch.

His face was turned toward me, his eyes shut. Dread clogged my throat as I pressed two fingers to his carotid. For the second time in less than twenty minutes.

If he was dead, it would be my fault for not calling 911.

But his heartbeat pulsed against my fingertip.

I nearly collapsed with relief.

I finally sucked in a breath, wheezing.

"James," I whispered, shaking his shoulder.

He didn't respond. He was out cold.

He was only ten feet from where the forest's understory grew dense enough to hide us, but there was no way I could drag him deeper into that cover.

Which meant I had to go with my original plan to draw them away from him. I'd told them he was dead. Maybe they'd believed it. If I could keep them distracted for twenty-five minutes, our reinforcements would show up to save us both.

I brushed my thumb across his cheek, swallowing back tears.

I could do this. I had to.

Rising to my feet, I started weaving through the scattered, smaller trees, staying a good ten feet from the forest's edge. I kept glancing back at James until the shadows swallowed him.

The moment he vanished from my sight, panic clawed at my chest. But I reminded myself it was the best way to protect him.

I had to believe that.

When I got far enough away, I quickened my pace, keeping my gaze on the area around the car. It was fully engulfed now. Maybe my plan had worked a little too well.

As I neared the corner where the terrain rose toward the road, movement caught my eye. Two men were descending the incline, their rifles sweeping with flashlight beams, cutting through the dark.

I didn't hesitate. I lifted my gun, aimed at the first man, and fired. A slight shift and I fired again. If they cried out in death, I didn't hear it over the roar of the flames.

More figures appeared at the top of the hill, weapons raised.

I bolted, plunging deeper into the trees as bullets pinged around me, splintering bark and whistling through the air. I didn't feel the sting of a gunshot, but I knew not to trust that.

Adrenaline could lie.

I started to climb the hill, toward the road. My original plan had been to distract them, but taking out two more had emboldened me.

The darkness gave me the advantage. A figure descended through the trees about ten feet to my left, his body backlit by the headlights of one of their vehicles.

I darted behind a tree, raised my rifle, aimed for his chest, then pulled the trigger.

He dropped like a rock, the brush crackling beneath him.

"Grayson!" a man called out.

I continued my ascent, pushing deeper into the woods. It was harder to see them through the trees, but another man appeared at the edge of the tree line.

Hiding behind a tree trunk, I slowly lifted my rifle. The

trees obscured my shot—until the man stepped forward, exposing his chest and head.

"Grayson!" he shouted, just as I pulled the trigger.

He fell in a heap, but he was close enough to the clearing that his buddies saw him fall.

A storm of bullets rained on me.

I flattened against the trunk, praying it was wide enough to give me complete cover. My heart raced as I listened for footsteps.

"Got him!" a voice yelled.

My heart dropped.

I chanced a glance and saw two men carrying a lifeless-looking James toward one of the SUVs.

I never should have left him.

Panic surged through me. I tried to line up a shot, but the shooters to my right fired again, forcing me to take cover.

I struggled to think clearly through the panic. If they got away, I might never find him, and I had no doubt they wouldn't let him leave alive.

I drew a deep breath and let it out slowly.

I couldn't let them take him.

More bullets sprayed around me, wild and unfocused. They were shooting blind, hoping to get lucky. I decided to take a risk and trust the cover of the trees. Darting up the hill to a larger trunk about five feet away, I pressed my back to the rough bark and tried to catch my breath.

The men were slightly below me now, advancing. I raised my rifle and waited. When one of them peered around a tree, I took my shot.

He cried out in pain, but he didn't drop.

I shot a glance at the SUV. They had the back passenger door open and were lifting James inside. I wasn't sure I had a clear shot, and even if I did, they might drop him on the asphalt. What if they dropped him on his head? I didn't know much more damage his head could take.

Before I could act, they tossed him inside and slammed the door. One guy moved toward the front passenger door. The other circled around the front of the SUV, out of view.

I lowered my rifle a few inches. Maybe I could take out a tire. I tried to get it in my sights, but bullets slammed into the tree I was hiding behind, splintering the bark in every direction. I dropped lower, hugging the trunk and praying I was still out of sight.

I was in serious trouble, but so was Malcolm.

What the hell was I going to do?

I'd lost track of how many shots I'd made. I popped out the used magazine, dug a fresh one from my pocket, and slid it into place.

Just as I heard the soft click of it locking in, a face appeared to my right. A man grinned at me, smug that he'd snuck up on me.

We were too close to use our rifles, but mine was already in hand. I rammed the butt into his gut, then whipped it up to smash his nose.

He doubled over, howling. Seconds later, more shots rang out, and the man next to me dropped.

His own partner had shot him.

That didn't bode well for Malcolm. My urgency increased.

I spotted the revolver of the man on the ground next to me, hanging from a holster on his waist. I dropped to a squat and reached for it, hoping I didn't take a bullet. More shots hit the trees around me, but I yanked the gun free and ducked back behind the trunk.

Just in time to see the SUV peel away from the shoulder.

Fuck.

I raised my rifle and released a round at the rear of the SUV. Bullets pinged off the metal, but the vehicle sped off, tearing down the county road—heading toward Malcolm's tavern.

Were they after the papers?

Malcolm would die before giving them up.

Panic mushroomed inside of me. Even if I got away from these assholes, Malcolm's car was a burning heap. How was I supposed to follow them?

Then I spotted the second SUV.

I just had to take care of the rest of these guys and go after him.

Rationally, I knew it was an insane plan. Hell, it wasn't a plan at all. More like a wish, but I was determined to make it happen.

I turned and peeked around the tree. I spotted a man sprinting up the hill. I pulled the handgun from my waistband and braced against the tree, firing three quick shots toward his chest and neck.

He stumbled, clutching his throat. I was close enough to see the bewildered look in his eyes as blood streamed between his fingers. He dropped to his knees, his rifle swinging from the strap over his shoulder.

I stepped out from behind the tree, pointing the handgun at his head.

"Where are they taking him?"

His eyes filled with fear, but not of me. He knew he was dying.

"Where are they taking him?" I shouted. I knew there wasn't a chance in hell he'd tell me, but I had to try.

He opened his mouth to speak. Nothing came out, but I could easily read the *fuck you* on his lips before he fell to his side, the light fading out of his eyes.

Dammit.

I shoved the handgun back into my waistband, raised the rifle, and scanned the trees.

The woods were silent other than the crackle of the flames and creaking of the expanding metal.

Then I heard it.

A moan.

It came from farther down the hill. I saw a pair legs sprawled on the ground, the upper body propped awkwardly against a tree.

I crept closer, rifle ready, praying for answers but prepared for another fight.

The wounded man's face was pale. My earlier shot had caught him in the shoulder. The wound gaped open, soaking his shirt in blood.

He was bleeding out.

He glanced up, flinching when he saw me, bracing for the end.

"I'm not going to kill you," I said, stepping closer. "But only if you tell me where they're taking him."

He licked his cracked lips. "I know I'm dead anyway. No one's coming to save me."

My heart dropped.

I could torture him, but I hadn't sunk that low.

Not yet.

"Why are you tryin' so hard to save him?" he asked with a soft shake of his head. "That man ain't worth savin'."

His words sent a chill down my spine. I knew James had been ruthless before—hell, I'd seen signs of it myself—but he'd never struck me as irredeemable. "Then I guess you don't know him like I do."

He made a face like my answer satisfied him. "I have a girl too."

I didn't like where this was going. It was one thing to shoot a nameless gunman hell-bent on kidnapping or killing me. That was survival of the fittest. But this made him real.

A person who was dying.

Because of me.

"I bet she'd do anything she could to save you," I said, my words thick.

"Nah." He gave a faint smile. "She's too soft. But I love her anyway."

"I'm sure she loves you. And if someone had taken you, she'd fight like hell to get you back. Just like I'm doing. *Please*—I'm begging you. Tell me where they took him."

He looked at me again, his gaze distant and unfocused. "You must really love him."

I was pretty sure lying to a dying man was some kind of unforgiveable sin, but I was out of options.

"You have no idea," I said. "I can't live without him. So, please. *Please*, tell me where they took him."

A ghost of a smile crossed his face. "An abandoned factory on the west side of town. That's all I've got. She's waitin' there for him."

"Nicole Knox?" I asked, but he didn't answer.

I'd killed this man.

Guilt clung to me like yoke, heavy and cold. But I'd had no choice. It had been them or us, and I'd chosen us.

I could deal with the guilt later.

Right now, I had to save James.

I patted the outside of the dead man's pockets, hoping to feel the outline of keys or a key fob. Nothing. I made my way up the hill to the next guy, and then next—still nothing.

Frustrated, I sprinted to the SUV and yanked open the driver's door. To my shock, the key fob was sitting in the cupholder like a gift from the universe. I muttered a quick thanks to whatever deity was watching over me as I started the engine, threw it into drive and hit the gas.

The warehouse was at least twenty minutes away. And they had a ten-minute head start.

I just hoped I wasn't too late.

## Chapter 34

I called Carter while en route to the warehouse and gave him a condensed version of what had happened after we'd been run off the road—including the fact that James had been kidnapped.

Carter let out a sharp gasp.

"I stole one of their SUVs," I said, my voice tight. "I'm on my way to get him right now."

"By yourself? I'll send the team to the warehouse. Don't go in alone."

"Your team won't get there in time," I said, my stomach churning. They might not kill him, but they'd sure as hell hurt him.

"Don't take any unnecessary risks and get yourself captured too," Carter said. "That'll make the rescue team's job twice as hard."

"Fuck you, Carter." I hung up, furious. I knew he was probably right, but there was no way I was leaving James in their hands a second longer than necessary. God only knew if he'd regained consciousness yet, or what kind of damage they might be inflicting to his concussion.

Carter tried calling me back, but I sent him to voicemail.

He wasn't going to change my mind, and I wasn't going to waste time for either of us by listening to him try.

I slowed as I neared the warehouse, pulling onto the shoulder. I parked a good fifty feet away and then approached the building through the woods. How ironic that James had wanted to meet my father at the very place Nicole Knox had ordered her henchmen to bring him.

He was right. Having prior knowledge of the layout gave me an advantage.

I exited the trees at the edge of the parking lot, wary in case she had called for reinforcements. A dark, bullet-ridden SUV sat out front, along with a black sedan that looked suspiciously like the one that had dropped Nicole off at my mother's house.

This was a rescue mission, but I was also here for answers.

I slipped through a back door, rifle slung over my shoulder, the handgun tucked into the waistband at my back.

Voices echoed through the open space—muffled words in a woman's voice, then Malcolm's unmistakable, "Fuck you."

Pride—fierce and undeserved—swelled in my chest. I wouldn't have expected anything less from him, but hearing it still made me beam. James wouldn't go down without a fight.

And now, he had me to fight for him too.

I took cautious steps through the darkness, weaving around machinery that hadn't run for years, probably decades. I knew the front of the building had multiple rows of empty metal shelving that reached about fifteen feet high, but there was also an open area.

Drew Sylvester had used that space to lure me in with little Ava Peterman taped to a chair. Would Nicole Knox do the same?

But first, I had to pass a block of offices that separated the warehouse into two halves.

I lingered in the shadows, mentally shaking my head at her lax security. No guards at the front or the back—just four men stationed out in the open area—two on each side. Sure enough, James was strapped to the same metal chair Ava had once been bound to. A woman stood in front of him, her back to me, but I recognized the salt-and-pepper bob.

Nicole Knox.

Malcolm's right eye was swollen shut, and dried blood streaked the side of his face. Rage burned in my chest at the thought that they'd beaten him, until I remembered it was from the accident. Still, he likely had other injuries I couldn't see.

Rope bound his arms and legs to the chair. Another looped around his chest, keeping him upright. I doubted it was out of concern that he might fall over.

"I'll ask you again, Mr. Malcolm," Nicole said, her cultured voice laced with a genteel Southern accent. "Where is the documentation that Sarah Jane Adams collected from her husband?"

"I don't know," James slurred. "Have you tried lookin' up your ass?"

She jabbed something metal into his side. His body convulsed and the room filled with the crackling sound of electricity.

She was jabbing him with a cattle prod.

Rage surged through me. The men who'd chased us were sloppy. Could I be lucky enough that these men were too? Or at least be slow to react? I was almost certain they were the only guards.

From the shadows behind the shelves close to the offices, I had a clear shot at all four men. I wasn't sure I could take them all down at once, but I was damn well going to try. I just had to make sure James and Nicole weren't caught in the crossfire.

Hiding behind a row of racks, I rested the rifle on a shelf, lining up the nearest target. I drew a breath, finger hovering over the trigger, then Nicole's voice rang out.

"Where's Paul's daughter? Why haven't they brought her yet?"

Two of the men flinched, one casting a sidelong glance at the other, but neither answered.

She stepped toward them, her free hand curling into a fist. "You said the others would bring her here *any minute*. I'm done waiting. Call them again."

"They're not gonna answer," James slurred, his chin still on his chest. "She's keepin' 'em busy."

Nicole spun to face him, her eyes icy as they swept over him. "Then you'll pay for her tardiness." She started toward him, the cattle prod extended.

I knew I was about to do something stupid, but there was no way I was going to let her shock him again.

I needed her alive, so shooting the prod wasn't an option. A ricochet could hit Malcolm.

Before I could think it through, I aimed for her extended forearm and squeezed the trigger. Her scream confirmed I'd hit my target.

The men were already turning their weapons up. I dropped the closest two in quick succession. The remaining two opened fire. I ducked and took out the third, then swung to the fourth. He dove for cover behind a shelf. He died before he hit the floor.

Nicole clutched her bleeding arm and scrambled behind Malcolm's chair, using him as a shield.

I emerged from the shadows, the rifle trained on her. "I heard you were looking for me."

Her eyes widened slightly.

Malcolm lifted his head, giving me a grim look, not that I'd expected him to give me a wave and a smile. I knew exactly what I'd just set in motion. James had left this life behind, and I'd dragged him right back into it. Sure, he was after Simmons's successor, but if Gerry Knox wasn't that guy, then I'd just made a powerful enemy—and brought him straight to James's door.

Gerry Knox wouldn't forgive me for taking out so many of his men, even if they'd struck first. And James would be caught in the fallout.

"If you wanted to talk to me, all you had to do was ask, Nicole." I took two steps closer. "Because I want to talk to you too."

She cast a nervous glance at the dead man a few feet away, then swung her gaze back to me. Some of her poise returned, but I saw it for what it was: false bravado.

"You have something I want," she said.

"Yeah, I know," I said dully. "I saw you at the bank, trying to get it yourself. I take it you planned to forge my mother's signature?"

She didn't answer. Instead, she countered with a question of her own. "Where is it?"

"Somewhere you can't access it," I said. "But if you tell me exactly which document you're after, maybe I can get it for you."

Her upper lip curled. "You expect me to believe you don't already know?"

"There are *several* documents," I said, "You'll have to be more specific." I grinned when panic flickered across her face. "Then again, you're probably not surprised. I'm sure your hands are filthy enough if you killed my mother for them."

She didn't deny it, which, to me, was as good as an admission.

"I know you showed up at her house last Tuesday," I said, each word clipped. "What I don't understand is how you got her to trust you." When she stayed silent, I said, "Or how you got that burner phone number to her."

"That part was easy," she said with a short laugh. "Your mother was so gullible."

"Funny. *Gullible* isn't a word I'd ever use to describe her."

She rolled her eyes. "People believe what they want to."

"How'd you know she had the documents?"

"A month ago, your father warned me that your mother had been collecting papers for years. He was concerned she might have something that could incriminate my husband and our family. I told him to make certain it was recovered—or we would do it ourselves. Of course, I never expected Paul to come through. He's incompetent on his best days. But my foolish husband had a soft spot for him."

None of this surprised me, and I wondered if their meeting had taken place by the lake. I was guessing Dad's partner had seen this meeting, not a lover's tryst.

"So I took matters into my own hands," she continued. "Your father had left her in a last-ditch move of desperation. He was hoping to scare her into handing them over, but she wouldn't budge. I befriended her at the grocery store. I told her a sob story about my husband leaving me. It took a couple of 'coincidental' run-ins before she trusted me enough to tell me she was separated too. A few coffee dates later, she admitted she'd collected evidence of illegal activity."

She was discussing this so casually, as if my mother's life meant nothing. Like she was merely a pawn in Nicole's game.

"When I asked how she kept them safe," Nicole went on, seemingly proud of her deception, "she said she'd put them in a safe deposit box. But she wouldn't tell me which bank, no matter how I pushed. "

"Where did the burner phone number come from?" I asked.

"You found out about that, huh?" She chuckled, then winced as her injured arm shifted. Her pain must have been covered by her adrenaline and the endorphins flooding her system as she regaled her accomplishments. "I gave her the number the last time we met for coffee. I told her to call me if she was ever in danger. It only took her two days to call." Her smile turned cruel. "The threatening messages she started getting helped nudge her along."

My mother had met this woman the Sunday before her death. I'd been too drunk to realize she'd even left the house.

And when I'd cancelled on her for the luncheon, she'd turned to *this* woman. Nicole Knox had baited the trap and waited for my mother to spring it.

She may have murdered her, but I'd helped lead her there. Even if I hadn't meant to.

The older woman's face looked strained. She was pale, and blood dripped steadily from her arm. She was going to need more than her hand to stop the bleeding, but I wasn't about to offer any help.

As if reading my mind, she gave me a smug smile. "She might still be alive if you'd only let her bring you into her confidence last Tuesday. That's why she called me, you know. Because *you* refused to help her."

"That's bullshit," James spat, lifting his head part way. "Sarah Jane had plenty of chances to tell Harper what was goin' on. But I suspect *you* convinced her not to."

The triumphant look in her eyes made my finger twitch on the trigger, but I forced myself to tear it away. I wasn't done with her yet.

"So you went to her house on Tuesday to help her?" I asked sarcastically. "And after you left, what? You tried to get her to open her bank box, and she refused?"

"She said if the papers left the box, she wasn't going to be the one to remove them," Nicole said with a sniff. "By then, she'd realized I'd never planned to help her. At least not in the way she thought. She started getting suspicious of my persistence. I'd picked up the Zoloft Paul said he had filled for her, and popped a couple in her drink, hoping I'd get her loopy enough to agree." Disgust twisted her face. "She was a stubborn bitch."

"So you killed her."

"You think I'm going to admit to that?" she asked with a laugh. "I'm not that stupid."

"But you had her murdered all the same," I said. "You drugged her with her own meds, put her behind the wheel of her car, then had your men run her off the road."

"I'm not admitting to any such thing." But the proud smile on her face said everything.

"You're definitely not denying it," I sneered.

"Which isn't an admission of guilt," she countered. "I plead the fifth."

This woman was *gloating* about murdering my mother.

"Why capture James?" I asked, gesturing my gun toward him. "I'm the one who has the papers. Not him."

"My issue with James Malcolm is a separate matter. It was just a lucky coincidence you were both together. Then again, I'm not surprised. I know he's been snooping around. If *he* had the documents, it would lead him straight to us."

I shot a look at James. Did he want me to press her further? He didn't meet my gaze, but then again, he looked like he was about to pass out.

I had to get him out of here. But I had to figure out what to do with her first.

"You need to free him," I told her. "Then we'll talk about what happens to you."

"What happens to *me*?" she laughed. "Oh, you stupid fool. You should be worried about what happens to *you* after shooting me and my men. And if you even think about killing me, not only will you sign your death sentence, but it will be slow and agonizing."

"You think whatever you like," I said. "But right now, you're going to untie him."

"Like hell I will," she sneered. "I'm walking out of here, and you'll count the days until my son tracks you down and makes you pay for what you've done." Then, like she was the damn Queen of England, she spun around and headed to the front door.

My finger curled over the trigger, and for one vivid moment, I could picture pulling the trigger, her falling to the ground. Getting justice for my mother. The fantasy felt so real I could taste it.

But James lifted his head, his eyes locking with mine. He gave a slow shake of his head. "Let her go."

*Let her go?*

The words hit me like a physical blow. She'd practically admitted to murdering my mother—she'd tricked her, drugged her, hit her over the head, and pushed her into the river to drown. What kind of sick, twisted person could do that? Now she was walking away, smug as ever, promising her son would come for me next.

"Harper," James said, his voice firmer this time.

I swung my gaze to him, my hand trembling around the gun. Did he really expect me to let her go? She'd killed my mother! Wasn't the whole point of this finding out who'd murdered her so I could seek retribution?

"She murdered my mother," I whispered, my voice breaking. "She murdered my mother and she's going to get away with it."

"I know," he said quietly. "But not like this."

Not like this?

I sucked in a shaky breath, fury and heartbreak churning in my gut.

What was I doing? This wasn't how I dealt with criminals. I'd collected evidence and let a judge and jury decide. It wasn't up to me to decide or dole out punishment.

Even though every part of me burned to do so.

Maybe I could turn the evidence over to Mason Deveraux. Following the evidence trail might keep him busy enough that he'd forget his vendetta against Malcolm. But James would never agree to it. And even if he did, she'd hire expensive attorneys and get away with everything she'd done.

"*Harper.*"

His voice was soft and low. Like he knew how hard it was to lower the gun.

Drawing a shaky breath, tears blurred my vision. I slowly let my arm drop. I needed to untie him and get him out of here.

Before I changed my mind about Nicole.

I dropped to my knees in front of him, letting my rifle clatter to the floor. Nicole was almost to the door, walking away like she'd just completed a shopping trip to the mall.

My eyes burned as I blinked and focused on the knot binding his right wrist. Every part of me wanted to go after her and wipe that smug expression off her face with the barrel of my gun.

But I didn't.

Not yet.

"What the hell happened?" James asked.

I blinked, trying to ground myself. "You'll need to be more specific."

The knot was tight and not budging. I bent down and bit it, tugging it until it loosened just enough to wedge my finger underneath.

"In the woods," he said. "We were running, and the next thing I knew, I was in the back of their car." His eyes locked on mine, blazing. "I thought they'd killed you."

"The car explosion worked a little too well," I muttered. "You hit the ground and got knocked out cold." I dug my nails in and finally yanked it loose. "I couldn't wake you up, so I tried to draw them away." My words turned bitter. "Obviously it didn't work."

"Why the fuck would you do that?" He tossed the rope onto the floor, then bent down to work on his leg while I tackled the knot on his left arm.

"Are you serious?" I shot another glance at the entrance, half-expecting Nicole or one of her henchmen to burst in and finish what they started. "It doesn't matter. I botched it. They captured you anyway, and I left a hell of a mess behind."

He looked up at me, brow raised, waiting for more.

"There're more than a few dead bodies out there." The reality of the carnage I'd left hit me center mass. "I don't know how we're supposed to explain that."

His face softened. "Carter'll take care of it."

"How can he take care of *that*?" Panic crept in. "What if someone saw the fire? What if they called it in?"

He reached up, cupping my cheek with his freed hand. "Deep breath. I won't let anything happen to you, okay?"

The tenderness in his voice broke something in me. A tear rolled down my cheek before I could stop it.

He brushed it with his thumb, still watching me. His pupils were slightly dilated, but he was more focused now than he'd been since the crash. "Do you believe me?"

I nodded. Maybe it was like believing in Santa or the Tooth Fairy, but in that moment, I knew he'd burn the world down to keep me safe.

Just like I'd done for him.

"Good," he said, brushing his lips against my forehead. Then he pulled back. "Let's finish untying the piss-poor binding job and get the hell out of here."

"Yeah." I dragged in a breath. I'd held my shit together this long. Falling apart now wasn't an option.

I finished untying his left arm, then moved on to his leg. We both worked on the knots in silence, and when we reached the rope around his chest, he lifted his hands to help.

I batted his hands away. "I've got it."

"You scared the hell out of me," he said, his voice low and husky, as though the last hour was sinking in.

"You scared the hell out of *me*," I shot back, sharper than I meant it.

His jaw flexed. "You were a fool to risk your life for me."

Anger flared in my chest. "Why? Because you're not worth saving? Don't bullshit me, James. You would've come for me. Hell, you already did last week."

I yanked the knot loose, and he pushed the rope off his chest as he rose to his feet. He swayed, and I stepped closer on instinct, ready to catch him if he fell.

"You need to go to an ER," I said, slipping an arm around his waist as he took an unsteady step. How hard had he hit his head after the blast? And God only knew what kind of damage they'd done tossing him into the SUV.

"No ER." He took another step, but his knees buckled slightly. I reached out, catching his weight against my side.

"You might be seriously hurt," I said, my breath catching. "We need to check for intercranial bleeding."

"We'll figure it out." His voice was firmer this time, gritty with pain. "No ER."

I could've thrown him in the car and taken him anyway, but I knew better. If James Malcolm didn't want to end up in a hospital, there was a damn good reason. Still, we needed help. I could only hope he had someone in his network—a private doctor, a medic, or the woman who'd stitched me up last week. Someone off the books but qualified.

We managed a few more stumbling steps. He was leaning on me harder now, almost sagging. Every shift in his weight increased my concern.

*He's worse than he's letting on.*

As soon as I got him loaded in the car, I was calling Carter. James might not trust hospitals, but I trusted Carter to know how to keep him alive.

I lifted my gaze to the front entrance of the building, now in view. "How long do you think I have before Gerald Knox comes for me—and my mother's papers?" If James was out of commission for even a few days, let alone weeks, we'd have to go into hiding. But as long as he was conscious and breathing, I knew he wouldn't let me face this alone.

"He's comin' for *us*, Harper," he said, turning his head toward me, wincing as pain flashed across his face. "I bet good money he thinks I'm comin' for him now too."

My stomach clenched. "This is my fault. You're only involved because I dragged you into it."

"Dragged me into it?" he echoed in disbelief. "I *shoved* my way into it. And let's not pretend I didn't make it clear from the start—I was after whatever your mother was hiding."

I released a hollow laugh. "So now we're both on Knox's most-wanted list."

A dark smile curved his lips. "Let him come. Only we're not waitin'. We'll strike first."

I didn't know what that looked like, not yet, but I trusted he had a plan.

We'd reached the front door, what was left of it. The glass on one side had been completely blown out. The sedan was gone. A small, twisted part of me had hoped Nicole would still be there so I could finish what I'd started.

"Why did you stop me from shooting her?" I asked.

He pulled me to a halt, turning to face me. "Because she was unarmed."

"So?" I asked, my voice sharp with a pain I didn't bother to hide. "She killed my mother, so what if she wasn't armed?"

He cupped my cheek. "You're not stooping to her level."

"I already did," I whispered, my voice cracking. Images of the men I'd killed came back in violent flashes. "You didn't see what I did out there."

"No," he said gently. "There's a difference between killing in self-defense … and killing for revenge. You don't want that dark mark on your soul."

*Like me.*

He hadn't said the words, but they were unmistakable, all the same.

My shoulders stiffened. "If I see her again, I can't guarantee I won't kill her."

His gaze softened with understanding, and a tenderness I still didn't know what to do with. "Then, for your sake, I hope she's armed."

## Chapter 35

At Malcolm's insistence, I drove him to the tavern, calling Carter on the way. He sounded like a mother hen, fretting over Malcolm's injuries. He promised he'd have a car waiting at the tavern for us, along with a couple of guards to make sure we made it to James's house without any further incidents. He also promised to send someone to look over James's injuries.

"He needs someone good," I insisted, casting a sidelong glance at James in the passenger seat. He was struggling to stay conscious. "Not some quack. A qualified medical professional who won't screw this up."

"You're worse than Skeeter," Carter said with an impatient sigh.

I grinned. "That's quite the compliment."

"It wasn't meant to be," he grumbled.

Malcolm shook himself awake and grilled him about what had been done to contain the situation on the county road as well as the factory. Carter assured him he had it handled and told James to focus on getting better.

"And preparing for war," James growled.

"Not if we can help it," Carter said, hesitation thick in his voice.

Malcolm leaned his head back against the seat. "You know we've been gearing up for it."

"Maybe so," Carter said, "but it sounds like you're in no shape to go to war with anyone. Not in your state. Get well, then we'll come up with a plan."

Malcolm flicked his gaze to me, and I knew he was thinking about Nicole Knox's threat to send her son after me.

"We'll figure it out," I said, my tone leaving no room for argument. "But Carter's right. In your current shape, you're no help to anyone. You're a liability."

He looked at me, startled, and Carter turned so silent I thought we'd lost our connection. Then James started laughing.

"What the hell is so funny?" I demanded.

"No one's talked to him like that for a long time," Carter finally said. "Anyone who tried would have been cut down before they finished the sentence."

"Who called him on his bullshit before me?"

Both men went silent, James turning sullen. Had it been Jed? But no, that didn't fit. Something told me it had been a woman.

Jealousy reared its head, sharp and ugly. But I reminded myself that we both had pasts. And declarations a man made when his brain was still scrambled couldn't be held against him.

Even if his kisses still burned on my lips.

Next, I called my father.

"I met Nicole Knox," I said, catching the flash of anger in Malcolm's eyes.

"Oh, Harper! No." My father sounded gutted.

"She came to *me*," I said. "But you know she killed Mom, right?" The words caught in my throat.

He was quiet for a long moment. "I suspected."

"She sought Mom out. She befriended her, then pretended she wanted to help protect her, all so she could get those documents."

"Harper…" his voice broke. "I had no idea about any of that."

"Maybe not," I said, "but you had to suspect something. You *told* her you left Mom to coerce her to hand over the documents."

He was silent again, before meekly asking, "Did you give them to her?"

"No," I said, my back stiffening. "She'll have to kill me first. Just like she killed Mom."

He sucked in a sharp breath. "Harper—"

"Don't worry," I said, my voice icy. "I don't plan on giving them to the authorities. But you might want to watch your back. Nicole Knox already promised me a slow, painful death, I'm sure she has something creative planned for you."

"You're not going to the sheriff?" he asked, his voice small and hollow.

Had he always been like this? Why had my mother stayed with him?

"No," I said. "Not the police. Not the sheriff. Not even the attorney general's office. Your secrets are safe from the law."

I paused.

"But God help you from the criminals who come knocking."

Then I hung up.

A flicker of guilt prickled the edges of my resolve. He'd sleep easier if he had those documents in his possession, but he also had no guarantee there weren't copies out there some-where. And I had no doubt Gerald Knox would make him pay for being a thorn in his side.

If Nicole Knox didn't get to him first.

When we got to the tavern, I parked around back. Two black SUVs were waiting, both engines running. As soon as I stopped, the front doors of one SUV opened, and two men climbed out.

My heart stuttered. I was prepared to throw the vehicle in reverse, but James's hand lightly covered mine.

"They're ours," he murmured reassuringly.

I turned to look at him, my heart now racing.

"It's okay," he said. "They're gonna take us home."

The men approached, one on each side of the car. They opened our doors, helping us out and guiding us toward the back of the SUV. James moved under his own power, slightly steadier than before, but I could tell he was still struggling.

Once we were inside, they shut the doors and then one of the men got behind the wheel and took off, leaving the other guy behind. I turned around to see him get in our stolen vehicle while our second SUV followed behind us.

James cast me a glance. "They're gonna dump Knox's vehicle somewhere."

I nodded. That made sense, but I was too tired to ask where *somewhere* might be.

When we pulled up in front of Malcolm's house, the house was lit up like it had been the night before. The second SUV pulled up behind us.

James opened his door and was out before the driver could reach him. When the man moved to help him walk, James let out a low growl while he gave him a death stare. The man wisely backed off. He and the other men stayed at the bottom of the steps. I could hear them discussing setting up security around the property.

It took James multiple attempts to enter the code on his door, but once it pushed open, I hustled him inside. He refused to go to his bedroom, insisting I help him to the leather sofa instead. I turned on a couple of lamps and turned off all the overhead lights, hoping to dim the light.

"Get me a handful of Advil," he grunted, his eyes clenched shut. "Please."

"Not until you've been examined." Not that I expected a real diagnosis without a CT scan. Somehow, I doubted Malcolm's backwoods doctor carted one around in his trunk.

A surprisingly short time later, a middle-aged man with a soft paunch and thinning hair knocked on the front door. He wore green-and-white striped pajamas and glanced nervously around the porch before peering over my shoulder at James on the sofa.

"I'm here to examine the patient," he said.

He didn't introduce himself, and neither did we.

After doing a few coordination tests, a brief physical exam, and a check of his pupils, the doctor stitched up James's head near his temple, then handed me a plain white business card with only a phone number printed on it. He said James had a concussion and likely didn't have internal bleeding, but if he started talking nonsense, got confused, or if his pupils became uneven, I should call him immediately.

Then he hurried out the door and into his car as though he feared for his life. I stood in front of the window, watching his taillights disappear around the curve in the road, while two men with semi-automatic weapons stood in front of the house.

"He was already talking nonsense," I mumbled, still uneasy.

"I wasn't talkin' nonsense," James said softly behind me.

I spun around to face him, my stomach fluttering. "You need to go to bed."

The corners of his mouth tipped up. "Only if you come with me."

My heart skipped a beat. "Of course I'll help you to bed. I plan on checking on you throughout the night."

"You'll be able to assess me better if you're sleepin' next to me."

I drew in a breath. My pulse pounded so loud it drowned out everything else. I leaned back against the window for support. "Tomorrow, you're going to regret everything you're saying."

He slowly shook his head. "No. I won't."

"I can sleep in a chair in your room. Just like you've done for me."

"No," he said firmly. "In my bed. I need you next to me. I need to know you're safe."

I tried for a teasing smile. "I think that's my line."

He huffed out a laugh, then winced. "All the more reason for you to sleep with me tonight."

I stood there, teetering on the edge of something dangerous. A relationship with this man would torch what was left of my reputation, yet I couldn't seem to care. Before Malcolm, I'd been sleepwalking through life. Now I felt wide awake. I didn't want to miss a second of it.

I had no illusions. We were two broken people, clinging to the only other person who understood our pain. But I was okay with that. I'd take this for as long as it lasted.

Or however little time we had before Nicole Knox—or her son—tried to finish us off.

---

Want to read a spicy bonus scene? Scan the QR code or use the link below.

subscribepage.io/LutDBS

# About the Author

**Denise Grover Swank** was born in Kansas City, Missouri and lived in the area until she was nineteen. Then she became a nomad, living in five cities, four states and ten houses over the course of ten years before she moved back to her roots. She speaks English and smattering of Spanish and Chinese which she learned through an intensive Nick Jr. immersion period. Her hobbies include witty Facebook comments (in own her mind) and dancing in her kitchen with her children. (Quite badly if you believe her offspring.) Hidden talents include the gift of justification and the ability to drink massive amounts of caffeine and still fall asleep within two minutes. Her lack of the sense of smell allows her to perform many unspeakable tasks. She has six children and hasn't lost her sanity. Or so she leads you to believe.

denisegroverswank.com